We hope you enjoy this book. Please return or renew it by the due date.

You can renew it at www.norfolk.gov.uk/libraries or by using our free library app.

Otherwise you can phone 0344 800 8020 - please have your library card and PIN ready.

You can sign up for email reminders too.

NORFOLK ITEM

30129 086 483 394

NORFOLK COUNTY COUNCIL
LIBRARY AND INFORMATION SERVICE

D1513062

It
Must
be
Love

Caroline Khoury was born in Beirut to a Lebanese mother and Welsh father, and grew up in suburban London. She recently returned to the UK after more than a decade in Hong Kong, Japan and America. It Must Be Love is her debut novel.

Caroline Khoury

It Must be Love

PENGUIN BOOKS

PENGUIN BOOKS

UK | USA | Canada | Ireland | Australia
India | New Zealand | South Africa

Penguin Books is part of the Penguin Random House group of companies
whose addresses can be found at global.penguinrandomhouse.com

Published in Penguin Books 2022
001

Typeset in 10/15.2 pt Palatino by Integra Software Services Pvt. Ltd,
Pondhicherry

Printed and bound in Great Britain by Clays Ltd, Elcograf S.p.A.

The authorised representative in the EEA is Penguin Random House
Ireland, Morrison Chambers, 32 Nassau Street, Dublin D02 YH68

A CIP catalogue record for this book is available from the British Library

ISBN: 978–1–529–15645–4

www.greenpenguin.co.uk

To my mother and brother, for always believing in me

Prologue

Destiny. Fate. Call it what you want. I never believed in either. But that was then, and this is now.

I tugged at the locket around my neck, pulling it back and forth along its chain. An imprint. It always left one, an impression of the metal against my skin. Bringing the pendant to my lips, I closed my eyes. A picture lay inside one half of the silver heart: a memory of a day long ago. I hadn't got around to filling the other side yet. There never seemed to be the time.

The chill of an April afternoon made me shiver as I stared out to sea. I pulled my pale blue shawl up over my shoulders; soft wool, cosy against my goose-pimpled arms. It had been hand-knitted by Mum, a bestseller at her shop in Mumbles, a stone's throw from here. But this one was a special creation. Three names had been embroidered in the corner to mark today's occasion.

My sleeveless dress was better suited to a warm summer's day. But I would have worn it whatever the season because it held so many memories within it. It skimmed my knees and had been adjusted at the waist.

I stepped over rock pools and pebbles, aching to reach the water, the soles of my feet growing numb with cold. In the distance stood Mumbles lighthouse; a white beacon of salvation for centuries, visible from any point along the five-mile sweep of Swansea Bay.

Deep breaths in and out, in time to the waves breaking against the shore, steadied my heartbeat. Salt wash intermingled with vinegar filled my nose and my toes scrunched the wet sand beneath my feet.

I should have called him. All those years ago, I should have called him. And when we said goodbye, why didn't I have the courage to do something? If I had, things might be different.

'Abbie?' A voice drifted over with the breeze, its gentle tone always a comfort.

I turned to see my best friend, Liz, walking towards me, carefully stepping over the rocks in her heels, her dress swinging around her knees.

'You found me,' I said.

'Your mum said you'd probably be here. Oh, sod it,' she said, peeling off her shoes. 'I'll wash my feet later.'

I smiled, pulling the folds of my shawl tightly, my hair blowing around my face in the wind. Lots of suggestions had been made as to how I should style it today; I had opted for down with a simple clip.

Liz placed her hands on my shoulders and rubbed my arms. 'You OK?'

'It's healing, this beach.'

'Mary just called me. She's picked everyone up from the station. They'll be here in ten minutes. Are you ready?'

I nodded. And this time I was sure. Very sure. I only wish we had got to this day differently. But I knew it couldn't have happened any other way because this was our destiny.

1

Now

December

I tapped the pen against my forehead. *Focus, Abbie, focus.*

Nope. It was no use. A large pile of paperwork sat in front of me; an immigration case that needed my undivided attention to get the judge to rule in my favour. Three items littered my green leather-topped desk hindering that outcome because I couldn't stop thinking about them.

Exhibit A: *The Legal 500* directory – hot off the press – containing my ranking and review. One of my colleagues had brought it in earlier to show off his 'rising star' status and to laugh at my entry. I was grateful he had departed soon after leaving me alone in our office – his gloating was insufferable.

Exhibit B: a manila envelope filled with details of the annual immigration conference in Paris I had been roped into attending this weekend but not yet opened. Mary Baker – my best friend's wife – had asked me to step in. The delegates would no doubt be expecting her expert input, not someone who had only been qualified a few years.

And finally, Exhibit C: a heart shaped Post-it with a message on it from my boyfriend Charlie which I had stuck on my computer's screen.

My mobile vibrated beneath my papers. Amy's name flashed on the screen and I tossed the phone into my handbag. No time for a catch-up. My big sister loved to talk but I was desperate to come up with at least one winning argument for this case by tonight.

Surveying my desk, I sighed and tugged at my low bun. My hair was always scraped back in this style even when I wasn't in court; ready to don my wig at a moment's notice like I was Supergirl waiting for the call of someone in distress.

The landline rang and I picked it up without a second thought.

'Abigail Jones,' I said with a lilt in my voice.

'Hey, sis, why didn't you pick up your mobile?'

My shoulders slumped. 'I'm at work.'

'This won't take long,' she said with a raised voice over what sounded like a hairdryer.

'Are you in the salon?'

'Yeah, just finishing up with one of my regulars.' Amy owned a hairdresser's in the heart of Mumbles called Hairway to Heaven – a nod to her heavy metal teenage years. 'So ... what do you think? Cedar or walnut?'

I placed the receiver in the crook of my neck and sifted through the bundle of papers looking for a witness statement. 'Cedar or walnut what?'

'The shabby chic wooden sewing box for Mum. Her Christmas present. I sent you an email with the link last week.'

'Did you? Must have missed it. Sorry.' I brought my mouse to life and did a quick search for Amy's message in my emails. One click took me to two identical-looking boxes. 'Umm. Walnut?'

'Great. You'll order it, right? It takes a week to get it hand engraved and delivered.'

'Why can't you order it?'

'I'm busy.'

'So am I.' My desk groaned under the weight of everything that needed my full attention.

'I'm a single parent with two kids *and* I run my own business,' Amy said defensively. 'Besides, *I* thought of the gift. Done my part.'

'Fine,' I acquiesced as I copied and pasted the link into my 'To Do' folder which loomed large.

'So, what are you wearing?' she asked, her voice almost singing the question.

I looked down at my outfit. 'Black trousers and a green jumper. Why?'

'No, stupid. Not now. For your big dinner tonight with Charlie.'

'How did you know about that?'

'Mum told me.'

'It's only dinner,' I said, doodling my and Charlie's initials on my notepad and drawing a circle around them.

'No, it's not. It's your three-year anniversary and he's taking you to Chez Pierre. I looked it up. That place has a three-month waiting list. He's *so* going to propose.'

OK. I rest my case. Exhibit C had my head in a spin. All week Charlie had been leaving notes around our flat reminding me about dinner tonight. This morning's memo was on his pillow when I woke up. He had been due in court extra early for the start of a big corporate case and I hadn't seen him before he left. Now, I peeled it off my computer screen.

Tonight's the night! I'll see you at the restaurant. Love you. xxx

'Stop speculating, Amy. Charlie has sworn off ever getting married.' I crossed out my scribblings. 'We're just going out for a nice meal.'

'Oh yeah, forgot he was once jilted at the altar. Poor sod.' She laughed and the hairdryer cranked up a notch. 'Still, it's obvious he's gonna do the deed. Lucky you. All I got from Barry was a Full Platter at Nando's.' She tutted. 'I even had to pick up the tab when he realised he'd left his wallet at home. I reckon Charlie should suck up those misgivings. He's in his forties and you're not far off.'

'*Hey*, I'm thirty-four, thank you very much. Listen, if there's nothing else—'

'Yeah, well ... I'd better go anyway, my four o'clock is here.'

I looked up to the clock on the wall. 'They're a bit early, aren't they?'

'Nah. They're bang on time.'

I did a double take as I noticed the second hand on the wall clock was merely going backwards and forwards and was an hour behind the digital display on my computer. 'Crap. I'm going to be late for Liz.'

After a quick goodbye and a promise to text if I had any news later tonight, I wrapped my case up in its tape and slid it into my work bag along with the conference envelope. I would have to carve out some time to work after meeting Liz.

The winter sun was making a brave attempt to burst through the clouds as I stepped outside of chambers, and the pavement still had a slick of last night's snow. Turning the corner of Middle Temple Lane onto Victoria Embankment, I quickened my pace. A message pinged on my phone.

How are you? Call me when you can. Love you more than ever. Mum x

No time to call her now. Her bi-weekly 'check-ins' to make sure I was eating healthily and not over-working, and to fill me in on all the latest goings-on in Mumbles never lasted less than an hour and I had been looking forward to this coffee date all week. Liz and I hadn't seen each other on our own since she had come home from the hospital with Maddy – hers and Mary's firstborn.

My phone buzzed again. It was Liz. *Going to be a bit late.*

How late? Have you left yet? I typed back. No instant reply.

I made my way through Embankment station and reappeared the other side onto Villiers Street. A cold blast whistled around me and drove me forward.

And that's when I saw it. *Café d'Amour.*

Images of a day fourteen years ago flickered in my mind until they settled on one frame: two strangers sitting at the table by the window; conversation, laughter, happiness. I suddenly felt light-headed and my breathing became shallow. I reached into my coat to retrieve my inhaler and took a quick puff, shaken by the resurgence of those memories that hadn't surfaced in years. I walked past the café and didn't look back.

Standing at the Charing Cross tube exit, I waited for Liz. Five minutes passed before I called her. It rang and rang and rang – until finally a muffled sound came through. A sob. Then another followed by the sound of Maddy wailing in the background.

'Liz, what's the matter? Is everything all right?'

'I. Can't. Do. This.' Raspy intakes of breath punctuated each word.

'Do what?'

She mumbled something indecipherable. I held my finger in my ear to drown out the noise of the commuters around me. 'I didn't hear you.'

'I can't come to Charing Cross,' she screamed. 'I haven't even left the house. She won't stop bloody crying. Please, Abs. Please come over.'

I held my breath, thinking of all the work I had to do at home before heading out to dinner. But these thoughts evaporated immediately.

'Of course, I will. I'll be there as soon as I can,' I said.

'Thanks, Abs. And bring supplies. I'm fucking starving.'

There was a hint of relief in her voice and I took it as a good sign.

I rang the doorbell to Liz's home half an hour later and was greeted by a tear-stained face. The near constant screams of baby Maddy filled the hallway. Liz flung herself at me, burying her head into my shoulder.

'It's OK, it's OK,' I soothed. 'But I am about to drop these cakes on your doorstep if you don't let me come inside.'

She pulled back and I followed her into the living room. Maddy was lying in her Moses basket, arms and legs flailing. The coffee table was littered with nappies, baby powder and cabbage leaves. Liz was still in her nightdress with her dressing gown hanging loose over it, her wayward blonde curls unbrushed.

'Please pick her up, Abs. I'll go and make some tea.'

Before I could protest, she had already gone to the kitchen. I shrugged off my coat and took several deep breaths as I stared down at Maddy thrashing about in the basket. I gingerly lifted her ... No. I couldn't do this. As I went to put her back her wailing increased. What was wrong with her?

I placed her against my shoulder and stroked her back in a circular motion, changing the movement in my body from up and down to side to side. A burp and a fart came out almost simultaneously and the writhing eased. Before long, the wailing stopped.

'How the bloody hell did you do that?' Liz said from the doorway, a mug in each hand.

'I guess she had some wind.'

'Right. You are never leaving.'

I smiled as I slowly laid Maddy back down into her basket, relieved it could be that simple.

'Thanks,' I said, taking the mug Liz passed over.

She sniffed, grabbing a tissue and blowing her nose, before sinking into the sofa. 'I tried winding her. I fed her, I jiggled her, I changed her nappy for the fourth time, but nothing. I haven't slept in days. Mary left for her case in Sheffield this morning, and I told her I would be fine but I'm not. Where's this so-called maternal "instinct" that's meant to kick in once it's dropped from your vagina? It's a lie.' She rocked back and forth.

'Hey, hey,' I said, squeezing her knee. 'It's fine, I'm here. I can stay a bit. Everything's going to be OK. Have some cake.'

Liz bit into a millefeuille. 'This is heaven, thanks, Abs,' she mumbled as flakes of pastry spilled down her chin. 'I didn't think it'd be this hard. Mary does her best, but I think she expects me to know what to do all the time, and I don't. I've even started counting down the days until I go back to work.'

A cry then pierced the air. A gap, then a wail.

'See!' Liz said, plopping her cake on a plate with a half-eaten wilting sandwich on it. 'Not even five bloody minutes.'

I looked to Liz and waited, but she didn't pick up Maddy. She seemed paralysed as she sat there, her eyes wide and glassy.

'It's OK, I've got her,' I said.

I tentatively picked Maddy up again and did a similar rocking motion. Bodily functions passed from both ends again and she closed her eyes.

'Maybe I should keep her on my shoulder for a bit longer,' I said.

Liz nodded and the panicked look appeared to fade. 'Are you sure? My arms start to ache after I've held her a while. The health visitor came yesterday and said she was almost twelve pounds. She's a bruiser.'

'I think I can manage twelve pounds for a few minutes. I remember lugging almost thirty when we got dropped by that bus almost two miles from the train station in Zagreb when we were Interrailing.'

Liz flopped back onto the couch. 'God, I remember. You were cursing me for having misread the timetable.' A smile suddenly appeared on her face. 'I know.'

'What?'

She didn't elaborate but padded out the room in her slippers.

Maddy squirmed and I shifted her back into my arms. She cooed and a tight knot nestled in my chest as I took in her big blue eyes. Is this what it might have felt like? I wrestled the thought away and rocked her back and forth.

'This!' Liz suddenly said from the doorway, brandishing a photo album with palm trees on it. 'Please say you'll stay. Wouldn't it be fun to go through it? It's been years since we did this.'

I knew exactly what was in there – and that she had another three albums where it came from. They contained photos of the trip we took after graduation, fourteen years ago.

I looked at the clock on the wall. Five-thirty. 'I'd love to, Liz, but I've got dinner with Charlie tonight, remember?'

'God, yes, I forgot.' Her face fell instantly, and she gripped the album tightly to her chest. 'It's just ...' She chewed her bottom lip. 'I don't really want to be on my own right now,' she said in almost a whisper.

I looked at Liz's pleading face and settled back into the sofa. 'OK, maybe one album.'

As we flipped through the last page of the *fourth* album, swapping memories of crazy escapades along our travels, I noticed Liz's eyes begin to droop. Maddy stirred in her basket and emitted a familiar, throaty cry. It wasn't long before it reached a wail.

'Maybe I should feed her,' she said. As she brought Maddy to her breast, Liz grimaced, narrowing her eyes.

'Is that painful?'

'It's the mastitis. Still hasn't cleared up. The doctor gave me some antibiotics, but they haven't kicked in. Come on, come on,' Liz pleaded, trying to direct her nipple into Maddy's mouth. 'No, not there, there.' She sighed heavily.

'Can I get you anything before I go?'

'Yes, please. A large glass of water would be great.'

As I was in the kitchen, I could hear Maddy start up again.

I returned to find Liz sitting on the sofa, her head in her hands, shoulders shaking. Maddy was back in the basket, writhing about.

'What happened?'

Liz glanced up with a defeated look in her eyes, which were now rimmed with tears. 'Why can't she tell me what she wants?'

I put the glass down on the table and rocked the Moses basket from side to side until her cries lessened. Surely it couldn't be that easy again. I didn't deserve the satisfaction of being the one to soothe her.

'I ... I can't ...' Liz was gasping and struggling for breath.

'It's OK, Liz. Here.' I grabbed the paper bag on the table, shaking out the cake crumbs. 'Breathe into this.'

The bag deflated and inflated rapidly. She gripped the edges so hard, I feared it would rip. In, out, in, out. Liz's breath slowly began to steady until it returned to normal, and she took the bag away from her mouth.

'I'm scared, Abs,' she finally said. 'This morning, I seriously thought about walking out and leaving Maddy alone. I knew you'd be worried and would come over eventually. You know where the spare key is. I wanted to get in a car and drive away, even though I don't have a bloody licence.' She let out a sound resembling a laugh, but it was tinged with sadness and her hazel eyes glazed over again.

I held her hand in mine. 'I'm no expert, Liz. But I think you need to talk to someone. Your GP, your mum—'

'No way, I'm not calling her.' Liz shook her head rapidly. 'I'm fine.' She smiled wanly. 'I'm just missing Mary, that's all. And the last thing I need is Mum. She'll come over and make it all about her. I'm sure this is a one-off,' she said, lifting the paper bag up. 'I have a newborn, for heaven's sake. What is it they call it? Baby blues. That's what the midwife said at my first check-up. All completely normal, Abs. It'll be your turn soon and you'll see.'

'No, thank you. I love my sleep too much.' Maddy gurgled in her basket as if she knew my response was fabricated.

'She's wide awake,' Liz said, yawning. 'Maybe she wants to be pushed around in her buggy. We haven't been out all day and it's dark now.' She stroked wisps of hair on Maddy's head and Liz's eyes suddenly widened, as if fending off sleep.

'Why don't I take her for a quick outing? You go and have a nap. You'll feel much better once you do.'

'Really? You'd do that? But what about your dinner with Charlie?'

I looked at the clock on the wall again. Six-thirty. No time to get home to Baker Street and change into my new dress and get to Piccadilly, but time enough to take Maddy for a quick walk, change here and then do some work after dinner.

'I'm sure he won't mind if I'm a little late. Could I have a shower here, borrow something from your wardrobe and raid your make-up stash?'

'Of course. Anything.'

It wasn't long before Maddy drifted off on our walk and I circled back towards Liz's house. Pushing the buggy into the living room, I dimmed the lights and removed the pram's cover.

Tiptoeing up the stairs, pausing every time a floorboard creaked beneath the carpet, I reached Liz's bedroom to tell her I was going to take a shower. But she was curled up in a tight ball, snoring loudly.

'Liz,' I whispered softly, gently nudging her arm. 'Liz.'

No response. There she was, totally checked out, finally able to let go.

What should I do now? No way could I leave Maddy alone downstairs without letting Liz know. The panic attack that I had seen grip her earlier worried me too.

Creeping back down to the kitchen, I pulled out my phone. Charlie's mobile went straight to voicemail. I took a deep breath when I heard the familiar beep.

'Hey, it's me. I'm at Liz's. She's having a hard time with Maddy and I'm really worried. I said I'd stay a while. She's fallen asleep and I can't leave right now. I'm so sorry.' My shoulders dropped. 'I'm not going to make dinner. I'll probably be another hour or two. Maybe we can catch last orders at Seymour's and have a late-night bite? Oh, and I forgot to tell you, Mary asked me to step in for her at the immigration conference in Paris tomorrow and Sunday. Can't wait to tell you all about it. My train leaves at eleven so we could have a leisurely breakfast. Love you. I really am sorry.'

I tossed my phone onto the kitchen table and pulled open Liz's fridge, a feeling of disappointment setting up camp inside me. But was there a sliver of relief mixed in too?

A half-bottle of rosé sat on the shelf inside the door. Pouring myself a glass, I took a big swig. God, that helped.

What now? One small consolation. I had clawed back some time to work. At the mere thought of the impending case and conference, my head throbbed with a sharp pain. I noticed a packet of paracetamol by the bread bin and swallowed a couple.

Taking my glass through to the lounge with my work bag, I flopped back on the sofa, knocking the last photo album to the floor.

As I picked it up a photo slipped out. It was of me; the last one Liz had taken in Bulgaria – the penultimate destination on our trip – before she had to suddenly go home. Her mum had needed her, and Liz had never forgiven her for spoiling the end of her holiday.

I fingered the picture. A dumb grin was plastered across my face and I was holding a guidebook to the last secret destination Liz had booked. What had I felt in that moment? The journey ahead was a long one and I was about to do it alone – an 'adventure of a lifetime', Liz had called it. But if I had known going there would change the course of my life, would I have ever gone?

2

Years Earlier

June

His fingers caressed my cheek and moved down to my shoulder and along my arm. Kisses on my lips roused me further from my slumber.

'Wake up, Abbie,' he said.

'What time is it?' I murmured, not wanting to open my eyes just yet. My other senses were already heightened: the feel of the soft cotton sheet that bound our naked bodies, the scent of his skin – a mixture of aftershave and that distinctive citrus smell, his voice – everyday words that did something to me every time he spoke and the taste of his kisses – always sweet.

'It's time to wake up,' he said.

I groaned and turned over, away from him, prising one eye open. Streetlights outside the window shone into the room. We hadn't even got round to closing the shutters last night. 'No, it's not. It's still dark.'

He spooned me tighter, moving his hand to my stomach where his fingers circled. I tingled at his touch. Maybe he was instigating a repeat of last night's exploits.

'It's five and I want to take you somewhere,' he whispered against my ear before brushing his nose against it.

'Then I am certainly not waking up. We only drifted off a few hours ago. Go back to sleep.'

'I haven't slept. I have waited years to be in your arms again and I don't want to waste a single minute sleeping.'

I melted at his words and drew his hand from my belly to my lips.

He kissed my neck and shoulder before pulling me back towards him. 'Please, Abbie. I want to show you something, but we have to be quick. We can sleep later in the car.'

My eyelids fluttered open and I instantly smiled. I had never woken up next to him in bed and my heart sang as I took in his face: those eyes, that smile.

'OK,' I said with a conciliatory tone. 'But can I go back to my room and change at least?'

'There's no time. Last night's clothes are fine.'

He stepped out of bed and I took in his nakedness, the muscles in his arms as he stretched, his smooth olive skin. I willed him not to get changed but to return to bed and into my arms, to make love to me again. He rifled through his suitcase and pulled out a crisp white T-shirt.

'Here.' He handed it to me. 'You can put this over your dress. It will warm you against the morning breeze.'

I dragged myself out of bed and changed as he dressed quickly. He led me out of the hotel holding my hand, picking up a package from the reception on our way out. 'For later,' he said when I enquired what the mysterious contents were.

He led me back to the spot where we had talked heatedly last night, to the rocks by the sea – where he had told me he had never stopped thinking of me and that he was glad that destiny had brought us back together.

There were fewer people by the water now, unsurprising given the early hour; some with fishing rods, others chatting quietly in foreign tongues and holding steaming cups. The only illumination came from lamps spaced evenly down the promenade and the early morning light.

He clutched my hand tighter as I stepped over the railing before pulling me down onto him as he sat on the rocks. Sea spray splashed our legs.

'Are you cold?' he said.

'No, I'm fine.' My body was still on fire – that post-sex glow that I never wanted to be extinguished.

He wrapped his arms around me, and I leaned back and rested my head on his shoulder.

'Any minute now. Do you see?' He pointed somewhere far into the distance. 'The lighthouse has been lit through the night to protect the boats coming into the harbour, and … there.'

I focussed hard and in an instant the light went out and a burst of orange emerged on the horizon and cascaded along the water in ripples, breaking against the rocks. The sight literally took my breath away. He squeezed me tighter.

'I don't want to move, ever.' I couldn't see his face, but I could feel his smile behind me. 'Though I wouldn't say no to a coffee at some point.' I looked up at him and grinned eagerly. I had noticed some stalls opening on the promenade and people gathering to make breakfast purchases.

'Your wish is my command.'

He broke free from our embrace and reached into his rucksack for the package the concierge had given him, revealing a flask and a tray of pastries. As if on cue, my stomach growled.

'Oh, you are a god.' I smiled as I cradled the cup, and he poured the brew. It was a strong black roast – not something I was used to drinking but it hit the spot perfectly and had a sweet aftertaste. We shared the coffee and pastries in companionable silence.

'What will we say to the others when they pick you up?' I said after a while. 'How do we explain this and the fact that I am coming too?'

'Do we have to?'

I chewed a mouthful of croissant and shook my head.

'Let's keep it as our secret for now,' he said. 'We can say we met at breakfast and I persuaded you to come. Before I forget.' He reached into his shorts and fished out his mobile. Holding it up in selfie mode, I saw our image – the glow of sun on our faces, a look of pure bliss in our smiles. 'I want to send this to you, so you have my number. I never want us to let this many years pass again.'

I typed my number into the phone and hit send.

When we finished the last of our breakfast, he held my hand in his.

'Abbie,' he whispered, leaning closer. 'This moment is like a dream. I feel alive for the first time in years.' His eyes held mine and I was under their magic spell once more.

He touched my mouth with his again. His lips were warm from the hot liquid and the taste of his tongue was exotic and

19

befitting of this crazy city – a city of contrasts, a melting pot – a city I wanted to visit again, with him.

The kisses were gentle at first before becoming more urgent and probing. I groaned as his hands clasped me tighter, so our bodies merged even more.

Could he hear my heart thundering beneath his T-shirt? Did he know how much I wanted him again? My thoughts were crystallising and that's when I realised; he had entered my soul and there was no other person I wanted to be with forever except him.

3

Now

December

'Abbie?'

'Hmm.'

'Abbie, wake up,' Liz said.

'What time is it?' I mumbled, my head fuzzy, eyes trying to focus on her face.

'Half six. In the morning.'

'What?' I shot up, noticing the empty wine glass on the table and daylight spilling through the blinds. A blanket was knotted at my waist and my stomach growled audibly. 'What happened?'

'I think you were having an orgasm in your sleep.'

I looked at her quizzically.

'You were moaning and groaning. Must've been some dream you were having.'

'How can it be morning? Didn't you try and wake me last night?'

'I did, I promise. But you were dead to the world; I even tried shaking you. I took Maddy up to my room when she stirred and went to bed. Sorry.'

I undid my bun and ran my fingers through my hair, trying to tease out the knots.

'I don't even remember falling asleep. I poured myself a glass of wine, took some paracetamol I found on the kitchen counter and sat down here, waiting for you to wake up.'

'The tablets by the bread bin?' She shook her head like a mother about to scold her child. 'That's Mary's codeine. She left a packet on the side. She's got a dodgy knee. Christ, Abs. I didn't think we needed to childproof everything yet.'

'Oh no, Charlie.' I picked up my phone from the coffee table and saw two missed calls and three text messages from him.

'It's fine. He called me late last night and I told him you were staying over.'

'Was he OK about it? I feel bad I cancelled our dinner and then I told him I was only going to be a couple of hours.'

'Of course he was OK. Charlie's the most understanding guy I've ever met.'

I tilted my head to relieve a crick in my neck and rubbed the bridge of my nose.

'Is everything OK, Abs?' Liz asked, holding the baby monitor and a cup of tea in her hands. 'You and Charlie aren't having problems, are you?'

'No, we're fine. I just haven't been sleeping well recently and it's making my nerves frayed.'

And now I had lost a whole evening where I could have been thinking up at least one winning argument for my case and prepping for the conference. If Mum knew I was overstretching myself, there would be a lecture of epic proportions. She loved to remind me what happened the last time I took on too much. I pulled at my locket, swinging it back and forth on its chain.

'I'd better go,' I said. 'I need to get myself ready and packed for Paris.'

'Already? Can't you stay for a cuppa?' She wafted the steaming cup in front of my nose.

I inhaled the brew. 'OK, just a quick one.' I smiled and took a little sip, letting my fingers warm against the cup.

Liz shifted beside me. 'God, this takes me back, having you crash out on the sofa. Remember when you were at law school in Guildford sharing that flat with Nada? All those evenings when I came down to see you and had to stay over when I'd missed the last train back to London?'

I smiled at the memory. Nada had been an international student from Lebanon, studying journalism at the University of Surrey. It had been a blast living with her. Even though she had moved back to Beirut after a year, we still stayed in touch religiously, but I missed seeing her.

'I wish we could go back to those days,' Liz said. 'I think I would do everything differently. Certainly wouldn't have wasted all those years living at Mum's doing all those crappy temp jobs and then thinking PR was the best career path. I would've travelled more, volunteered in Africa or something like that.'

'But you got your dream job in the end.'

'Only ten fucking years too late.'

For the past four years, Liz had worked in the communications department of a charity funding research into childhood illnesses and problems in pregnancy. I had never seen her as happy in her professional life. She loved to tell me about the families the charity had helped, but some of the loss stories were hard to hear; an ache always settled deep inside me.

'But if you hadn't had all those terrible PR jobs,' I said, 'then you wouldn't have been the right person for the job you have now.'

'Suppose,' she said, passing the monitor between her hands. It suddenly burst into life, causing her shoulders to tense and her breathing to shorten. She was soon in the grip of the same panicky gasps she had struggled to control yesterday.

'It's OK. Let her cry a bit,' I said, turning the volume down. 'She might settle herself. Look at me and breathe.' I took her arms and rubbed them up and down, trying to get her to focus on the measured movement of air in and out of my lungs.

Several minutes passed before Liz regained her composure, during which time Maddy's complaints had stopped.

Liz gripped my hands. 'What's happening, Abs? Please stay.' Her bottom lip wobbled. 'Please don't go.'

My stomach twisted. I had already cancelled on Charlie twice and had the weight of the conference and next week's case balancing precariously on my shoulders. But none of that mattered right now. It was still early and the latest I needed to be at King's Cross for the Eurostar was ten.

'I'm going to go and check on Maddy and make you another tea,' I said. 'But I want you to do me a favour.'

She didn't answer. A mixture of fear and anxiety had crossed her face.

'I can stay a little longer, but I want you to call your mum as well.'

There were no protests this time, only a simple nod.

I wiped away the tear trickling down her face and brushed her curls behind her ears.

She picked up her phone and scrolled through her contacts before placing it to her ear.

'Hey, Mum. I'm sorry it's so early. No, no, she's fine. But ...' And that's when the tears came freely.

Giving her arm a quick squeeze, I walked out and up the stairs.

I hadn't wanted to tell Liz I knew exactly what my dream had been about. It was of a day years ago. A day when ... when the decisions I made would have far-reaching consequences. Looking over the photo albums must have triggered the memory. But what good did it do me thinking about the past? All this talk with Liz about doing things differently. The only thing I needed to focus on this morning was getting Liz the support she needed and racing back home and making it up to Charlie.

The teaspoon clinked against the cup three times. It rattled as Charlie placed it on the saucer. A rustle of newspaper followed. He was sitting at the kitchen table of our flat. Technically, the flat belonged to his parents – an investment they made when he graduated from Oxford and started at Bar school in London – but he paid them a token rent and I began contributing once I moved in a year ago.

'Hey,' I said.

Charlie flinched and looked over his shoulder. 'Christ, you gave me a fright. I didn't hear you come in.'

He stood up and brushed my lips with his. 'Here, come and sit.' He pulled me down onto his lap.

I encircled my hands around his neck and sank into his embrace, feeling his warmth against my hands. 'I'm so sorry about dinner and not coming home last night,' I mumbled into his neck, leaving a kiss close to his Adam's apple. The familiar scent of his shower gel lay there, and it was comforting.

He pulled back a fraction and stroked my cheek. 'It's OK. But I was *so* worried about you. When I got your message at the restaurant, I headed home and waited. I tried calling you. Thank God I got hold of Liz.'

His green eyes widened with concern beneath his spectacles. I loved the way his sandy blonde hair fell onto the black frame and how when he was holding them, he chewed the temple tips, lost in thought.

'I made a stupid mistake,' I said. 'I'd picked up some of Mary's codeine by accident and mixed it with wine. Knocked myself out, literally, and Liz couldn't wake me. You got my text this morning though?'

'About staying with Liz until her mum arrived?'

'Yes. It took a lot of courage ringing her – they still have a strained relationship. And it's hard with Mary not around either.'

'Maybe we should send some flowers to cheer her up.'

I put my hands on either side of his face. 'That's so thoughtful,' I said, leaning in to give him a long, lingering kiss on his lips. 'I love you, Charlie Logan.'

His smile widened. 'And I love you, Abigail Jones.'

'I really am sorry for missing our anniversary dinner. I was so looking forward to it.' My bottom lip protruded.

'You don't need to keep apologising. It was just dinner. We can go there anytime.'

I pulled back from his embrace, my hands twisting in my lap. 'I thought it had a three-month waiting list.'

'Where did you hear that?'

I decided not to tell him what Amy had been speculating. 'I think someone at work mentioned it. So ... it wouldn't have been a special evening?' My brow wrinkled.

He clasped my hands and squeezed them. 'Of course it would've been special. Every date with you is special. But it's no big deal that we didn't get to go.'

'Oh.' I struggled to hide the disappointment in my voice. I sat up then went over to the sink and filled the water tank of the coffee machine. Placing a pod inside, I pressed the button and waited for my mug to fill with an espresso.

'Shall I make you some breakfast?' Charlie said.

'That would be great. I have to pack for the conference.' The machine came to a spluttering stop and I inhaled the roasted beans before blowing away the steam and taking a sip. 'Can't believe I'm off to Paris.'

'Neither can I. I'm going to miss you.'

'Why don't you come with me? That would be amazing. There's some time tonight after the dinner. We could do some late-night sightseeing.'

'I wish I could. But yesterday's case didn't go quite as planned. I'll have to, umm ...' He cleared his throat. 'Meet with the solicitor tomorrow to go through some points.'

'On a Sunday?'

He shrugged. 'Can't afford for Monday to go the same way.'

I brought my mug to the table and sat down on the chair next to Charlie's. 'That's a shame. I was rather hoping you could be there to … well, to support me.'

'You'll always have my support, Abbie, but you don't need me to be physically there. I have faith in you. You'll do great. Has Mary filled you in on what you'll be doing?'

'She prepared a pack for me, but I haven't had a chance to go through it or do enough prep for Monday's case.' I rubbed the back of my neck with my hand to try and ease out the knots of tension. 'And did you see what *The Legal 500* directory called me? "Approachable and patient." I'm hardly going to be inundated with requests based on that review.'

Charlie reached out his hand and pulled me back onto his lap, taking over from my feeble attempt at a massage. 'I'm worried about you,' he said softly. 'I don't want you running yourself into the ground.' He pressed his fingers deep into my shoulders and up and down my neck and I groaned in ecstasy.

'Don't be worried. I'm fine. Oh, that's so good,' I said. 'You have the hands of a … oh, I don't know, a magician.'

He chuckled. 'I aim to please,' he said cheekily as he laid a few kisses on my bare neck. 'And I for one think you are much more than just approachable and patient.'

'You would say that, though, you're my boyfriend.' The tension began to ease even more as his fingers kneaded harder. 'Hmm. Maybe I could spend the train journey reading the conference pack,' I mused. 'I'd rather have this massage go on forever and a fry-up.'

'Consider it done. And I can help with your case on Sunday night if you need to bounce any ideas around. I know it's not my specialism, but I know a thing or two about the law.'

I looked over my shoulder at him and he gave me a wink.

I kissed him again, flinging my arms around his neck, practically knocking his chair backwards as I shifted to sit astride him. 'You are the most thoughtful guy, Charles Fitzpatrick Logan. And I am going to miss you this weekend.' I leaned in to kiss him hard on the lips before removing his glasses and trailing my lips from his mouth down his neck, before peeling back the folds of his dressing gown.

His return kisses became more passionate until I yelped as his hands met my skin under my jumper.

'That tickles.' I giggled and gazed into his eyes again. 'I know this is going to sound crazy.' I bit my bottom lip. 'But . . . I thought you were going to propose last night.'

The shocked look on his face reinforced what I had surmised from his earlier comments. There had been no planned proposal. It was *only* dinner. I dropped my arms from his neck.

'Oh, Abbie.' He paused to put his glasses back on and pull up his dressing gown. 'I'm sorry if I gave off that impression. I just thought it would be nice to do something a little different for our anniversary. And we've both been so busy at work and hardly spent much time with each other recently. I thought it would be fun to go somewhere a little fancy.'

'Of course, I knew that.'

He shifted his position on the chair as if my weight was a sudden burden. 'I like things the way they are now, don't you? Remember I told you how I felt about marriage?'

'Uh huh.' I nodded.

It was true. We'd had a talk about marriage not long after we got together, and he had told me about how his university girlfriend had jilted him at the altar to go travelling around Australia. But that talk was almost three years ago. And the build-up to this anniversary and what I'd thought was Charlie's not so obvious hints had made me think he had changed his mind.

But Charlie was right. Things were good between us. Why change anything? Getting married would inevitably lead to the subject of having kids and I wasn't ready to have that conversation again.

Charlie got up awkwardly, pushing me to one side, and began fiddling with pots and pans, pulling out eggs and bacon from the fridge. I guess that meant the discussion was over. Now he would never know what my answer would have been. But did *I* even know?

Paris. The city of love, passion and about three hundred thousand protesters. Of all the weekends to hold a conference – the same time as France was gripped in a political movement concerning workers' rights and deteriorating standards of living. In front of me was a sea of people, the majority wearing yellow Hi-Vis vests, with raucous chants filling the air I couldn't understand, but then I had never made it past GCSE French.

A pulse of excitement filled me at being back here. The last time had been on my and Liz's Interrailing trip. Then it had been a budget hostel and 'all you can eat for ten euros' restaurants. My destination now? The five-star Marriott Rive Gauche in the fourteenth arrondissement of Paris, a twenty-minute ride on the RER B line from the Gare du Nord.

I gripped the handle of my overnight case and readjusted the shoulder strap of my laptop bag. The protest roared around me.

'*Excusez-moi,*' I said, attempting to push my way through the mass of people filling the tree-lined avenue.

But it was no use. The crowds were building, not thinning. It had been a wall of protesters as soon as I had stepped out of the Metro. My first session at the conference was in around an hour, but if my progress continued to stay at nil, then I would be cutting it fine to make it to the hotel in time.

Then something strange happened. It was like a straight line had been carved along the road, causing heads to part so I could see far into the distance.

That's when I saw his face. A face I could never forget. My mouth opened to call out his name, but my breath caught in my throat and in a blink he was gone. Was my mind playing tricks?

Another surge of movement and there he was again, proving this was no figment of my imagination. But he was too far away to hear me calling him even if I tried. I reached into my coat to grab my inhaler. Clarity struck again after the medicine filled my throat, and I became rooted to the spot. Protesters buffeted me as they marched. I couldn't move.

Was this fate or destiny? Who knew?

And then he turned, and our eyes met. Brown meeting caramel with flecks of burnt orange; an image singed in my mind forever.

The chants of the protesters quietened; the thumping of my heartbeat all I could hear.

It was like being sucked into a tunnel to the past; memories surfacing which shouldn't be stirred.

He smiled – that familiar smile – and I closed my eyes for a second. When I opened them, he was gone.

5

Fourteen Years Earlier

February

'Where are you, Liz? If I don't make it to Hyde Park by two to hear the speeches, I'm screwed. It's already half twelve.'

I hit the 'end call' button on my mobile, noticing the single bar of battery flashing at me like a detonator. Brilliant. That was the third voicemail I had left her.

Behind me, streams of people poured out from the depths of Charing Cross tube. The voice of John Lennon asked everyone to give peace a chance from a loudspeaker, and ahead, the view was a sea of placards – thousands of them – and a glimpse of the statue of Charles I, sitting on his horse at Trafalgar Square. The absence of red double-decker buses and black cabs was conspicuous. The streets had been given over to the people.

I chewed the inside of my cheek and checked my watch. Fifteen minutes. I had given up waiting for Liz fifteen minutes ago and moved barely three hundred feet since then. By my calculation, it would take another five hours to march the mile and a half to Hyde Park. *No, no, no.*

A tightness gripped my chest, and I rubbed my hand over my jumper, brushing the scratchy wool of the Christmas present Mum had knitted for me.

There's no need to panic, Abbie, I tried to reason with myself.

A chopper hovered overhead and a chant swept across the crowd, which was about forty deep now. Whistles added to the din. A group to the right of me moved forward and I took a small step in that direction.

'Ouch,' I yelped, as a heavy weight bore down on my foot.

'Pardon,' someone said, right as I blurted 'Sorry.'

'Are you OK?' they asked.

The thick accent cut through the February chill and caused me to look up, surprised at the interest in my welfare.

A tall guy with dark hair – long and wavy up top, shorter on the sides – held up his hands in apology. Concern was etched into his forehead and there was a hint of stubble against his olive skin, lips parted.

I caught myself staring at them and realised he was waiting for a response. 'I'm fine,' I said, even though my little toe throbbed inside my boot. A shove in the back thrust me forward but a mass of bodies in front instantly checked me. 'We're not moving particularly fast. I'm sure I can manage with one foot.'

He looked at me, perplexed, tipping his head into the upturned collar of his dark grey puffer jacket. His hair ruffled in the wind.

Before I could think of an explanation for my attempt at sarcasm, another wave of 'Not in Our Name' began to build. The guy turned away and lifted his arm high, shouting the words along with the crowd.

I attempted to join in, but I was wheezing. I lifted my inhaler from deep within the pocket of my parka. Three shakes and one hard press on the pump. Barely a puff emerged. *Crap.* I thought I had replaced the canister last week. I dropped it back in my coat and my fingers touched the note; the note I had received yesterday from my politics supervisor. I didn't need to read it again; three words burned in my brain: 'Could do better.'

My heart rate picked up and a prickly sensation passed over my limbs. I sucked in the cold air, filling my lungs with as much oxygen as I could, but it did nothing to moderate my breathing.

Another surge knocked me forward, and I pressed up against a woman in front of me. Now I felt dizzy. Please, no. An asthma attack was not an option right now. The message 'Keep hope alive' rippled on a banner behind me, and I hoped it was an omen.

A thought smacked hard against my brain. The six-point plan. That was it. I had to remember this sequence of steps to ward off an attack. Mum wrote it out and laminated it for me when I was seven. She even pinned it to my school bag once. It's filed in the multi-purpose case Dad gave me on my first day of university – two and a half years ago – along with a talk. In return, I had given him the promise – *the* promise – to stay focussed on my studies. A promise I would never go back on.

But in this environment – nothing. None of the six points came to mind. I pulled my inhaler out again with the hope of shaking one more puff from it. But another push forward knocked it from my grasp and onto the ground. *Shit.* I dropped my head to scan the ground around my feet; all Timberlands and Uggs.

'Excuse me, excuse me,' I said, but my words were lost in the chants. I gasped, airways tightening.

Everyone around me swayed. *Where's my … why is everything tilting?*

Darkness. Weightlessness; then voices – a burst of non-English words before more familiar accents took their place. I fought to breathe until a mask was placed over my mouth. The relief was instant.

Forcing my eyelids open, images began to take shape. A police officer – with a shiny EIIR police badge on her helmet – peered down, along with a paramedic adjusting a tube attached to a pump and a group of people behind them.

'Breathe deeply,' said the paramedic.

The cylinder hissed and crackled as I sucked in the medicine until my breathing normalised.

'Can you tell me your name?' the paramedic asked finally.

'Abigail,' I said, my voice muffled, steam coating the mask.

'Does anything hurt, Abigail?'

I wiggled my feet which were perched on the arm of a bench, my boots bumping together. My head was resting on something soft and grey but wooden slats pressed into my lower back. No other sources of discomfort. I shook my head.

'You gave us quite a fright,' the policewoman said. 'It's a good thing this young man was here to catch you.'

From the crowd, a tall man stepped forward. He was wearing a black T-shirt and blue jeans and looking like he had stepped out of a Levi's commercial from the nineties – all sculpted shoulders, muscled arms. *Wait* – that's the guy who trod on my foot earlier on. The cushion propping my head was probably his coat. He must be freezing without it. Hold on, he caught me? I rolled my eyes. Had we acted out a scene from a romcom? The hapless female saved by a dashing hero – the London backdrop faded and romanticised.

He crouched beside the bench as sunlight leaked through the clouds, giving him a halo. That same look of concern was etched even deeper into his face.

'You dropped this.' He held out his hand to reveal my inhaler. As he steadied himself with the arm of the bench, I noticed a scar peeking out from his sleeve – a line about four inches long, with a faint indentation of old stitches, pink against his darker skin tone.

'Thanks,' I said, curling my fingers around the canister. As I did so, a tingle of static passed between my fingertips and the palm of his hand and he smiled. Dimples formed in his cheeks as he stepped back.

The paramedic leaned down to remove my mask and lift me up. He held my wrist and checked his watch as I stole glances at black T-shirt guy who continued to watch the scene unfold.

'Hmm,' the paramedic murmured. 'Your pulse is quite high.'

I looked down at my boots and gripped my inhaler tightly.

'You're asthmatic?' the paramedic continued, putting a blood pressure cuff on my arm and inflating it.

'Yes. But I'm fine now. I felt dizzy and the canister was empty and then I think I began to panic.' My teeth chattered.

Black T-shirt guy reached out to grab the coat from the bench, but instead of putting it on, he slipped it around my shoulders. It was like an ignition switch lighting a burner, and I stopped shaking. 'Thanks,' I said, pulling the folds together in my free hand and involuntarily taking a sniff – a distinctive aroma of citrus and spices.

The paramedic stared at me with an eyebrow raised as he took the blood pressure cuff off. 'Your vitals are fine, but I think it's best you went home, Abigail.' He began to pack his bag.

'But no,' I protested. 'I have to make it to Hyde Park.'

'You need to take it easy first.' He flicked his head in the direction of black T-shirt guy. 'Why don't you go and get a cup of tea and a slice of cake with your boyfriend before heading back on the march.'

'My boy—' I looked over to him, my cheeks reddening.

The guy didn't flinch. Perhaps he only heard the word 'friend'.

'This isn't my boyfriend,' I muttered, shifting on the bench.

'He's her knight in shining armour,' the police officer said, nudging the paramedic. They both chuckled as I pulled at the collar of the puffer, trying hard not to look back at black T-shirt guy.

The paramedic lifted his bag onto his shoulder and then sighed. 'Seriously, though. Fainting isn't something to be taken lightly.'

That fact I knew. Mum had reminded me constantly since the first and last time it had happened.

'You could also suffer from outdoor claustrophobia,' he continued.

'Claustrophobia?'

'Possibly. Outdoor claustrophobia isn't common but could be one of your asthma triggers. Now,' he said, shifting his bag, 'keep your inhaler filled and book an appointment with your GP on Monday for a health check. All right?' He smiled before turning back towards the crowd.

The police officer nodded her head. 'Stay safe.'

'I'll try,' I said.

She left and the crowd around her dispersed.

Over my shoulder, protesters filed past, peace signs painted on cheeks, placards raised. The Beatles' song 'All You Need Is Love' rippled across the crowd. I pulled the puffer jacket to my chin. What now?

I had to find a way to Hyde Park without another incident. If I didn't, my chance of getting a first for my degree would lie in tatters. My politics supervisor had told me my first draft of my dissertation – twenty per cent of my final exam – wasn't good enough for the top grade and that listening to the speeches might give me some inspiration. Clearly, he didn't think my quotes were relevant enough. But how would I make it there now when there was a rumour only the first surge of protestors would be let through the gates and with my inhaler empty?

'Shall we have some tea?'

I swivelled back to the one person still standing in front of the bench – black T-shirt guy. 'Sorry?'

'The doctor said tea.'

I smiled. He had taken it as a serious diagnosis. 'You don't have to have tea with me.'

'I would like to.' His voice was earnest and soft. 'To make sure you're OK.'

'That's kind, but …'

And there it was. The word BUT. The 'get out of jail' card. But what? Mum would say don't talk to strangers while Dad would remind me that my deadline for my dissertation was looming. My big sister Amy, on the other hand, would say something crude like there is no but. He's bloody gorgeous. Say yes, and then shag him senseless.

'I'm fine, honestly. I can take care of myself.'

He nodded. 'I understand.' But he didn't move away. He cupped his hands, blowing air into them, and then rubbed them together.

'God. I'm sorry,' I said, pulling off his jacket from my shoulders. 'Thanks for your coat.'

'*Rica ederim,*' he said.

Our fingers touched briefly, and another, bigger jolt of electricity pulsed through them. We both flinched before looking back at each other. His dimples deepened as his smile broadened. He really did look like he'd stepped out of a commercial. But there was an air of shyness and self-deprecation about him – like he would laugh at the mere idea of gracing the cover of *GQ*.

As he turned and walked back into the march shrugging his arms into his coat, I felt another surge of light-headedness. Crap, not another asthma attack. But this feeling was different; deeper. Liz's voice wormed its way into my subconscious: *Why did you let him go?*

Don't be ridiculous, I would say to her. I don't have time for guys right now: dissertation due in two days, finals in three months, and I'm sure he was just being polite.

Come on, Abs, live a little! You're turning twenty-one tomorrow! And it's only a cup of tea for flip's sake.

I chewed the inside of my mouth and checked my watch. Springing up from the bench, my knees buckled. 'Wait!' I called out. But he had already disappeared into the crowds.

6

I pushed my way back through the rally, staying near to the barriers this time, rising on tiptoes to scan the sea of heads. A glimpse. All I wanted was a glimpse of his dark grey jacket. *Agh.* At least two-thirds of this crowd were wearing dark grey jackets.

This was stupid. What was I doing? Chasing after a guy who had rescued me and flashed me a heart-stopping smile? No. I was chasing him to say a proper thank you for catching me and carrying me to get medical attention. Only being polite, I reassured myself.

Wait. Over there.

Oblivious to any disapproving glances, I pushed my way into the centre, my heart hammering in my chest. I tried to sidestep a pushchair with a screaming toddler straining to get out. But while pirouetting, I lost my balance, stumbling towards the nearest person. They caught me, but the word 'thanks' stuck in my throat when I looked up into those eyes again.

It was like everyone else was flying past at speed, but we were locked in slow motion. Oh boy. Was this cementing my role of ditzy female in the romcom we were enacting, rescued yet again by the handsome stranger?

He put me on my feet and released his grip.

'We've got to stop meeting like this,' I said, but my words were lost in the chants around me.

He looked at me expectantly as other protestors bumped into us. Another push from behind propelled me flush against his chest. Misty clouds of breath from our mouths collided.

'Umm ... so ... tea would be perfection,' I said.

He looked confused.

I tucked wisps of hair from my too-long fringe behind my ears. 'That is, I changed my mind. Tea is probably a good idea. Paramedic's orders, right? I wouldn't want to faint on the way home, what with my inhaler being empty.'

I giggled nervously. I never thought I would see the funny side to an asthma attack. But I had survived it, despite years of Mum saying it would be the death of me, even though it had been a terrifying experience.

'There's a café on Villiers Street. Fancy it? I owe you one.' I dipped my head, letting my fringe fall back over my face. 'A cup of tea, that is ... for rescuing me ... umm ... twice.' Crikey, why had he reduced me to such a stuttering mess?

'OK,' he said, with a grin – dimples appearing again on cue.

Slipping through a small gap in the barriers, we made our way back to Charing Cross. Going against the crowd felt wrong, but a burst of excitement pulsed inside me as though I had been given a blank canvas with free rein to splash colours over it. A feeling I hadn't felt before.

We turned onto Villiers Street – a narrow cobbled walkway shut off to cars and trucks during the day. Shops on either side brimmed with weekend shoppers, and the smell of cooked onions from a nearby hot-dog stand gave the air a thick, sweaty quality. Hundreds of people continued to filter up from Embankment station towards the peace rally.

'I'm Abbie, by the way,' I said, peering at him before gazing down at my boots.

'Özgür.' A hand outstretched, and I took it in mine. The grip was strong and firm, and warmth spread through my fingers.

'Are you from London, Özgür?' I said, stumbling over the pronunciation of his name.

'No, I am from a district of Istanbul called Beşiktaş.'

'You're Turkish?' I nearly slapped my forehead with stupidity. 'I mean, you're Turkish. Statement, not question.'

'Yes, I am Turkish. And you are ... English?'

'Half. My dad's Welsh but he moved to the West Midlands when he was young.' I pulled up the collar of my jacket. 'Are you on holiday, then?'

'I complete a year at University College as part of my masters. It has a course linked to my university. I have also been studying intensive English.'

'Your English is amazing.'

His face lit up. A megawatt smile. And those dimples in his cheeks were big enough to hold a pound coin in. 'Thank you. You are kind. But I think I need more practice.'

Let him practise on you. Liz's words – laced with innuendo – sprang into my thoughts and a flush crept over my cheeks.

'And please, call me Oz. All my British friends do,' he said, holding the door to the café open.

44

Oz insisted he be the one to go and get the drinks, despite my objections, so I slid into an armchair beside the window and shrugged off my coat. He returned from the counter a few minutes later with a tray and lifted off a cup of tea, a mug of coffee and a plate. On it was a heart-shaped gingerbread cookie with pink icing.

'For you.' He pointed to the biscuit.

'Thanks.' The flush in my cheeks deepened. I never had been able to control the way they blushed every time I was caught in various degrees of discomfort or embarrassment. It had been a source of school teasing as the shade wasn't far off from my hair colour.

Oz peeled off his coat and sat down. 'My sister suffers from asthma also and her doctor said ginger could help. This was all they had.'

'Right, of course.' I suddenly felt foolish for thinking the gesture meant anything else.

It had slipped my mind what day it was as I had been so preoccupied with my dissertation. Liz had been nagging me to come to the King's Valentine's dance tonight, but I had told her I didn't have the time. My birthday weekend plans would have to be postponed until next Saturday.

I broke off a piece of the biscuit. 'I didn't know ginger had that secret power.' The spice tickled the back of my throat as I chewed. 'I don't usually make a habit of fainting. Thanks for catching me.'

'*Rica ederim.*' He took a sip of his black coffee.

'What do those words mean? You said them to me by the bench.'

'They mean "you're welcome". I forget sometimes which language I am speaking.'

'How many do you speak?'

'Four.'

'*Four* languages?'

'Not fluent. Turkish and English are my main languages, but I also studied Arabic and French as part of my degree.'

'Wow,' I whispered, pressing my spoon against the teabag, and adding a splash of milk.

He placed his cup back on the table and settled back in the armchair. 'Are you also a student?'

'Yes. At King's, London, studying PPE.'

'I don't know what that is.'

'Philosophy, politics and economics.'

'You will work for the government one day?'

I shook my head, munching a mouthful of cookie. 'Law school,' I said behind my hand.

'You want to be a lawyer?'

I nodded. 'A solicitor. Corporate. It's a good profession – excellent career progression.' My stock response tripped off my tongue like it had since I was thirteen. 'What about you?' I blew ripples across the surface of my tea. 'What do you want to do after your course?'

He leaned forward, lost in thought, cradling his mug. 'This experience, travelling and living in England. It excites me.' His eyes twinkled. Lifting his coffee off the table, his arm flexed. The scar was even more apparent in the harsh lighting of the coffee shop. 'I wish to do more travel.'

'And do you always spend Saturdays rescuing fainting passers-by?' I said, raising an eyebrow.

His smile broadened. '*Hayır*. No. Normally, my friends and I, we go to the cinema. It is a way to practise our English comprehension. There is a small screen in Leicester Square called the Prince Charles. It shows classic movies. They even show them all night.'

'Really? I don't know that place.' At night, I never usually ventured far from my room on Stamford Street – about a twenty-minute walk from here across Waterloo Bridge – or the Strand campus without Liz by my side. Safety in numbers. And there was an Odeon a stone's throw from our halls of residence.

'What's your favourite movie, then?' I asked.

He considered my question for a moment. '*Raging Bull*.'

'De Niro? That boxing movie?'

'Not only boxing. It is about the human spirit, and there is also a love story.'

I spluttered on my tea. 'There is?'

'But it is a destructive love.'

'Sounds heavy going.'

'It is a dark story but with excellent acting. You prefer a different kind of movie?'

'*Before Sunrise* is my favourite.'

'I haven't seen it.'

'It was released years ago.'

'What is the movie about?'

'Umm … I guess it's about taking a risk. An American guy meets a French girl on a train. He persuades her to get off in

Vienna, before her stop in Paris. They spend one perfect day together and then he leaves – back home to the US.' I took a sip of my tea.

'It is the whole story?'

'Pretty much. They agree to meet six months later back in Vienna.'

'And do they?'

'You don't know at the end. But I've seen the sequel.' I raised my eyebrows up and down.

'I will have to watch it then.'

'Do. It's beautiful. Very little plot but intense conversation and gorgeous scenery. They have this connection, the two characters. It's incredible.' My mind wandered off to the setting of the sequel – Paris.

'Would you do that?' he said.

My cup hovered by my lips. 'Do what?'

'Get off a train in Vienna with someone you had just met?'

'No!' I said emphatically.

'Why not?'

'Well, to start with, I can't imagine being on a train travelling around Europe on my own. And Vienna's very nice, I'm sure, but Paris? The architecture, the museums, the food.' I breathed in as if I was taking in a whiff of freshly cooked croissant. 'I don't think I'd pass up an opportunity to spend an extra day in Paris.'

'You haven't been?'

I pulled at my leggings to make the hole at my knee smaller. 'No, I haven't. I've spent every summer on the Welsh coast with my family. Have you?'

He nodded. 'It is as beautiful as you have imagined.'

'My best friend – Liz – has been nagging me to go Interrailing with her this summer. You know. Six cities in ten days.'

He shifted in his chair. 'Sounds fantastic.'

'It does. But ...' I pulled at my sleeves. 'I looked into the costs. The train ticket alone would be a couple of hundred quid, and once you calculate the expenses: hostels, food, incidentals ... it all adds up. And I should work all summer – save for law school and my accommodation.'

'So much responsibility, so young.'

That sounded like something my grandpa would say.

'*Yani*, I mean, it is a shame that is what you have to do when there is a world out there to explore.'

He stated it as though he had been hired by Turkish Airlines to do an infomercial.

'I'm sure the world will still be waiting for me once I get a job.' I pursed my lips and looked down at my cup.

'*Tabii ki*, of course. You recognise your ... *eh* ... priorities. But I think if you want to change your mind, there is always a way to do something meaningful; see the world, experience another way of life, another culture. Even if one's resources are limited, there is always a way.'

I fiddled with a bit of wool poking out from one of the sleeves of my jumper. The recruitment fair I had attended two weeks ago came to my mind. There were so many other possibilities after university I had never even imagined, and I couldn't deny my head had been turned several times.

'I bet Istanbul is beautiful,' I said after a pause. 'It's a blend of Europe and Asia, right?'

'Yes. A crazy city, where you could travel between two continents in a day. So much history, beauty—'

'And hot sun?'

'Yes. The summer sun is hot. It is also a city rich in culture, reflecting the many empires that once ruled it. But I have not been to Vienna and would like to.'

'Me too. It looked lovely in the movie. I'll have to watch it again somehow – refresh my memory. My sister broke my DVD.'

'I know well how annoying siblings can be.'

'Tell me about it. But it wasn't as bad as her locking me in a shed for four hours during a game of hide 'n' seek when I was eight.'

He bit his bottom lip to stop himself from laughing. '*Üf ya*. How cruel.'

'I'm scarred for life,' I said, holding my hand over my heart. Oz let out a laugh – his face lighting up with those dimples stretched wide. I caught myself staring at them.

'So …' I pulled my gaze away. 'What's the worst thing your sister's done?'

He pondered the question. 'She tore up my collection of football cards and flushed them down the toilet. I was ten.'

I pressed my fingers over my parted lips.

'I know. Crazy,' he said.

'What did your mum do?'

He tutted, with a quick flick of his head. 'She didn't care. I think she took my sister's bicycle away for a day.'

'And your dad? Was he harsher?'

Oz moved his head to the window. 'My father died when I was young.' His jaw tightened, and his fingers reflexively covered the scar on his arm. He rubbed it as though he was trying to erase a bad memory.

'I'm sorry,' I said in a whisper.

A barista tapped out a portafilter and a low hum of conversation filled the space around us along with the gentle croon of a French singer on the sound system.

'I will miss London,' he said finally.

'Why? Where are you going?'

'I leave tomorrow.'

'You what?' I said, a little loudly. 'I mean, that's a shame.'

He turned back to me and tipped his head. 'Yes, a great shame. My flight to Istanbul is at seven in the morning from Heathrow. My backpack is in a locker at Marble Arch station. At six today, I go to a farewell party with my friends at a Lebanese restaurant on Edgware Road, then I will spend the night at the airport.' He drained his mug of coffee and pushed it to the side. 'And now, I must go back to the march.'

'Oh.' I turned my cup on its saucer, sloshing dregs around the sides.

'Come with me.' He spoke so quietly his words didn't register immediately.

'Sorry?'

'Come with me, back to the march. You drank your tea and ate the biscuit. You are better, yes?'

I nodded. 'Yes, I am. But I have to go back to my room, to work on my dissertation.'

'On a Saturday?

'It's due on Monday.'

'What is it about?'

51

'Whether the UK has a perfect democracy.'

'How interesting.'

'I was meant to listen to the speeches at Hyde Park to get some quotes for it, but I don't think I'll make it there now. I still have loads of reading to do as well.'

'What will you do for quotes now?'

I shrugged. 'No idea. Go up to people on the march and ask them what they think?' I let out a half laugh.

'Yes,' he said enthusiastically. 'We can meet those from different backgrounds, different beliefs. Ask them why they are here, and whether they believe the will of the people will persuade the government to back down. Then you must come to the farewell party with my friends. You can interview them, too.'

'Go up to random people and interview them about their views on democracy?' I laughed.

'Why not?' he said.

A lady who had sat down at the table next to us cleared her throat and clutched her book closer.

'Well ...' I leaned over our table, so I could lower my voice. 'That's not what you do.'

He smiled. 'British people are so reserved.'

'We're a stereotype for a reason.'

'But you are different.' He rested his arms on his knees. 'You are not afraid to have a conversation with a stranger. I have faith in you. You could approach people on the march and ask them whether they believe they can change the course of history. And my friends will be honoured to speak with you, to explain how their governments compare.'

I positioned myself on the edge of my seat. 'I'm sorry. I'd love to, but it's probably not a good idea. I'm also running out of time.'

'You won't get a fail, yes?'

'No, I won't, but—'

'And you also have tomorrow to read? One day, you will be asked what you were doing on this day – this incredible, historical day. What will you say?'

God, he made it sound so easy, as if I had a choice to head back into the march with him and then go out to a party. My supervisor's comments were vague. He couldn't tell me where exactly I needed to strengthen my arguments. That was frustrating, after I had spent weeks, even months on it. And tomorrow was my birthday. My reputation as 'square Abbie who has no life' would be cemented forever.

'You can't always find the answers in books,' he said. There was a teasing expression on his face.

Oz's eyes held mine. Those caramel eyes were drawing me in when I knew exactly where my priorities should lie.

I could easily imagine Liz's advice. Smoking-hot guy is asking you to dare to do something different; her fist would be pumping, with 'go for it' written all over her face. My sister would disagree. If the long-term prospects weren't going to lead to a rock on her finger, a trip down the aisle and a semi in Solihull, what was the point in heading off with him for a few hours? But what did I think?

Oz stood and cleared the plate and cups away before putting his coat back on. 'Will you come with me?'

7

Now

December

The automatic doors of the Paris hotel swung back behind me as I entered. A board showcasing the immigration conference was on full display in the lobby. Delegates mingled with cups of steaming coffee, a gentle hum of various languages swirling around me. At the reception, I handed over my room confirmation sheet.

I had decided to come straight to the hotel before I was any later. What good would it do me to trawl the streets of Paris looking for Oz? What would I even say to him after all these years? I had moved on from the last time I ever saw him when he had shattered all hope of us ever being together. I'd read the conference pack during the entire Eurostar journey, and knew I needed to rehearse some of the things I wanted to say at the meetings I was due to attend this afternoon before the first talk kicked off.

'Ah, yes, Ms Jones,' the receptionist said with a strong French accent and a hint of humour lacing his words. 'We have you for one night in our top suite.'

'Um, no, I don't think so.' I retrieved the confirmation sheet from the counter. 'Double standard, it says here.' I pointed at the description underneath the picture of the room layout. 'There must be a mistake.'

'*Mais, non*. I have it here on my computer. You are booked into the suite and we have already arranged lunch in your room, so please hurry.'

I looked at him, puzzled, his overfamiliarity out of place. 'I should call my office and check what's going on. I don't think I'm meant to be booked into a suite. If you'd give me a minute.'

Before I could reach for my phone, the receptionist had stepped around the desk and was instantly by my side.

'Please, *mademoiselle*. There is no need to call your work. I assure you this is where you are booked in. It is, ah ... a special upgrade.'

Reluctantly I accepted the key card and resolved to take up the issue with one of the clerks at chambers on Monday.

The lift pinged as it reached the top floor, and I dragged my wheelie case along the red carpet towards a set of double doors. I looked at the key I had been given and matched it with the sign above the door: PRESIDENTIAL SUITE.

Good grief. What a mix-up. I stepped inside and my eyes bulged. A vast living room with a sofa and two armchairs stood on one side with a table and chairs on the other adorned with a lavish array of food and cakes and wine. Purple velvet drapes festooned the windows and elaborate patterns swirled around the carpet.

The doors to my left suddenly burst open. 'Surprise!' came a familiar voice.

I stepped back in shock. Charlie glowed in the pool of sunlight filling the bedroom behind him. Dressed in his navy pinstripe suit and pink tie, he looked ready for court. 'What on ...? What are you doing here?'

'I came to surprise you.'

'Why?'

'Why?' he said with a beaming smile, opening the doors wider and stepping towards me, taking a moment to reach to a side table and pull out a single rose from a vase. 'Because I love you,' he said, handing it to me. 'And because there was something I wanted to ask you. And I had so desperately wanted to ask you last night but it wasn't to be, so I rearranged everything to make sure, this time, nothing could get in the way of what I wanted to ask you.'

I stood rooted to the spot, my mind a jumbled mess. 'How did you get here?' I asked.

'I was on your train and had the good sense to take a taxi to the hotel. Thankfully the driver knew about the protest and the best way to make it here. I knew I would be cutting it fine, but the hotel was in cahoots and knew to stall you if I wasn't here before you.'

I laughed. 'I can't believe you did this.'

'This isn't the half of it. You should've seen what I had planned for last night.'

'But you said it was just a dinner.'

He nodded with a sheepish look. 'I had to throw you off the scent.'

My mouth widened. 'I don't know what to say.'

'Please, can I?' He silenced me with a pleading look and raised hand.

I clamped my lips shut, my heart thumping in my chest.

Charlie stepped towards me and held my hands – my fingers still holding the stem of the rose. He cleared his throat.

'Abigail Lily Jones. When I first met you fourteen years ago, I knew you were someone special. I admired your gumption.'

I stifled a giggle and cast my eyes downward.

'It's true. You weren't like any of the other students who walked past my booth that day at the recruitment fair. And the fact you didn't call me made me think about you constantly. But I resolved you were a determined woman who was incredibly headstrong and didn't want to deviate from the path you'd set yourself. Then when you walked back into my life all those years later, I knew it was fate.'

I flinched a little at the word.

'What were the odds of you turning up at my chambers? So poised, so beautiful.'

He stroked my cheek and I melted at his touch, leaning into his hand where I pressed my lips.

'All I wanted to do the day we went for our first coffee date was kiss you. Who knew it would take another two years to break down your resolve?'

'Was I hard to ask out?'

'So now you're telling me you would've gone out with me sooner?' He raised his eyebrows, causing several lines to appear across his forehead.

'Well, no, you're right. I was pretty determined on not dating someone from work.'

'Or anyone, it seemed. You mentioned something that day about giving up on the whole dating thing altogether.'

That much was true. But I hadn't divulged *why* I felt that way.

'Anyway, the last three years have been amazing. Being with you, sharing your life, moving in together. I know I said when we first met that I wouldn't take the plunge again, but I had no idea then that such an amazing woman would still be in my life three years later.'

My heart burst from beneath my ribcage as he reached into his jacket and produced a small velvet box. Pulling it open, I was momentarily blinded by an enormous diamond catching a ray of sunlight coming through the window. The jewel was flanked by two sapphires and set in an elaborate gold band. Charlie went down on one knee and I held my breath.

'Abigail. Will you marry me?'

I hesitated. Not what any guy wants when they ask their girlfriend to marry them. I opened my mouth, but the word stuck in my throat. Why was it so hard to reply?

A flashback to the streets of Paris burst into my mind like an old-fashioned camera taking a snapshot – a snapshot of the face in the crowd. No, that couldn't be the reason.

'You said this morning that things were fine the way they are now,' I said.

'They are. Of course they are. They're great, amazing in fact. But your intuition was spot on. I *have* been planning this for a while and I was gutted when you cancelled last night. But you were just being a good friend. And that is one of the many things I love about you.'

'Oh, Charlie.' My heart swelled, and as I brought my hands closer to my face, I inhaled the luscious scent of the rose. 'This morning really threw me, and I thought—'

'Could we possibly discuss later why it took all of my strength to hold back from telling you earlier that of course I was planning to propose and how I hated seeing that look on your face when I said I had no interest in marriage, because my knee is fizzing, and I think I might collapse.'

I laughed and helped him up until we were face to face.

'I love you,' he said, his tone turned serious. 'I want to take the leap, with you. Will you, with me?'

He held the side of my face with his free hand, stroking my cheek, his eyes eagerly searching mine.

'Yes,' I said without hesitation this time. 'Yes, I will marry you.'

Charlie jumped on the spot and let out a whoop which made me laugh again. He then composed himself and lifted the ring from the box. His fingers trembled as he placed it on my finger. Before I had a chance to gather my thoughts, Charlie had lifted me into the air and was spinning me round and round before placing me back down and planting kisses all over my face.

'It's stunning, Charlie,' I said, finally able to admire it as he held my fingers to his lips.

'Logan heirloom. Huge history behind it. I asked my father for it when we last visited.'

That was five months ago. I couldn't believe he had been planning this for so long.

'It's beautiful and I'd love to hear the history of it, but ... I have to get to the conference. The first talk is beginning in a few minutes and I desperately need to freshen up.'

'I'm sorry. My timing is awful. I just couldn't wait another moment and thought how wonderfully romantic it would be to propose here.'

'It was. I loved it.' I kissed him hard on the lips. 'I wish I didn't have to go, but I have to make an appearance at all the seminars.' I pulled myself from his embrace and headed to the bathroom. 'Why don't you wait up here for me,' I called over the running tap. 'I can come up when this session finishes in forty-five minutes, have some of this feast.' I dried my hands and returned to the sitting room to pick up my work bag. 'And we could go out and celebrate tonight after the official dinner.'

'OK.' Charlie pulled me back for another kiss. 'I'll be waiting,' he murmured in my ear.

I smiled at him before closing the door. On the other side, I paused and took a quick look at the ring. *I'm engaged.* I wanted to call everyone and tell them the news but knew I needed to stay focussed on the task in hand. Instead I held my hand up and took a quick picture before sending a group text to Liz, Mum, Amy and Nada with several celebratory emojis as well as the words 'look what just happened'.

The door to the main auditorium was ajar and I slipped inside, taking a seat towards the back, by an aisle. Flicking through the first sheet in the conference pack, I saw that someone from a Turkish NGO called Small Projects Istanbul was due to speak about the plight of Syrian refugees coming into their country, the speaker's name unfamiliar.

An older man stood at the podium. A ripple of applause followed his introduction before someone dressed in a dark suit stood up from the front row to take his place at the lectern. I stilled as the man turned around.

Had I stopped breathing? It couldn't be. It was Oz. His opening words were in French – the one language I had never heard him speak – but as he slipped into English I shivered, despite the warm room. His voice was unmistakable: the tone, the depth, the effect it always had on me.

I listened as he talked with passion about the problems he had encountered in his work, but it wasn't long before I struggled to focus on his words. Memories of our time together surfaced like a tidal wave as if a collection of photographs had been displayed on the projector behind him detailing every minute we had ever spent together.

Silence. He had stopped talking as his eyes met mine. There were at least a few hundred delegates seated in the hall, yet he had found me. It was as if the room had been plunged into complete darkness and there were two spotlights: him and me.

For a few seconds, he narrowed his eyes. Checking I wasn't a mirage? When I smiled, he began talking again. But every few beats, he addressed me, and me alone. He kept smiling before clearing his throat and continuing, only to pause again before looking down at his notes and gripping the lectern.

He looked good; happy, even. I knew then there was no chance of avoiding each other later now he had seen me.

The auditorium erupted into applause at the end of his speech. But Oz didn't shift his gaze from my direction. I could see him mumble apologies to people who tried to stop and talk to him as he left the podium. A beeline. That's what you would call it. From one place to another; from the stage straight to me.

'Abbie,' he said. His smile was broad, and those dimples were even more prominent than I remembered. He kissed my cheeks, his scent stirring old memories, which I fought to banish. 'It must be ...'

I knew what he was going to say but I couldn't finish the sentence for him.

'How come you are here?' he asked.

I clutched my conference pack close to my chest. 'I'm standing in for one of my colleagues. I'm an immigration barrister now and—'

'Me, too. *Yani*, I'm not an immigration barrister,' he said, smiling shyly, 'but I am also standing in for one of my colleagues. It really is ... *eh* ...'

It was no use. Coherent sentences weren't forming in my mind, or clearly in his. We stood there staring at each other, taking in every inch. There were more creases on his face, his hair was shorter on top, but his eyes were exactly as I remembered them.

'Great speech,' a delegate said, breaking the silence, extending his hand to shake Oz's.

'*Teşekkür ederim,*' Oz said before a brief conversation passed between them in Turkish.

'There is coffee outside in the lobby, would you like one?' Oz said.

'Umm. Maybe a quick one.' My voice cracked as I said the words. I knew Charlie was waiting for me upstairs, but after all these years I couldn't just say a quick hello and goodbye.

We weaved our way through the crowds, pausing each time someone came to offer a comment on Oz's speech.

At the drinks station, he handed me a cup of black coffee.

'How have you been?' I asked, not having a clue what else to say.

'Good, good,' he said, unbuttoning his suit jacket.

The saucer trembled in my fingers as I lifted the cup to my mouth, not daring to look up at him. The coffee burned my lip, and I blew ripples across the surface.

'You work for an NGO now?' I said finally.

'Yes, I do. It has been a while that I work there ...' He shook his head and stepped forward a fraction. 'Abbie, there is so much I want to talk to you about. I can't believe you are here. I saw you in the crowd, outside, on my way to the conference. You saw me too, yes?' His voice had become softer and deeper.

Heat surged through me.

'I ...' I held onto my cup more tightly. 'I did see you, but then you disappeared.'

'I searched for you.'

'You did?'

He nodded. 'I almost missed the start of my speech.'

I hadn't noticed how close he was standing now. The air around us became charged – we would likely combust if a match was lit close by. The chatter around us quietened, and the backdrop faded.

'You haven't changed since the last time we saw each other,' he said. 'You are still so—'

'There you are.' A hand snaked round my waist and drops of coffee spilled from my cup. Charlie kissed my cheek.

'Hi.' I placed the cup on a table, fiddling with the buttons of my work jacket, a flush creeping up my face.

'I was waiting for you upstairs,' Charlie said. 'How did the first talk go?'

'I'm sorry, it ran over a bit. It was good. Great, in fact. This is …' I struggled for the right introduction. 'This is the keynote speaker, Oz. I mean Özgür Arsel. Özgür is …'

The memory of fainting on the march popped into my head: when he stepped out from the crowd of protesters, his face full of concern as I lay on the bench, my head propped up by his coat.

'I am an old friend,' Oz said, breaking the awkwardness, his hand outstretched to Charlie.

'Pleasure to meet you. Charles Logan. Where do you know Abbie from?'

Both of us opened our mouths but struggled again to say anything.

'Our student days,' Oz said finally. 'I met Abbie at an anti-war demonstration when I was studying in London.'

'Sounds like my fiancée. Always fighting for the right cause. Her and her best friend haven't missed a protest in all the years we've been together.'

Oz looked stunned. 'Fiancée?'

Charlie reached to my left hand and lifted it to show him the ring. 'Yes. As of today.' He beamed.

'*Tebrikler.* Congratulations,' Oz said, loosening his tie. 'When is the big day?'

'Oh, we haven't had a chance to—' I began.

'Maybe next Christmas,' Charlie spoke over me. When I met his eyes and gave him a surprised look, he gave a slight shrug. 'Hopefully.'

'Well, I wish you both all the best,' Oz said. 'I am afraid I have to go. There are some people I am meeting soon.'

'Are you here the whole weekend?' I asked casually.

'Sadly, no. I leave before the dinner this evening. It would have been lovely to catch up, but I am now busy with meetings until I go.'

'That's a shame. Do you ever come to London?' The words were out of my mouth before I had time to retract them, and I didn't know where they had surfaced from.

'I come once or twice a year. *Aslında*, I mean, actually I will be there in April. Sixteenth and seventeenth. There's a property exhibition I agreed to attend with my brother. Istanbul's might and power in the twenty-first century is the theme. There will be many displays of recent projects my family are involved in there in London.'

'Sounds interesting,' Charlie piped up. 'My father has several property businesses. I'll have to mention it to him; we must see it.'

'Please do. Here.' Oz reached into his jacket and produced his business card. 'I would be honoured to host you and your father. And Abbie, too, of course.' He held my gaze a little too long and my eye began to twitch – a nervous tic that had plagued me for years.

'Thanks,' Charlie said, as he tucked the card away. 'Nice to meet you, anyway.'

Oz gave a small nod and turned to me. 'Abbie. As always, a pleasure.'

I shook his outstretched hand, and it took all of my resolve not to show that a spark had fizzed between our fingers just like it had the day we met. A dizziness made my legs feel like they would buckle at any moment. No. It shouldn't. I grabbed hold of Charlie's arm for support.

'Are you, OK?' Charlie whispered by my ear.

I nodded. 'Fine, absolutely fine.' I regained my composure and smiled. 'Lovely to see you again, Oz. Please excuse me.'

I spun on my heel, not daring to look back at either of them. Rushing towards the ladies' bathroom, I tripped over my feet as I entered, and the door swung behind me. Smacking my head on the back of it, I covered my face with my hands. This was ridiculous. Why did I let him have that effect on me again? Why?

Oz was the past. Charlie was my future, yet there I was casually allowing my fiancé to make plans to meet up with Oz again. *Christ, Abbie. Get a grip.*

I pulled out my phone, desperate to call Liz, but I couldn't do it. Was I scared of what she would say? Anyway, she had enough problems of her own trying to cope with being a new mum.

Splashing water on my face, I stared at my reflection in the mirror above the sink, stretching out the skin beside my twitching eye, longing for it to stop pulsing. Merely tiredness, I thought. Thank God it was Christmas in a couple of weeks. A time to recharge and refocus. Christmas. A special time of year, and maybe Charlie was right, a lovely time of year to get married. I held up my ring to the light.

Seeing Oz again shouldn't change a thing, yet I couldn't banish the thought that if Mary had been here or Oz's colleague had been available, we would never have seen each other again. If that day fourteen years ago had played out differently, then maybe it wouldn't have mattered that we had.

8

Fourteen Years Earlier

February

Head back to my room and study or go on an adventure with Oz back to the march. The decision suddenly became easy to make as I looked into the warmth of his eyes.

'OK,' I finally relented. 'Yes, I'll come with you.'

Oz smiled. Those dimples again. A fluttering sensation tickled my insides. *Get a grip, Abbie.* This isn't a date. He's trying to help you from messing up your degree by encouraging you to pursue your own idea that might well be simply brilliant. I stood up with purpose and grabbed my coat.

We left the café and made our way back up Villiers Street. After approaching various protesters and scribbling down their comments on a notepad I'd brought with me, we met a group of four Turkish women who worked at their home country's embassy near Green Park. Oz slipped into his native language after the introductions, his tone passionate. He spoke to the women for several minutes as we shuffled along before one handed him her business card. I couldn't help noticing how she eyed him flirtatiously and touched his sleeve before moving on.

'Friends of yours?' I said.

'No. They invited me to an embassy drinks reception tonight.'

'Oh.'

'But I said I leave this evening and have a party to attend. She gave me a business card with the details in case I change my mind.' He shrugged as he slipped the card into his wallet.

We stopped a few other protesters after the Turkish group, and I was continually struck by how willing everyone was to share their views on democracy. The pace slowed as we edged nearer to Hyde Park until we came to a halt. Oz checked his watch.

A chill spread to the tips of my fingers as I clutched my notebook and pen. 'These quotes are golden,' I said. 'I ... um ... don't want to hold you up if you have to be somewhere else.'

'I wanted to visit one more place in London before the party, but I think it closes soon. I have been before. It is fine if I don't go again.'

'What? No, you must go. Don't miss out for me. Like I said, I have a lot of great quotes.'

'Are you sure? You will be OK to go to Hyde Park?'

I swallowed away my disappointment; he had clearly forgotten his earlier invitation to go with him to the party. 'It'll be fine. Honest.'

'It was a pleasure, Abbie.'

I clutched his outstretched hand. Warmth spread through my fingers again, but this time it spread deeper into my body.

'What,' I squeaked, before I cleared my throat. 'I mean, where is the last place you want to see?'

'An art gallery, about a ten-minute walk from here.'

'Oh.' I pulled my coat tightly around myself and hopped on the spot. 'God, I wouldn't say no to diving into somewhere warm. Should've brought a hat and scarf with me.'

'Why don't you come to the gallery then?'

'Um … sure. Why not. I'm not sure I need to go to Hyde Park any more anyway.'

His smile broadened. 'Great.'

As we walked away from the crowds through Grosvenor Square, we discussed the responses we had received from our fellow protesters and how much fun it had been to talk to people from such varied backgrounds.

I wasn't sure where we were. But then sometimes I still felt like a tourist navigating around London. As a child, visits to the big city had been rare. A trip to a pantomime aged seven and a shopping spree for my sixteenth birthday were the only two days out that had made a lasting impression, although the former memory where I had my first ever asthma attack wasn't a pleasant one.

When we rounded Manchester Square, Oz stopped outside a red-brick mansion house with a columned entrance: the Wallace Collection.

'My grandmother has a love for eighteenth-century French paintings,' Oz said. 'It is a love she has passed on. *Hadi.*' He gave a flick of his head in the direction of the main door.

I followed him into a hallway with a sweeping staircase, and we bore right. Every room was filled with canvases framed in gold, set against vivid walls with ornate furniture dotted around. The air was thick with the smell of wood polish and the floorboards creaked with every step.

We stopped by one piece, and Oz gave a potted history of it. I nodded repeatedly, noticing the curve of his jawline, a well-defined cheekbone, the fullness of his mouth and how he sometimes licked both lips when he paused for thought. I idly wondered what it would be like to kiss them before realising he was looking at me waiting for a response. I murmured some kind of agreement and hoped I hadn't made a complete fool of myself.

We came to a room filled with seventeenth-century paintings including Poussin's *A Dance to the Music of Time*.

'I know this one,' I said. 'I studied it at school.'

'What figure are you most – how do you say – drawn to?' he asked.

My memory of the class where I had studied it was hazy, and I didn't recall ever being asked my opinion. I scanned the picture with fresh eyes. 'I'd probably say the dancer representing pleasure. I love the mischievous grin she has. Like she has the secret to life and all its trappings. What about you?'

'Wealth.'

'Really? Why?'

'I am interested in the world's desire to gain it. And at what point are we satisfied with what we have. And if one is born wealthy, what place do the dancers on either side – those that represent labour and pleasure – what role do they then play?'

Without realising it, we had both sat down on the bench in front of the painting. Time began to slip by the more we chatted and analysed each work of art. I couldn't think of a nicer way to pass an afternoon.

Darkness had fallen when we stepped out of the museum – the security guard having turfed us out and locked the door as we left. The streets of London now had a magical quality; a light fog touched the pavements. Our misty breath filled the space between us.

'Are you hungry? Would you like to go to the party with me?' Oz asked, putting his puffer back on.

He *had* remembered. My heartbeat picked up a beat. *Yes, no. Agh. I dunno.*

There was something in Oz's smile which was having a strange effect on me. And his voice. It was drawing me in like I was Odysseus unable to resist the call of the sirens. But if I said yes, my whole birthday would be spent rewriting my dissertation.

'A quick bite to eat does sound good,' I said. That would still give me a few hours to work on the essay, especially if Oz had to leave for Heathrow soon for his flight.

'Where we are going, you will have a feast. Are you tired? It's a ten-minute walk to the restaurant.'

'I think I'll make it.'

'No more fainting?'

I smiled. 'I promise you won't need to use any first aid on me tonight.' *Except mouth to mouth.* I looked away, hoping he couldn't read my mind.

When we entered the glass doors of the Lebanese restaurant, a gentleman with a white wispy beard and big belly hanging over his belt threw his arms in the air. An outpouring of Arabic – or so I guessed – issued from his mouth. He embraced Oz and patted his back as he greeted him. The older man didn't want to let go. Another embrace followed, then more handshakes.

When Oz brought me into the conversation, the look he gave me made my insides churn. His words were unintelligible to me but lyrical. When he mouthed my name, it sounded a hell of a lot better than 'Yeah, this is Abbie.'

The older man stepped towards me and took my hand in his. *'Ahlan wa Sahlan.* Welcome, Abbie.' He patted my knuckles gently. 'Özgür is right. You are indeed beautiful. Come, come. *Yalla.'*

My mouth dropped open. I was wearing an oversized fawn cable-knit jumper, charcoal miniskirt and black leggings, with a hole at the knee getting bigger by the hour. I was dressed for a rally in central London, definitely not for a night out, yet Oz had introduced me as beautiful? Perhaps he meant 'of spirit' or something. I couldn't recall anyone ever using that word to describe me before.

A thought came into my head. It was evening already, and I hadn't seen Liz all day; she didn't even know where I was.

'Excuse me, do you have a phone I can use?' I asked the man, touching him gently on the shoulder. I looked to Oz. 'I need to call my friend and tell her where I am.'

'Of course. Please. Come,' the man said, gesturing for me to follow him.

I slipped behind the counter and picked up the landline receiver. While I punched out the digits of the phone in our halls of residence, Oz disappeared to a private room out the back. The girl who answered the phone said she would go and see if Liz was in her room. There was music and laughter in the background – everyone getting ready for the Valentine's dance, no doubt.

'What?' Liz's voice grumbled.

'That's a terrible way to greet people.'

'Abs? That you?'

'Uh huh.'

'Where the hell have you been? I called you like a million times.'

'Where have *I* been?' I turned back to the entrance as a group of young men came through the door. A waiter stepped from behind the bar to greet them. I raised my voice over the sound of their hellos. 'Where the hell were you? *You* said you'd be on time.'

'Something came up with Mum and I was only half an hour late. I'm sorry. I did try calling you once I got there.'

'I forgot to charge my phone last night, so it didn't have much battery and then it died.'

The waiter appeared again to usher the noisy group to the back.

'Where are you anyway? And who's hollering in the background?'

'I'm at a Lebanese restaurant on Edgware Road.'

'What the hell you doing there?'

'I'm at a party with someone I met at the march.'

'You met someone? Spill. Details.'

'Just some Turkish guy.'

'Is he hot?'

I laughed. 'He's dreamy,' I said in a mock Southern American drawl.

'Are you bringing him to the Valentine's dance? Don't you dare go to his! Always bring a guy back here.'

'Liz!'

The barman stopped wiping the counter and looked in my direction.

I wrapped my hand around the mouthpiece and lowered my voice. 'I'm not some slag who picks up guys and sleeps with them.' The waiter went back to his cleaning duty. 'And anyway, he's going back to Turkey tomorrow.'

She tutted. 'Don't be so flipping judgemental. And don't knock it until you try it. Besides, you said you weren't interested in dating that barrister guy—'

'Which barrister guy?'

'The one who gave you his card at the recruitment fair.'

'You mean Charles?' I recalled the business card he had given me two weeks ago that I had done nothing with: CHARLES LOGAN, BARRISTER, GREENCOURT CHAMBERS.

Liz had dragged me over to his booth when she caught him staring. She had challenged him to convince us to join the Bar. He kept clearing his throat and readjusting his tie as he talked passionately about his job. He had passed over his card, insisting I could call anytime if I had further questions. He was charming and handsome, in a preppy, well-mannered way. And there was definitely a touch of Ralph Fiennes from *The English Patient* about him, in his accent, sandy blonde hair and deep-set green eyes. I couldn't deny that I was attracted to him.

'Do you think he was interested in me?'

'Of course he was interested in you. Even though you told him you didn't want to become a barrister, he kept trying to persuade you just so he could keep the conversation going; there was a massive queue of people behind us. And that look he gave you.' She whistled. 'He's probably waiting by the phone right now.'

'What should I do? I don't think I'm ready for something serious and he's *so* much older, got his life all figured out already.'

'Then hot Turkish guy is perfect. One night. That's it. No complications. Now go and take your scruffy jumper off, let your hair down and go and get some action.'

'Liz!' But my reply fell into the void, or rather the monotone of a disconnected call. I would have to tell her later why Oz couldn't come to the dance. And she had clearly forgotten about my dissertation crisis.

There was more music coming from the back and I saw a staircase leading down into the basement. A quick scan of the restaurant showed it was half full of diners, but no Oz. He must be down there somewhere.

I pulled off my coat and jumper to reveal a black Lycra top and climbed down the stairs, releasing my hair in waves from its tie. The room was packed and the lights were low. Music blared from a sound system on a platform in one corner, and tables filled with glasses and bottles of water lined the perimeter.

'I thought you'd left,' Oz called from behind.

I swung round. 'And miss the food? Never.'

He leaned down and whispered in my ear. 'Come and meet my friends.'

'Um … sure.' I stuttered, feeling foolish for thinking he was about to kiss me. What had got into me? It must be the lack of air in the room, stifling any sense of decorum I should have.

Oz introduced me to Yusef from Syria and Yaman from Turkey. They both kissed my cheeks and asked me questions about where I came from, what I was doing in London, and how I had met Oz. The hugging continued. It was their last night all together and they had obviously bonded during their time in London. A pack of photos appeared and was shared around like a tourist's guide to the city, the group of friends standing smiling in front of every monument.

'Would you like a drink?' Oz asked, turning to me.

'Yes, please.'

He held a finger in the air, and a waiter appeared with a tray of glasses.

Several tumblers brimming with ice and a cloudy liquid were perched on his salver. Oz handed me one, and we clinked. A strong smell of aniseed invaded my nostrils. 'What is it?'

'Arak. A speciality of the Middle East.'

I took a sip and spluttered; it was like drinking paint stripper with a heavy liquorice aftertaste.

'Too strong?'

I grimaced. 'A little.'

Oz took a silver jug and spoon from the nearest table. He poured until the liquid reached the top of the glass and then he stirred it. 'The taste is hard to get used to, but you can mix it with as much water as you want.'

The next sip went down more easily.

'Better?' he asked.

I nodded and the more I drank, the more I liked it.

In a sudden flurry of activity, waiters filled the tables with an assortment of dishes as well as colourful bowls of vegetables. Oz led me to a table, and we sat against a mirrored wall on a black leather couch. He told me the names of the dishes which were spooned onto my plate. Tabbouleh – a salad of chopped mint and parsley, with tomatoes, onions and bulgur wheat; baba ganoush – a darker hummus made from aubergines, and kibbeh – a medley of ground beef and pine nuts, fried into an oval shape. Waiters brought hot, puffed pitta bread which Oz and I broke apart and dipped in the various bowls.

'Have you ever tried any of this food?' he asked.

'No, I haven't. Mmm,' I moaned, crunching a lettuce leaf filled with a scoop of tabbouleh. I licked a splash of lemon juice from my lips.

Oz leaned his arm on the top of the couch. '*Sahtein.*'

I swallowed my mouthful. 'What does that mean?'

'Arabs say it when you have a good appetite.'

'This is the best meal I've had since Christmas at Mum's house.'

'This is only starters.'

'What? Oh no, I'm almost full.'

He tutted, raising his eyebrows with a slight tilt of his head. 'It would be an insult not to keep eating. I am always told this by the owner of the restaurant.'

'Well, in that case.' I shrugged and took another forkful of fattoush salad, full of tomatoes and croutons. The arak was slipping down easily now, and I wasn't paying attention to how often my glass was being refilled.

As the main course of shish kebab and rice was cleared away, Turkish coffee and sweets appeared. The room suddenly plunged into darkness before a single spotlight highlighted a woman with her belly on display and a jewel nestled in her navel. Soft waves of dark hair hung around her beautiful face.

Her hips swayed with the rhythm of the music, the folds of her red dress billowing around. The music picked up pace, and she moved faster. I joined in the applause, my mouth wide. Her sensuousness was mesmerising. Joy and laughter filled the room and tables were pushed back to create more floor space. When the song finished, the belly dancer bowed and gave a small speech. Catching my eye, she approached me and stretched her arm out.

I looked at Oz. He shrugged and leaned in. 'She wants to teach you some moves.'

'God, no. Surely not.' I shook my head.

'It would be an insult to say no, I think.'

Crikey, was everything in the Arab world an insult if you said no? The guests started a slow clap, and another song came on. OK, so the chances of seeing anyone in this room after tonight were close to zero. What did I have to lose? Only my dignity and leaving a lasting impression with my new Turkish friend that I wasn't the least bit cool, and a lousy dancer.

With a slight shrug and a gulp of arak, I grasped her hand, manoeuvring myself past several diners' knees to make my way out from the table. She stood behind me and grabbed my hips with her bejewelled fingers and began to sway. I probably resembled my grandad: dancing at Christmas after he'd had a couple of whiskies.

But when I looked at Oz, he wasn't laughing. In fact, nor was anyone else. His gaze didn't leave mine even for a second. Once I found my rhythm, the belly dancer held my arms in the air, and I let the music guide my movements. A heady feeling engulfed me: the music, the arak and the most gorgeous guy smiling at me with … with *what*? I didn't know him well enough to know.

The song came to a climax and I flopped back down, my chest rising and falling as though I had done ten laps of a track. Other victims were plucked from the audience and asked to dance before couples began to crowd the room, dancing to an even more upbeat tempo.

Oz handed me a glass of water, and I knocked it back in one. I wiped my chin and willed my heartbeat to steady. But when he squeezed my hand for a second, it was like a blood pressure cuff had been pumped with too much air and the pressure had burst it off. I shuffled closer to him.

'You were incredible,' he said.

The arak was beginning to dismantle my defences. My mouth opened and my hot breath tickled my wet lips. The spotlight picked out the line of his scar and a sudden urge to touch it caught me off guard.

'Do you want to dance?' I raised my brows in the direction of the dance floor.

'I wish I could, but I have to go. I can't miss the last tube,' he said. 'Please stay and enjoy the party. Yusef said he would make sure you got back to your university safely.'

Go? Already? I wanted him to stay longer, hear more stories about his life in Istanbul and listen to him talk effortlessly in four languages. That smile. And those eyes? *Mayday, mayday.* Send me a raft before I drown in them.

I held his gaze and my eye twitched. 'I'd like to go with you. To the station, I mean. I probably should be getting back anyway.'

He smiled again. '*Tamam.* OK. If you're sure?'

When we stepped outside, the night air hit me hard. I quickly pulled on my jumper and parka. The stroll down to Marble Arch tube took us past a long stretch of other restaurants and shisha bars, filled with music and merriment.

We strolled at a slow pace, as though we were prolonging our time together. I couldn't quite be sure if I was walking in a straight line. The arak was much stronger than the cider I usually drank at our student bar.

'Are you sad to be leaving England?' I said.

He nodded. '*Evet.* Yes. London is full of so much excitement, opportunity and freedom.'

'I bet your family has missed you.'

Oz shrugged and faced a shop brimming with colourful vegetables. 'I am not so sure.' It was the second time a dark expression had crossed his face. He hadn't divulged much about his family since we had spoken at the café earlier, only that he also had an older brother who tormented him growing up, almost as much as his younger sister.

'I wish ...' he continued, *'belki* ... perhaps life will be different now. I think there will be troubled times ahead ... in the Middle East. We should stand up to those in authority who mean harm.' He stared at the pavement, his hands shoved deep in his coat pockets.

His words confused me. He had moved from his family to world politics and hadn't elaborated on why his family would not have missed him. The arak was dulling my senses and I couldn't think of anything else to say.

'Will you be OK getting back to your halls?' he asked.

'I'll be fine. There's a bus that goes from here straight to Stamford Street.'

Oz retrieved a large khaki backpack from a locker inside the entrance to the tube and hauled it onto his back. He bought a single ticket to Heathrow from the machine and twirled it in his fingers.

'I guess this is goodbye, then,' I said, rocking on my heels.

When I lifted my eyes to his, he was looking at me intently. 'It was a fun farewell, thank you.' He shifted his backpack straps. 'It will always be ... unforgettable.'

Suddenly an idea came to me. 'And I think I can find a way for you never to forget,' I said brazenly, tugging at his arm as I turned back towards the exit.

'Where are we going?'

'You'll see.'

In the corner, next to a newsstand, there was a Photo-Me booth which I had spotted on the way in. I popped a couple of pound coins into the slot while Oz rested his backpack on the floor. He lifted the curtain and I stepped inside.

Naturally the booth only had one stool and suddenly my idea seemed foolishly forward.

Oz perched on the edge, leaving me a little room. We giggled as we attempted to position ourselves. I followed the instructions displayed until our heads filled the screen for the four-shot 'fun' option. But we were both half outside the circle.

'We need to get closer,' I said, pushing my hair behind my ears.

'Like this?' He rested his head flat against the side of mine.

'Yes,' I whispered, breathless.

A flash.

'Whoops, I think I blinked.' I smiled and tried to compose myself before the next shot.

'Your ear is cold,' he said.

'Is it?' Another flash. 'Flip, I think my mouth was open. These pictures will be a disastrous memory.' I turned and my nose brushed against his cheek.

'Your nose is cold, too.'

I reached out to rub it, accidentally smacking him in the face as the flash came again. 'God, I'm so sorry. I didn't mean to do that. Did I hurt you?'

'It's OK,' he said, rubbing his cheek, stifling his laughter.

'There's one left,' I said.

Oz struggled to keep a straight face, the creases by his eyes deepening as I stared at his reflection. 'Come on, Oz, it has to be good.'

'I'm sorry,' he said, trying to compose himself.

But I could see it was pointless even attempting to get one perfect shot.

I turned to him in exasperation but my breath caught as our eyes met once again. Then it happened. Our heads moved closer until there was no space left between them. I closed my eyes as the fourth flash went off.

His lips were warm on mine, and he gently stroked his thumb down the side of my cheek. I was spinning, melting into the moment, and my heart pounded beneath my jumper.

We pulled apart. 'Oh,' the only word I could muster.

Fumbling as we tried to get up, we bumped heads.

'Sorry,' he whispered. 'I'm sorry. I should not have done that.'

'Right, yes. I shouldn't have … umm.'

We both looked anywhere and everywhere except at each other as we stepped out of the booth. When the photos slid out into the slot, Oz took them and carefully bent them in half before tearing them down the middle. He handed me one side and pulled out his wallet, placing his between the leather dividers.

'Thank you, Abbie. This will always be … memorable.' He pulled his backpack onto his shoulders. A small bow and then he strolled to the gate. I followed behind. He put his ticket in the slot and slipped through to the other side. But he stopped instantly and doubled back to be thwarted by the barrier. 'I wish I could …' He sighed deeply. 'My English escapes me. Goodbye, Abbie.' And with those words he began to walk away.

'Come to England again,' I called after him.

He looked over his shoulder. '*Inşallah.*'

I didn't know what the word meant, but I hoped it was as good as a yes. As he disappeared down the escalator, my heart sank. That was a crap goodbye. I touched my lips. What did he mean by I shouldn't have done that? The kiss or the clashing of heads? I guess I'll never know.

Why didn't I ask for his number or his address even? We could write, become pen pals. My head sank into my shoulders. What was I – fourteen years old, on a French exchange? I looked up at the clock on the wall. If his flight left at seven, why couldn't he take one of those night buses to Heathrow? Yeah, I remembered Liz taking it with her mum when they went to Lanzarote last Christmas. If he took it, he could come to the Valentine's dance with me, and ... well. Oh, flip. My head was all fuzzy. I couldn't think straight.

Then it hit me. I knew what I wanted to do.

9

I fished out my student railcard. A few extra hours with Oz weren't going to totally ruin my future, I resolved, as I raced through the gate to try and stop him from leaving.

Running down the escalator towards the Central line, I could see the tube was already on the platform, and some way into the distance I saw Oz boarding with a group of others. 'Oz! Wait!' I screamed.

The doors closed and the train pulled away, along with my hopes of ever seeing him again. As it clattered away through the tunnel, passengers who had stepped off pushed past me to get out. My shoulders sagged. Probably for the best. After a large glass of water to sober me up from the effects of the arak, I would be ready to tackle my rewrite.

But before I turned to go a figure up ahead caught my attention. Oz. He smiled as we walked towards each other. My face lit up.

'I thought you'd got on the train?' I said.

'I heard you call me, and well ... I had to know what you wanted to say.'

'I ...' My mind was blank. What did I want to say? I swallowed. 'You said something to me in Turkish and I wanted to know what it meant. When I said I hoped you'd come to England again?'

'*Inşallah*? It translates as "God willing". It's Arabic; people in Turkey often say it when they want to express a wish, a hope, for something to happen.'

'Really? Well ... thanks.'

Another tube pulled in and more passengers thronged around us. The brakes screeched, and as the doors opened I came out with what was on my mind.

'There's a bus. You can take it to the airport. It runs through the night from Victoria coach station and it's a cheap taxi there from my university. That is, I wondered if you wanted to hang out a little longer, with me, back at my halls?' My mouth was dry. God, I could really do with that glass of water.

He pursed his lips, and his eyes widened so he looked like a little lost boy. Flip, had I completely misjudged what had happened between us in the photo booth?

'We could take the open-top bus to my university – one more look at London by night – Waterloo Bridge, Houses of Parliament; be a tourist for a couple more hours. More fun than sleeping on some airport chairs. What do you say?'

People rushed past us to get on the train, and an announcement warned us to stand clear of the closing doors.

He opened his mouth. 'I say ... yes.'

As we got to my halls of residence on Stamford Street, the music we could hear as we approached became much louder.

'There's a Valentine's dance tonight.'

'*Ölye mi?* Sorry – I mean – is that so?'

'You don't need to apologise every time you say something in your mother tongue. I'll be near fluent by the morning.' I laughed nervously. 'My room is on the third floor.'

But it was no use. We were rumbled before we even made it to the stairs.

'Abs!' Liz hollered from the entrance to the common room. Her blonde curls were loose around her face and her red tube dress – which showcased her curves – had been teamed with a pair of Dr Martens.

'I've been waiting for you.' She rested her hand on my shoulder. 'And this is?'

'This is Oz. Oz, Liz.'

'The best mate,' Liz declared as if she had rubbed her scent all around me.

Oz stepped forward and offered his hand which she shook. '*Memnun oldum.* It is nice to meet you, Liz.'

Liz's features softened and she turned to me as Oz looked over at the disco behind us. 'Fuck, he's hot,' she mouthed, raising her eyebrows.

I shot her a look. 'We were going to do some work on my dissertation,' I said, not daring to say what I really hoped we would be doing.

'Na-ah. I am taking this gorgeous guy to get his free drinks and *you* are going to go and make yourself more presentable,' Liz said, giving me a once-over that would have been offensive, had it come from anyone else. Before either Oz or I could protest, she had linked arms with him and led him away, letting him drop off his backpack and coat at the reception desk. He gave me a shrug over his shoulder and I raised an eyebrow, letting him know there was no point protesting.

In my room, I surveyed the scene: scattered books, an unmade bed and balls of paper surrounding my bin. Two Diet Coke cans and a tube of Pringles were on one side of my desk with the two politics books lying unread on the other. I tidied up and pulled out a Top Shop miniskirt and my favourite burgundy crushed velvet top from my chest of drawers. Wriggling out of my day clothes, I slipped them on and applied some lip gloss.

I caught my reflection on the way out and teased my hair with my fingers. What was I doing? Tarting myself up for a one-night stand? This was so unlike me.

Back at the dance, Liz was sitting in a booth with Oz, chatting away. Her mouth dropped open comically when she saw me. She leapt up and whispered in my ear. 'Oh. My. God. Love him. Don't let that one slip away!' And with that she was off, sashaying her way back into the crowd.

Oz stood and came towards me, holding two plastic cups.

'You look … *güzel* … sorry, no, I'm not sorry.' He smiled. 'You look beautiful.'

'Thanks.' I took the cup he offered, glad he couldn't see my flushed cheeks in the semi-darkness. 'What is it? I asked, staring down at the bluish, greenish liquid.

'I am not sure,' he shouted over the music. He showed me the top of his hand which had two heart stamps on it. 'These were for the free drinks I was given.'

I nodded to the beat as I swigged my drink and before I knew it, it was gone. 'Would you like to dance?' I said.

He nodded and put his cup on the nearest table. The music had a sultry, Spanish beat pulsating through it. Oz grasped my hand and spun me around and giggles surfaced as I bent back my head. He brought me close to his chest and moved with me, sometimes breaking away to spin me again.

As the next song began, I knew it instantly: Solomon Burke 'Cry to Me'. And in that moment, I was acting out that scene from one of my other favourite films – *Dirty Dancing*.

Smart and hot and he can move, too? Surely too good to be true.

We danced and danced and lost ourselves. In the heels I had put on, I could almost look directly into his eyes. His breath was on my neck one minute, fingers stroking my back the next, as we swayed and yelped with laughter. The only break from dancing was to down my free drinks between us.

Time slipped away. My feet throbbed but I wished it could go on forever. What were these feelings? Delirium fuelled by alcohol?

The next song was 'Unchained Melody', a slow track, signalling the dance was almost over. My arms wrapped around his neck tightly and his hands circled my waist. We swayed gently before I tipped my head back, my lips achingly close to his.

The lights suddenly snapped on and the music screeched to an end; the moment lost.

I grabbed his hand and tugged him in the direction of the stairs, stumbling as I went, until we reached my door. As we fell inside, I rubbed up against him while trying to close it behind us.

'Sorry,' I mumbled.

He pinched at his T-shirt to let in some air as I flicked on my table lamp.

'It is very hot in here,' he said.

'Old radiator. I can't control it, I'm afraid. Usually I sleep with the window open.' I kicked off my heels, feeling petite again by his side. 'You can take it off if you want,' I said brazenly, indicating his top.

He looked at me, his eyes twinkling, before pulling it off in one swift move, his hair flopping back on his forehead.

Oh boy. Don't drool, Abigail. He had a chain around his neck with a dog tag hanging from it; I resisted the urge to reach out and inspect it.

He noticed a pile of papers on my desk. 'Is this your dissertation?'

That last word sobered me up. 'Yes, it is.'

'Can I read it?'

'Umm ... sure.'

As he sat there flicking through the sheets, it was impossible not to focus on the curve of his abs, the waistband of his boxers and the happy trail that led from his belly button down to his briefs. I wondered whether that tag meant he had done military service and what it would be like to caress the scar on his arm. Would he flinch at my touch? A wave of something was coursing through me and my breath had become shorter, my skin warm.

'Water,' I suddenly said, causing him to look up from my papers. 'Let me go and get some water. I'm hot from all the dancing and the ... Yup.'

I slipped out to our communal kitchen and the fridge lit up my face in the darkness. The display on the oven showed it was almost midnight. He probably had a couple of hours, at most, before he had to leave.

I dropped some ice cubes in two glasses and filled them with water, taking a large sip. Liz had a lot to answer for. A one-night stand. Sex with no strings attached. Could I do it and move on, just like that?

Back in my room, Oz was hunched over my desk, pen in hand. He turned and smiled. 'This is very good. *Bence*, I think you have made some excellent arguments.'

'Thanks.' I beamed. 'I wish I knew what my tutor meant by his comments, and where I could improve though.'

'I hope you don't mind but I highlighted the areas where I think the quotes could fit. Your tutor's comment? I think he means this essay has to come from here.' He held his hand over his heart before moving to his head, 'and not only here. And I think you can do this, if you add these … *eh* … insights, these messages from the protesters.' He laid my papers down before picking up the politics books. 'I don't believe you need to add any more theory.'

'Wow. Thanks, I appreciate it. That'll make the rewrite easier.'

'*Rica ederim*,' he said with a wink. I might have drunk a fair amount, but I could remember what those words meant.

He moved to the stack of CDs next to my portable player and lifted up a few. 'Your music is … eclectic. Is that the word?'

'If you mean, I have a habit of buying a CD because I like one song, then yes, my taste is varied. Charity shops are the best for building up a collection.'

'Ah, I have this one,' he said, brandishing one of my Coldplay albums. 'I saw them last June at the Camden Palace.'

'You did?'

'Yes, they were fantastic.'

He pulled the CD out and slid it into the player, studying the case before pressing the play button. 'This is one of my favourites.'

I immediately recognised the opening chord of 'What If'. It was one of my favourites, too.

Oz held out his hand. 'Dance with me?'

I nodded.

He crossed the distance between us and laid his hands on my shoulders, sliding them down my arms before interlocking his fingers in mine. He brought my hands up to his chest and left them there before resting his on my waist. His skin was moist, and the smell of his chest was intoxicating.

'What if ...' he began.

I looked up into his eyes. 'What if what?'

He gave a slight shrug. 'What if this was our one time together? If we never saw each other again. Would you ...'

Was he asking my permission?

'A one-day affair? I think I'd be OK with it.' *Really, Abbie? Would you really?* 'Unless ... we could arrange to meet again sometime in the future, then it would make it less ... Well, in *Before Sunrise*, they have' – I cleared my throat – 'sex because they talk about meeting again.'

'Ah, your favourite movie. So, the sequel was six months later?'

'Actually, it was nine years later.'

'*Niye*? Why?'

'The heroine's character couldn't make their agreed meeting and because they didn't swap details, it wasn't until nine years later they met again in Paris.'

'They didn't exchange numbers? That's a little … what is the word?'

'Contrived?'

'Yes.'

'I guess, but it made it all the more exciting for the sequel when they did meet.'

'Then we will have a date in nine years? Nine years from today?' he said.

'Nine years? It'll be the day before my thirtieth birthday.'

He stopped moving. 'It is your birthday tomorrow?

I nodded.

'*Doğum günün kutlu olsun*,' he said. 'It means—'

'Happy birthday?'

'Yes.' He smiled before bringing me close to him again, my nose brushing against his warm skin, lips tantalisingly close to his naked chest. 'We will have a date in nine years,' he said. 'A movie?'

'OK. At the Prince Charles cinema? At seven?' I giggled at the absurdity of it all. Was this clearing our consciences? 'But what if we're not single?'

'Then you must have my number,' he chuckled, 'so I don't fly all the way to London and find you married with kids.' He broke his hold and grabbed the pen that he had used to mark up my dissertation.

'Kids? No, thanks. I'll be a successful solicitor by then. I'll probably have to squeeze you into my busy schedule for the date.' I couldn't hold back my laughter now.

'We will watch whatever is playing that night. Where shall I?' He looked around for something to write on.

Seductively, I turned away and tugged at my skirt, revealing a patch of flesh on my back by my hip. 'Write it here.' I caught his gaze and bit my bottom lip.

Oz dropped to his knees slowly, not taking his eyes off mine. He then dipped his head and placed his lips against my skin, and I caught my breath sharply.

The biro was cold as he wrote the digits. He blew onto where he had written before climbing to his feet. Lowering his head, he rested his forehead against mine. 'Your smile. It's … *nefes kesici*. Breathtaking.'

The song 'Fix You' came on and we began moving slowly to the beat. The music swirled around us and I was lost. Completely lost. My hands moved up over his chest, down his strong arms and back up again to encircle his neck. I let his body guide my movements as we danced, and shut my eyes.

When I opened them, he lifted my chin with his fingers and pressed his mouth to mine. My knees buckled and he held me steady in his arms. His tongue met mine and this time we didn't pull back nor did the music stop. The intensity was thrilling.

But when the song moved up a gear in its second half, Oz finally broke the kiss and began twirling me around and around, moving with me, laughing. And we didn't stop until I toppled backwards onto my bed, taking him down with me. He lay on top of me, his tag caressing the skin above the low neckline of my top, his arms supporting his weight.

'You are so beautiful.'

He stroked my cheek before moving in for another long, lingering kiss. His lips moved down my neck and across my shoulder, his hand roaming freely under my top, his fingertips igniting my skin with his touch. Our kisses became more urgent and I sighed happily, giving myself up to the rhythm of his body as it moved with mine.

A knock. Then another.

'Abs? You awake?'

I prised one eye open. Daylight was streaming through the window and my head throbbed. I lifted myself to reveal a pool of drool on my pillow. Oz was gone and a sinking feeling sat in my stomach along with a wave of nausea.

Liz opened the door and sniffed. 'Sex. It smells of sex in here.'

'Ha, ha,' I mumbled.

'You look like shit and your family's here.'

I bolted upright, clutching my head as a jolt of pain shot into my temple. 'My what?'

'Yup, they came to surprise you for your birthday. You weren't picking up your phone, so the security guy called me instead.'

'They can't be. I said I had plans. And now I have to rewrite my ... shit,' I said, tumbling out of bed, getting caught in my sheets and hitting the floor with a thump. 'Ow!'

'Don't stress. It'll be fine. But you have about two minutes to fumigate this room and put something decent on, so they don't find out what you were up to last night.'

'I wasn't up to anything,' I said, rubbing my shin, my eye twitching. OK, so it wasn't only nerves that brought on my tic, but lies, too.

'So, you normally fall asleep half dressed?'

I immediately yanked down my skirt.

'I want to hear all the deets later. First up.' She reached into my wardrobe and pulled out my dressing gown. 'Put this on.'

'What shall I tell them?' I said, wrapping myself in the robe.

'Nothing. You're twenty-one, for heaven's sake. You're entitled to a love life as well as studying,' she said, giving the room a few spritzes of my body spray.

'Knock, knock,' came Mum's voice. 'Is there a birthday girl in here?'

The door swung open as I tightened the belt and there in the doorway were Mum, Dad and ... 'Amy?'

She pushed through and stood in the middle of the room, chewing gum, arms folded over her pink jacket. 'Three-line whip. Here.' She thrust a card in my direction. 'Happy birthday. God, what's that smell?' Her nose wrinkled, overcome by the powerful fragrance of orange and lily.

'Thanks,' I said, fanning my cheeks with the card. 'Why didn't you tell me you were all coming?' I looked from one face to another.

'We wanted to surprise you, pet,' said Dad, his arms opened wide.

I sank into his warm embrace – the wool of his navy coat soft on my cheek. Mum joined in the hug, squeezing me so tight I could hardly breathe.

'We knew you'd been studying so hard and wouldn't get much chance to celebrate,' Mum said, 'so we thought we'd take you out for a nice meal.' She looked around my room, clocking the empty Pringles tube. 'And you know we never like to miss an opportunity to feed you up.'

I forced a smile. 'That's so thoughtful.'

'Who's Oz?' my sister asked, brandishing a note she had picked up from my desk.

I shot Liz a 'please help me' expression.

'Oz is this Turkish girl we met recently.'

'Why did she say, "Last night was amazing. I'll see you in nine years?"' She thrust the note in my direction.

Liz grabbed it and crumpled it into a ball. 'It's mine. I brought it to show Abbie, to ask her whether it meant she liked me or not. It was just a hook-up.' She looked at my parents, who were doing their best not to look aghast. 'She said she'd be coming back to London … in nine years?' Liz looked at me for back-up, but I remained tight-lipped. No way could I contribute to this conversation without my twitchy eye going into overdrive.

'Yes … well.' Mum straightened her jacket. 'We should let you get changed and we'll meet you downstairs.'

'What about the presents?' Dad said.

'Ooh, yes,' Liz screeched. 'I'll go and get mine.' She shot out the door, leaving me alone to handle any further interrogation.

Amy sat on my desk. 'Open mine.'

I ripped the seal of the envelope to reveal a card showing a washed-out-looking woman with smeared lipstick, swigging from a bottle of champagne. The message inside had as much warmth as a fortnight in Bognor in February. A coupon for twenty pounds off a facial slipped out. 'Is this where you work?'

'Yeah. You're welcome.'

'It expires in two months and I have to get up to Birmingham?'

'God, don't sound so ungrateful. Mario said he'd give you an amazing facial. Special deal.'

I gave her my best 'you shouldn't have' smile. 'Thanks.'

'And now for ours.' Dad presented me with a small box. 'It ... well.' His voice tightened, as it always did when he was trying to find the right words. 'It belonged to your great-grandma, on my side. I think your great-grandad made it by hand, as an engagement gift. Anyhow, your mum and I thought you might like it.'

I popped open the lid. Inside was a silver locket on a chain; a heart-shaped pendant with a floral pattern engraved in it. 'It's beautiful.'

Dad fished it out and unhooked it. 'We thought it might bring you luck for finals and it's a special birthday so we thought something with meaning would be fitting.' He placed it round my neck and fastened it as I held my hair up. 'It was passed on to my mother and she always said it brought her good fortune. It was the only thing left to me when she ... well ... when she passed. And I thought you'd appreciate it.'

Dad's eyes had become watery. He never liked to talk about the past; memories he had buried long ago after he had left Wales in search of a brighter future.

I didn't look at Amy, but I could feel her eyes boring into me.

'There aren't any photos in there,' Dad continued. 'I thought you might like to put someone special in it. Not now, of course, but one day. You've got big things coming up, graduation, law school. But when the time is right, and you meet someone nice, or you get yourself a cat and put its picture in.' He chuckled.

I tucked my arms by my sides, as if Oz's phone number could be seen through the fabric of my dressing gown.

'Pass me a bucket,' Amy muttered under her breath.

'What was that, dear?' Mum said.

'Why didn't I get anything special or for good luck on my twenty-first?' Amy shot back.

'You didn't go to university,' Dad said, very matter-of-fact. 'And besides, you asked for cash. Abbie doesn't need cash because she's careful with her money.'

Amy's eyes burrowed into mine.

'How's the law school fund coming along, pet?' Dad continued.

'It's great.' I had a job at a dentist's office on a Wednesday and Friday, late opening, which brought me a small wage. But I was holding out for a sponsorship from one of the top solicitors' firms to get me through law school. Interviews were in a few weeks and I had to stay on course to graduate with a first-class degree.

Crap. Why had I let myself get carried away last night? If I had known my family was coming today, I wouldn't have hauled Oz off the train. I should have known they would materialise at some point. There hadn't been a single birthday I had spent without them.

'I'm back!' Liz announced as she burst into my room. 'This is for you.' She handed over an envelope like she was entrusting her firstborn to me. 'I hope you like it.'

The room was silent. Mum and Dad sat down on my bed while Amy swung her legs back and forth under my desk, looking as sullen as the minute she had walked in.

I unpicked the seal and removed the contents – one sheet of paper with the words Eurail Pass at the top. My hand went to my open mouth.

Liz squealed, jumping up and down.

'Liz, I can't accept this. This is … huge.'

'What is?' Amy said grabbing the sheet from my hand. 'You're going Interrailing? She bought you a flipping Interrail ticket? That's worth hundreds.'

'I won't hear another word.' Liz clapped her hands together and gave a small bow in front of my parents. 'Mr and Mrs Jones. I am sure you will agree Abbie works extremely hard and deserves a break once her finals are over, and of course before she embarks on her glittering career as a solicitor. She said she couldn't go away this summer because of the job at the sailing club in Mumbles, but I hope you'll help her smooth it over with the manager and spare her three weeks while I whisk her around Europe.'

'That's incredibly generous of you, Liz,' Mum said, taken aback.

Liz threw an arm around my shoulder and squeezed me tight. 'It's going to be brilliant.'

Three weeks travelling around Europe. It was a dream come true. Where would we go? Paris, Rome, maybe Vienna? This is what I needed to focus on: getting a first, a sponsorship and then spending the summer touring the continent with Liz before starting work. Last night was fun but that's all it was, one night. Yesterday with Oz would be nothing but a memory held in those four Photo-Me photos.

10

Now

January

'Drink, madam?'

'Ugh,' Liz groaned, flicking her hand. 'Please take that away from me.'

The waiter looked startled at Liz's response to the tray he had offered her bursting with tall flutes of champagne.

'Abs, please have another one for me,' she said, reaching across to grab a tumbler of orange juice.

'I'm already on my second, Liz.' I gave the waiter a signal I was fine, and he moved on.

'Who cares? It's your engagement party and you aren't breastfeeding.' She cast her eyes downwards. 'Or taking anti-depressants,' she added in a whisper.

I squeezed her arm. 'Hey, it's going to be OK,' I said. 'You're doing great. Look at you. You look stunning.'

She swept her arm down her scarlet dress. 'I look like a cross between the devil and a Jersey cow.'

'Your boobs were always big.'

'I know,' she said giving them a squeeze, 'but they're so heavy now. I thought I'd expressed enough for tonight, but I think I'm going to have to go into the ladies soon and relieve myself with my pump.'

'Words I thought I'd never hear you say.'

'Me neither. It's all-consuming, Abs. I've been looking forward to this night for days, even painted my nails,' she said, wiggling her crimson-tipped fingers at me. 'But the first thought that came into my mind when Mum came around to babysit was ...' She paused and screwed up her face. 'I sooo want a nap.' With a dramatic flourish, she flopped her head on my shoulder.

'Liz,' I said, stroking her bare arm. 'You have no idea how much it means to me you came.' She lifted her head up. 'But I won't mind if you sneak off to the coat cupboard and get a few winks.'

'What, and leave you to Charlie's parents? No way. I'm here for you.'

'They're not *that* bad.'

'They'll steamroll the whole event. Remember it's your wedding, not theirs, even if it's some mystery date far into the future.'

I took another sip of champagne. 'I'm not sure I would mind if they did take over. It's not like I have loads of time to be trawling wedding magazines right now, making decisions. And it has to be just right – perfect, in fact – and that takes time.'

'But that's what I'm here for. I'm on maternity leave, remember. Best to get the ball rolling now while I can,' she said with a yawn.

'You should be focussing on getting better, not figuring out whether I should be having salmon mousse as a starter for the wedding breakfast or haggis croquettes.'

Liz made a gagging motion. 'The former, clearly. How on earth has it even come up in conversation if you haven't set a date?'

'Over Christmas at Charlie's parents. He asked me to humour them and not emphasise the fact this might be a long engagement.'

'Remind me again why it is?'

'We've got too much going on this year,' I said. 'You know from Mary that Charlie is hoping to try again to become a QC, and I want to win something high profile and maybe even build on the conference I did last month.'

'But that's why I'm here. Please, Abs.' She tugged the sleeve of my black velvet dress. I had picked it up in the New Year sale last week when Charlie had sprung the news of the party on me. 'You could come round, and we could go through all the magazines together. I want to be involved in everything.'

'You will be eventually. You're my matron of honour, of course.'

She beamed. 'Am I? You never said.'

'Thought it was a given.'

'Nice, Abs. Classy way to ask your best mate to be probably one of the most important people in your wedding party.'

'Sorry.'

'Forgiven. But please let me take over. I can do all the research and then give you the options, so when you do set a date, you'll have this kick-ass folder with all the details. It'll be a doddle for you to organise it then.'

'Really? You'd do that?'

'Of course. First up, venue. I'm guessing small, intimate in Wales?'

'Abigail, darling,' Charlie's mum called from behind, her voice silky and smooth. Elena Logan – the most elegantly turned-out seventy-year-old I had ever met. She was very Helen Mirren, with her silvery blonde hair in a neat bob. I don't think I had ever seen Elena look anything short of fabulous – even when she was out walking the dogs on the family estate.

Charlie got his height and angular nose from her and his warmth and thoughtfulness from his dad, who was currently propping up the bar with a guest I didn't recognise, knocking back a couple of whiskies. Charlie was their only child and it always showed in the adoration they heaped on him. But it didn't make him spoiled. Quite the opposite; he was the most selfless person I knew.

'Great news, Abigail,' Elena said. 'Auchen Castle in Dumfries is free the last weekend of December.'

Liz spluttered on her orange juice. 'I thought you hadn't agreed a date.' She shot me a pissed-off look. I knew it all too well – eyes bulging and nostrils flared.

'Well no, we haven't actually—'

'Darling, Abigail.' Elena touched my arm lightly. 'I am sorry. I had no idea. Charles said you'd agreed to Christmas-time, so it was more a question of when the castle was free, not whether it fitted into your calendars. Besides, he assured me you never take on cases over the Christmas period.'

I opened my mouth to say that wasn't entirely true but held back, not wanting to come across as confrontational.

Charlie had once commented that I always sounded defensive around his mum. I had no idea why she made me feel like I had to be.

'It's very thoughtful of you to have arranged that, Elena, but it's probably best if I consult Charlie first.'

'As you wish, dear. It is your special day as well.' She gave a slight shrug. 'Only problem is my mother is getting terribly frail these days. Travelling long distances doesn't agree with her. One of her last remaining wishes is to watch her grandson get married. You weren't contemplating a Welsh wedding, were you?'

A prickly heat crept up my neck. I hoped it wasn't noticeable in the low lighting of the venue which had been chosen to celebrate our engagement. Charlie's parents had organised this evening. They had wanted it to be a surprise, but Charlie had thankfully given me a heads-up, so we didn't have a repeat of me bailing on him like I did the night he had wanted to propose.

The Parlour room of Six Storeys on Soho exuded opulence in its heavy silver drapes and crystal decanters illuminated in the mirrored wall behind the bar. Charlie's dad often did business in town and knew the owners of the venue well. The room was filled with a lot of his work associates and Elena's acquaintances from the Women's Institute. In fact, did I even know half of the people in this room? An overnight storm had hit the south of Wales, causing travel chaos, and no one from my family could make it tonight, so I was more than grateful Liz was here. The event's short notice also meant Nada couldn't coordinate one of her trips from Beirut, but she had sent a case of Lebanese wine to the flat as an engagement gift.

I straightened up. 'It is tradition though, Elena, for the bride's family to organise everything. And my family is based in Wales.'

She pursed her lips. 'Of course. I see I might have got carried away. My apologies, darling Abigail. I'm just so excited for Charles. He's the only child I have,' she said wistfully. 'You will have to rein me in, I'm afraid.' She smiled, though it only reached one corner of her mouth.

An arm snaked around my waist. 'There's my beautiful bride to be,' Charlie said, and I leaned into him. 'What have you all been discussing?' he said, looking from one face to the next.

'Well, it seems, Charles dear,' Elena began, 'I might have overstepped the mark with your fiancée. I was only trying to help, of course.' She gave a wounded look.

Charlie rubbed his hand up and down my back, waiting for her to elaborate.

'Your mother said Auchen Castle is free the last weekend of December,' Liz piped up to clarify things.

Charlie's eyes lit up. 'It is? That's fantastic.' He reached out to embrace his mother before turning back to see the look on my face.

'Sorry, Abbie. I only mentioned December as a possibility, but honestly, trust me. Wait until you see the place. Remember the restaurant we went to in Dumfries last summer after our walk? Remember the view?'

I thought back to that trip. It had come at the end of an arduous five-day case I had won. A mixture of exhaustion and contentment had flooded me when we had arrived at the most exquisite hotel in the middle of the town. I had quizzed him about the cost, but he had brushed the comment away saying we deserved to splurge now and again. Charlie had booked me an afternoon at the hotel's spa as a treat and then we had taken a taxi to this restaurant where we had watched the sun set from the beer garden, snuggled up in tartan blankets, sipping wine. And yes, the view had been breathtaking.

'Yes, I remember,' I said, wrapping my arm around his waist.

'Auchen Castle is on the other side of town with an even more spectacular view.'

Charlie continued to discuss specific details with his mum and I suddenly felt like an inactive participant. But what could I add to this conversation? There hadn't been any time for us to sit down and discuss how we wanted the day to pan out. After Paris, my next three cases – only one of which I had won – had led straight to Christmas Day.

Yet suddenly there was now a date and a venue without so much as a consultation.

A familiar tightness gripped my chest, and I held my hand over my locket. My inhaler was in my coat which was hanging in the venue cloakroom.

I fanned my face with my hand. 'I think I need some air,' I said once a lull in the conversation materialised. 'Can you all excuse me?'

Liz gave me a 'do you want me to come with you' flick of her head. I mouthed I was fine and unwound myself from Charlie. 'I'll be back in a bit,' I whispered by his ear and left.

Outside, cold air mingled with that fine English drizzle which had coated every night this January. I shivered and my teeth chattered.

I thought back to what Elena had said about Wales. Had I always dreamed of a Welsh wedding? No, not really. Amy was the one who had kept a shoebox under her bed in the room we shared growing up, with clippings of various celebs in their gowns from Mum's copies of *Hello!* and *OK!* magazine. She used to talk about the perfect dress, the perfect proposal. In the end, all she got was a shotgun wedding at the Manchester registry office when her boyfriend of six months – Barry, a car salesman from up north – popped the question after she had told him she was pregnant. Mum and Dad were disappointed not to be involved when they got the call a week before to say it was happening. That was nine years ago. My family had always hoped to host at least one Jones wedding in Wales, but now it looked like it would never happen. And a winter wedding. *Brr.* Even in summer Dumfries was sometimes nippy – I couldn't imagine how freezing it would be in December.

The front door to the venue opened, and Charlie stepped outside.

'There you are,' he said before focussing on my trembling lips and immediately swaddling me in his arms, wrapping his coat around me. The cashmere wool was soft against my cheek and I inhaled the woody scent of his aftershave that lay on the lapel.

He pulled back and rubbed his hands up and down the sleeves. 'You're freezing out here. Come back inside.'

'It's refreshing. I get a bit claustrophobic in tight spaces.'

'Thought it was the outdoor kind you suffered from?' He pressed his cheek against mine and clasped my shoulder. 'I know she can come across a little overbearing sometimes.'

I looked up into his eyes with a slight tilt of my head. 'Sometimes?'

He smiled. 'She means well, but it's not her day, it's ours. If you don't want to get married at the castle, it's fine, we'll find somewhere else.'

'Really?'

'Of course. We could compromise. Do it in London.'

'But your mum said your gran couldn't travel. Isn't she in her mid-nineties?'

'Nana Fitzpatrick? She's made of fine Scottish blood and we can always fly her over. The only small issue is there's about two hundred on our side. We'd have to find a big enough venue to host everyone and enough hotel rooms for them to stay overnight.'

'Two hundred!'

'At least. Last time we drew up a list, we had to do some serious culling.'

A pang of guilt hit me, remembering the fact this was second time round for Charlie. On my side of the family, we could barely count relatives on two hands. Mum was an only child and her parents long gone and Dad's sister – Aunt Betsy – had never married. But as much as I loved our holidays in Scotland, nothing could beat my little corner of heaven in South Wales.

'What's so special about the castle, anyway?'

Charlie held my hand, circling the engagement ring around my finger. 'Nothing really.'

I studied his face. 'Come on, tell me. It obviously is.'

'It's silly really. When I was a boy, I used to visit the castle with Dad and loved all the stories he told me about the clans that lived there from the thirteenth century onwards. I used to imagine becoming a chief and finding a beautiful princess to marry and that I would usurp the owner and have the ceremony there.' He dipped his chin.

'That's so sweet.' I smiled.

'Embarrassing, more like.'

I squeezed his arm. 'No, it's not,' I reassured him. I thought of Mumbles. The only landmark that meant something to me was the lighthouse and you couldn't get married there. 'You know what? I think Dumfries would be a lovely place to have a wedding.'

'Really?' Charlie beamed, nudging his glasses upwards.

'My only issue is the cost. How on earth can we afford to host so many people?'

'We?'

'Yes, you and me. Equal partners.'

'Abbie, I appreciate the sentiment, but my parents are insisting on bearing the cost of the wedding.'

I pulled back. 'We can't let them do that.'

'They insist. Listen, you always bristle when we talk about money, but you have a lot of commitments in your life. If you want, we can agree to pay for the things which matter to us, your dress, my suit, the photographer. But there's no way my parents will expect us to pick up the tab for such a large-scale event. We're saving for a new place to live, right?'

I nodded.

'Let's not make this into a big deal. It'll still be our special day. And the banquet room in the castle is spectacular. Imagine it. Roaring fires, candles everywhere.'

'You put forward a very convincing case, Mr Logan. I just never imagined it being a large wedding. And December feels a little close.'

'Not really. It's almost a whole year away. Come on, let's do it. We can have our diaries set from now, so we don't take on anything around then. And we can go up there as many times as you want to check out everything, get it all booked. And if a smaller wedding is what you want, I'll talk to Mum and see if we can get the numbers down. Anyway, the chapel is small, so that part of the wedding will be intimate. It seats eighty max. Other guests can join for the reception.'

I tipped my head to the side. Charlie was trying hard to compromise and please me, but still the image of what the day would look like seemed hard to picture. But I was certain that it would begin to take better shape once we had gone back up to Scotland.

He leaned down to look into my eyes and his forehead wrinkled. 'No second thoughts?' He stroked my cheek and placed a kiss on my lips.

The earlier tension I had felt in my chest began to dissipate as I stared into his eyes, though a small, nagging feeling of doubt remained buried deep inside my ribcage. Maybe this dress was too tight.

'No second thoughts,' I said with conviction.

Charlie smiled broadly and held my shoulder tighter, steering me in the direction of the door. 'Then everything will be great. You'll see. It'll be the best day of our lives.'

As we stepped inside, Liz and Mary were standing at the reception desk.

'You're leaving?' I said, dropping my arm from Charlie's waist and stepping towards them.

'I was looking for you to say goodbye,' Liz said, stifling a yawn.

'I am taking my beautiful wife home,' Mary said, holding out Liz's jacket to her. Liz leaned back onto Mary and kissed her cheek. In return Mary planted a soft kiss on Liz's lips. They still acted like newly-weds around each other, even after five years of marriage. It was adorable and I hoped that would be me and Charlie in a few years.

'Sorry, Abs, I can't keep my eyes open.' She laughed but her lips were compressed and I knew something was up.

Liz and I hadn't seen much of each other since the conference. Her mum or Mary had been there on the three occasions I had managed to go round, and tonight was the first proper chat we'd had since the weekend I went to Paris. I'd debated whether or not to tell her who I had seen but resolved to let it go. It was no big deal.

I hugged her and she squeezed me tight, almost too tightly. When I drew back and saw her eyes welling up with tears, I pulled her sideways.

'Guys, can you give me a few minutes with Liz? I want to arrange a date for some wedding planning.'

Charlie headed upstairs back to the party while Mary left through the front door, just in time before Liz's tears began to roll. She pushed them away with her thumbs before reaching into her handbag for a pack of tissues. The coat attendant was in spitting distance, so my voice was low.

'What's the matter?' I asked.

'They're not working.'

'What's not working?'

'The drugs. The antidepressants. I cry *all* the time; the panic attacks are easing but the insomnia is worse. And now Maddy has colic and ...' She couldn't finish her sentence as the tears flowed faster.

I let her cry on my shoulder until I felt her take a deep breath.

'Feel a bit better?' I asked.

She nodded.

'Have you spoken to your doctor about this? Maybe they need to up the dose, or try another type? He might have some colic treatment for Maddy as well.'

'I'm seeing him Monday morning. Mary will be in Sheffield and I don't want to worry her, and Mum's out of town.'

'Want me to come with you?'

'Would you?'

'Of course. I'm not in court and can bring some papers with me to work on afterwards. I can even stay a couple of nights until Mary comes back.'

She sniffed. 'You're the best.'

I pushed her curls behind her ears. 'It's all going to be fine. The hardest part was asking for help. You've just got to keep on asking. No one expects you to be all happy and in control straight away. It'll take time. Hey, I can even stop at Smith's this weekend and clear them out of wedding mags. We can make a start on planning.'

Her tears dried up and a genuine smile appeared on her face. 'I'd like that. Are you really getting married in a castle? And in Scotland?' She grimaced.

'Scotland's not that bad.'

'I thought you said you wanted a long engagement, small wedding, preferably in the summer.'

Absent-mindedly I pulled my locket back and forth along its chain. 'I don't know what I want, Liz. Small, big, Wales, Scotland. Isn't it supposed to be every girl's dream to plan their wedding?'

'Not always. And it can get overwhelming pretty damn fast. The expense, the guest list, demanding families. Same happened with me and Mary. Then I thought, sod it. This shouldn't be so hard. It's why we eloped to Thailand, aside from being an amazing chance to go back to where we first met. It was our special day and the only way we could do it on our terms. Sometimes it's about being spontaneous, doing something crazy. You and Charlie could elope tomorrow if you wanted.'

My eyes widened. 'I'm not spontaneous nor do I ever do anything without mapping it all out and having a detailed plan.'

'You weren't always like that.'

'Yes, I was.'

'I can remember a time you weren't. I've known you for seventeen years and there have been glimpses of wild and crazy Abigail Jones.' Her eyes sparkled.

I knew exactly the times she was referring to but didn't want her to bring up any of them.

Spontaneous Abbie didn't exist in the now. She belonged to the past. Although I valued my best friend's advice, following Liz's wild ways hadn't always worked out.

No. Charlie had painted a picture of a lovely wedding, and a trip up to Scotland next month would make me feel involved. Between us we would ensure it would be a memorable day, carefully planned. I knew all too well that being spontaneous only led to heartache.

11

Fourteen Years Ago

July

My shoulders sagged under the weight of my backpack. The soles of my feet had hardened from pummelling the streets of Paris, Munich, Zagreb, Belgrade and Sofia – one city I had always dreamed of visiting and the other four, places I would never have imagined turning up in. The farmer's tan had progressed along the way – Liz's bronzed arms versus mine which looked like a pair of burned salmon fillets.

I wriggled out from under the burden and sat down on the bench in front of Sofia's Central station – our designated meeting place. I had left Liz back at the hostel because I wanted to fit in one more trip, to the Alexander Nevsky Cathedral. The Byzantine interior with its cool air infused with incense had left me calm and reflective.

On our last day in each city, Liz had surprised me by revealing our next stop. We had travelled so far east, I was secretly hoping the last place would take us halfway back to London. Italy, maybe? Only so the train journey home wouldn't take two days.

'Abs,' Liz called from behind me.

'There you are. I was about to send out a search party.' Her face was smeared with tears. 'What's wrong?'

She dropped her backpack by my feet and sat down next to me. Cars hooted as they drove by.

'Just got off the phone to Mum.' She sniffed.

'What's happened?'

'She collapsed in the middle of Waitrose. They rushed her to hospital and ...' Another sniffle. 'They pumped her stomach.' Liz's lower lip wobbled as she looked up at me.

'Shit. Is she OK?'

'Yeah, she'll be fine. She'd mixed too much Mirtazapine with the bottle of Prosecco she'd necked before going late-night shopping. Stupid cow.'

Liz's relationship with her mum had always been strained. They'd lived on their own in a two-bedroom Camden flat since the day her dad walked out on them, when Liz was seven. Money had been tight until a distant relative died a few years back and left them a windfall. Aside from splurging on expensive holidays and treating best friends to Interrail tickets, the money had fuelled her mum's drinking habit.

'I have to go back,' she said.

'*We* have to go back.'

'What? No, I'm not dragging you into my stupid life back in London. Mum will be fine, but I spoke to her in the hospital and she needs me. I booked a flight out of here. It leaves at ten, takes a little over three hours.'

'Why didn't you check with me? I can't leave you to face all that alone back home.'

'I'll be fine. I'm just a bit pissed off I don't get to do this last stop with you.'

I swallowed hard. 'But I don't want to go somewhere without you.'

'Come on, Abs. It'll be fine. An adventure of a lifetime.'

'Which you have yet to fill me in on.'

'I can't believe you haven't twigged yet.'

'You haven't exactly been leaving many clues.'

'My favourite book?'

I shrugged.

'*Murder on the Orient Express*.'

'I vaguely remember the movie – everyone did it. But doesn't the Orient Express go from London to Paris or Vienna?'

'There's one more route, the one we've taken the last two and a half weeks. I took some liberties with a couple of the stops. But ultimately this trip will end where the book began. Istanbul.'

My eyes widened. 'Turkey? How long does it take?'

'Here.' She handed over a ticket with 'Balkan Express' printed on it. 'About ten hours or so. I've booked a two-person sleeper, so you'll have the compartment to yourself.' She reached into her bag and unearthed a folded piece of paper which had obviously once been crumpled up. 'Go find him.'

'Find who?' I asked, unfolding it. The note was from Oz – the one he had left on my desk after the night we'd spent together. 'I thought this had been tossed in the bin!'

'I fished it out.'

'Why?

'Cos he left his address on it. And you were pissed off when you' – she did quotation marks with her fingers – '"lost" his number after you took a shower before lunch with your family.'

'It was a joke, Liz. He left me his details so I could let him know in nine years if I couldn't make the date. That's why I didn't give him any paper. It was a—'

'Yes, I know it was a reference to that movie you made me watch once: two actors blathering on about love and life.'

'Hey, they were two people who were obviously meant to be together but couldn't, because of circumstances.'

'Exactly.'

'Wait, I wasn't referring to me. That was a movie, fiction. Totally made up. Didn't happen. Couldn't happen.'

'Yes, I know what fiction means,' she said with a hint of annoyance. 'But he's "the One".'

I slumped back on the bench. 'You know I don't believe in all that.'

'Listen, Abs. He left you his details for a reason. He doesn't want you to wait nine years. He left his address. As an insurance policy, in case you showered off his number. And this is your chance to find him.'

I decided to humour her. 'And then what?'

She shrugged. 'Hadn't thought beyond my superbly romantic plan to get you there. I heard Turkish women are gorgeous too, and now I don't get to go.' She pouted and folded her arms. Liz had already swapped numbers with two girls on our trip – an American student in Croatia and a German tattoo artist in Munich.

I swatted her on the arm. 'You're insane, you know that?'

She nodded. 'Yes, I am. And maybe you won't want to come back home.'

'Liz, I have to. The job at the sailing club, Guildford law school, my training contract with McKenzie's. That's my life.'

'And it's boring.'

Her words shocked me, but I decided not to have it out with her. She was clearly in an emotional state. 'Look. I know what this is about. You'll figure things out, too. There's a job waiting for you somewhere.'

'Where?' She frowned and fiddled with the straps of her rucksack. 'I'm scared, Abs. Everything was great at university. I had you, I belonged to groups and organisations I cared about. But now? What have I got to look forward to? Holed up at Mum's with zero career prospects.'

I threw an arm around her and rubbed her shoulder.

'I'm sorry, I didn't mean it about your life being boring,' she said. 'It's not, honestly. You've got it all figured out, and I'm proud of you. But ...'

'But what?'

'I lied about being over the rejection from UNICEF. I was so sure our applications would get us onto their graduate scheme, and it would be the most amazing thing ever to work with you, have you live with me at Mum's, do something worthwhile.'

'But law school is my path. I only put in the application because you forced me to.'

'I know. You're right.'

'Let me come back with you, Liz. It won't be the same without you in Istanbul. We can work out some other jobs for you to apply to. I'd have three whole days before I have to get back home. And Oz was … was a one-day flirtation. One hot night of … It was nothing.' My eye began to flicker and I casually rubbed it with an index finger as I leaned my arm on the bench.

'Nice try. You can't hide that tic of yours from me.' She popped open the clips of her rucksack and pulled out a Ziploc bag. 'I want you to look at these.' Opening it, she handed me two photos.

Two pictures of me and Oz dancing.

'Where did you get these?'

'I took them. You missed the start of the dance when they were handing out disposable cameras. I took them when you guys were doing all that dirty dancing.'

I blushed at the memory.

'Look how happy you were.'

In one we were laughing as he had bent me backwards. 'I was drunk.'

'Nah-ah. I've seen you properly drunk.'

I looked at the second picture – my arms around his neck, his around my waist. Our eyes were fixed on each other.

'It must be love,' Liz said.

'Love?' I spluttered. 'It was not love.'

She nudged me in the ribs. 'He did something to you. And neither "Salamander Steve" nor "Pete that toad" ever came close to being worthy of my best mate.'

I laughed at the mention of my two university boyfriends and Liz's nicknames for them.

'I think you'll regret it for the rest of your life if you don't at least go and try to find him,' she said.

I stroked the photograph, battling to suppress the memory of how the night ended. 'But I can't roll up unannounced. Maybe I should write him a letter.'

'What do you think this is? Nineteen ninety? Look him up on Facebook, message him, meet him, have wild sex again and ... well, the rest is up to you.'

'How do I look him up? I don't know his last name.'

'It's Demir.'

'How do you know?'

'I beat it out of the Information lady at UCL. She gave me their student magazine which had an article about the programme he did there. Did you know he was studying business and management as well as intensive English?'

'No, I didn't. But, Liz, that night was ... well, it was supposed to be a one-night stand.'

'Says who?'

'We agreed.'

'Well change the agreement. This is your last chance to do something completely wild and spontaneous, and then you get to go and be boring back in London.'

I gave her a dirty look but my pulse was quickening. A wave of excitement was building. Would I have the nerve to go through with it without my best friend by my side?

12

The bus from Halkali station wound its way east to the district of Sultanahmet. I had every intention of counting the thirty stops it would make before having to get off, but once I had found a window seat and settled, I lost track. There was so much to absorb as the coach headed deeper into Istanbul: the thick, chaotic traffic; the street hustlers; the pink-fronted shops. I noticed a beautiful mosque wedged between a block of flats and a Domino's pizza – a jarring juxtaposition of old and new. I wanted to drink it all in. Suddenly I was relieved I hadn't bailed and gone home with Liz.

'Blue Mosque,' the tannoy announced about an hour later, snapping me out of my trance.

I hauled my backpack off the bus and stood in awe at the monument ahead. My sandals slapped against the cobble-stones until I reached my hotel, the Sarniç. When Liz had told me I would be staying there, I wondered why. The hostels we'd stayed in had been great so far, and cheap. She had gone all out for our final destination, knowing I would give in, thrilled at the prospect of a private room after two and a half weeks of sharing with other people and getting little sleep.

This was her treat, she had insisted. 'What if you want to ask Oz back to yours?' she had said with a wink.

I had smacked her on the top of her head with the Lonely Planet guide to Istanbul she had handed over, along with everything else she had organised, including a flight home – and not, as I had feared, a two-day train journey.

The Sarnıç looked like a yellow chocolate box; perfectly symmetrical with tall windows, and brown terracotta tiles wrapped around the frame of the building. Flowerpots brightened the five steps to the entrance.

Up in my room, I picked up the landline at the side of my bed, remembering the promise I had made to Mum and Dad that I would check in at every new destination. There was only one ring.

'Hello.'

'Hey, Mum.'

'Abbie, sweetheart. I'm so happy to hear your voice. Where are you?'

'Istanbul.'

'Goodness, how long will it take you to get home?'

'Only a few hours. Liz booked me, I mean us, a flight back to London.' My eye twitched.

'That's very generous of her.'

Heavy breathing filled my ear. 'Hey, Dad.' I twirled the telephone cord between my fingers.

'Hey, pet. How did you know I was here?'

'I can hear you breathing.' I chuckled.

'Phil, I'll tell you everything she says, you don't need to be on the other receiver.'

'But I want to hear her voice.'

'Then put your hand over the mouthpiece.'

It was like a comedy sketch. Every single time I called, the same repertoire.

'What are your plans in Istanbul?' Mum asked.

'Just sightseeing, the usual,' I said, my eye continuing to pulse as I thought of the photos Liz had given me of Oz and what the real motivation was for choosing this city.

'Please be safe, sweetheart,' Mum said. 'Make sure you have your money separate from your bank card, don't go out late at night, and don't forget your inhaler.'

'I will. I'd better go. This will be costing a lot.'

'Pet, before you go,' Dad said. 'An envelope came from McKenzie's and I opened it in case it was important. It was a reminder to sign your training contract. I thought you'd organised all that before you left.'

I twisted the cord tighter around my finger. 'Umm ... There were lots of forms to fill out. I didn't want to rush it. It only came the day before I left, and I wanted to make sure I made no mistakes.'

'OK, pet, I'll put it in your bedroom for when you get back. Bye, love.'

I hung up and my shoulders slumped, relieved I had sidestepped any further investigation as to why the contract I had received a week before I left was still sitting buried in one of my university boxes, unsigned.

After eating breakfast at the rooftop restaurant and taking snaps of the incredible 360-degree view, I sat at the guests' computer in the lobby and logged into my Facebook account. Typing Özgür Demir into the search field produced eight results. I prayed he had a plain photo of himself and not some fancy posed image like mine. My thumbnail was a side-shot of me in a large sun hat looking out over Bracelet Bay, my favourite spot in Mumbles. Every summer, Dad and I loved to trek to the lighthouse there at low tide; the scramble to get there, when the sand gave way to seaweed-strewn rocks, was always exhilarating. When I was little, Dad and I would make up stories of shipwrecks and lost souls stranded there by the tide. He would always put me on his shoulders and carry me back to shore when the tide started to come in. It made me feel safe when I wrapped my arms round his neck and the water splashed at my feet. Amy went with us once but hated that she was expected to wade back, so after that she stayed on the sand with Mum who couldn't swim.

I scrolled up and down but none of the pictures were of my Oz. Nor did any of these guys live in Istanbul. Looked like I would have to turn up at his address and hope he was home.

That journey proved fruitless, however. The address took me to a gated compound where neither of the guards recognised Oz's name, nor could they speak any English. I ducked into a café across the road for a welcome respite from the scorching sun.

A waiter appeared to take my order as soon as I sat down. The table to my left had a gaggle of girls with heavy make-up and expensive-looking clothes. I was sure my sensible sandals and Primark skirt and T-shirt combo would not impress them.

The waiter brought my coffee and I winced at the first sip; it was as thick and bitter as tar. He passed me a cup of sugar and I spooned in three servings.

'Excuse me, can I ask you a question?' I asked before he could retreat.

'My English is not so good.'

'Oh. Well, um. *I* am looking' – I pointed to myself – 'for a man. A man called Özgür Demir.' I held my breath.

He stroked his chin, a half-inch of stubble brushing under the touch of his fingers. 'Sorry.' He shook his head. 'This name I do not know.'

I sighed and unzipped my bag, retrieving my purse. I had slipped in the photos of us dancing that Liz had given me. It was a sideways shot of Oz, probably not the easiest form of identification.

'Are you sure? Maybe he comes here for coffee,' I said, pointing to the coffee cup, hoping I wasn't being rude about his level of English comprehension. 'He gave me his address which I think is over there,' I said, pointing across the road.

'Burak!' he yelled to another waiter – an older man wiping glasses behind the counter. An outpouring of Turkish followed; all I could decipher was Oz's name somewhere in the middle. The other man shook his head, and I sank further into my seat.

'Sorry, Miss.' He shrugged and walked away.

I tucked the photo back into my purse and took a bite of my croissant. This was ridiculous. How had I let Liz talk me into this? Anyway, I had tried. It was time to get back on the tram, explore the city. No time to waste, chasing a guy who ... who ... I bit my bottom lip. OK, I'll admit it. It had been hard to get that day and night out of my head. After I handed in my dissertation, I had spent a lot of time stressing about the mark I was going to get, but also daydreaming about Oz. I had endlessly stared at our Photo-Me pictures and hid them under my pillow until they began to get crumpled. So far, I thought I had managed to shut him away into a part of my brain I used to store those amazing experiences you have once, and once only. No guy could be that smart, attentive, great in bed *and* a good dancer. They just didn't exist.

A tap on the shoulder brought me back to the present. I turned around to see a beautiful young woman standing behind me. Her pleated red skirt barely covered her thighs and her three-inch heels revealed manicured toenails of the brightest yellow. She flicked her wavy black hair over her shoulder and straightened her polo shirt.

'Excuse me,' she said with a thick Turkish accent. 'I heard you say the name Özgür Demir.'

I sat up straight. 'Yes, do you know him? Wait, I have a picture.' I tugged at the jammed zip of my bag. A lip balm, loose change and a pack of tissues spilled out. 'I'm so sorry, excuse me,' I said, fumbling around the floor at her feet, where I couldn't help but notice a Jimmy Choo logo on her sandals. I scooped everything up, lifting the photo from my purse. She took it as if her fingers were tongs.

'I met him in London a few months ago, and a friend took this photo. He gave me his address, but it doesn't look like he lives there.'

Her nostrils flared. 'Are you English?'

'Yes, I am.'

'And you've come here to Istanbul to find him?' She placed her hand on her hip and arched an eyebrow.

'Yup.'

She smiled – full lips painted the same shade of red as her skirt – and handed back the picture. 'I know him. Our families are friends for years and years.'

Excitement shot through me. 'Do you know where I might find him?'

She flung her thick black mane over her other shoulder and that's when I noticed two equally glamorous girls sitting at the table behind her. They were whispering and glancing over, stifling giggles.

'Today Özgür is out of town with his mother. But tomorrow we will all meet at the Golden Beach Club. Please join us, at eleven. I am sure he will be happy to see you again.'

She sauntered back to her table and clicked her fingers, mumbling something under her breath. One of the other girls gave her a pen and a receipt. She could barely write the words, her talons struggling to gain purchase on the biro.

'Give this to a taxi driver and he will know where to bring you.' She thrust the paper at me.

'Thank you ...'

'Dima. My name is Dima.'

I stretched out my hand. 'Abbie.'

She took it, but something resembling a sneer appeared on her face as my sweaty palm made contact with her hand. I didn't care, though. I couldn't wait to message Liz. I had done it. I had found Oz.

The tarmac sizzled in the sun the next day as I strolled the mile or so from the bus stop to the Golden Beach Club, having opted to use public transport and not accept the extortionate taxi fare quote. It was set well back from the road, giant palm trees swaying by a lush expanse of lawn. Two doormen opened the glass doors as I approached, both bowing low.

I gasped at the waterfall which dominated the atrium, the soft furnishings scattered around, and the giant fans overhead. Along one wall was a long counter with two well-presented gentlemen standing behind it, rows of white towels stacked behind them.

I gripped the strap of my handbag and approached. 'Excuse me.'

'*Hoşgeldiniz*. Welcome. How can we help?'

'I am meeting someone here.'

'Do you have a name?'

'Yes. Yes, I do. It's Dima.'

'And her second name?'

I took off my sun hat, scratching the side of my head where sweat had accumulated. 'I don't know her second name.'

'We have over a thousand members at this club. I am afraid I cannot permit you to enter without the name of the guest. Perhaps you can call her?'

'I don't have her number. Wait, there's someone else. A man called Özgür Demir.'

He punched some keys on his computer. 'We have no record of this name.'

I sighed and puffed out my cheeks, fanning my hat, annoyed with myself for not extracting more details from Dima.

'Is there anywhere I can get a water?'

The man pursed his lips. He was clearly under strict instructions not to admit anyone who resembled a scruffy tourist. It must cost a fortune to have a membership here.

He tipped his head to an area at the back. 'You may use the drinking fountain. Please, be our guest.' He smiled tightly.

I picked up a glass beaker and pulled down the handle, which caused water to pour out much faster than I had expected. The splash hit my shorts, forming a wet patch around my crotch. *Just great.*

The sparkling water of the pool beyond the glass wall appeared inviting, sun loungers dotted around the edges. A man got up from a seat and stretched his hands high in the air as he prepared to dive in. I squinted. *Oz?*

He emerged from the other side of the pool – far enough away he couldn't see me if I were to start frantically waving, but near enough for me to be sure, his swimming trunks wet and clinging to his skin, leaving little to the imagination – the muscles on his chest and arms glistening. I nibbled my bottom lip, thinking back to that night in London.

Oz sauntered back to his spot, where a woman in a white micro-bikini passed him a towel before practically throwing herself at him, circling her arms around his neck. He reached behind his head to grab her hands, but not before I saw her lean in. Had she kissed him?

As he reclined back on the sun lounger, the girl pushed her sunglasses onto the top of her head and flicked her hair behind her. *Wait, I know that flick.* She glanced briefly over her shoulder, and there was no mistaking it was Dima. I stuck my head back behind a fern and peeped through its leaves.

'Miss!'

I jumped, kicking over the glass at my feet, which – thank God – didn't shatter. 'Hi,' I said, locking eyes with the man I had spoken to at reception.

'Would you like me to call a taxi for you?'

I shifted my bag on my shoulder. 'No, that won't be necessary. I'll wait outside for my friends. I'm sure they will come out soon,' I replied lightly, smiling, before scuttling outside.

The sun burned brighter, the shade from the palm tree above providing little respite.

An hour later, the doors opened to the sound of laughter. A group emerged; Oz was in the centre, Dima's arm circling his.

'Oz?' my voice squeaked; throat parched.

He turned towards me, pulling his shades off. As recognition dawned, his eyes widened.

'*Yok artık.* No way. *Abbie?*' He dropped Dima's arm; his smile broad – those familiar dimples deepening. 'Is that really you?'

He stepped nearer, drawing me in with his eyes, taking in every inch. The memory of his lips on my body, the heat from his skin on mine, flamed my already hot face.

Taking hold of the top of my arms, he planted kisses on both my cheeks. He left a heady aroma of coconut and citrus as he leaned back. His caramel eyes sparkled in the sunlight; they were deeper and more intense than I remembered. The white T-shirt he now wore emphasised his tanned skin.

He ran a hand through his towel-dried hair. 'What are you doing here?' he asked.

'Dima invited me,' I said, tipping my head to acknowledge her presence.

He turned to look at her, arms stretched out, palms upwards.

She mirrored his pose. '*Sürpriz!*' The corner of her mouth curled as she stepped forward. 'Dear Abbie. We waited for you. I wonder you change your mind.'

I shook my head. 'They wouldn't let me in without your full name.'

Oz continued to run his hands through his hair. 'I don't understand. How did you meet Dima?'

This was not exactly a private conversation. The same girls who had hung out with Dima in the café were by her sides, and three guys milled around in the background, studying their phones, periodically looking up at the unfolding drama.

'I met Dima at a café yesterday, and she said she knew you. She invited me here today to see you.'

'But the ... *eh* ...'

'Coincidence?'

He smiled and tapped his fingers on his forehead. 'Yes, that word.'

'I've been travelling around Europe by train with my friend, Liz. Do you remember her? She planned all the cities, and this was our last destination, but she had to go back to England suddenly.' I shrugged my shoulders. 'Dima heard me ask the waiter in a café if he knew you. She invited me here, but I failed the entrance test.' I wrinkled my nose with a glance towards the club.

He stepped closer. 'You came to Istanbul to find *me*?' His words were a whisper, his nearness causing a familiar warmth inside me.

Suddenly a car pulled up. 'Özgür!' a male voice hollered. '*Hadi ama.*'

'One minute,' Oz said, his hand held up. 'How long are you staying in Istanbul?'

'A couple more days.'

'Do you have any plans?'

'Just sightseeing. I've ticked off a few of my top ten.'

'How sweet,' Dima said. 'We could show Abbie some things of Istanbul tomorrow afternoon.'

'That would be nice, thank you. I'd love to see some parts of the city only the locals know. Are you free tomorrow morning as well?' I asked Oz hopefully.

His mouth opened to answer, but Dima interrupted. She burbled on in Turkish at Oz, and he replied with a note of irritation. I felt like I was intruding on a lovers' tiff. One of the guys stepped forward and slapped Oz on the back, before wading in. It was a proper soap opera right in front of me, but I had no subtitles to follow.

'I'm sorry, Abbie. In the morning, I have to be somewhere. We will have a big party to celebrate my brother's birthday on Wednesday, which I have to help plan. You must come.'

At that suggestion, Dima turned on her heel and stomped to the waiting car.

'I must go now, but can I call you to arrange tomorrow?'

'Actually, my SIM card doesn't work abroad. But I'm staying at the Sarniç hotel.'

'OK, maybe we can come and pick you up at two?'

I nodded. 'Sounds great.'

Oz leaned in once more to kiss my cheeks. A sudden urge to run my fingers through his hair and kiss him hard and long on the lips caught me off guard. The scorching midday sun must have turned my brain to mush.

'Can we get you a taxi? Or give you a lift?' Oz asked.

'I'll be fine. It looks like you're busy.'

His lips twitched. 'It's so good to see you.'

'And you, too.'

He shook his head slowly. 'Abbie. My mind is ... Ah, my English. I can't think of what I want to say.'

'That's OK. I know it's rather strange I am standing here, but it must be lo—' I stopped myself before I used the same word Liz had. 'It must be fate.' I laughed nervously. This wasn't fate. A meddling best friend who meant well, more likely.

'*Kader*, they say in Turkey. Destiny.' His voice was low and deep. 'It is something I—'

'Özgür!' Dima's voice was sharp, from the rolled-down window.

I resisted the urge to tut and sigh. Was she planning on interrupting our every attempt at conversation? 'I will see you tomorrow?'

'Yes, I cannot wait.' He put his sunglasses back on and walked away, turning briefly to show me that smile, which brought me right back to the time he had appeared at the bench after my fainting spell.

The rest of Oz's friends were still waiting for their cars once he had driven off and they looked at me, puzzled. On a whim, I signalled to the valet and pointed to the taxi sign. *Sod it.* At least I would leave in style.

The car's cool interior was welcome and I sank into the leather, my head spinning. I wasn't so delirious as to give the driver the name of my hotel, though. He shrugged as he drove away before pulling up about a mile later at the bus stop where I had got off this morning.

My pulse hadn't settled since I had left the club. Why? Memories of the time we had spent together in London came flooding back and I couldn't help smiling. Although there was a strong undercurrent of unease over something I couldn't figure out: Oz's relationship with Dima. They appeared close, very close. I was sure I had seen him kiss her.

Would I get an opportunity to see him alone to ask him more about their relationship? It didn't seem likely, yet I had scored an afternoon of sightseeing plus an invite to his brother's party. Maybe I could find the right moment. Or maybe it would become blindingly obvious if she continued to drape herself all over him. Honestly, what had I expected?

That he would spend nine years in a state of suspended animation, pining away for Abbie Jones?

I shook my head to banish the thoughts. This was stupid. Until two days ago, I had never expected I would see him again. I had forced myself to park our time together in the depths of my subconscious. Surely it was a good thing for my future if that's where it remained. Only ... what if Liz was right? What if he was 'the One'? What if there was an entirely different path I was supposed to be on?

13

A horn roused me from my spot in the lobby of the hotel. When I had returned from dinner yesterday, the concierge had handed me a phone message: *I have cancelled my plans and can pick you up from your hotel at 11 a.m. tomorrow. Hope you are free. Oz.* My heart had done a triple flip.

I heard the horn again and peered through the window. Oz was sitting on a scooter, alone. I took a deep breath, smoothing out the pleats of my beige skorts. My pink T-shirt was about a shade lighter than my current skin tone which was struggling under the Turkish sun.

I skipped out of the doorway with a wave to the concierge.

Oz removed his helmet and shook his hair out.

'Hi,' I said with a low wave.

'*Günaydin*.' He swung his leg over the bike and settled it with a turn of the handlebars. He walked over and kissed me on both cheeks. I felt a tingle along my spine as his skin brushed mine. I breathed deeply; the scent of citrus and sun cream mixed with freshly laundered clothes. His navy short-sleeved shirt was unbuttoned over a crisp white T-shirt and his beige cargo shorts skimmed his knees.

'*Günaydin*,' I repeated. 'Nice bike. Pink suits you.'

'And you too,' he said, nodding at my top. 'The scooter is my sister's. I borrowed it for the morning and can't let it out of my sight, so I apologise for not coming into the hotel. She will kill me when she finds out.' He smiled mischievously. 'But it's worth the risk. You said you wanted to see a different side of Istanbul.' He patted the back of the scooter's seat. 'This is the best way. Here.' Opening the seat to reveal a small storage area, he took out the other helmet and I put my sunglasses and bag inside. 'Let's go.' He swung his leg over the bike and started the engine.

'Are we going far?'

'To a place east of my hometown. It's quite a long way but the view from a car would be boring. Put your feet on this bar and hold onto me tight. Don't let go.'

I nodded and squeezed on behind him. Circling his waist, I held him lightly. The bike lurched forward, and I almost tumbled backward. I grabbed him harder, cursing myself for not heeding his warning.

Once out of the city centre, the bike took a straighter path. I looked around; flawless blue sky and trees more verdant than any I had seen before. It was exhilarating seeing Istanbul from this viewpoint.

A while later, a briny breeze filled my nose as we arrived at a small town with colourful single-storey houses. The motor slowed as we bumped over a narrow track leading to the harbour.

'We're here,' Oz said, removing the keys from the ignition and taking off his helmet.

Once the engine cut, I was conscious of the cries of seagulls overhead and water lapping against a flotilla of small fishing boats.

'Where are we?'

'This is Arnavutköy. I used to come here when I was a boy and fish with … my brother.'

Oz hung the helmets on the handlebars and we stepped towards the water. He slipped off his shoes and sat down, dangling his feet off the dock.

'It's so peaceful here,' I said, sitting beside him and unbuckling my sandals. As I dipped a foot in, I yelped. 'It's freezing.'

He laughed. 'Go in slowly.'

I gradually submerged my foot and ankle, and he was right. It was refreshing – a welcoming cool from the midday sun. Leaning back on my hands, I smiled. 'So tranquil.'

Oz was leaning forward, his shoulders tensed and his brow furrowed. I splashed his legs with a kick of water.

'Hey,' he protested.

'You look so serious.'

'I was thinking how you came to be in Istanbul.' He squinted from the sun in his eyes.

'All down to Liz. This is our last stop after Bulgaria.'

'I remember you said you wouldn't go Interrailing.'

'Twenty-first birthday gift. From Liz. A last chance to let my hair down before starting law school.'

'To become a solicitor. Is that right?'

I took a deep breath. 'Yup. I got a training contract with quite a good firm. But not top tier like I'd hoped. My degree wasn't one of the best.'

'*Tebrikler,*' he said, reaching out to squeeze my hand. 'Congratulations. The dissertation was good?'

'I got a starred first for it. "A bright future in journalism" was one of the comments.'

'*Harika.* How wonderful.'

'I struggled more with the final exams though, so they brought the overall result down. But I owe you so much for helping me.'

'I did nothing.' He cupped his hands on his lap, looking thoughtful.

'And what about your travel plans, now your masters is over? If you haven't been to Croatia, I highly recommend it.'

He shrugged and focussed on his feet moving in the water. 'I join the family business now. Study and travel are over. I have to work.'

'That's a shame. What's your family's business?'

'Property. My brother already works there, and it is my destiny too.'

There was a note of resignation in his voice.

'I have to sign my training contract when I get back home,' I said. 'It's weird. I thought it'd be the easiest thing to do. It's just a signature. But ...'

'It is hard to take a step which will affect the rest of your life.'

I let out a puff of air. 'When you phrase it like that, yes, it is hard.' I thought back to the day the contract had arrived. It wasn't the only job offer I had received that day, but I couldn't tell anyone else about the other one, especially not Liz.

'To thine own self be true,' I mumbled.

143

'What did you say?'

I repeated it with a sweep of my arm this time.

'That's very poetic.'

I smiled. 'I can't take credit. Shakespeare wrote it. Not sure why I said it.' Liz liked to quote at me regularly, and I had clearly picked up her habit.

A cheeky grin spread across his face. 'Ah, British humour.' He tickled the water with his fingertips before flicking drops in my direction. 'I have missed it.'

'Hey.' I shielded myself before scooping some water of my own and sending it back at him. But he continued to splash with ever-faster shots of water. 'OK, OK. Stop.' I looked down at my top, which was becoming see-through. I gave him a look.

'*Pardon.*' He chuckled again, emphasising his dimples. Those little indents I had often stared at on the photo booth pictures.

'It's fine. Very refreshing,' I said wryly. I leaned back on my arms again and breathed deeply. 'How are your friends doing? The ones you met in England.'

'*Aslında* – I mean, actually, Yusef is visiting Turkey tomorrow and I will show him some of my country. Yaman is still in Ankara. Sometimes we email.'

'It'd be great to meet Yusef again.' Gathering some courage, I opened my mouth to ask him about Dima. But Oz turned away and shouted to a man in the distance. He pointed at the boats and out towards the sea.

'*Hadi,*' he said, standing, reaching his hand out to me.

'Where are we going?'

'For a trip on the water. You can swim, yes?'

'I can swim, but ...' I scanned my outfit.

'No, no. We will be in the boat, not swimming. But in case we fall in,' he said, deadpan, before giving me a wink.

'Ha, ha. Funny,' I said. 'You're catching on to British humour.'

Oz led me back to the shore before untying one of the wooden paddle boats. 'Watch your step.' He extended a hand to me again, his grip tightening as I stepped in and the boat wobbled.

'Don't worry, I have you. You won't fall in,' he reassured me.

I sat down on the seat at the back – a blanket underneath me – and held onto the other side of the boat. In one swift move, Oz pushed us away from the harbour with his foot and grabbed the paddles, nudging them left and right until we were on a straight path. His knees knocked into mine every time he stretched forwards.

My fingertips trailed on the surface. It was so clear, I could see little shoals of fish darting about as the boat cut through the water. As we rowed further from the shore, the arc of the harbour became more obvious, framed by colourful houses like scoops of ice cream in a banana-shaped dish. Restaurants had opened and checked tablecloths lay on tables outside, a few of them filled with diners.

Over my shoulder, the distant view of the Bosphorus Bridge and endless blue sea. I had no idea how far we were going to drift, but I didn't care.

'It's beautiful out here,' I said. 'I never used to like being out on the water.'

'*Neden?* I mean, why is that?'

I wrapped my arms around myself. 'When I was ten, my sister persuaded me to take a dinghy out from Mumbles Pier, close to where we stay every summer, and go out sailing together. We got caught out in a rip tide and lifeguards had to rescue us. It was terrifying. Our parents were furious – grounded Amy for weeks.'

'Did you escape punishment?'

I nodded. 'They were so relieved I was alive and mad at Amy for leading me astray, even though I knew she hadn't got their permission to go out in the first place.'

'It is interesting how parents treat their children differently. My sister was always getting into trouble when we were young, but every time, my mother put the blame on me or my older brother. My sister is the much loved only daughter. Cherished.'

Perhaps Amy felt the injustice, too. I remember she had stood on the beach after we were rescued, sobbing, her wet hair sticking to her face while our parents hugged me so tight, I could've shattered into pieces.

'Do you feel safe out here on the water with me?' Oz asked, his eyes sparkling in the sunshine.

I smiled. 'Is it likely we will get caught in a rip tide?'

He shook his head. 'The water is calm today.'

'Then yes, I feel safe.'

He held my gaze steady with his before lifting the oars clear of the water and resting them on the side.

'Here.' He patted the seat next to him. 'This is the better view of the bridge.'

I stood up gingerly but as the boat wobbled, I began to lose my balance. Oz reached out and grabbed me, but somehow I managed to collapse on top of him.

'Well now I don't feel so safe.' I laughed as he helped me position myself beside him.

'I'm sorry.' He bit his bottom lip and looked very contrite. 'I thought it was a good idea.'

'It's OK. It's not your fault I have a habit of falling into your arms.'

He looked down shyly as he stretched his legs out. They pressed into mine and the warmth heated my skin. A flashback popped into my mind of our legs entwined on my dorm room bed and heat flamed my whole body at the memory.

A faint tune began to play on Oz's lips.

'What are you humming?'

'It is a song from a show my sister loves to watch. The TV is always turned high and I think it got into my head.'

'It has a nice melody. What are the words?'

He cleared his throat and licked his lips before singing the sweetest song in Turkish.

'That's beautiful,' I said once he had finished. 'And you have a lovely voice.' *Sings, dances, a linguist. What* else *could he do?*

He grinned, looking down again. '*Teşekkürler.*'

'What do the words mean in English?'

'*Eh.*' He gazed at the sky. 'Let me see. Forgive my translation. "Where can I put myself? Where shall I hide and cry? Where can I ... find myself? Shall I go to the seaside and dream?'" He finally turned his head and held my eyes steady again.

Goosebumps rose on my arms and I couldn't help but focus on his lips. 'That's ... very moving. I might write it down.'

A breeze picked up and rocked the boat gently from side to side and our shoulders touched. I wondered if he was thinking of the last time we were together and whether he would lean in and kiss me.

'I can't believe I found you,' I said, looking into his eyes. 'I lost your number, or rather, I accidentally washed it off.'

He smiled and those dimples formed again, and I ached to reach out and stroke them.

'And when I went to your address, the one you left me on the note, the security guard was insistent you didn't live there. In fact, it's strange. The beach club didn't recognise you either. Liz got your surname from UCL, from a magazine which had details of your programme.'

He looked away and his arm tensed – the scar appearing paler in the sunlight. He reflexively covered it with his hand. 'I registered at UCL in my father's name, but here, I am known by my grandfather's name – Arsel – the same as my mother.'

'Oh,' I said, not sure whether I should press him further.

'We should eat before we meet my friends,' he said, moving over to where I had sat, picking up both oars. 'Do you like seafood?'

I nodded.

Oz strained his arms and pulled us back into shore. I felt as if I had spoiled the moment by bringing up my confusion over his surname. But I didn't want our time alone together to end. Out here on the water, the two of us, I felt a connection that was beginning to run even deeper than before. And couldn't he feel the electricity between us, like a current running through a circuit every time we made contact?

The owner of the restaurant greeted Oz like an old friend. But then again, it seemed everywhere I went, everyone knew each other. He placed an assortment of fried calamari, fish balls and salted bonito in front of us, proudly displaying the restaurant's specials with a sweep of his arms. A fresh green salad and bread basket accompanied the vast array of dishes Oz ordered.

'This all looks delicious.'

'*Afiyet olsun.*'

'What does that mean?'

'We say it at a meal to wish you a good appetite.'

I nodded, tucking into some olives and bread before spearing a fried ring with my fork. The batter was light and crisp and the calamari not in the least bit chewy.

'How often do you come here? Everyone seems to know you.'

'I try and come once a month, more in the summer, but my friends prefer the beach club.'

'It looked like quite a place.'

'I'm sorry you did not get to experience it.'

'That's OK. I'm far happier here.' I took in the sweep of the harbour. 'In fact, this village has a similar feel to Mumbles.'

'Where you spend your summers with your family?'

'Yes. Of course the weather's better here. We're usually bundled up in a raincoat at this time of year. Wales seems to have its own microclimate.'

'I miss that fine British rain,' he said with a hint of humour.

'Really?' I raised an eyebrow. 'Actually, I don't mind it either. It's quite refreshing and never stops us from going in the sea.'

'I'd like to go there one day. To your Mumbles.'

I caught my breath at the thought of seeing him again. 'I'd like to show it to you. We could have cockles and lava bread at Colin's seafood café.'

'What's lava bread?'

'It's seaweed and it's really good for you.'

'I'd love to try it.' He smiled more broadly, making my heart skip a beat.

We shared more stories of summer breaks, places we wanted to visit in the future, and I wondered if we would travel to all these places together.

'So, what's the plan now?' I said, brushing a few breadcrumbs from my lap after we had finished the meal and I had my feeble attempt to help pay the bill rejected.

Oz wiped his mouth with his napkin and pushed back his chair. 'An art gallery. My friend Mert is the boyfriend of the owner of the studio and will tell you the story of every painting.' He shrugged. 'I think it is modern art.'

'Sounds interesting.' I followed him back to the bike, thanking the restaurant owner on the way.

'Then we will stroll through the bazaar. The girls will take you to the best shops. Then …' His eyes sparkled. 'A sunset cruise.'

'Can't wait.'

He patted the bike's seat. *'Hadi gidelim.'*

'What does that mean?'

'Let's go. And this time, hold on.' He winked.

I nestled back on the bike and wrapped my arms tightly around him, resting my cheek against his back. As we sped off, I moved one of my hands over his T-shirt until I could feel his steady heartbeat. I sighed. He looked back for a moment and smiled, leaning his back into me. His hands tightened around the handlebars and the rhythm of his heart quickened under my fingertips.

I closed my eyes, and in a flash, I was back in my room at university; the heat from the radiator throbbing beside me, adding to the warmth coursing through me from his kisses which had trailed from the bottom of my legs all the way up, lightly brushing the inside of my thighs; the teasing way he had removed my underwear before everything blurred into a blaze of pleasure.

I squeezed my legs around him, the motor humming underneath me, my hands caressing his chest, wishing to be back there, back in my dorm room, where—

A horn hooted at the same time as I groaned, snapping out of my fantasy. We slowed to a halt and I tried to gather myself and dared not look into Oz's eyes once we got off the scooter. I blamed this heat. Still not used to it, not even after the last two and a half weeks.

In the distance Dima stood with her posse of girls. The guys appeared bored as they tapped away on their mobiles. No one looked especially delighted to see us. I snatched a look at my watch – well past two, our designated meeting time. A girl broke from the crowd and remonstrated with Oz before speeding off with the bike. I assumed it was his sister.

After the trip to the art gallery and a lazy spell of browsing in the bazaar, Dima led our group outside. The sun had sunk low, throwing an orange glow around the square in front of us. Ahead, the port at Eminönü was crowded. Gaggles of camera-wielding tourists were assembled in what can't ever be described as a 'queue' for the cruise – well, at least not to a Brit. Dima puffed out her cheeks and the other girls folded their arms. We waited for a few minutes before we started shuffling forward.

When we got to the front, one of the stewards – with the tour's name emblazoned on his shirt – held up a palm, his other hand bearing a rope. As Dima spoke to him, he replied with a two-fingered signal, then pointed to the boat swaying low in the water, tourists almost spilling over the sides. Dima stamped her foot and raised her voice.

I didn't dare ask what was going on, but at a guess, I would say the boat had reached capacity. I was about to say to her it didn't matter, that I could catch one on my own tomorrow, or that I had already had the best boat ride, the one with Oz on our private little dinghy. But as my mouth opened, I felt a tug on my hand.

In one swift movement, Oz had grabbed it and pulled me forward. He ducked under the rope, lifting it high enough to let me through. We skipped along the gangplank without a backwards glance.

'Özgür!' Dima hollered. She repeated his name, but her call was lost in a churn of water as the engines started. Oz gripped my hand tighter as we leapt over the gap between the boat and the harbour's edge.

My heart hammered against my chest and I giggled, in between gasps for breath. Oz didn't relax his grip but led me through the crowd to the back of the boat, up a flight of narrow steps, and then weaved through the upper deck crowd to the bow. He gently prised his elbow into a small space between two passengers, said *'pardon'*, and brought me towards him so I could see the view from the barrier.

We could see Oz's friends, standing down below. Dima's arms were folded across her chest again, but the guys were waving, probably relieved they wouldn't have to do this tour with us. Mert stuck his thumb up and pointed to the bag of souvenirs I had left behind, before waving. Oz waved back and shouted something in Turkish. I picked out my name from his words.

As the boat pulled away their figures shrank, until they blended into the backdrop.

'What did you say?'

'That you were staying for such a short time, how could we let you miss one of the highlights of our city?'

I smiled and the breeze picked up, my hair buffeting my face. I barely had any wriggle room to pick off strands. 'I feel bad we left your friends behind.'

He tutted. 'No. Don't feel bad. They will go out for a meal or drink in a café. I am sure they will be there when we return.'

'They're very nice, your friends. But I don't think Dima likes me much.' I paused, waiting for a hint on their relationship status.

'Dima is hard to get to know, but she is a loyal friend.'

I pursed my lips. That didn't help much. 'Is she—'

The loudspeaker blared out a message in three languages, cutting me off. Although one of them was in English, I could barely make out enough of it for it to tell me anything. Oz pointed ahead and became my own private guide.

Crap. The moment had passed. How could I bring her up again now?

Oz pointed out the palaces of Dolmabahçe and Beylerbeyi, and the Yalis – wooden houses dating from the Ottoman Empire. I fished out my camera and took several shots, but it was hard to focus on some of the buildings through the lens with Oz in the frame. Using the zoom button, I studied his face as he talked: eyes dancing with excitement with every word, his lips soft and inviting. When one of the two suspension bridges loomed ahead, I leaned forward more. It was lit up like a Christmas tree. As we sailed under, we passed another cruise boat. The water slapped between our vessels, and ours lurched to one side. I grabbed Oz's hand, and he steadied me with his arm.

'Thanks,' I whispered. The boat eased into its earlier groove and I released my grip to tidy a few strands of hair.

The sun dipped lower, the coastline of Istanbul glowing with strings of lights against a backdrop of a marmalade sky.

Oz nodded at my camera. 'Shall I take some of you?'

I handed it to him. 'That'd be great.' I struck a few poses; some were flamboyant, and I could see Oz's smile behind the camera. Someone to our right offered to take one of the two of us and we shuffled together. Oz's arm lightly touched my shoulder. I leaned in and he grasped my arm tighter – our heads touching. We thanked our photographer and turned back to the water. I snatched a quick look at the frame and smiled before placing it back in my bag.

I inhaled deeply, the salty air filling my lungs. 'Your home is beautiful, Oz.'

'It is a lovely city. But London ... London is exciting and colourful. The extra courses I studied were so ... enlightening. The museums I visited – so interesting. I felt free when I lived there.' Oz gripped the railing and looked back out to sea. 'Do you ever wish you could run away?'

I snatched some air and focussed on the shore, where the outlines of buildings were merging in the fading light. 'It's never crossed my mind before.'

'I sometimes think it is easier to run than face the consequences of declaring you no longer want to be on the path set for you. *Yani* ... We are told as children to dream, but what good is a dream if it goes against the order of life?' He leaned forward on his forearms, lost in thought, before looking back over his shoulder. 'What did you want to be when you were a little girl?'

I laughed. 'A vet. There was a TV show I loved called *Blue Peter* which had a golden retriever on it, called Bonnie. When she had puppies, that was it. I was convinced being a vet was the greatest profession of all.'

'How old were you?'

I wrinkled my nose. 'Six, maybe seven. But that dream lasted about two years, until the day my dad ran over a squirrel with our car. My sister loves to tease me about how I threw up on the side of the road when I saw its innards smeared across the tarmac.'

'*Úf ya.*' He smiled sympathetically. 'But then you created a new dream?'

My shoulders sagged. 'When I was thirteen, something happened with my dad and it kinda snowballed from there.'

'Why, what happened?'

I chewed the inside of my cheek. I had never opened up before to anyone. 'He came home one evening upset. I was upstairs reading and crept out onto the landing to hear what he was saying to Mum.'

Looking out to the water, I could imagine the scene again, me crouching by the banister, straining to hear the voices downstairs, growing chilly as I huddled there in my nightdress.

'He'd received a letter from the head office at the bank he worked at, a local branch in my hometown. At the time I didn't know what it said. Next thing my sister Amy bursts in, declaring she's leaving school. They had a huge fight. I remember the exact words he told her. "Why can't you be more like your sister? She'll make something of herself. She'll be a lawyer or a doctor. Not a dropout like you."'

'What happened then?'

'A door slammed. I knew it was Amy leaving, but then I heard Mum screaming.' The scene was still vivid in my mind: sirens and flashing lights, a paramedic's soothing words. 'A heart arrhythmia. That's what the doctor called it. They rushed him to hospital. I saw him wheeled out on a stretcher with a mask over his mouth. Mum left me and said she'd call when they got there and when she had more information.'

'I'm so sorry.'

My eyes misted over. 'For hours I thought he was going to die. Those fears spun around my head haunting me for months. He was fine in the end; needed medication, told to avoid stressful situations. I remember him telling me weeks later some new guy who was a qualified accountant had got the promotion Dad had been hoping for. That was what the letter had been about. He didn't have any qualifications – never went to university either. He'd worked his way up from junior clerk. No one knew the bank better than him yet still he didn't get the promotion he'd worked thirty years for. He always said, "If I'd had a certificate, it would've been me." That was the year I had to make my GCSE choices – the exams we take at sixteen. Like I told you, the sight of blood makes me throw up, so I decided I wanted to become a lawyer, get a qualification, and picked all my subjects based on that career path. Silly, right?' I swallowed hard.

'No. Not at all.' His look was so earnest.

'My sister always caused him so much stress, and I was desperate for him never to be put in that situation again. I even thought as a lawyer I could protect him.' I gave a half laugh, realising how childish it all sounded. 'But he was so chuffed when I told him what I wanted to be.'

'Chuffed? I don't understand this word.'

'It means pleased, satisfied.'

'But now? There is something on your mind. A conflict?'

I shivered and looked into his eyes. Could he read my thoughts?

I nodded. 'I've wanted to be a solicitor for so long, well, I thought I did. Three years at King's changed a lot for me; rallies, demos, writing for the student magazine, so much to experience. I probably should've chosen to do a law degree – that would've been simpler and wouldn't have turned my head. But then the day I met you, I remembered what you said about the world being out there for me. Something hit me. I can't quite put it into words. Anyway, Liz wanted to get a job at UNICEF. We'd done some volunteer work for them during our second year: handing out leaflets, stopping people in the street with clipboards, trying to get donations, that sort of thing. She persuaded me to apply for a position on their graduate scheme, saying it would be fun to work together. She didn't get it … but I did.' I let out a puff of air.

'That's amazing.'

I shook my head. 'No, it isn't. I can't tell her I got it. She'd be crushed. It was *her* dream, not mine. She was just too scared to apply on her own. Only … I can't deny the idea of working for them …' I trailed off, looking out into the darkness. 'Doesn't matter. I can't take it.'

'You would sacrifice your happiness for hers?'

I searched his eyes. 'I'm not sure. I don't know what to do. It's not only Liz I can't tell. Dad would be bitterly disappointed if I told him I'd changed my mind. He's already framed the acceptance letter from Guilford law school and hung it on the wall.'

He squeezed my hand. 'I am sure your father will be proud of you no matter what you decide.'

'Maybe. What about you?' I asked, realising I had moved my gaze from his eyes to his lips and lingered too long on them. 'What did you want to be when you were younger?'

He grinned. 'Footballer. I hoped to play for my team, Beşiktaş.'

'And how did that turn out?'

He shrugged. 'When the scouts came to watch a junior high school game, I failed to impress them.'

'Sorry.'

He tutted and tipped his chin upwards. 'It's OK. It is a goal shared by many but only a few will succeed. A silly dream, my mother called it.'

'And now?'

'Politics. But there is no way my family would agree to me leaving the family business. Perhaps the way to pursue that dream would be to run away. I researched last night. There is an international student programme which offers parliamentary internships in London. I read you can work with a member of the House of Commons as a research assistant.'

My eyes widened. 'Wow, that would be incredible.'

He fixed my gaze, and I couldn't look away. 'When you appeared yesterday, I remembered when I was in London a few months ago and it was possible to have such a dream.'

I smiled.

'I'd like to see *you* again, too.'

My breathing became shallower. 'You would?'

'*Evet*. Would you like to see me again?'

I nodded without hesitation.

The backdrop melted away and suddenly it was just me and him. Only then did I realise he was still holding onto my hand after he had squeezed it earlier. And it felt like the most natural thing.

The fingertips of his other hand tucked a stray strand of hair behind my ear. The softest, most tender touch on my skin, yet a charge ran down my spine.

'I can't believe you're here. Of all the cities in the world, you chose Istanbul,' he whispered.

'Well ... I ...' Words and feelings were crowding my head, leaving me unable to form a sentence.

'Burada olduğun için çok mutluyum.'

I didn't ask for a translation because what it meant didn't matter. All the other sounds around me were dropping away, including the hum of the engine and the chatter of tourists.

He inched closer and my lips parted, his nose brushing against mine. The boat dipped under a bridge and bathed us in darkness.

His lips were warm. He held the side of my face and I leaned into him, and into the kiss. It was deep and sensual. I didn't care who saw us, I was so lost in the moment, and in the way our mouths merged perfectly together.

My body swayed with the rhythm of the boat; head held steady in both his hands now as my arms slipped around his waist, the heat between our bodies intensifying. His thumbs stroked my cheeks. It felt like if he ever let go, I would collapse onto the deck.

Cold air tickled my mouth when his lips left mine as he pulled away to smile. As the boat swung round in a semi-circle, back under the bridge, he leaned in again, his lips tugging at my top lip this time. When we finally broke apart, I nuzzled into his neck and inhaled the warm scent of his skin. The lapel of his shirt flapped in the breeze, which had picked up pace as we ploughed back towards the harbour. Oz held his arm around my waist tighter, and steadied us with his other, leaning against the handrail.

'If you get the chance tomorrow, you must visit inside the palace of Dolmabahçe,' he said, casually resuming the role of tour guide. 'It housed six sultans before the Ottoman Empire was destroyed. Fourteen tons of gold were used to decorate the ceilings. The history is interesting. I would love to know your views about it. There is even a chandelier your Queen Victoria gave as a gift. It is the largest in the world.'

'Hmmm. I'll add it to my list,' I whispered, still tingling from his embrace. I longed for him to look down and kiss me again.

But as the harbour began to come into view, I felt his grip around my waist loosen. He leaned over the barrier and clenched his hands on the rail, knuckles whitening.

He suddenly turned. 'I forgot. I got you this' – a silver bracelet emerged from the back of his shorts – 'from the bazaar. It is a small souvenir of your time here.' He unclasped the hook and placed it on my wrist. Etched into the oval shape on top was an inscription – *Türkiye*.

I rolled it round. 'I love it, thank you.' I leaned in and kissed him on the cheek. He smiled shyly before turning away.

By now crowds were gathering by the stairs to disembark. Oz broke away to join them, but I wanted him to hold back, for a second; to be in his arms again, to talk about the kiss and what it meant. Christ, what was I, sixteen again, filling out some quiz in a teenage magazine?

Question one: if a guy kisses you, does it mean:

a) he's totally into you.

b) he took pity on your lustful advances. Or

c) his girlfriend wasn't around, so he thought he had nothing to lose.

Oz's friends weren't too impressed at having been abandoned. Strike that; Dima wasn't impressed. She slapped Oz's arm and gave him what sounded like a bollocking in Turkish. So many sighs and tuts and flicks of the hair. The guys were less fussed; Mert told me they had been sipping beer in a café nearby. They all insisted on walking me back to my hotel, firing questions in English about what I thought of their city.

Oz stepped forward. 'I will send a car for you tomorrow evening. I am sorry I can't sightsee with you in the day,' he said sadly.

'That's OK, I understand.'

'Özgür!' Dima said. '*Hadi, hadi.*'

I had heard the word often enough to know it meant 'come on'. But from her, it sounded more like a command.

'Bye, Abbie.'

As I lay in bed that night, I stroked my lips which still bore traces of his touch. Why did he have to leave? Why didn't I ask him to stay? We could have gone out for dinner or even back to the hotel. I closed my eyes and let my mind loop: his embrace, that kiss, our night together in London, his mouth on my skin. The dreams we had shared today were so intimate; there was an ease I felt talking with him. His accent did crazy things to my heartbeat and those eyes could see deep into my soul.

I turned and folded the pillow under the side of my head. I could almost hear Liz saying: *'It must be love.'*

14

Now

February

'*How* much?' Amy spluttered, almost choking on a garlic prawn.

I twitched on my seat, embarrassed that I had said out loud the extortionate sum the wedding reception would cost.

'It still doesn't feel right to be accepting such a huge handout from them,' Mum said as she tucked into her fishcake starter.

Mum, Amy and I were sitting round a window table at the Waterfront bar and restaurant to celebrate my thirty-fifth birthday. The room was flooded with light from the sun which had finally appeared after a dull wintry morning and half the tables were full. A low hum of chatter and occasional laughter gave the space a warm and inviting atmosphere. Amy had already clocked the cute waiter and flirted with him every time he came near.

This particular seafood restaurant overlooking the Thames had been a favourite birthday haunt for years since the day my family had surprised me and taken me here when I turned twenty-one, and even more convenient now it was walkable from chambers.

'It's not a handout, Mum,' I said, taking a sip of my sparkling water. 'More like a wedding gift,' I tried to justify, though it still did rankle with me that the offer had remained. Something off our gift list would've been more than enough for me, but Charlie had kept insisting that they wanted to do this for us.

'If you'd both considered the sailing club, things would be different,' Mum said.

'Yeah,' Amy agreed. 'And Davy Hughes might be free that night. He's the best Tom Jones impersonator in the whole of South Wales.'

I stifled a giggle, hiding my smile behind my serviette.

'What?' Amy said, blotting her mouth with her napkin and leaving a scarlet lipstick stain on the cloth. 'That not good enough for you?'

'No, of course not. I love a bit of Tom Jones. I just can't see Elena Logan grooving to "Delilah" on the roof terrace. And besides, the sailing club could only accommodate fifty in the beer garden, and Mumbles is a long way for most of Charlie's relatives to travel.'

'Scotland to Wales isn't far,' Mum said.

'We're talking about the Outer Hebrides. It's about a fifteen-hour drive.'

'How about your honeymoon?' Amy said, lifting her glass up, trying to attract the waiter's attention for a refill of Prosecco.

'We're thinking of somewhere tropical, maybe the Maldives or Brazil for a bit of adventure.'

'All right for some. I didn't get a honeymoon.'

'I thought Barry bought you some diamond studs instead.'

'He did.' She thanked the waiter for the glass of bubbles with a cheeky wink. 'But it wasn't until I tried to pawn them after we broke up that I discovered they were fake.'

Mum patted Amy's hand. 'That's all in the past now. Maybe you can go with Abbie and her friends somewhere nice for her hen party.' Her voice sang with excitement and her head tipped from side to side – her Doris Day styled silvery-auburn bob swishing.

'I don't want a fuss,' I said. 'A nice afternoon tea in a London hotel would be fine.'

'I'd be up for that if there was champagne on tap and we could go out clubbing after.' Amy flipped her hair over her shoulder. 'Couldn't drink at my hen do. But then I never expected to be knocked up and then have to plan a wedding.'

Mum pinched her lips and shifted in her seat. 'Have you started dress shopping, sweetheart?'

'Ooh yeah, I saw a fab Vera Wang knock-off at Sally's in town,' Amy said, licking the garlic sauce off another prawn.

'No, I haven't got round to going to any dress shops. I've got a lot on at the moment.' That was task number five on my ever-expanding list. I picked up a fried calamari ring and dipped it into the seafood sauce.

'You always have a lot on, Abbie,' Mum said. 'I thought the advantage of being a barrister was you could work for yourself, make time for other things, like planning your wedding.'

'Not when I'm still so junior. I need to take on as many cases as I can to build my reputation.' I didn't want to tell her

I was on the back of two defeats which had rocked my confidence.

'Hmm.' She took a deep breath before sighing and I braced myself for the lecture I knew she was keen to deliver.

'I wish you would take more time away from work.' She reached out to clasp my hand. 'I worry about you. You look tired. Are you sleeping well?'

I resisted rolling my eyes. It was the same question she asked every time we met up. 'I'm fine. And yes, I am sleeping.'

'It's silly really,' she continued as she picked up her fork. 'I had hoped you would consider having the wedding in Wales as it would give you an excuse to come and see us more and we could help you get everything organised, ease some of the load.'

A pang of guilt hit me hard in the chest. 'We can still do things together. You can come to London anytime and help me organise things. I wish I could come to Mumbles more but it's hard to find the time when I spend so many weekends working.'

'I know it's hard, sweetheart. I don't expect you to come all that way just to see us. I would love to come to London more. Wouldn't you, Amy?'

Amy nodded and mumbled in agreement.

'Maybe you can organise one of those wedding dress afternoons,' Mum said, 'like the ones you see in movies.'

I smiled. 'That would be great. I'll ask Liz to look into it.'

'How is Liz? Is she still finding motherhood hard?'

'I think it's getting better. Maddy is getting into more of a routine, and her mum has been involved a lot.'

'I can't wait until it's your turn.'

I dropped my fork and it clattered on the plate. 'I ... we ... It's not really come up in conversation,' I said before retrieving my cutlery and piercing another battered ring.

The truth was it was a discussion I knew Charlie wanted to have but was too sensitive to bring up. A stabbing pain shot into my side. Maybe it was indigestion.

'Why not? You're thirty-five, Abbie. You're not getting any younger. And it gets harder to fall pregnant the older you get. I hadn't planned to have you and Amy when I was so young, but I'm so glad I did.'

'Really?'

'Why do you sound so surprised?'

'No reason,' I said, not wanting to bring up a conversation I'd had with Dad about it for fear it would upset her. 'I don't think Charlie and I want kids just yet – we like our life the way it is now,' I said. 'Besides, things were different in your day. Now many women have babies in their forties; I could even freeze some eggs.'

The wrinkles in Mum's forehead intensified and she carefully set her knife and fork down. 'Is this what you want, Abbie? Does Charles make you truly happy?'

I flinched at the question. 'What? Why would you ask?'

'Getting married, starting a family. They're big decisions. You've always been such a determined girl; very driven. But despite that, I imagined when the time came to settle down, you'd feel more excited.'

'I am excited.' My voice had risen an octave with those words, but I could tell from Mum's expression she wasn't convinced. 'But "settling down" is such an old-fashioned saying. It makes me think I have to live a calmer life, slow down at work.'

'It doesn't necessarily mean that. I take it to mean you're convinced the person you have beside you is worth everything and you no longer need anyone else.' She paused, lost in thought. 'Did I ever tell you how I fell for your dad?' She looked expectantly at me and Amy.

'Something about him losing your number and that it was by chance he found you?' I said.

'Didn't an art gallery feature?' Amy said.

Mum folded her napkin and placed it gently beside her plate. 'That lovable fool hunted the length and breadth of the country looking for me.'

'Remind us again how he did?' I said.

'He took a chance. He remembered an artist I had told him I liked and discovered there was a week-long outdoor exhibition of his work in Regent's Park. He came down for the whole week and turned up every day from morning until the park closed, hoping I would come to it, even though he didn't know if I was still living in London at the time.'

'But you were?' I asked.

She nodded and looked away wistfully. 'He even brought a picnic with him every day, too. I almost didn't go, but something drew me to the park on the last day. We took a boat ride on the lake and that's when I knew, when he told me how he had spent the last few months looking for me. It's true love when you know in your heart the crazy things you would do for someone. After that, there was nothing he could've asked me I would say no to. That's how in love we were. You feel the same way about Charlie, don't you? Abbie?'

I hadn't realised I had switched off towards the end of her tale. My mind had lurched somewhere else – somewhere far off in the past. I struggled to pull myself back but knew I had to.

'Yes, of course I feel that way about Charlie.'

'You're not just after his money then.' Amy nudged me in the arm and my hand reflexively knocked into my glass, sending it flying onto the table, water cascading onto her.

'Oh, flip. I'm soaked. Thanks a lot,' she huffed, dabbing at her skirt with her napkin.

'It was an accident,' I replied defensively.

'Go to the ladies and use the hand dryer,' Mum said.

Amy stood up and drained her drink. 'Might stop at the bar on my way back.'

She left and I took her absence as a good excuse to change the subject. 'So ... the shop. How's it going, Mum?'

'Well ...' She picked up her napkin again and twisted it in her hands.

'What's happened?'

'Nothing serious. Bob looked over those reports you told me to send him and he's a little worried. Something about "a going concern", he said on the phone. He wants to meet with me next week to talk about it, but I know I'll be hopeless at understanding anything he has to say. I'm not good with numbers.'

Oh no. Going concern. That didn't sound good. Mum had been running a shop in Mumbles for several years now a few doors down from Amy's salon, selling her hand-made clothing creations. She was even dressed in some of her finest work – a lavender-coloured twinset. Last year's numbers showed sales were slowing considerably despite her best efforts. She hardly ever took a day off, and on days like today, she would pay a neighbour to look after the shop.

'I'm sure everything will be fine,' I said brightly. 'I'll call Bob next week if you'd like, get him to fill me in. And I've told you I'll help you out in any way I can, you only have to say the word.'

'On top of all the other things you've done. I couldn't, sweetheart.'

Mum was making a fuss. All I had done was help get her back on her feet a few years back. But Amy knew nothing of the extent of it and I wanted to keep it that way.

The waiter appeared to clear our plates.

'Your sister is always on at me to do more online,' Mum said once the waiter retreated.

'You should, Mum,' I said. 'It'll help sales no end. Remember the idea you told me about – the one with the patchwork quilts where people send in their fabric squares for you to create a one-of-a-kind keepsake? That could go viral if you posted the best stuff online.'

'Going viral doesn't sound good.'

I laughed. 'Viral is great. You'd be inundated with orders once they see what you could make.'

'I'm sixty-three, Abbie,' she said, stroking her hair. 'Far too old to be taught new tricks. If the business has run its course, then there's not much more I can do.' She looked down at her lap.

I noticed Amy standing at the bar talking animatedly to our waiter.

Grabbing Mum's hand, I leaned in. 'I've told you, I can issue you another line of credit. You just have to say the word. All I want is for you to be happy and not have to think about slowing sales and flagging foot traffic.'

'But I worry you're running yourself into the ground to help me again and now you have a wedding to think of and you're planning on moving this year, too.'

'Mum, I can handle everything.'

'I love you dearly, Abbie. All I've ever wanted was your happiness. Everything I have ever done, it was always because I was trying to do what I thought was best for you. And I know I might not have always gone about things in the right way. That is …' She tightened her lips. 'Please promise me one thing.'

'What?' I whispered expectantly.

'Promise me there are no doubts in your heart.'

I stilled. Where had that statement come from? Was this what they called a mother's intuition?

It was true. A strange feeling had been bothering me ever since Paris – a hollowness tinged with sadness which felt unshakeable. But I could never confide in Mum that I was having a few doubts about marriage and my work. That would mean trawling through events from the past which were better left buried. Bringing them up would only cause Mum sadness. And I knew what mistakes she was probably referring to. But it didn't matter. They were events that didn't need to be rehashed. And I was happy, wasn't I?

'Your dreams are important,' she continued. 'Remember that.'

Dreams. The word transported me someplace long ago. It felt like I was in a developing room – rows of images clipped onto a line – showcasing the photos I had taken on the sunset cruise in Istanbul and the one of me and Oz. That was the last time I had spoken of dreams.

No. Plans were more secure than dreams. A well-formed plan meant less chance of getting hurt.

15

Fourteen Years Ago

July

It felt decidedly decadent to be picked up the next evening – my last in Istanbul. I had expected a taxi but was surprised when a Mercedes pulled up in front of the hotel. I felt a lot like Cinderella going to the ball.

My eyes widened when we came to the gated community I had visited a couple of days ago. The guard who hadn't let me through before nodded and ushered the car in. A plaque inscribed with the words 'Arsel Holding' was positioned to the side of the booth. The car wound its way along a road for a mile or so, and we passed tennis courts and other sporting facilities before houses began to appear.

Each property appeared grander than the one before. The car parked, and I stepped out into a green oasis, lit by a million strings of lights. Another security guard opened the gate and directed me in. My sandals clacked along the winding path and my eyes bulged. I was looking at a white marble two-storey palace – yes, it could hardly be described as a house. This was where Oz lived?

Another guest slipped past me and headed off to one side. I followed, clutching my handbag by my side, fiddling with the bracelet Oz had given me, which had settled halfway up my arm. At the back was the garden. But not a garden like the one attached to my parents' terraced house in Evesham, barely big enough for an apple tree and a swing set. It looked more like the exterior of the Golden Beach Club. There was a pool, with underwater lighting, and tables arranged around it. Garlands hung around pillars, and a marquee with a stage was set back in the distance. This was no intimate gathering for a few friends. Half of Istanbul seemed to be here.

A waitress stood by with tall flutes on a silver platter when I reached the end of the path. I thanked her and took a glass, the champagne bubbles catching at the back of my throat. I swallowed a cough.

I weaved my way through the crowds until I saw Dima. She was wearing a halter-neck gown – black and long, slashed to the thigh. But when I saw who her arm was draped over, my stomach flipped. There by her side was Oz, dressed immaculately in a tux. *GQ* eat your heart out.

When Oz saw me, he stepped forward, smiling. Dima's arm was limp as he pulled away. His lips were warm on my cheeks and skin smooth against mine; a hint of aftershave pricked my nose as he leaned in. I closed my eyes for a moment remembering that kiss on the boat and longed for him to take me in his arms and embrace me again. Maybe there was a chance we could slip away after the event – just the two of us – go back to my hotel and repeat the events of the first time we met.

'You look beautiful,' he whispered, before taking a step backwards.

I looked down at my outfit. 'This old thing?' The red dress Liz had shoved in my backpack before saying goodbye had an elastic scooped neckline, exposing untanned flesh which had been covered by the T-shirt I had worn earlier.

Dima's gaze was on me, her eyes narrowed, nostrils flared.

'Ah, Dima, honey, honey,' Mert said, appearing beside her. He spun her around and whistled. She rolled her eyes and stomped off with her arms folded across her chest. Her characteristic pose. I was amazed she could walk in heels that high. She stopped beside her group of girlfriends and they spoke animatedly, occasionally glancing over towards me.

Oz appeared agitated. He kept tugging at his bow tie and the stiff collar of his shirt. Someone patted him on the back, and he turned. The man gave Oz a couple of playful slaps on the cheeks and spoke to him in Turkish.

'Forgive me,' Oz said, turning to me. 'This is my brother, Sinan. And this is Abbie, a friend I met in London.'

The likeness was uncanny. It was obvious they were brothers, yet you could tell Sinan was older. A few more creases lined his eyes. He was taller, too.

Sinan nodded. *'Memnun oldum.'*

I remembered the same greeting Oz had given Liz back in London. 'It's nice to meet you, Sinan. Happy birthday.'

He laughed. *'Evet*, happy birthday to me.' He raised an eyebrow.

'It is our mother's excuse to hold another one of her parties,' Oz said, by way of explanation.

It did seem there were an awful lot of guests who were not in Sinan's age bracket.

A photographer appeared and took a snap of the brothers – momentarily dazzling me with the flash.

'Excuse me, Abbie. I am being called to greet another guest I don't know. It is good business though.' Sinan shrugged and walked away.

I sipped my champagne. 'What did that mean?'

Oz took a glass from a passing waiter. 'There are a lot of people here tonight connected with Arsel Holding, the family business. It is Sinan's duty to meet with them. There is a big project which my family wants to start, on a piece of land of some importance. They need approval for it. This party is—'

'Not really to celebrate Sinan's birthday?' I scanned the scene around me, shifting my dress down a little. 'You didn't tell me you were so ... um ...' How could I say it without being impolite?

'Rich?' Oz said.

'Well, you're not exactly poor.'

'I never believe a man should display his wealth. It's very—'

'Like the sultan in the palace?'

He laughed. '*Evet*. You went there?'

'Yes, it was quite a place. The harem?' I whistled. 'Quite a contrast to the luxury of the sultan's quarters. There was a woman begging outside. It seemed ... wrong.'

'A relief the empire was destroyed.'

I nodded; except I was hardly one to pass judgement on Turkey's past. My history A level had limited me to the British monarchy from the Tudors onwards. 'How ... how big is your family business?'

'We built most of this town and have many big projects taking place around Istanbul and abroad.'

'Oh.' I felt the eyes of several guests on me – their pinched looks disapproving. Dima was there in my peripheral vision, still staring. I tugged at my dress's neckline, noticing how the fabric hung like a hessian sack. The material wasn't ideal for this humidity either. It was sticking to my back and I feared sweat patches were visible.

Oz caught my eye. 'Is everything OK?'

I nodded.

'Don't worry, I will make sure you sit with Yusef, so you won't be bored tonight.'

'Can I not sit with you?'

'*Keşke,*' he replied with a sigh.

Before I could ask what that meant, someone approached from behind and slapped Oz on his back, causing a few drops to spill from his glass.

Oz swung round. 'Yusef!'

'*Marhaba.*'

Yusef was barely recognisable; hair short, almost a military buzz cut. They hugged.

'*Marhaba. Keef halak?*' Yusef said.

'Good, good. You remember Abbie?' Oz gestured towards me.

'Of course. London Abbie. Ah, if Yaman was here, it would be a proper reunion.'

'*Inşallah.* One day,' Oz said.

A string quartet struck up and we chatted for a while. Canapés of asparagus and crab and other delicacies were offered as we talked. I gazed at Oz as he spoke. Among the three of us, he was the most animated, his grin broad. But when he talked about the wars in Iraq and Afghanistan, his free hand gesticulated and his forehead became etched with concern. He talked of the plight of civilians caught up in clashes. Conversation with his Turkish friends, in contrast, was always light and he seemed less interested in participating.

An announcement cut our conversation short and Oz excused himself as he left for the top table, where he was immediately joined by Dima, who sat next to him. Several glasses of champagne had slipped down rather too easily, though I couldn't be sure of the exact number, as my glass had been topped up so often. It was a relief when they began serving the meal – something to line my stomach and soak up the alcohol.

Yusef and I chatted about his life in Syria and how he planned to go to Lebanon after his finals for a year's placement at the University of Beirut. Politics was his major and we shared stories of our classes.

I shuffled in my seat to try and catch a glimpse of Oz, straining my neck to see over the other guests. This was my last night in Istanbul – heck, my last day of travels – the end of three incredible weeks. The mere idea of going back took the edge off my excitement. I needed to find a place to live and sign the contract. But what about the UNICEF job? That role would have meaning but the salary, at least in the first few years, would be nowhere near enough to live in London. How could I stay at Liz's house and do the one job she had wanted to do? Maybe on the flight back, my head would be clearer. But no. My mind *was* clear. Liz was my best friend. Surely, she would understand my decision.

When sweets and Turkish coffee were brought, I took the opportunity to head off to the bathroom. As I applied a slick of lip gloss, the door suddenly swung open and high-pitched squeals filled the room. Dima and her two girlfriends stopped short when they saw me.

'Abbie, hello,' Dima said, air-kissing me. I hadn't realised we had become so familiar.

'Hi, Dima.'

'You leave tomorrow?'

'Yes, I have to go back to London.'

She pouted. 'So sad. I hope you will come back to Istanbul.'

'Yes, I'd like that,' I said, trying to manoeuvre past her to leave the bathroom.

She laid her hand on my arm to stop me from leaving. 'You will come to the wedding, yes?'

'What wedding?'

'When I marry Özgür.' His name cannoned off the walls of the bathroom.

'I, I …' My response stuck in my throat.

'He didn't tell you? We haven't set a date yet, of course. It is still a secret,' she said, her two immaculate rows of teeth on display, 'but we will announce our engagement soon. OK, bye bye.' And with that, she waved me off and pulled a compact out of her bag. She fluffed the brush over her cheeks and her friends giggled as they resumed their gossip.

I reeled out of the bathroom, my mind exploding like a party popper having just been released.

Had I been hoodwinked? Was Oz playing me? No. Surely this couldn't be true. I had to find him and ask him for the truth.

I began to make my way back to the party, still utterly thrown by what Dima had told me, but a figure stood in my path – her hair platinum blonde with a hint of dark roots. Her make-up was heavy and her features stretched, the work of only the best surgeon, I thought.

'Are you Abbie?'

I nodded.

She extended a hand, sheaths of creamy silk dangling from her arm, a gigantic diamond solitaire ring erect on her middle finger. '*Merhaba*. My name is Ayla Arsel. I am the mother of Sinan, Özgür and Eylül.'

The handshake was brief and limp. I grinned, probably too broadly, glad I had checked my teeth in the bathroom mirror for traces of food.

Retracting her hand, she placed it on her hip. She towered at least five inches above me. Intimidating was an understatement.

'My son tells me he met you in London.'

I wasn't sure whether this was a question or a statement. 'Yes, we met on a march when he was studying at UCL.'

She arched an eyebrow. 'I hoped that would be the end of his rebellious phase. My son has a good heart, but his head is too easily distracted.'

Her English was near perfect, but I couldn't grasp her meaning. I smoothed the creases from my dress.

'What do you do in London, Abbie?'

'I've just graduated. I am trying to decide whether to be a lawyer or work for a charity.' *Whoops*. No idea why I told her that. She was a complete stranger.

She tilted her head, looking me up and down. 'I am sure your parents are proud. Özgür will be joining the family business soon.'

I thought of making some comment about him not wanting to do that, but I held my tongue.

Her expression hardened. 'I know he has a mad plan to do something different,' she said, folding her arms.

Crikey, was she reading my mind?

'This is why he needs no distractions. It would be a great shame if he decided his future lay outside Istanbul or in politics. I am sure you understand he will not go back to London again this year. And his greatest achievement will be when he marries Dima, and our two families will be united. The Tara family is an important one to ours, and this will be a great union. We are – how do you say – equal.' An eyebrow arched again as she scanned my outfit once more.

I could feel the colour draining from me. Was I even breathing? A tightness gripped my chest; a familiar feeling creeping over me like the day on the London march.

'They will have a lavish wedding. No expense will be too great. If you will excuse me, I must make an important announcement.' She turned on her heel with a flourish.

I blinked furiously as she left, the train of her dress sweeping over my toes. There it was: confirmation. And from his mother, no less. I was kicking myself for not pressing him further when he was trying to explain his relationship with

Dima. But now maybe I finally had the whole picture; they were destined to be together.

Pain pulsed at my temples and I rubbed them in the hope of erasing the words that I had been told. How could I have been so stupid? Swanning around town with Oz when all this time he was with someone else.

A ripple of applause spread around the garden and I looked at the stage to see his mother take the microphone. Every few words drew another small burst of clapping. She beckoned for others to join her, and all three of her children came up on the stage. I shuffled forward, peering at them from between the heads of other guests. Oz had his arms folded.

Another group joined them – Dima and two older people. Her parents? She beamed as she linked arms with Oz. I didn't have a clue what Ayla Arsel was saying, but when she moved her arm around her son's waist, Dima squeezed in further. Then Dima grabbed his face and kissed him. On the lips. He didn't pull away.

My heartbeat pounded in my ears. I walked backwards, careful not to trip over anyone's feet, before turning and beginning to run. The alcohol was making me unsteady, causing me to stumble.

Did I need any more proof than that? I groaned inwardly. What was I to him? A last fling before he accepted this union, which had been sanctioned by his family?

'Abbie,' a voice called. I knew it was Oz's but dared not turn around. 'Abbie, wait!'

A grasp on my elbow forced me to stop.

'Abbie, please. Don't run.'

My cheeks prickled with heat, and I was breathing heavily. When I looked back at Oz, I could see anguish on his face.

'Please. Let me explain.'

'Explain? I think it was obvious what I saw. How do you begin to "explain" that?'

'You don't understand, Abbie. My life is …' He licked his lips and ruffled the back of his head. Guilt. That's what the gesture was. When I met him at the beach club unannounced, he hadn't been pleased to see me; he had been embarrassed. Full of guilt. Worried his girlfriend would find out what had happened between us a few months before.

'Your life is what?' I didn't know why I was shouting at this point. He hadn't made any promises to me back in London. I had been swept up in Liz's ludicrous notion that he was 'the One' and it must be love, when all along he had been with someone else, someone who he had just got engaged to. 'Well? Your life is what?'

That's when I noticed the crowd of guests gathered around us, including Dima, his mother, brother and an elderly man who shot me a look of pure disdain. Oz opened his mouth while scanning the faces of his family. No words came out.

'You have nothing to tell me? You're going to stand there and not give me any reason not to walk away? That kiss on the boat, the time we spent together in London, what was that?' The silence was agonising, as I awaited his response.

'Can we go somewhere private?' he said finally.

'No. Anything you want to say you can say to me now, right here.'

He drew himself up, his eyes darting back and forth to the faces around us, but he didn't speak.

Please, Oz. Say something. Say anything to stop me from walking away.

No words came. The longer I stood there, the more embarrassed I became as everyone's eyes bored into me.

'Goodbye, Oz,' I said and turned away.

The security guard let me out through the gate and showed me towards a line of taxis. I stepped into the first and gave the driver the address of the hotel. I didn't care how much it would cost, I had to get away. Oz didn't follow me. It spoke volumes.

'Agh,' I shrieked into the still air in my hotel room, throwing my clothes into my backpack. I didn't belong here. A different culture. Hell, a different world. One that couldn't be further removed from my own. How could I compete with all this when I had been born to a suburban working-class family from the West Midlands? Dad's father had worked down the mines in South Wales while Oz's had built the town he lived in. That word 'equal' had rankled with me. It was clear what Ayla Arsel meant by it. She probably considered me nothing more than a gold digger, trying to haul myself above my status. And all the talk on the boat about dreams and running away. Were those empty words just to get me to kiss him?

It was stupid to waste a night by not sleeping here, but the flight Liz had booked me was at the crack of dawn anyway, so what did it matter if I lay on the hotel bed, glaring at the ceiling, or scrunched up on a couple of airport chairs?

As I passed the security check of Atatürk airport, I took a quick glance over my shoulder before the glass doors of the departure hall swung shut. A familiar figure passed by but was swallowed up in a sea of people.

'Oz?' But it was too late. The doors closed and when they reopened there was no sign of him. I shook my head. It couldn't have been him. He was no doubt still at the party, celebrating his engagement.

I heard someone shouting from far away. Was that my name? Before I could turn, a swarm of passengers thronged around me, their voices ringing in my ears – a cacophony of foreign tongues. I managed one more glance over my shoulder, but the departure doors were firmly closed.

I gritted my teeth. *Grow up, Abbie.* I had let this silly pursuit get in the way of making proper, level-headed decisions. What had happened to me, the girl who wouldn't dare lie to her parents, or hesitate in forging a successful career as a solicitor? No way. I wouldn't let this trip threaten the promise I had made to Dad all those years ago.

16

Now

April

'OK, this calls for wine,' Liz said, hopping off the sofa, walking in the direction of my kitchen, flapping Oz's business card in the air. I had been rumbled. It had escaped my notice that Charlie had left it lying on the coffee table, but it was the first thing Liz had spotted when she'd settled on the couch tonight. I resolved to move on from the discussion as soon as I could, since I knew she would make it into a big deal when it wasn't at all.

Rain battered the windows, and the heating was turned up. It was Thursday and near the end of another long week of work. I had met Liz at Baker Street tube and we had raced to my flat under one umbrella as Liz had been caught unprepared. We were both drying off our clothes on the radiator. I had changed into leggings and a jumper and lent her a similar outfit.

Liz swung the fridge door open – the light instantly illuminating her face in the semi-darkness – and pulled out a half-empty bottle of rosé. 'Is this all you got?'

'There's probably another one in the cupboard next to the sink.'

'I'll stick it in the freezer then. This' – she shook the bottle – 'is not enough.'

'Are you making up for lost time?'

'Don't make me feel any more guilty for giving up breastfeeding than I already do. I've had enough lectures from the boobfeeding mafia.'

'The who?'

'That woman Mary and I went to see – the lactation consultant who made me sit bolt upright on the hardest chair with my feet on a Yellow Pages and expose my breasts to get a perfect position when it was freezing in her front room. Both me and Maddy sat there bawling our eyes out.' She shuddered at the memory.

'Poor you.'

'Maddy and I are scarred for life. Ugh.' She grimaced, unscrewing the lid of the bottle. 'I still have nightmares about her grabbing my nipple and trying to direct it into Maddy's mouth. She'd been losing weight and I was freaking out, which is why we booked the appointment in the first place. If it wasn't for my amazing health visitor who said I shouldn't beat myself up about not continuing after that, I don't know what I would've done. But the guilt's still there.'

'I'm sure you're doing what's best for Maddy.'

'I hope so. I never told you, but the first day I gave Mads her bottle she held up her hands and grabbed it. I can't deny it was like a light switched on in my brain and suddenly the anxiety and panic attacks began to lift. It felt like we had finally bonded.'

'That's great news.'

'I guess,' she said, pouring the wine into two glasses.

'But I thought you couldn't drink with the antidepressants.'

'Shit.' She smacked her forehead and began to pour her glass into mine. 'I forgot. I'm thinking of asking the GP if I can slowly wean myself off them. I've got my first NHS counselling session next week, so I was hoping I would no longer need them.' She shrugged. 'I just don't enjoy feeling like I'm not myself. Maddy is over her colic, she's got a routine that I can handle, but I know I need some kind of additional support. Maybe talking therapy is the answer.'

'It's all a step in the right direction, Liz.'

'I hope so.'

Liz had come around for our monthly sleepover. It had been a sacred part of our friendship for years, but this was the first one we'd had in ages. Charlie was working up in Birmingham and staying overnight and Mary was on baby duty, made all the easier now Maddy was on formula. Liz reached back into the fridge and got out a can of lemonade and brought the drinks over.

The first sip of wine slipped down nicely. Too nicely. I hadn't eaten much all day and I certainly didn't have any motivation to prepare any food. Charlie and I loved to cook together at the weekends when we had more time to spend on getting ingredients and making something special from scratch. We had an agreement that mid-week, whoever was working late would come home to something made or bought by the other. On nights when we were both working late, we would head to the Japanese takeaway place around the corner from chambers and bring home tasty teriyaki chicken or a beef rice bowl and slouch in front of the television. We were creatures of habit.

'Shall we order a pizza, too?' Liz asked. 'I'm starving. And I noticed you have nothing in your fridge that looks like it would take less than three hours to cook.'

'Sounds good.' I picked up my phone and found the website of our local takeaway. 'The usual?'

'Yes, please.' Liz shuffled around the kitchen, opening cupboards while I placed the order. 'Eureka,' she squealed. 'A tube of Pringles. This will tide us over,' she said, sitting on the couch next to me. 'Why didn't you tell me you saw Oz in Paris?'

I puffed out my cheeks. 'You were preoccupied, remember?'

'Still. I'm your best friend. And this is huge.'

I propped my head up, leaning my elbow on the back of the sofa. 'It wasn't.'

Liz wrinkled her nose and took a swig of her lemonade. 'I beg to differ. Your eye is twitching.'

'That's tiredness. Why does everyone always assume it flickers when I'm lying?' I said defensively, reaching for the crisps.

Liz narrowed her eyes. 'Whatever. So, what did he say, what was it like to see him again?'

'It was ... unexpected.'

'No shit, Sherlock. And with Charlie there, too.' She pulled a face.

'Liz, you're making this into a much bigger deal than it was.'

'Did you talk to him?'

'No, not really. We exchanged some pleasantries. He's left the family business and is working for a Turkish non-profit organisation, but I don't know why. And I told him about being a barrister. But then Charlie interrupted us, and the conversation ended.'

'Was he wearing a wedding ring?'

I shot her a look.

'What? Just interested.'

'Well, I didn't notice because it makes no difference if he was or not.'

She leaned her arm on the sofa and studied my face before picking up her mobile from the coffee table.

'What are you doing?' I said.

'Googling him.' She whistled. 'Yup. Mmm-hmm. Still fucking hot, even at what ... thirty-seven?'

'Let me see.' I stared at the frame Liz had zoomed in on. It was of Oz kneeling, surrounded by a group of laughing kids. There was so much warmth in his expression and one of the kids had her arms wrapped round his neck. My stomach twisted when I looked at those dimples on his face and the feeling left me uneasy. I looked back up at Liz.

'What? Why are you looking at me like that?'

'I don't know. There's something you're not telling me.'

I ran my finger around the rim of the glass. *Crap.* Liz knew me too well.

'There so is. Spill, Abigail.'

'He's coming here. To London.'

Her mouth dropped open.

'Tomorrow and Saturday for some property exhibition he's attending with his brother.'

'And you're meeting up?'

'No. Well, yes, sort of. Charlie told him we would go to the event with Charlie's dad. That's why Oz gave him his card. But I never thought Charlie was being serious until he mentioned it to me again last week. I stalled. Said I'd see how work panned out during the week.'

'You have to go.'

'Why?'

'You need "closure".' Liz did speech marks with her fingers.

'This isn't an episode of *Friends*, Liz.' I brushed some Pringles crumbs off my lap. 'I don't think I can see him again, especially if Charlie will be there.'

'Doesn't he know you used to be together?'

'No. When Oz introduced himself as an old friend at the conference, I bottled it and didn't correct him. I never thought I'd actually see Oz again, and now it would seem really weird if I said he was much more than just an old friend.' I downed a large gulp of wine, then placed my glass on the coffee table.

'OK, calm down. Maybe you don't need to correct him. After all, you only want to clear the air. You're not sneaking off to have some illicit affair.'

'Of course not,' I said, lightly punching her in the arm.

'You just want a few minutes alone.' She folded her arms, lost in her own thoughts. 'I'll come. Get my mum to stay another night. I can direct Charlie and his dad to one part of the exhibition while you take Oz to another to talk.'

'That sounds like the very definition of "sneaking off".'

'Well then, how else can you see him alone? Come on, Abs. We both know he's the reason why you're so screwed up when it comes to guys.'

'I am not screwed up, thanks very much. I've been in a committed relationship with Charlie for over three years.'

'I know, but I still think Oz is there at the back of your mind. The last time you guys met, you told me it was all over between you, but I could see there was still something about him you couldn't let go. If you met up with him again under different circumstances, maybe you could find a way to finally bury that part of your life.'

'Hmm. Maybe you're right. I thought I had eliminated him from my past. Seeing him again in Paris has made me trawl up old events. I keep rehashing them, wondering if things had happened a different way, then ...'

Liz leaned back on the sofa and stroked my arm. Her gaze fell on a DVD case on the coffee table. She lifted it up. 'You got out *An Affair to Remember* for us to watch?'

I chewed the inside of my mouth. 'And?'

'Should I be reading anything into your choice?'

I grabbed the case off her and held it to my chest. 'What? No, of course not. I am truly, wholeheartedly committed to Charlie. I adore him. My feelings for Oz are old news. He just has this silly effect on me; makes me feel like I'm young again. Stupid, isn't it?'

'No, not stupid at all.' She emptied her can of lemonade and put it on the table. 'We all want to escape sometimes when life gets a little complicated. And it's inevitable that you might start to have doubts when you're about to commit to someone for the rest of your life. When Mary proposed, I got swept up by it all but then I started to trawl through my previous relationships, wondering why they hadn't worked out, why this was different. So many thoughts filled my head. I even rang a couple of ex-girlfriends who I had thought I had been in love with.'

'Really?'

'Yeah. Something clicked when I heard their voices. I felt nothing. I knew then Mary was my "forever". If Charlie is yours, meeting Oz again shouldn't be a big deal.'

I had no idea at what point during the movie Liz fell asleep, but I couldn't blame her. It was hardly an action-packed film full of explosions and fight scenes that would keep someone still sleep deprived awake.

As the credits rolled, I manoeuvred Liz into a lying position on the couch, wrapped a blanket around her and cleared up the remnants of our pizza. I didn't have the heart to wake her when I knew getting enough sleep with a baby was a challenge, nor did I want to revisit the conversation we had earlier.

But why? Was it because I was scared of feeling something for Oz when I saw him again and what it would mean?

The next night I stood outside the entrance to the exhibition and checked my watch. The event had begun an hour ago and I could see through the glass window people mingling in front of photographs on walls and displays of property developments created in miniature. Tuxedos and fancy gowns abounded, and champagne flowed. Charlie was due to arrive any minute and Liz was late as usual.

My mobile rang and I saw Liz's number flashing up. 'Where are you?' I whispered, as if I was on a heist.

'I'm so sorry. Mum called me and cancelled. She's come down with something. Probably caught the cold Maddy has and Mary isn't back yet from work. I'm sorry, Abs. I can't come.'

My heart lurched. 'It's OK. Honestly, it's fine. Charlie will be here soon anyway.'

'Go talk to Oz now, then. Arrange to meet.'

'I can't do that, Liz.' I could hear the distant wail of Maddy in the background.

'Listen, Abs. I have to go, but do it. You'll regret it otherwise. I'll speak to you later.'

She hung up and I stood there shivering. Spring still hadn't made an appearance and I regretted not going home to change into something a lot warmer and smarter. I had left my suit jacket back at chambers in my rush to get out. I pulled the collar of my shirt up to my chin and filled the space between my neck and the fabric with hot breath.

And then I saw him. His back was to me, but I could tell it was him. An elegant blonde woman placed an arm on his shoulder, and I knew instantly who it was – his mother. What was she doing here? He turned and I stepped back into darkness. But he hadn't seen me.

An arm snaked around his waist and I froze. Dark hair, svelte body. I knew exactly who that was. She squeezed in tighter and he rested his hand on her back.

I couldn't go in. I couldn't face them all again even though I was desperate to know why he had changed his name back to Demir – the name he carried on his business card – and to find out what had happened in his life since we last met all those years ago. And what would I say to Charlie when it was obvious I knew everyone in that group? The whole truth of our relationship would have to come out.

'Abbie!' Charlie called from behind and I jumped. 'Sorry, gorgeous.' He leaned in to kiss me. 'I didn't mean to startle you. Dad's just parking the car. He'll be here in a sec.' He studied my face. 'Are you OK? You look a little worried.'

'Umm. I just got a late email from the solicitor on tomorrow's case. I think I need to bail.'

'But my dad has come all the way down from Scotland. Couldn't you at least stay for one drink?' His eyebrows knotted beneath his spectacles.

'My head also hurts.'

He reached out and touched my forehead, his fingers warm against my cold skin.

'My throat is a little sore, too.' My eye twitched as I held a hand on my neck.

He brushed a stray hair out from my eye. 'OK. I'll explain to Dad. He'll be disappointed though. I'll see you back at home. Why don't you have a Lemsip?'

A pang of guilt dropped down on my chest at the fib I had told. Another silk thread had been added to the web of lies. But this was for the best, I resolved – for the best that I never saw Oz again.

I walked away from the venue along the street, but before I turned to go down into the tube, I heard my name being called from a distance.

I turned and my heart lurched. Oz was running down the road towards me. Thoughts began to spin in my mind. I shouldn't have turned but it was too late now.

Oz stood in front of me, breathing heavily. 'Abbie ...' he whispered, struggling to catch his breath. 'Why are you leaving?'

'How did you know I was here?'

'Charles. He said you had to rush off and I had so hoped to see you again.'

My throat felt tight as if my earlier excuse was coming back to bite me. 'I have a lot on at work. It's best if I head home.' I looked nervously over his shoulder in case Charlie's dad might suddenly appear. 'I noticed your whole family is here.'

'Yes. It's been a long time since we have all been together. *Yani*, there is a lot that's happened to keep us apart. Are you sure you can't stay? Even for one drink?' His eyes bored into mine and I knew I had to look away. No way could I let myself be cast under their spell, and how would I explain to Charlie my reason for reappearing at the event?

I noticed a small bistro to my right. Oz clocked where I was staring and looked at me expectantly.

Liz's words about reconnecting with old lovers swirled in my mind. She had known the second she heard the voices of her past girlfriends that they no longer meant anything to her. And here I was, completely incapable of denying the effect his voice was having on me. Would these feelings be suppressed over a glass of wine?

'I'm sorry, I can't. Goodbye, Oz.' I turned and walked away.

17

Now

May

'The architecture is stunning.'

'I was hoping you would like it,' Charlie said as we stood outside a whitewashed detached house close to Belsize Park. It was unusual in its design, with a Mediterranean feel to it. Set back from the main road alongside a cluster of four similar-looking houses, it was akin to something you would see in one of those property magazines.

'But why are we here?' I said, placing the bottle of ice-cold water – which I had just bought from a newsagent around the corner – against my cheeks and forehead.

It was an unusually hot Saturday morning and spring was in full bloom. We had walked from the flat through Regent's Park and up Primrose Hill. I had wanted to sit for a while and enjoy the sunshine at the top, but Charlie had insisted we keep walking and find somewhere for brunch.

'We have a viewing,' he said.

'What? Why?'

'Why?' He spun me around then reached into his grey shorts and produced a set of keys. 'Because I got a tip-off and put a holding deposit on it.' He clenched his teeth and sank his head into his shoulders.

My jaw dropped. 'You what?'

'OK, so I knew you would freak, but hear me out. I spoke to Dad about our house search and he thought our remit was all wrong. He said we should be bolder. It's a buyer's market and there's little point in investing in a house we would possibly outgrow in a few years when the market will have picked up.'

'But this looks palatial. We've been looking at three-bedroom terraced houses in places within our budget. This is a brand-new construction a forty-five-minute walk from where we currently live. There's no way this is affordable.'

His shoulders sagged. 'You're right. I knew you would hate it.' He shoved his hands into his shorts and began to walk away.

'Charlie, wait.' I reached out to hold his arm. 'I didn't say I hated it. It's beautiful. But I wish you had consulted me. This is a monumental decision and surely we can't afford it.'

'Well … *we* can't, but Mum and Dad decided there was little point in keeping the flat in Baker Street and have found a buyer. They want to reinvest the money in another property and thought we could all pool our resources.'

'How exactly would I be involved in this purchase?'

He slowly turned me back around to face the house. 'Look, with Dad's investment the mortgage will be affordable, and we will be paying it jointly, I promise. I know you wanted us to put down a deposit together, but with you bailing out your mum last month—'

'You said it wouldn't matter.' I folded my arms across my green polka-dot summer dress.

'Hey.' He unfolded my arms and placed them around his waist before clasping my shoulders. 'I never said it *would* matter. What you do for your mum is heroic.'

I looked down. 'No, it isn't.'

He lifted my chin so I could look back into his eyes again. Leaning down, he placed a gentle kiss on my lips. 'Yes. It is. It took you, what, two years to save that money that you gave her.'

It was true. I had been saving that money for a deposit on a house for years, long before Charlie and I had got together, but after talking to Mum's accountant, I knew it was a clear case of helping her out or letting the shop close. And I could never let that happen. No matter what she had been alluding to at my birthday lunch about things in the past, I still couldn't abandon her.

'Listen, Abbie. You and I will always be a joint unit, no matter who puts in what amount, where or when. It's what being a couple should be about. So just because you're not in a position right now to help buy this place, shouldn't mean we can't at least *think* about getting it.'

'But why didn't you at least tell me before doing it? I might've been open to the idea if you'd put that argument to me.'

'I guess I wanted to surprise you. I'm sorry.' His bottom lip pouted. 'Dad was always one for grand gestures. That's how he bought our family home. Mum loved the gesture. I thought you might too. And I had to move fast. These houses will sell out in a minute once they're put on the market. They're not even available to move into until October.'

I drew a deep breath and looked up at the house. It *was* beautiful. There was something about it – in the arched windows and the columns beside the front door – which appeared familiar and inviting.

'These are the keys to the show home.' Charlie rattled them. 'You can help me decide which plot we buy. How about we look around? No pressure. If you really hate it or don't feel comfortable about how we would buy it, then we'll walk away. Fair?'

Charlie had put a convincing argument forward, but would it feel like home if I hadn't contributed to the purchase?

Ever since I got my first job at the dentist back at university, it had been a goal of mine to buy my own place, but as the years had gone by, that goal had slipped further away. Maybe it was time to let it go. Maybe Charlie was right. I should start seeing us as a team, not always equal in finances but a team nonetheless.

'Sounds fair.' I smiled and he clasped my shoulder tightly and steered me towards the house.

'Come on,' he said. 'Let's go inside. It's amazing.'

As we toured the downstairs and the small, manicured garden at the back, it was hard not to get carried away by Charlie's enthusiasm. He opened up every kitchen cupboard, marvelling at the soft-closing doors and the hidden larder which made me giggle. The rooms were vast but a little lacking in features. Cosy was certainly not a word I would use to describe the place.

He held my hand as he led me upstairs, my other still clasping the water bottle.

'And I was thinking here,' he said, pointing to the large bay window ledge in the master bedroom, 'and ...' He dragged me quickly into the next room and pointed at a similar window. 'Maybe here.' In the third bedroom there was another which overlooked the garden. 'And definitely here.' His eyes twinkled.

'What were you thinking about doing here?' I said, narrowing my eyes, tipping my chin towards the window.

He tugged me forward, walking backwards until his legs met the ledge and he sank down onto it, pulling me flush against him. He took my handbag from around my neck and put it on the ground, then grasped my water bottle and held it against my neckline. I yelped at the coldness. It left droplets of water in its path as he set it down on the whitewashed sill. Leaning down, he kissed each drop away as they dripped towards my chest. I groaned as his lips moved further down, caressing the skin behind the folds of my dress, his hands reaching out to grasp my bottom and pull me closer against his hardness.

I leaned my head back, my heart racing. 'But, Charlie, surely we can't.'

'It's OK,' he whispered, his breath against my hot skin. 'The agent isn't collecting the keys for a little while.'

'Oh,' I moaned as his fingers traced up my thighs to tug at the lace trim of my knickers. The sudden thrill of being caught made me feel even hotter than I already was despite the window being partially open and a cool breeze drifting in, bringing with it an exotic scent of flowers from the garden below. I began to slowly unbutton his crisp white shirt which he had rolled up at the sleeves, stroking the smattering of hair on his chest.

'Do you like it?' he asked as he trailed even more kisses over me. 'Do you like the house?'

'Yes,' I said as he pulled the folds of my dress further open. I reached down to pop the buttons of his shorts.

'Shall we buy it?' he said.

I panted as he rocked me gently against him.

And in that moment, I was so lost to this heady feeling that I wasn't even sure whether the 'yes' I moaned was in agreement or something more primal.

My phone buzzed in my bag continuously. I was too far gone to interrupt the moment but hadn't completely been able to banish some niggling thoughts.

This house was nothing like the one I had dreamed of living in. But maybe that dream was a childish one. My family home in Evesham was small and on a busy road. Sharing a bedroom with Amy until she moved to Manchester had meant that all I had wanted was a room of my own with a double bed and wardrobe just for me – preferably a small cottage somewhere in the countryside. But now here I was about to become joint owner of a five-bedroom detached house in north London. We hadn't even got round to discussing what we were planning on doing with all these bedrooms. And I wasn't sure if I was ready to discuss that. I finally parked all these thoughts and let myself go.

As Charlie buttoned up his shorts, I readjusted my dress and fished out my mobile. Nada's name was by the missed

Skype call notification. Noticing she had also sent a text, I opened it up.

'Who called?'

'Nada. She said ...' I scanned the first two sentences. 'She got our save the date card and she can make it.'

'That's great.'

As I scrolled down her message where she filled me in on her life over the last few weeks, I froze when I saw the attachments she had sent.

'Is that you?' Charlie said over my shoulder.

'Yes,' I said, casually dropping the phone back in my bag.

'Hey, let me see.'

I hesitated before handing it over to him. He narrowed his eyes, fingering the screen to enlarge it. 'You look gorgeous. Is that Nada in her wedding dress?'

I nodded.

He moved across the image. 'I recognise him. Yes, that's the guy from the property exhibition. The one we met at the conference. I thought you said you met in London when you were students.'

Heat coated my neck. 'Yes, we did, the first time. But it turned out we had mutual friends,' I said lightly, hoping he wouldn't press me further.

'Well, we have a lot to thank him for.'

I stilled and looked up at him. 'What do you mean?'

'I told you I met him and his brother at the property event last month. They promised Dad they would let him know as soon as the first units were available to buy, before they went onto the open market. This is one of their family's developments.'

I couldn't believe it. This house was built by Arsel Holding? Oz's family was building the house I was going to live in.

'There isn't a problem, is there?'

'No. No, not at all.'

The web of lies had more strands. But how could I live here now when all I would ever associate it with was Oz?

Charlie left the room and I looked at the screen again. Three photos. My heart lurched as I took them in. Nada had begun reminiscing about her wedding when she got news of mine. I switched off my phone. I couldn't let myself go back to that time. The memories were too painful.

18

Nine Years Earlier

June

'You look sensational.'

'I do, don't I?' Nada said as she admired herself in the mirror of her aunt's bedroom, a cheeky grin plastered on her face, her hands holding up her black curls in a makeshift up-do.

Her wedding dress was simple but elegant, beads lining the scooped neckline. Folds of silk fell to the floor. It had been worn by her mother and grandmother and had needed some last-minute alterations before her wedding tomorrow.

'*Bijannini, bijannini,*' her aunt said.

'She's saying "beautiful",' Nada translated.

I had arrived at Rafic Hariri airport an hour ago and stepped out into a haze of heat and smog before being whisked straight to Nada's aunt's flat downtown to pick up the dress, and I was doing my best to stifle my yawns. I had snatched about an hour of sleep on the overnight flight from London to Beirut, at most, despite the in-flight drinks and my profound state of exhaustion. There was too much on my mind about work, and a call late last night from Mum had made me doubt whether I should have made the trip at all. She was worried about having to go to Manchester suddenly if Amy had her first baby – even though she wasn't due for a few weeks – while Dad wasn't feeling well. He had sounded OK on the phone, but Mum had told a different story once he put his receiver down – something about constant indigestion. I was sure she was making a fuss. There had also been a bomb explosion in downtown Beirut a few days ago and Mum was understandably worried.

'I still can't believe you came,' Nada said to me once her aunt had left the room to get some tea. 'Sad Liz couldn't make it. It would've been like old times; the gang back together.'

'She was gutted.'

'So, how's the world of corporate law?' Nada asked as she began to change out of the dress.

'You really want an answer?'

'Maybe once I've had a couple of drinks tonight to celebrate my last night of singledom.' She winked.

I feigned a look of shock.

'Joking, I'm joking. But I'd much rather hear about your love life than your job.'

'What love life?' I rolled my eyes.

'It didn't work out with that guy?'

'Which one? The actuary who got a highlighter out when the bill came after dinner? Or the FX trader I met at a coffee shop who then kept dropping to do press-ups when we went for walks in the park?'

'*Ya' Allah*. Jerks.'

I laughed. 'They were both lovely guys. I just don't have the patience or the motivation for anything serious. I barely have enough time to keep my fridge stocked, let alone put in the hours needed for a relationship.'

'You make it sound like a second job.' She chuckled.

'God, I've missed you. It's been so long. How's life as an international reporter?'

Her face lit up. 'It's insane. Too much to write about, but I'm not complaining. The troubles of the Middle East are good for my career. I've dreamed for so long to write for the *Financial Times*. And who knows, one day I might get a transfer to London, and we can see each other more.'

'That would be amazing.'

I smiled through a sharp pang of jealousy. Nada had it all figured out – the job, her relationship, her future. Three years I had worked at McKenzie's – one of London's top one hundred law firms. The work was relentless, but the pay was great. I lived on my own in a smart one-bedroom rental in Clapham and I was a junior associate trying to scale the next rung of the ladder. But once I got there – what then?

I had squeezed in a quick drink with Liz a week ago and we had talked about how we both felt like we had come to an impasse in our lives. She'd had a string of bad dates recently and was struggling with her new boss. I, for my part, couldn't shake the feeling this was not where I wanted to be. But I had no clue where I *did* want to be, or what to do about it. I was stuck. Receiving Nada's wedding invitation was the excuse I needed to escape for a while. I hadn't met her fiancé yet because this was the first time we had seen each other since she'd left London four years ago.

'So ... if you're not dating then ...' Nada had a cheeky look on her face as she put her shirt back on.

I tugged at the sleeve. 'Wait. You're not going to stick me on one of those singles tables, are you?'

'Me? Matchmaker? *Never.*' Her mouth dropped open comically. 'But I think you might have something in common with someone I've sat you next to. He's lived in London before and I promise you, he likes to pick up the tab occasionally and only does press-ups at the gym.'

I let Nada's enthusiasm excite me. Who knew, she could have found my perfect man.

After a quick shower and a change of clothes at my hotel, we spent the next few hours driving around. What struck me most about the city of Beirut was the depth of the chasm between rich and poor. BMWs and Rolls-Royces were vying with beat-up Rovers and Mazdas. We would turn down one street to see signs of a city ripped apart by a civil war which had lasted fifteen years, with many buildings still untouched by reconstruction and bullet holes lining flats long ago abandoned. But take another turn and the backdrop changed completely: restaurants filled with young, rich-looking Arabs, decked out in designer gear.

We met with Nada's friends from the American University of Beirut where she had studied journalism and political science, including the year abroad at the University of Surrey. They took me on a tour of their old haunts on the stately campus, lifted high above the chaos of the city, where a strong scent of pine filled my nose.

After hours of touring and a feast of Lebanese food and wine, we headed to a club after another quick shower and change, where a tray of cocktail glasses filled with milky pink liquid was brought to our table. They were so refreshing

I downed two of them in rapid succession, the garlic from the food having made me thirsty. We huddled around a low, round table, talking about work, men and politics.

We moved to the dance floor when it became too loud to be heard, but not before I had drained my third drink. The room spun, and I reached for Nada's arm to keep me upright.

'You OK?' she said.

'I feel dizzy,' I shouted into a mouthful of her hair.

'Drink some water. Those cocktails are quite strong. You're probably not used to the heat, either.'

'What's in them?' I slurred. 'They're delicious.'

'Strawberry cordial, cream and double shots of rum.'

I hiccuped, and a snorting kind of laugh spilled out of my mouth. *Whoops.*

We danced and danced until sweat poured down my back beneath my white silk blouse. I spun continuously, delighting in the way my short skirt fanned out.

The clock pushed into single digits, and Nada announced she was calling it a night. With the wedding the next day, she wanted to get at least a few hours' sleep. I begged her to stay for one more song, but she shook her head. Draining one last delightful strawberry cocktail, I swayed out of the club with Nada and her friends. They tipped me into a taxi and gave the driver instructions and a couple of notes.

I was grateful for the assistance. By this point, I didn't know what day it was, let alone what hotel I was staying at. My parents would be horrified. Liz, though, would be giving me a gigantic high five. Alone and drunk in a strange city. I snorted again and high fived myself.

I must've nodded off for a bit because I jerked awake when the taxi came to a sudden halt. '*Shukran, shukran, shukran,*' I said to the driver.

All day I had heard this word of gratitude in Arabic. It was lovely to thank someone so many times and for it not to sound ridiculous. I said it another three times. The driver grinned at me in his rear-view mirror.

I stepped out the door, but my arm was tangled in the seatbelt and I tumbled onto the pavement, smacking onto the concrete with my knees and elbows. Pain shot through me, overcoming the numbing effects of the alcohol, and a chorus of voices rang around me in rapid-fire Arabic.

No need to make a fuss, I'm OK. A hand up would be good, though. A glance at my left knee revealed a trickle of blood down my shin. *Whoopsy.* I giggled again.

Someone took me under one arm and someone else on the other side. On my left, the driver was horribly apologetic. He nodded and let go as an arm slid around my waist. I turned to see who my other saviour was. His features were blurred in my drunken haze, but still, I was stunned.

'Oz?!' I screeched.

'Can you walk, Abbie?'

It was like trying to tiptoe on one of those tiny beams resting on springs. So no, not really. He helped me forward, but my legs still weren't obeying. I rested my cheek on his chest and inhaled his distinctive citrus scent before being lifted. How the heck was he supporting me? I must've put on at least ten pounds with all the food and booze I had consumed tonight.

'Abbie, what floor are you on?' he asked, his voice straining from the effort.

'Yours?' I hiccuped. My arms encircled his neck, the hairs at the nape tickling my fingers.

He furrowed his brow.

'The top, I think. Key's in my purse.'

I must have blacked out for a moment, as the next thing I knew I was in my room and the light was snapped on. As I slid down his chest a sudden urge overcame me. I bolted to the bathroom, slammed the door, and heaved into the toilet.

After that my senses returned, by degrees. I pulled myself to the sink, splashing my face with cold water and gargling a little more, instantly feeling better.

Christ. What a sight in the mirror. Elbows grazed, showing flecks of gravel. At least the blood on my knee had congealed.

I grabbed the bathroom wall, tugging open the door. When I saw Oz sitting on the chair beside the dressing table, a breath caught in my throat. 'Hi there,' I said, with what I hoped was a husky, sexy voice. I couldn't tell though, because my ears were still ringing from the loud music in the club.

Oz rose. '*Hadi*, let's lie you down.'

'Only if you come with me.' I smiled, sashaying towards him. My ankle gave way and I stumbled again. He grabbed me before I tumbled.

'I'm always falling into your arms,' I giggled, with another hiccup.

He steadied me and I held onto the lapels of his shirt, drawing my nose closer and inhaling his scent.

'You smell lush,' I drawled, letting my fingers creep up to encircle his neck.

He removed them and pulled me down onto the bed, unclasping the buckles of my shoes before laying a cool sheet over me.

My head was spinning, and my eyelids were heavy. 'Why are you here? Where did you come from? Is this what they call fate?' I joked. Nothing was making sense.

'Get some rest, Abbie. I'll see you at the wedding tomorrow.'

'We're getting married?' I beamed at the thought of me walking down an aisle, with Liz flanking him at the altar. I began to hum the opening bars of the wedding march.

'No, but Yusef and Nada are.'

'How do you know Nada and Yusef?'

'Yusef is my friend from UCL. Remember, you met him in London.'

Nada's Yusef was Oz's Yusef? How did I not know this? My mind started to draw new connections, but the alcohol was stopping them from making any sense.

'Time for sleep,' he whispered, turning me on my side.

I tried to will my eyes to remain open. I hadn't even taken a good look at him. Still the same? Certainly smelled the same. So much I wanted to talk to him about. *Stay*. I wished he would lie down beside me, his arms wrapped around me. The feeling I was on a boat, with waves nudging it sideways, began to subside as I drifted into sleep, continuing to hum the wedding march.

19

Now

July

A black cab pulled up suddenly at the kerb in front of my flat and Liz stepped out.

'Why are you in a taxi?' I asked, perplexed.

'Secret wedding mission. Get inside. And that's an order.'

Before I could protest, Liz had shoved me inside. She had texted me half an hour ago to say she was coming round. I had been enjoying a leisurely morning with Charlie and the Saturday papers, but my suspicions had been aroused when I'd suggested he and I go out for a walk to grab some breakfast and he'd said we should stay in, even though the sun was glorious outside and it was stuffy in our flat. Now I knew why. I was being held hostage until my best friend turned up.

The taxi wound its way to Marylebone High Street and Liz sidestepped my interrogation as to where we were going until we pulled up in front of Browns Bride only a few minutes later.

'Surprise!' Liz said, paying the fare.

'But we've already been dress shopping.'

'A lunchtime stroll around the Debenhams bridal collection is not dress shopping,' she said sharply. 'And you have been dithering far too long about what you want so I took matters into my own hands. The wedding is in six months. I'm sure you're meant to have made a decision by now.'

I had vaguely recalled seeing a timeline in one of the wedding magazines Liz had brought round for last month's sleepover which had said to order it no later than six to seven months prior to avoid rush fees and to allow for various fittings. Another wedding magazine had assured me that a wedding dress straight off the peg could easily be adjusted within a matter of days, so my worry about getting one had been parked.

The door to the shop swung open and a middle-aged lady welcomed us with outstretched arms. She wore a beige silk blouse with a pleated long green skirt and had a tape measure around her neck.

'The bride to be,' she announced. 'Welcome to Browns Bride, I'm Olivia.' She ushered us inside.

An assistant thrust champagne glasses towards us, her toothy grin wide and keen.

The shop was intimate and exuded exclusivity. There were at most thirty dresses hung on three racks like a mere sprinkling of snow compared to the avalanche of white and cream we had seen at the department store. I gave Liz a panicked look, knowing I would dread asking what one would cost and the inevitable conversation where I would have to say 'I'll think about it' when I wouldn't.

Liz tugged at my sleeve so she could whisper in my ear. 'Sorry, your mother-in-law called and suggested this place.'

That didn't surprise me. Despite my best efforts, Charlie's mum had begun to take over with all the planning, berating

Charlie and me for not being able to take more weekends off to come to Scotland and help her. She had insisted it would be easier for her to organise and give us options.

'You don't have to buy anything,' Liz said. 'Just have fun. And there's a couple of surprises, too.'

'Welcome,' the assistant piped up again and I turned round and saw my mother hovering behind her.

'Mum!' I said, rushing to hug her.

It had been six months since my birthday lunch and I had failed miserably to organise any wedding-related activities for her and Amy to participate in because I had been swamped with work, so I began to feel more excited that Liz had organised this.

'I wouldn't have missed this for the world. Amy sends her apologies. Barry Junior isn't feeling well so she had to stay home.'

That was a relief, I thought but didn't say out loud for fear of annoying Mum. I loved Amy, honestly, I did, but she had a way of upstaging most events we were at together and the champagne would no doubt have disappeared in a second.

Olivia clasped her hands together. 'Do we wait for our last guest or shall we proceed?'

Liz checked her phone. 'She'll be here in about ten minutes but it's probably best we start. I want to see Abbie in everything.'

'Who else is coming?' I asked, but my question was ignored as Olivia and her assistant sat us down on a pale blue velvet couch.

'Our dresses are selected with the modern, independent woman in mind,' she began. 'A wedding dress is one of the most important and memorable purchases of your life, and to that end, we want you to have a wonderful experience today. We can make suggestions based on your shape, height, hair colour. Rest assured, when you leave here today you will have made a well-informed choice.'

I glanced at Liz and she gave me a knowing look.

She and Mum were invited to choose their favourite dress from a selection of ten Olivia thought would suit my figure and red hair, while I was drawn to another one.

'Mum, why are you crying?' I said a few minutes later after I came out of the changing room in the first dress – a poufy princess-styled one with a fitted bodice and layered skirt chosen by Liz.

'It's nothing, sweetheart.' She dabbed the corners of her eyes with a tissue from the box the assistant had discreetly placed on the table. 'You look so beautiful.'

'Like Cinderella,' said Liz, beaming.

I twirled for the full effect of the dress and allowed myself to get caught up in the moment. Striking a flamboyant pose, I lightened the atmosphere and Mum laughed through her tears.

'It really is lovely.' She tightened her grip on the tissue. 'I see now why you didn't want to wear my old wedding dress. It's better suited to a simpler affair – a marquee in the garden, perhaps, not a grand castle. This is definitely a contender.'

I looked back in the mirror and a tightness settled in my chest. Maybe the bodice was too snug.

'Go and try on another,' Liz urged before taking a large sip of champagne.

As I wriggled out of the gown in the changing room and slipped on my choice, I froze as I caught sight of a familiar face reflected in the mirror.

'Nada?' I squealed, taking in her beaming smile and throwing my arms around her. 'Oh my God, what a wonderful surprise. You came all the way from Beirut?'

'It was luck. I had some meetings at the office in London and Liz made sure to fix the date for today.'

'I can't believe you're here. We have so much to catch up on. How are the girls?'

'They're great. Growing too fast – eight and six now – and both feisty.'

'Like their mum.'

She shot me a mock offended look. 'Anyway.' She whistled as she held me at arm's length. 'Beautiful, Abbie. You look stunning.'

This dress was in stark contrast to Liz's choice. Fitted, with a French lace bodice and capped sleeves, and a column-shaped tulle skirt; it clung to my modest curves and felt simple and elegant. It reminded me of something ... I turned back to the mirror and admired it more thoroughly. Yes.

'It's like your wedding dress, Nada.'

She gave me a once-over and smiled warmly. 'Oh, yes. Yes, it is. Can't quite believe that was nine years ago.'

'Was it really that long ago?' My words surprised me. I could never ever forget how many years ago it was because it was a time that had left an indelible mark.

'Knock, knock,' came Olivia's voice as she pulled back the curtain. 'Have we found the perfect dress?'

I smiled nervously. 'I'll have to think about it.' I knew I shouldn't get carried away. At a guess I would say this dress was four figures with the first not under five. Such an extravagant purchase for one day. I thought about what Mum had said about not wearing her old wedding dress. It had been hand-made by her mother – a simple knee-length, A-line dress with lace trim, a family heirloom. That would definitely be a cheaper option. I had mentioned it to Charlie's mum a while back, but she had laughed and said there was no way it would be a suitable match for the groom and ushers' outfits. The truth was it was getting increasingly hard to imagine any part of the day, let alone what Charlie would look like.

'I appreciate it is a decision not to take lightly,' Olivia continued. 'But let me paint the picture. The eyes of your guests as you enter the church in this exquisite dress, your father on your arm, and the man of your dreams at the end of the aisle.'

She began humming the wedding march as a wave of dizziness traversed my limbs before a constriction in my throat left me struggling to take a breath.

'*Ya, Allah*,' Nada exclaimed when she saw me gasping. 'Are you OK?'

The concerned faces of everyone surrounded me as I stumbled back to the sofa and emptied the contents of my bag, reaching for my inhaler.

I drew two deep puffs, and the relief was instant.

'I'm fine,' I said shakily.

'Sweetheart.' Mum sat down beside me on the couch. 'What happened? What was the trigger?'

I shrugged. 'I'm not sure. Maybe this dress is too tight.' I tugged the fabric at the waist and turned away from Liz in the hope that she hadn't noticed the twitch in my eye. 'I've not eaten breakfast yet either, so I guess champagne wasn't the best idea.'

Mum shook her head slowly, gearing up no doubt to give me a lecture on taking better care of myself. But the truth was, I didn't have the heart to tell any of them that it wasn't only that I had drunk two glasses of champagne on an empty stomach; it was also the words the shop owner had spoken to me that had shaken me, because she painted a picture of a wedding that could never happen.

20

Now

September

My mobile's alarm pulsed into life on my bedside table. Something wasn't right. It was still pitch-black outside. I reached out to switch the phone off when I noticed the time. Three a.m.

Charlie stirred beside me, emitting a low grunting sound as he stretched out his limbs.

'Sorry,' I whispered. 'I must've set the wrong time.'

A minute later, Charlie's alarm sounded, too.

'No, you didn't,' he yawned. 'I reset it. It's time to get up.'

'But our flight isn't until eleven,' I said, propping myself up on my elbows as he switched on his bedside lamp.

'Surprise,' he said with a cheeky grin. He ran his hand over his face and eyes before picking up his glasses from his bedside table and putting them on.

'What's the surprise?'

He pulled back his duvet and swung his legs over the side of the bed. 'I am under strict instructions not to say anything except to get you out of bed at three and make sure you get into the cab which will be here in forty-five minutes.'

I sat further up in bed as he put his dressing gown on. 'Strict instructions from whom?'

He came around to my side of the bed and placed a kiss on my cheek. 'That would be telling.'

I tugged at his dressing gown sleeve as he tried to pull away. 'Charlie, what's going on?'

'Relax, Abbie. This is meant to be fun.'

'Four nights in Madeira? I've been counting the days, haven't you?'

Charlie had purchased a four-night getaway a couple of weeks ago, suddenly declaring we deserved a treat. We had spent little time together over the last month due to our workload, and with the wedding three months away, I knew we had to do some planning together before his parents took charge of every last detail. And I needed to feel that connection with him again. Our working lives were taking over.

'Sorry, Abbie. There never was a trip to Madeira. Get dressed and I'll make you some breakfast. Trust me,' he said, holding the side of my face with his hand and stroking my cheek with his thumb. 'You're going to have fun and you're still going abroad. Now get a move on, otherwise you'll be late.'

As the taxi sped off and I could no longer see Charlie from the back windscreen, I opened the seal of a card he had handed over as he had kissed me goodbye. Its poem baffled me.

> *Surprise! It's your hen do.*
> *Where we are going it's sure to be bright*
> *And don't worry it's always a delight.*

By its other name it could be eaten
But for this event, it can't be beaten.

This trip had Liz's name written all over it. We hadn't seen each other since a shopping expedition to Camden a few weeks ago where I had stumbled on a vintage dress store and found a beautiful inexpensive wedding dress which was hanging at hers ready to be altered closer to the big day. Liz had been too busy with working full-time again and Maddy to do anything else expected of the matron of honour, so the idea of spending four days with her filled me with excitement.

An hour later, the taxi arrived at Stansted airport. Inside the terminal, people thronged around me, suitcases by their sides. Everyone seemed to know where they were going except me.

'Abbie!' Liz's voice hollered from behind.

I turned to see her running towards me, pulling her case on its four wheels, her blonde hair bouncing with excitement.

'I knew it,' I said as she dropped the handle and embraced me. 'I knew you were behind this. It's very thoughtful of you but I would've been fine with afternoon tea at some hotel.'

She shook her head. 'Nothing to do with me, Abs. My big surprise was the dress shopping. First I knew I was going away was when Mum arrived last night with her suitcase, telling me I was off on a surprise hen do trip for you.' She bobbed on the spot. 'Even Mary was in on it. I am busting to find out where we're going. Also ... I have some news.'

'What?'

'I'm quitting my job.' She clenched her teeth.

'Oh my God, that's huge.'

'I know. But I think it's the right thing to do. I can't drop Maddy at nursery any more. I hate it: the stress, the tears – hers and mine. I don't want it to be this hard and Mary is taking on even more cases these days and ...' Her eyes began to well up. 'I feel like I was robbed of enjoying the first few months of her life and I miss her. But ... oh, I don't know, I love my job.' She looked skywards.

'Hey, it's going to be fine. You're doing your best for Maddy. I think it's a very brave decision and maybe it's the right one for now. I'm sure they'll welcome you back with open arms in the future if you change your mind.'

She nodded and smiled: the threat of tears thwarted for now. 'I'll bounce back. If I can handle post-natal depression, I can handle this. Anyway, this is your big trip.'

'But if you didn't plan this then ...'

I heard her before I saw her – heels clacking along the linoleum floor, that familiar wolf whistle. Amy. She waved frantically from a distance and then flung her arms around us once she drew near.

'Woohoo! You made it.' She clapped her hands together.

'It's really thoughtful of you to plan me a hen do, but I only wanted—'

'You think I'm going to let my little sister get married without a massive send-off?' She waggled a fake-nailed finger at me. 'No way. This is going to be epic. Mum is looking after the kids; Liz's mum is in charge of her sprog and we are going large. I'm still pissed off at you for not asking me to be involved in anything, so I thought I'd do this before you had a chance to organise whatever snooze fest the two of you had planned.' She pretended to stifle a yawn.

'It's just the three of us?' I asked for clarification.

'Nah. That Lebanese friend of yours happens to be attending a wedding where we're going and said she'd join us for some fun.'

I beamed at the prospect of seeing Nada again, but a pang of guilt dug me in the ribs. It was true, I hadn't asked Amy – or Mum for that matter – to be involved in much wedding prep since the dress shopping two months ago. Even the making of the bridesmaids' dresses that I thought Mum would oversee had been delegated by Elena Logan to some famous Scottish seamstress in her village. I had been persuaded it would be easier to make last-minute alterations.

Amy unzipped her suitcase and pulled out some pink T-shirts. It was hard not to notice all the hen-do paraphernalia clogging up one whole side of the case. Amy flung the shirts at us and my mouth opened wide when she popped open her denim jacket to reveal hers. It read: *Abbie's Hen Do, Istanbul. 14th – 17th Sept.*

Liz spoke before I could even form a coherent word.

'We're going to Istanbul?' She looked from me to Amy, wide-eyed.

'Yeah, did you not get it from my clues? A delight, Turkish delight; it's going to be bright and hot there; you can eat turkey. God, you two are slow. Got an ace deal with easyJet, seventy-nine quid return and a bargain on two interconnecting single rooms in a three-star hotel, too. I remember when you went Interrailing you told us it was your favourite destination. See. I don't forget these things. Thought you'd like to go back and reminisce.'

I opened my mouth to tell her I couldn't possibly go back to Istanbul, but she had already closed her case and headed to check-in. But how could I bail when everything was paid for? It was true, when asked about the trip by my family, I had told them how amazing it had been but left out the detail of Oz and how it ended. But what did it matter if I did return? It was a city of about fifteen million; there was no reason to bump into him at all.

The first two and a half days of the trip were crammed full of sightseeing, lounging by the hotel pool, eating and sleeping. Amy had crawled in at three the second night after we had gone to a nightclub while Liz and I had bailed after midnight. Amy had insisted on dressing me with a 'Bride to be' sash and tiara and we had drawn a lot of attention. Nada was in Ankara and joining us tonight for some celebrating. I knew nothing of what had been organised except I should wear the smartest dress I had packed. It was a pale blue cotton sleeveless sundress fitted at the top which fanned out when I spun around. I had been looking forward to wearing it on my holiday with Charlie, but so far this surprise trip had been more fun than I was expecting.

The sunset on the horizon of Florya Güneş Beach that evening was breathtaking – orange hues reflecting in the water as waves gently lapped against the shore. Nada had asked us to meet her here for a wedding reception she said we had been invited to.

A stage had been set on the beach with garlands of flowers hung in crisscross patterns from posts stuck in the sand. Tables were laid out with food and drink and crowds of partygoers mingled.

'Abbie!' a voice squealed, and I turned to see Nada running barefoot towards us dressed in a peach floral sundress.

'It's so good to see you,' I said. 'What are you doing in Istanbul? I can't believe the coincidence.'

She squeezed me tight. 'It is such good fortune. A friend of Yusef got married and there have been celebrations all weekend in his hometown of Ankara and here in Istanbul where his bride is from. This,' she said, sweeping her arm to the scene behind her, 'is the post ceremony party and you have been warmly invited. In fact, the groom said he met you once in London, Abbie. Yaman is his name.'

My eyes widened and I could feel a flush coating my cheeks. Liz noticed my expression.

'Yusef took our girls back to the hotel so I am a free agent. How about we go and get some drinks? Get our own little party started.' She wiggled her hips. '*Yalla*,' she said, ushering us forward onto the sand.

'Now you're talking,' Amy piped up, peeling off her stilettos, following in Nada's footsteps towards the bar.

I walked behind them with Liz, my arm linked with hers, whispering so they couldn't hear. 'You don't think—'

'That Oz will be here?'

'What are you two whispering about?' Nada said, looking over her shoulder.

'We need to get some drinks down us asap,' Liz said before lowering her voice. 'It's fine, Abs. This is your hen do, remember. Let's have some fun. Don't think about him, and besides, I'm sure it'll be OK if he comes. You told me back in April it had been fine seeing him, that you felt nothing.'

I bowed my head so Liz couldn't see my twitching eye.

Darkness came and with it the band took to the stage and began their set. It reminded me of the Turkish music I had danced to at the Lebanese restaurant Oz had taken me to in London all those years ago. We downed a few shots of raki – the Turkish equivalent of the arak I had drunk at Maroush, except this drink was neat and incredibly strong – and joined in a dance where we all linked arms in a circle and followed a sequence of moves.

It was getting close to ten and there had been no sign of Oz, and I hadn't had the courage to ask Nada about him and whether he was planning to attend. The mobile number that he had given me years ago still sat in my list of contacts and I had thought of texting him but decided it wasn't appropriate. It might not even be his current number.

I began to relax more as the evening wore on and we continued to dance, breaking periodically for another drink and some Turkish delicacies.

My head began to spin, and I clutched Liz's arm. 'I think I need to go and get some water and sit the next song out.'

'Need company?' she asked, pulling up the thin straps of her red dress which had slid down her shoulders.

'Sure,' I said, ceremoniously placing my hand on my hip so we could link arms, indicating to Nada and Amy we were heading to the bar.

A bonfire was lit on the beach in the distance and we swayed towards it, picking up a couple of bottles of water from the bar on the way.

'I'm wasted,' Liz declared. 'I haven't got this pissed since ...' She hiccuped. 'Who knows?'

We attempted to sit down beside the fire but ended up pulling each other down, soaking ourselves with the water bottles, giggling relentlessly. I dragged Liz back up, but she pulled me back down, so we were flat on our backs, snorting with laughter.

As we caught our breath, I looked up at the sky. A million stars twinkled. It reminded me of the sky I had seen when Oz and I took that tourist boat ride.

'He didn't come,' I slurred. 'Oz didn't come.'

'Did you want him to?'

I nodded. 'Yes.' Sitting up, I stared into the flames which licked the air.

'You did?' Liz propped herself up on her elbows.

I hiccuped. 'I think I did.'

'Well text him then. We've got all morning free tomorrow before our flight for you to see him.'

'OK,' I giggled as I pulled out my phone. The screen blurred in front of me as I typed his name in the search field and hit 'new message'. 'What shall I say?'

'Umm. You're hot. I miss your sexiness and want to see you for coffee tomorrow when I am not so pissed. Lots of snogs, Abigail Lily Jones.'

I typed out the words verbatim and hit 'send'. 'There,' I said, tossing the phone onto the ground. 'Take that, Mr Sexy, schmexy, Turkish heart-breaker. I am very, *very* drunk. I need to lie down again.'

I fell back onto the sand and a wave of nausea rose up my chest. 'Shit, Liz. That first trip to Istanbul. If things had turned out differently, we could've been together. I would have taken the internship offer at UNICEF, spreading peace around the world,' I said, with a dramatic sweep of my hand. 'And Oz would have come to London to work. We might even have got married.' I had no idea where those thoughts had come from. I really was too drunk to be making any sense.

Liz sat further up. 'Wait, what? You'd be working where?'

'You remember.' I sat up and nudged her. 'The internship we applied for. I turned down the offer.' I couldn't focus fully on her face because I was seeing double, but I noticed her smile had disappeared.

'I think I would remember something like that. Why the hell didn't you tell me?'

Her harsh tone sobered me slightly, and the realisation hit I had never told her.

'Because you pitied me?' she said, spitting out the words. 'Poor stupid Liz, not good enough to be accepted.'

'No. That's not what I—'

'And you kept this a secret for ...' She flashed her fingers one by one. 'Over fourteen years?'

'I didn't accept it because I was going to law school.'

'Oh yes, how could I forget? You were humouring me by applying because you thought you were destined for greater things. And then you went and bloody got it and now you're telling me you would've accepted it?!'

She stood up and swayed. 'I can't believe you never told me. I would've told you to take it, but you never gave me the chance. Why, Abs? You wasted your twenties doing a career you hated because you didn't have the guts to tell me you'd got this amazing opportunity to work in the one place I had always dreamed of working at.'

'You see.' I clambered to my feet. 'How could I have accepted it when it was your dream? You would've hated me, resented me.'

'Instead you don't tell me and bottle up all the resentment yourself?'

'No, Liz,' I said, reaching for her arm.

'Forget it.' She shrugged my hold away. 'I'm heading back to the hotel.'

'Let me come with you,' I pleaded.

'Whoop, whoop!' Amy said, appearing by our sides brandishing a bottle of Baileys. 'I nabbed this from the bar. What's going on here?' She swung her arm around my neck.

'I was just leaving,' Liz said. 'Stay. Enjoy the party.' Her smile – directed at me – lacked warmth and I felt numb as she walked away.

'Lightweight,' Amy mumbled, taking a swig from the bottle and offering it up to me.

'No, thanks.'

'Come on, Abbie. It's your hen do. It's meant to be wild. Do something unexpected.' She placed the bottle upright in the sand and began unbuttoning her dress, twirling on the spot. She wriggled out of it revealing a hot pink bra and knickers.

My jaw dropped. 'You're not skinny dipping, are you?'

Amy stumbled towards the sea, tugging at the straps of her bra before tossing it onto the sand. She waded in until the water reached her waist. 'I dare ya,' she hollered before she dived in and disappeared under the surface. She began thrashing around, her arms and legs flailing, but it wasn't long before she went under again. I waited for her to resurface but she didn't. Time passed.

A sudden panic gripped me, and I screamed out her name. Once. Twice. Three times. Nothing. I looked around. There was no one within shouting distance. The few partygoers that had sat by the fire near me and Liz had gone.

Without a moment's hesitation, I ran to the water, tripping as my feet made contact with the waves. I dived in and reached the spot where I had last seen her, treading water, dipping my head under to see if I could find her, swallowing a gallon of seawater in the process. But it was no use. It was too dark.

In a fountain of spray, Amy re-emerged, laughing. 'Got ya.'

'Agh,' I wailed into the night sky, slapping the water with one arm. I swam back to shore and dragged myself out of the water, my dress clinging to me, the light fabric now feeling heavy and uncomfortable. Of all the stupid pranks she had ever pulled, this had to top them all.

I grabbed the bottle of Baileys, took a swig and flopped beside the fire. Sand coated my wet legs, but it was pointless even attempting to wipe it off without caking my hands in it, too. I shivered and wrapped my arms around myself, sinking my face onto my knees. My head thundered beneath my fingertips.

'You really have a terrible sense of humour,' Amy said from behind.

I hauled myself up and looked squarely at her. She was clutching her clothes to her chest, hair dripping. 'Since when is pretending to drown considered funny? Have you forgotten what happened to us all those years ago, when we sneaked off and went sailing together in Mumbles?'

'Oh yeah, how could I forget? My little sister saved my life. As if you needed your family status to reach any higher than it already was.'

'What are you talking about?'

'Forget it. This hen do has turned lame. I'm heading back to the bar.' She staggered off back in the direction of the wedding party.

I finished the bottle of Baileys by the fire before hailing a taxi back to the hotel, texting Nada to say I would catch up with her tomorrow before we left. I stumbled over the threshold to my room having dropped my key card twice. The interconnecting door was locked from Liz's side and a sadness gnawed away deep in my chest. I knocked gently and called Liz's name, but she didn't come to open it.

Enough light spilled through the open window from the street down below to be able to see my way to my bed. I picked up the bin and placed it strategically beside me as I flopped down on top of the sheets.

Nausea along with an uncomfortable feeling that something else had happened tonight – something that I couldn't for the life of me remember – washed over me. I hoped to God it wasn't anything stupid. I hadn't been this drunk since that fateful trip to Beirut.

21

Nine Years Earlier

June

Hungover. Not a great look for Nada's wedding. I stepped out of the taxi in front of the church and held my clutch bag tight, readjusting the spaghetti straps of my mint-green dress. My shades were big enough for two purposes: to shield from the Beirut sun, which was blinding, and to hide my puffy, sleep-deprived eyes.

The entrance of the church had an arch bathed in a sea of jasmine, the scent intoxicating. Inside – darkness. The only illumination was from tea lights set on the floor beside the pews and the slivers of sunlight arcing through slits in the windows. A quick glance over my shoulder showed a sea of the lightest shade of blue. It merged with the sky. As I was wedged between Nada's friends from the night before, it was impossible to catch a glimpse of Oz.

I pulled at my locket, sliding it back and forth along the chain. Why didn't she tell me Oz would be here? Hadn't she worked out the connection between me, him and Yusef? But then why hadn't I? Nada never posted personal pictures on her Facebook page – it was mostly full of political commentary. She had sent me one snap of them together, but Yusef was wearing shades and had longer hair – unrecognisable from when I had last seen him in Istanbul.

The reception was at Al Falamanki restaurant, not far from my hotel, set back from the beach. A courtyard lay at the back, which was like stepping into a secret garden. Trestle tables were covered with white linens and there were more striking displays of jasmine. Fairy lights criss-crossed above us, giving the whole place a magical glow.

The bride and groom arrived, and I joined the guests to greet them and to throw handfuls of rice over their heads. I hugged Nada and kissed Yusef on the cheeks, telling him I had no idea he was Nada's fiancé until yesterday. I watched as they moved down the line, beaming.

'Abbie?'

I spun around with a nearly full glass of champagne, almost splashing it on the person behind me – Oz.

There he was, dressed sharply in a navy-blue suit, hair shorter but those eyes. Looking into them was like being given a portal to the past: the image of him on the rowing boat in Istanbul when the sun lightened their caramel colour, the day I had fallen deep and hard for him. The flashback was as clear as if it had happened yesterday, not five years ago.

My heartbeat escalated and our surroundings faded, bringing his face into sharper focus. I had no clue how long we stood there staring at each other. The humid Beirut night throbbed around us.

'Are you feeling better?' he finally said.

I lowered my glass as I remembered the events of last night. 'Yes, much. Thanks for helping me to my room.'

'There's no need to thank me, Abbie. I was happy to be there.'

I nodded, shifting my weight from one high-heeled shoe to the other.

'How have you been?' he asked.

'Good, good, thanks.'

He took a sip from his champagne. As the flute came to his lips, I noticed the gold band on his wedding finger and my face fell.

There were no further questions. He loosened his tie a little and popped the top button of his shirt. 'It's hot. Hotter here than Istanbul.'

'Are you here long?'

'I'll go to Damascus tomorrow with Yusef and Nada. They are visiting some of Yusef's relatives before going on honeymoon. I've never been, and it is a place I am interested in.' His tone had little of the warmth I remembered.

Someone squealed my name. Nada. 'I am so happy. You found each other,' she said, clapping her hands together.

'You planned this?' I said.

'I didn't know you knew each other until we were drawing up guest lists. You told me years ago about some gorgeous Turkish guy you met in London.'

I smiled at the memory of a drunken night with Nada in Guilford when we talked about previous loves; but I had told her that it had been a holiday fling.

'You mentioned he was studying at UCL and when Yusef said he was inviting a friend he had met in London doing a course there, I realised you had already met the love of my life and knew this handsome man.' She squeezed Oz's arm. '*Tati*. Come, come.'

She didn't elaborate but ushered us towards a table to the side, tucked away behind a pillar. 'These are your seats.' Our place cards sat next to each other. 'Enjoy.' With a flourish, she moved on and threw her arms around other guests as she made her way to the top table. Why would Nada sit us together as if she was matchmaking? Didn't she know he was married?

Oz drew back my chair.

'Thanks,' I murmured.

Others joined us, but after introductions the conversation continued in Arabic. Oz turned to me as I tucked into my salmon and pomegranate starter.

'I didn't know you knew Nada,' he said.

'I shared a flat with her when I was at Guilford law school.' I shook my head. 'I remember now. Yusef told me at your brother's party he was going to spend a year at AUB doing politics. That's what Nada majored in in her final year. She told me she had met a Syrian student and had fallen for him. I can't believe the coincidence.'

'You believe this is a coincidence?' He searched my eyes. The look was intense.

'Well …' I pushed some of the red seeds around my dish. 'I am not sure what else you would call it. You think there is some divine intervention behind this? Fate?' I said disbelievingly.

He shook his head. 'I once told you. In Turkey we only believe in *Kader*. Destiny.' His voice sent little shivers up my arms and I cursed myself for letting him have this effect on me again as I remembered how our last night in Istanbul ended.

As the main course of lamb and rice arrived, the gentleman to my left engaged me in conversation until he excused himself once the plates were cleared. By then a blanket of stars lay above us. A guitarist and violinist struck up a duet.

Nada suddenly thrust her head between us. 'Please, I beg you, come and dance. I don't want us to be the only ones.'

'I'm a terrible dancer,' I replied.

'Me too,' Oz said.

I frowned and he offered a slight shrug. I knew far too well he wasn't.

'Guys, the music is hardly frantic. I think you can manage to sway from side to side,' Nada said with an exasperated look. '*Yalla, yalla*,' she ordered, practically tipping us out of our chairs.

We pushed our way to an area near the top table, where Yusef was waiting to begin this important ritual with his new bride. They rested their foreheads together and began to move to the music.

Awkwardly, I held onto Oz's shoulder and clasped his hand. I couldn't look at him. The heat from his touch was putting my head in a spin. But I couldn't get over the memory of that scene on the stage at his brother's party – his future fiancée encircling his neck and then our confrontation in front of his family. My jaw clenched.

It was then I noticed he was squeezing my fingers unnaturally tight. I looked up. He seemed forlorn; sadness mixed with hurt and some anger. In the low light, his eyes were more dark chocolate than caramel.

'Is everything OK?' I said. 'You seem—'

'Why did you leave?' he interrupted.

I stopped moving and looked up again. His hand dropped mine and he took a step backwards, forcing me to move my other hand from his shoulder.

'Why did I leave the party at your house?'

He nodded.

'I gave you a chance to explain what happened up on that stage and you didn't. It was clear what it was, though – your mother announcing your engagement to Dima.'

'My *engagement*?'

'Do you have any idea how humiliated I felt that night?'

'I am sorry, but you misunderstood.'

'I don't think so. Your mother displayed the two of you with a grand sweep, you kissed Dima, and everyone burst into applause.'

'But that's not what happened.'

'What?' I said, a little too loudly for the intimate venue. Nada and Yusef paused their dance and looked over.

'I think we need to take this conversation somewhere else. There is a lot to explain,' he said.

My palms were clammy against my dress.

'*Gel*. Come.' He took my hand and we headed away from the courtyard. He didn't relinquish his grip until we had walked down one long street in total silence, my heels wobbly, grateful for his steady hold to stop me from stumbling on the pitted paving slabs.

The Corniche – a promenade running along the water as far as the eye could see – was crowded. Couples walked arm in arm at a slow pace, and a group of kids was chattering in the distance. The path was lit by candles, and a man sitting cross-legged was filling the air with a soft tune from a guitar. The waves lapped against the bank. We sat down on an empty bench, our knees touching as we faced each other.

'I don't understand. You're married,' I said.

He nodded.

'To Dima?'

'Yes, but—'

'Then there is nothing to explain.' I tried to get to my feet, but he held my arm and pulled me back down.

'Please, Abbie. Give me a chance to explain everything.'

I pulled my hand from his and folded my arms. 'I'm listening.'

He twisted his fingers in his lap, clearly searching for the right words. 'What you saw on stage that night was my mother announcing the business deal between my family and Dima's family, which involved a huge amount of cash from Dima's father. It was a celebration of the union of our families.'

'But your mother said to me she would announce your engagement soon. When I met her during the meal, she said it was your destiny, or something like that. And this was after Dima had told me exactly the same thing in the bathroom. What else was I supposed to think?'

He shook his head. 'Why didn't you let me explain? Why did you run off before allowing me to tell you my side?'

'I asked you to explain, but you didn't.'

'It was not something to say in front of my family. I needed to talk to you in private. And at the time, in front of them, I didn't have the courage to say what I was feeling in my heart.'

My arms remained folded. 'OK, they're not here. Tell me.'

'That deal for the land came at a price ... Me.'

I looked up at him, confused. A sharp line cut into his forehead.

'Dima and I had been good friends since we were little. It had been the family joke we would be together one day. It was my destiny to join the family business and my mother could not accept I had changed when I returned from England, that I no longer wanted to do what she wanted me to do. But the future of the whole company lay with this one deal. Arsel Holding had been in trouble. My grandfather had made some bad investments and the banks were getting nervous. It was my duty to help cement this deal. And family is everything to me. Dima's father wanted nothing more than to have his daughter married into our family. So ...'

I took a deep breath. This sounded like a script for a TV drama. But it was Oz's life.

'I had been persuaded this was how it should be – my happiness was a small price to pay for my family's business. But then you came back into my life ... and ... everything I said to you on the boat that day was real. It is what I felt. I wanted to run away but I didn't know how. And I wanted to tell you all this before you left, but you didn't give me a chance. I was a coward. I accept that.'

I let the words sink in. 'What difference would it have made? I didn't fit into your world, Oz. Your mother made me feel like I was not worthy of you. And as for Dima, she was always laughing at me. I felt clumsy around your friends.'

'Is that how you felt with me?' He placed an arm on the back of the bench, lightly touching my back.

A shiver ran down my spine. 'No, I never felt that way with you.'

'I left the party after a fight with my mother. I came to your hotel. Your flight wasn't meant to leave until the next day. The porter said you'd checked out, and I took a taxi to the airport.'

'It *was* you I saw,' I whispered, into the breeze.

His nostrils flared. 'Why, Abbie? *Why* did you leave?'

His harsh tone took me by surprise, and I stood up. 'I told you, Oz. Your mum and Dima convinced me you were getting married. I was twenty-one years old and felt horribly out of my depth. I was hurt, humiliated as well.'

His eyes looked misty and my heart lurched.

'Look, Oz, this was five years ago. So much has happened since. I can't remember every single word your mother and Dima said to me, but it was enough to make me want to run, to avoid having to hear the same speech from you.'

Oz held his head in his hands as he leaned on his knees.

Another thought burrowed away in my brain. 'Why didn't you try to find me to explain all this? You said you came to the airport, but what about the next five years? Why didn't you look me up online?'

I caught sight of his wedding ring again. 'You know what, forget it. You're married, and I hope you're both happy. I'm chilly, and I want to go back to the party and get my things. I think we've said everything that's been missing these last few years. It's been lovely reminiscing.'

I turned and began to walk away but Oz called after me to wait, forcing me to turn around.

'There were over two hundred Abbie Joneses on Facebook, and not one of them had your face.' He stepped closer. 'And I wrote to you, Abbie. Not long after you left, and my mother told me what she had said to you, I wrote you a letter. I rang your university and they promised it would be forwarded to you. And then I sent you postcards, one a month for six months. They were postcards of all the places you visited in Istanbul. Even if you were still upset with me, I wanted you to remember a happy time in my city. You came such a long way to visit me and I was responsible for ruining it for you.'

'You didn't write to me. I didn't receive any letter or postcards.'

'*Evet.*' He nodded. 'I did.'

It didn't make any sense. Surely Mum and Dad would have told me if I had received them. King's must have decided not to forward them on. They weren't the Royal Mail, for heaven's sake.

'For five years,' he said in a low voice, 'I thought you didn't care; that you'd read them and decided not to say anything.'

What would I have said or done if I had received his messages? How can you rewind history and make different choices, causing new paths to unfold?

One more look into his eyes – those bewitching eyes – and my defences would crumble. Pain pulsed at my temples. 'My head hurts. I need to go back. I'm sorry, Oz.'

He reached out and grabbed my arm. 'Don't you want to know?'

I tried to shake him away, but I was losing resolve. 'Know what?'

'Don't you want to know what I said in the letter? How I felt? How I feel now?'

His grip softened and I stopped trying to wriggle free.

'What does it matter, Oz? It wasn't meant to be. I had a life to go back to and so did you. You might say it's not what you wanted, but you accepted your destiny or whatever it was.'

'But I *never* stopped thinking about you,' he countered. 'I'd hoped my words, what I'd written in my letter, might find a way to your heart.'

What could I say? No words came. The truth? I had never stopped thinking about him either. Every date I went on after Oz had been spoiled by his memory. But I had moved on in the only way I knew how, throwing myself into law school and my new career. Once the sixteen-hour days became commonplace when I joined McKenzie's, it became easier to blame a lack of time for never getting beyond a few dates with someone new.

'I did have feelings for you back then, Oz, and I can't deny I thought about you a lot after that night. I kept replaying it in my mind and wondering if I'd been hasty in leaving and going straight to the airport. But your silence, or what I thought was your silence, made me think I'd done the right thing. But now ...' I shook my head. 'What good would it do me to know how you feel? It's too late.'

'It's not too late, Abbie. My life—'

'Please, Oz.' I held my hand up. 'Don't. I have to go. I'm sorry,' I said as I walked away.

It was the second time I had turned my back on him. But this time he didn't follow. With each step, a weight grew heavier on my shoulders.

'What happened?' Nada said as I grabbed my clutch from the table back at the reception. I didn't want to spoil her evening by filling her in. It was a time for curling up on the sofa with Liz, not pouring out my heart to a bride on her wedding night.

'Nothing. It was such a beautiful wedding.' I prayed my face didn't betray my turmoil. 'I hope you have a lovely time in Syria and on your honeymoon.' I hugged her. 'Thank you so much for letting me be a part of your special day.'

'You're not leaving already, are you?'

'I have a headache. Last night was wild.' I smiled. 'I'll see you in the morning before you go?'

'Definitely. I'll stop by the hotel with Yusef. We have to pick up Oz, anyway. I hope you two had' – she nudged me – 'fun.'

'So, you *did* plan this?'

'Yusef promised me not to tell.'

'You know about our past then?'

She nodded. 'And I couldn't think of a better way to bring you both back together.'

'But he's married.'

'Yes, but they separated a while ago. Yusef told me Oz had never truly loved her. His hand was forced for the good of the family. But finally, he made a stand. The divorce petition has already been submitted. They're waiting for a court to issue the final decree before announcing it to their families. I'd say that makes him a free agent.'

A guest came over to kiss Nada and give her a hug – her words ringing in my ears.

'Anyway, I'd better get back to my marriage duties.'

She left and the courtyard spun around me as I tried to digest this new information. Was this what Oz had tried to tell me when I cut him off? Why was I always turning away from him, not giving him the chance to explain?

I grabbed my clutch and wrap and began to run. My heels clattered on the paving stones until I reached the Corniche again. The bench was empty. I looked up and down the promenade but there was no sight of Oz. My breathing had become shallow and I fished out my inhaler and took two restorative puffs.

There was too much to absorb. Was Oz really separated and getting a divorce? Had he broken away from his life, his duty, his *destiny*?

What would have happened if I had read his words? Would I have gone to law school? Would he have come to London to study or undertaken that internship? Would we be together? Would I be living abroad?

'He never stopped thinking of me,' I whispered into the night air. I had to find him.

Back at the hotel I asked the concierge for Oz's room number, but he refused to give it. With a heavy heart I returned to my floor. I groaned into the silence of the hallway before putting my key card into the slot. That was it. Oz would leave in the morning along with all hope of me seeing him again.

A door opened a couple of rooms down and I turned. A head popped out. It was Oz.

When he saw me, he smiled – a look of bewilderment and joy crossing his face – his reaction mirroring mine.

I closed my door and ran to him, flinging myself at him, his body slamming into the door, our mouths clashing against each other's. Flashbacks popped in my brain: the tender kiss in the photo booth, the hot, frantic sex that night in my university room and the sensual embrace on the boat sailing around Istanbul. It should never have ended there.

His hands roamed from my neck, down my side, across my back. My skin lit up with his touch, all that pent-up desire suddenly unleashed – a longing that I had suppressed for years.

He pulled back, breathing heavily. 'Five years. I've waited five years to kiss you again.' He tilted his head to the side. 'How did it happen like this, Abbie?'

'I don't know, but we're here now. Nada told me everything.'

I pulled him back to me and kissed him hard, running my hands through his hair. His shirt had three buttons undone. The contours of his chest were visible, and I ached to stroke him. My fingers trembled as I did.

He breathed in and out deeply before moving in to kiss me under my ear, his nose brushing against a sensitive spot.

'Your smell. It's heavenly,' he whispered. 'Like that day. The day in London.'

'You remember that day?' I asked, panting.

'How could I ever forget? The girl who fell in my arms. A girl full of hope and excitement. You weren't afraid to try new food, new experiences. Very chatty, but nervous.'

I pulled back. 'I wasn't nervous.'

'You kept biting your bottom lip and pulling your hair behind your ears.'

I smiled at the memory.

'You were so ... what's the English saying? Down to earth?' He swept some strands of hair away.

'You mean boring?' I shot him a disapproving look.

He laughed. 'You are not boring.'

'Glad we cleared that up, but if this is part of your seduction routine, then it's failing miserably.'

He stroked my cheek with his fingertips. 'You want me to seduce you?'

As he said the word 'seduce', my knees buckled. I moaned as his feathery kisses moved across my collarbone, where the same spot below my other ear was even more sensitive.

'Well, I don't want you to think I'm a done deal.'

He stopped kissing me. '*Ne?* What is a done deal?'

'Never mind.' I pulled him back and pushed my hands through his shirt, revelling at the feel of his hard body and muscular chest.

When his lips found mine again, my body leaned into his. His hardness nudged between my thighs.

'I feel twenty-one again.' I giggled. 'I almost want to ask you to shut your eyes, so I can undress and slip under the sheets.'

'Let me undress you with them closed, then.'

'OK.'

His eyes shut, and I studied him unobserved, strong jaw, full lips, slightly parted. I placed a gentle kiss on them. Those dimples again. My thumbs followed their outline, cradling his head. 'When you smile, I want to dive right into these.'

'And when you smile, your nose wrinkles.' He reached across my forehead to the bridge of my nose. 'Right here.'

I tugged at his shirt, needing to have him naked right there and then. I pulled the fabric over his arms, so they were momentarily bound, the muscles in his shoulders more pronounced.

'I thought I was going to undress you first,' he said, arching an eyebrow.

'I changed my mind.' Once his shirt was off, I fumbled with his belt buckle and undid his trousers. I edged them down as he leaned against the wall, pushing his shoes off with his feet and pulling off his socks.

I placed his hands on my shoulders and he peeled the straps of my dress down with a delicate touch. He leaned in and kissed my chest, nuzzling with his nose. His kisses moved down to my breasts, his fingers tracing their outline against the silk of my bra.

'Oranges and lilies,' he murmured, catching the scent of my body spray. The anticipation was making me squirm.

My dress fell to the ground and pooled at my feet. He unclasped my sandals and took each one off before kissing all the way up my legs, working his way all over every part of me with his lips. My skin pulsed every time he touched me.

I pulled him forward until the edge of the bed knocked against the back of my knees. But it caught me by surprise and his weight tipped me backwards, taking him with me. We clashed heads and his eyes sprang open.

'*Pardon*,' he said, but I couldn't stop giggling, my body shaking under him.

But the laughter stopped when he scanned my semi-naked form, his eyes wide and hungry. 'You're even more beautiful than I remembered.'

I pulled him back towards me. After that, it was all tangled limbs, sighs and moans of pleasure. My own private firework display exploded in my brain. My thoughts were blurred, and nothing else remained except the sweetest sensation of belonging, of weightlessness and of desire, occupying all of my body.

It was hard to regain my breath once we finally pulled apart.

The sound of cars hooting and people talking on the street below filtered up through the open window. Oz pulled himself up, resting one hand behind his head, the other behind my neck, clasping my shoulder. I nestled into his side. Endorphins continued to course through me, in the same rhythm as the rise and fall of his chest.

'That was …' He finished his sentence in Turkish, the words tumbling out with a huge and crazy smile on his face.

He sat up suddenly. 'Come with me tomorrow, to Syria. I can't bear to leave you.'

My plan had been to check out and head into the mountains, where I had booked a room in a small and secluded resort. Byblos and Baalbek, the classic tourist haunts, were also on the itinerary. But without Nada, my guide, I wasn't sure how much fun it would be.

'A road trip to Damascus, with you?' I smiled up at him. 'I'd love to.'

His arm tightened around me, and he kissed my forehead. At the nape of his neck, I gave him one right back, before resting my head beside his.

He tenderly picked up my locket from around my neck. 'This is beautiful.'

'A gift from my parents for my twenty-first birthday. What about this?' I asked, holding his tag in my fingers.

'I did military service for six months after my degree, before I started my masters.'

As I caressed his arm, my fingertips touched the line of his scar and he flinched. 'How did you get this?'

He shifted up the bed, putting some space between us. 'It was a long time ago.'

'Does it have something to do with your dad?'

He covered it. 'Why do you say that?' His tone was defensive.

'I'm sorry,' I said, reaching up to be in his arms again, my hand stroking his chest. 'I don't want to stir any bad memories. It's just ... that's what you do, when I mention your dad, you hide your scar.'

'I didn't know I did that.'

'It's OK, you don't have to tell me.'

He paused, brow furrowed, before twisting his arm so he could study it more carefully. He took several deep breaths, steadying his heartbeat as it thumped under my fingers. 'There was a car accident. My father was driving me to football practice. I was six. *Harika ufaklık*, he used to call me. It means "little boy wonder". We used to kick a ball around for hours every day after school. He also loved to take me fishing at the place I took you to, where we rowed in the harbour. But that day ... the day of my morning practice, he had been drinking, so I was told, and ...' His jaw clenched and he edged further up the bed.

I positioned myself beside him, my shoulder pressing into his, hoping my silence would encourage him to continue.

'All I remember is waking up connected to many machines, bandages wrapping my arm. They moved my father to another hospital to have an operation. I never saw him again.'

'He died?'

He shook his head. 'No. He got better but ...' He paused. 'No one ever spoke of him afterwards. They said guilt made him leave, but he never said goodbye. And then a couple of years after, I was told he'd died from drinking too much. When I got older, my mother got angry with me every time I mentioned his name.'

'I'm so sorry.' Instinctively, I stroked the scar again and leaned across to kiss it. This time he didn't flinch. I looked back at his face and noticed his eyes were welling up and my heart ached for him.

He sniffed and ran his thumb and forefinger over his eyes before turning back to me. 'Tell me about your life in London.'

'It's' – I shifted the sheet under my armpits – 'crap.'

He repositioned himself on his pillow, leaning his head on his hand. 'Why?'

'I work sixteen-hour days as a solicitor: never having any time to see my family or my best friend. The work is nothing but contracts, dotting i's and crossing t's. It's soul-destroying.'

'I'm sorry.'

'I shouldn't complain. I earn good money and I'm saving for a place of my own in London. I might even make senior associate this year, which is another big bump in pay. But ...'

He stroked my hair, inching closer to me, his breath on my cheek. 'But ... what?'

'Now all I can think about is what might've been.'

'If you had received my letter?'

I nodded. 'Why did I run that night?'

'You were forced into believing something which wasn't true.'

'And I was humiliated.'

He held the side of my face and turned it towards him. 'I am so sorry, Abbie, for how you were treated that night. I'm sorry I didn't follow you straight away instead of fighting with my mother. I should've been braver. I should've told you how I felt in front of everybody.'

'It's in the past,' I said, with a thin-lipped smile. 'And who's to say what would've happened if I hadn't run, if I'd heard you out, or if I had received your letter after I got back. Let's not think about it any more.' I snuggled in closer to him.

He stroked my cheek before leaning in to kiss me again. My tongue met his, passion stirring deep inside me again. His kisses trailed from my mouth down to my chest and belly.

'Do you remember that night in London?' he said, his stubble tickling my skin.

'Yes,' I said, my breath shallow.

'When you called me off that train and invited me back to your room, I couldn't believe my luck. And now.' His kisses moved down further and further. 'Now good fortune has blessed me again.'

I melted and lost myself.

22

I used to think sunset was the most beautiful time of day until I watched the dawn with Oz. He had dragged me out from his hotel room at five this morning back to the Corniche where we watched it from the rocks by the harbour. I willed the sun not to rise any further – to stay in his arms which were wrapped around me, shielding me from the early morning breeze. I was scared that if we moved, the spell would be broken.

We held hands as we walked back into the hotel, dropping them instantly when we saw Nada and Yusef at reception. I tied the T-shirt Oz had lent me around my waist and ran my fingers through my matted hair, hoping it wasn't obvious what we had been up to last night.

'There you both are.' Nada threw her arms in the air. 'We went to both of your rooms and you weren't there. *Yalla*, Oz. If we don't leave soon, we hit traffic.'

'We … umm.' I looked down and realised I was still wearing my high-heeled sandals.

'I met Abbie at breakfast and persuaded her to come with us to Damascus.'

'Really?' Nada clapped her hands and squealed. 'Wonderful. Then both of you, hurry up and pack. I am giving you ten minutes to get ready.'

We smiled and turned away before I glanced back over my shoulder. 'We'll be down in twenty. I need a shower.' I looked back at Oz, biting my bottom lip, and he winked; my heart did a triple somersault.

Out on the road later, I rested my head on my arm and took in the scenery; nothing but mountains and crumbling rocks, interspersed with giant billboards promoting films, politicians or beer. Dotted here and there was the odd small village comprising a few streets of houses, a petrol station and a handful of shops. Yusef was driving Nada's jeep. The aircon was broken and we had to lower the windows. The breeze filled the car, making it impossible to tame my hair.

We crossed into Syria after our passports were checked by a soldier at the border. The landscape didn't change but the ground became more arid. Towns were filled with similar blocks of flats. But something appeared different. I lost count of the posters of the president plastered over walls, shopfronts and bus stops. It felt like he was following us everywhere. Women shuffled around with kids in tow; they wore black robes wrapped around their heads and bodies. Men wore mostly white robes and head covers.

Oz clutched my hand across the seat between us. I turned and smiled at him but pulled it away when Nada's gaze fell on us and she gave me a searching look. Oz and I had made a promise to keep this our secret. Everything felt too new and uncertain to share.

We spent the day walking around the sites of Damascus – including the enchanting Tekkiye mosque on the banks of the Barada and the Umayyad, a bigger, grander mosque in the old city. Nada had advised me to wear a long skirt and light cotton shirt, so I was able to go inside without any skin on display.

Yusef introduced us to his favourite lunchtime spot and we sipped tea later in the afternoon in one of the cafés he used to go to with Nada, when she came to visit during their courtship.

When it was time to say goodbye to Nada and Yusef, I hugged them tightly.

'Please, please come to London. Stay with me. I have a futon in my living room.'

'*Inshallah*,' Nada said.

'I hear this word so much. It sounds evasive, non-committal.'

'It's not.' She shook her head. 'If God wishes for it to happen, it will happen.'

They left with a belch of smoke from their exhaust, which merged into the dusty air of the city.

'Now what?' I asked Oz.

'This.' He pulled me into a side street away from the bustle of the main road and kissed me, deeply and passionately, bringing back thoughts from the night before and this morning in the shower when we were meant to be packing; that longing, desperate need to be with him, for him to be inside me. His fingertips found my waist beneath the cotton of my shirt. His touch. I couldn't control my pounding heart as he grabbed my hips. No one else had ever had that effect on me.

Chatter from a group of women broke us apart. They passed by and Oz loitered beside me, hands thrust deep in his pockets like a kid who had been caught stealing sweets.

We walked the streets hand in hand, hopped in cabs and stopped and stared in wonder at the architecture. Under the arch of the Al Azm palace, a sprawling, Ottoman-style complex, we sheltered in a patch of shade. Heat and dust. Even in the shade it was still excruciatingly hot. We sat down and leaned against a marble column and I fanned myself with the tourist guide to the monument.

'Are you thirsty?' Oz whispered, his lips gently caressing my ear, causing my insides to curl up.

I nodded.

He got up and strolled to a stand tucked away in the courtyard and handed over some money. He returned and placed an ice-cold bottle against my cheek, and I giggled. We shared it and in between sips, Oz placed his cool lips on my skin, at my neck and even my shoulder as he teased my shirt away from me.

'What would you like to do now?' he asked.

A wave of tiredness caused me to yawn. 'Sleep.'

He kissed the tip of my nose. '*Hadi*. Let's go and get dinner first and then we can go to the hotel. We have time tomorrow to explore.'

At a booth in a restaurant nearby, we feasted on hummus with warm pitta. The texture of the chickpea dip was smooth and creamy, and the puffed-up bread let out steam when our fingers broke it open. It reminded me of the delicious food I'd tasted at the Lebanese restaurant in London. I mashed a corner of the bread into the dip, then gave it a light coating of olive oil from the little pool in the centre of the dish before eating it. *Heaven*.

Music swirled around us from speakers on the wall and the air was dense with smoke from meat cooked on open coals and excited chatter from other diners.

We hadn't spoken about what we both planned to do next, and what this last day or so meant. After Friday, what then? A return ticket back to London, back to my old life?

Oz pointed to my face. 'You have a little hummus.'

I dabbed at my cheek. 'Where?'

He leaned in, kissing the corner of my mouth and gently licking it off, making my insides melt again.

I had been a total mess of hormones since we had made love. Our knees rubbed together under the small table. The hairs on his legs tickled my skin. He stroked my thigh, and I bit my bottom lip, beginning to be overtaken by the urge to get him back to the hotel and have sex again. Who cared about sleep?

'What are you thinking?' he asked. 'This line' – he stroked my forehead – 'appears sometimes.'

I stared down at the plate, my fingers passing a piece of bread between them. 'Aside from wanting to go back to bed with you, I want to know what we're doing,' I said boldly.

'Eating the most delicious food in Syria.'

'I mean "us". God, I sound like a teenager. All that crap about what "us" means.'

He squeezed my hand. 'We are enjoying this time together. I want to be with you, Abbie. *Inşallah*, we will find a way. Soon I will be free, I hope.'

I sighed. 'I don't know what to do, Oz, about going back to London. I hate my job.' I let out a puff of air – it felt good saying it out loud. 'Listening to Nada talk about journalism took me back to the time when we spoke about our dreams on the boat. And now I can't stop thinking about how life might've been different if I'd accepted the job at UNICEF.'

'Me, too. I wish I'd had the courage to return to London and do the internship or something more worthwhile, like work for a humanitarian organisation – build shelters, make a difference to others' lives. Instead, my job is knocking down old apartment blocks, displacing families, then building luxury towers where they stood.'

A moment of clarity struck me. 'Why don't we?'

His smile mirrored mine. 'Why don't we what?'

'Nada told me about an organisation in Beirut she wrote about – Habitat for Humanity. Why don't we both quit our jobs and go volunteer in Beirut. My rent is up for renewal soon. I need to give three months' notice at my work, that's all. I've saved a lot of money for a flat, but what's the point in buying one and having to maintain a mortgage by staying in a job which makes me unhappy?'

His eyes shone. 'Are you sure?'

'I don't think I've ever been surer.'

'OK.' He leaned in and kissed me gently on the lips. 'Let's do it.'

'Really?' I hadn't counted on such a response. I didn't want to think about any possible repercussions, or the fact it was a plan devoid of any details. We would have to figure things out along the way. Together, we could.

Lying in his arms later that night, a bedsheet wrapped around our naked bodies, I stirred, and a thought popped into my head. I had neglected to check in with my mum since I had arrived at Beirut airport. A quick text would reassure her that I was having the time of my life. Oz was sleeping peacefully, and I carefully unwound myself from his embrace.

I shuffled out of the bed, slipping into a bathrobe, and rooted around for my mobile. It was dead. I hooked it up to my charger and once it had enough power it buzzed continuously: a text, a voicemail and five missed calls. Surely my over-anxious mother, trying to establish I was still alive. I read the text message first. As the words registered in my brain, the phone slipped out of my hand and clattered to the floor.

23

'Abbie! Where the hell are you?' Amy's voice cut right through me as I listened to her voice message for the third time. 'For God's sake, call me back. Dad's had a heart attack.'

The next few hours were a blur. Oz woke once he heard me shouting when the call connected. My sister's voice was quivering; sobs intermingled with words, with an infuriating delay. Cardiac arrest. Critical but stable. Evesham general hospital.

I calmed her by promising I would get on the first flight out. But once I had hung up, I started shaking. Oz rubbed my arms as he held me tightly.

He took charge after that. A late-night taxi service was called from reception and a rate agreed with the driver. Oz's Arabic was good enough that I didn't even have to think, except to put one foot in front of the other. He called the airline and had my ticket changed so I would be on the next flight to London.

I kept dozing off in the cab, my head lolling in the crook of Oz's neck. Every few minutes a jolt would shake me awake to a brief moment of disorientation. Outside the taxi was total darkness. The street signs in Arabic, illuminated by headlights, were incomprehensible to me.

At immigration, tears were streaming down my cheeks. Oz pushed them away with his thumbs, holding my head. 'Please, Abbie, please don't cry.'

'I ... I don't know what to think, what to say.'

'There is nothing to say. Your family is your priority. You have my number. Call me when you can. Don't think about us. Your father. He is the most important thing in the world to you right now.'

I shivered, my teeth chattering. Caffeine kicking in, no doubt, after the coffee Oz and I had ordered after we arrived at check-in.

'Thank you for getting me here.'

'*Her zaman*. Always, Abbie, and forever.' His lips caressed mine briefly.

I lost myself once more in his eyes, seeing flecks of burnt orange hidden in the depths of the melted caramel before he hugged me. As his warmth radiated throughout me, a thought occurred to me: when would I see him again?

This wasn't how we were meant to say goodbye. We needed to talk about our plans, but how could I give them even a second of my time when Dad was lying in a hospital bed thousands of miles away?

I showed my passport to the man at the gate and laid my handbag down on the conveyor. I kept turning my head to catch one more glimpse. Oz stood there behind the barrier and didn't move; his jaw set, arms folded, as if hugging himself. I retrieved my bag at the other end, turned for one last look and waved. The automatic doors closed behind me, cutting off my view. I staggered to the nearest bench and sobbed.

'What a lovely sight.'

I sprang from my slumber, spilling the last few drops of water from my paper cup onto the floor. 'Dad! You're awake.' I pulled my chair to his bedside.

He was connected to all manner of machines, indicating his heart rate was steady and blood pressure measured. I knew what the numbers on the dials meant from the health check I'd had at work last year, the one the company insisted on making its employees take every year.

His big, rough hand was nestled in mine. Bruises lined the IV drip which had found a spot among the wrinkles.

'You scared us, Dad. Mum is in a state.'

'She does fuss, your mum.'

'I think she has every right to. You had a heart attack and broke your knee when you fell.'

'I'll be fine.' He coughed. 'Can you get me a sip of water, pet?'

'Sure.' I poured him a cup from the metal cylinder which the nurse had brought in earlier, and brought it to his lips. He strained to lift his head and take a sip.

'Ah, that's better. My mouth is parched.'

A knock on the door and Mum and Amy came in. Mum looked awful, as though she hadn't slept in days – her hair scraped back, shirt untucked from her gardening trousers, one of her hand-knitted cardigans wrapped round her

265

shoulders. My sister waddled in, her pink maternity dress stretched over her watermelon-shaped bump. She waved away my attempt to give her my seat.

'If I sit, I'll never get up again.' She chuckled.

'Oh, Phil. You gave us such a fright,' Mum said, as she perched at the end of his bed, stroking the blanket on his legs.

'I'm fine, Jean. Why did you have to go and ruin Abbie's trip?'

'By the time you came out of the operation, she was already in the air.'

The message I had received upon landing had come as a relief. Amy ordered me to go home first and grab a few hours' sleep before I drove over. She said Mum wouldn't be able to handle it if anything happened to me as well.

'We called her, I promise. But I'm so happy to have her here with us.' Mum leaned over and squeezed my hand which was still clasping Dad's.

I hadn't had a chance to talk to the doctor yet. I had heard conflicting accounts as to how serious Dad's condition was. The broken knee alone would need weeks if not months of physio, as he couldn't put any weight on it. No doubt in my mind, though. I would have come back regardless of the diagnosis.

A nurse popped her head through the door. 'Time for your medication, Mr Jones. And visiting time is coming to an end. Sorry everyone, but he needs his rest.'

I kissed Dad's forehead, the scent of clinical soap on his skin. He held onto my arm a little longer and waited for Mum to step outside the room with Amy. The nurse was checking his drip and within earshot, so his voice was low and calm.

'Look after your mum, pet. She's had quite a fright. She's worried about how she's going to care for me and be with your sister once the baby's born. You're the strongest one in the family. I can rely on you, right? Take good care of both of them. Always.'

'Don't talk like that, Dad. The doctor said you're going to be fine.' I stroked his grey hair.

'Five minutes,' the nurse said to us, before leaving the room.

I sat back down on my chair wanting these five precious minutes with him – minutes I thought I might never have again. During the agonising flight over when I didn't have any updates on his condition, I was so sure I would never be able to talk to him again.

'How's work going?' Dad asked. 'Did you have that meeting with the partner? What does he think of your chances for promotion?'

'Umm. It's all looking good, Dad.'

'I'm so proud of you, pet. You'll be in his partner shoes one day, I know it. Then you could add to that deposit and spring for a two-bed flat. Wouldn't that be something. My little girl, a homeowner. Your future is as bright as that lovely face of yours.' He smiled before flinching in pain.

'What? What's the matter?' A wave of panic rose.

'My knee. Every time I move a fraction, it … Agh.' He clenched his teeth.

'Shall I call the nurse back in? Maybe they need to increase the painkillers.'

'It's OK, pet. I'll be all right. The pills are here.' He lifted a cup with two capsules inside and popped them in his mouth, straining to wash them down with a gulp of water. 'You'd better go and be with your mum. She needs you.' He laid his hand on mine. 'And please, remember what I said about looking after her and Amy. Promise?'

'I promise,' I whispered, trying to keep my emotions in check.

How could I tell him the truth about my plans now? He would be crushed.

Later that evening, once Barry had collected Amy and taken her back to Manchester, I excused myself and headed to my childhood room. I flopped onto my bed and cradled a pink fluffy cushion. I wanted to call Oz, but it would be well after midnight in Beirut. Sod that, I wanted him to walk through my bedroom door, kiss the top of my head, hold me and tell me it would all be fine. We had exchanged a few texts when I arrived at Heathrow before taking the tube back to my flat and later when I was leaving the hospital.

I scrolled through my contacts, and punched in Liz's number. The rings were endless.

'Abs?'

Her voice was soothing. 'Hi,' I whimpered.

'What's the matter?'

'Everything is terrible.' I pulled some pink fluff from the cushion and threw it on my bedspread. 'I'm at home.'

'London home?'

'No, my parents' home.'

'I thought you weren't coming back until Friday.'

'I was, but Dad had a heart attack and—'

'Shit. Is he OK?'

'He broke his knee when he fell. He's out of surgery and recovering, but I got the first flight back. My head feels like it's going to explode. I hooked up with Oz at the wedding and we made plans to quit our jobs and live together in Beirut, but my dad thinks I'm still on the road to make partner.' I sniffed and dabbed the snot from my nose on the sleeve of my jumper.

'Slow down, Abbie, you're talking too fast and not making any sense. Did you say you hooked up with Oz? Turkish sex god Oz?'

My shoulders slumped, and I placed the cushion behind my head as I sank back into my bed. 'Yup. Nada played matchmaker, and we ...'

'You shagged him?' Her voice rang with excitement.

'Several times.' I bit my lip.

'Abigail Jones, you total slut.'

I gave a half laugh. 'But it was so fraught when I left him. I haven't got a clue what I'm going to do. We didn't start planning anything. I'm staying up in Evesham until Monday and I'm not sure how to tell my parents about what I've decided. And how can I leave when my dad is so sick?'

'You're really going to quit your job and move to Beirut?'

'Yes.' There wasn't a lot of conviction in my voice and I knew what Liz was thinking. How could I leave her?

'Hmm. Maybe now's not the time to tell them your grand plan. Will your dad need care forever, or only 'til he's walking again?'

'Probably a couple of months at least. I need to go and chat with the doctor in the next day or so. I don't think Dad's giving us the full picture. Can you come up next weekend? I would love to talk it all through.'

'Course I can.'

Hearing her voice gave me a sense of clarity. Things had seemed dark a few minutes ago but now I had a plan, of sorts. The problem was, it was shrouded in lies and secrecy.

A few weeks later, I settled on the couch after dinner at my parents' house. Dad had been discharged a few days before with three different sorts of medication and a set of crutches. The dining room had been transformed into a bedroom, and a private carer came six hours a day to cover the hours when the NHS nurse wasn't there. Amy was getting close to her due date but still no sign of the baby. Oz had been busy with various projects. A work trip had taken him to China, and I was trying not to get paranoid about the lack of communication. During our last conversation, he suggested we park our plans until my life had settled down a bit, but I was itching to hand in my notice at work and to my landlord so we could begin planning our future.

The TV hummed in the background. Dad was sitting in his armchair, left leg outstretched, trying to complete the crossword he had started that morning. Every few minutes he clenched his jaw. I knew he was in pain, but he was irritated when Mum fussed at his slightest movement.

'How are things at work, sweetheart?' Mum asked, as she settled next to me on the sofa.

I took a sip of tea. This was as good a time as any to come clean. 'There's something I wanted to talk to you about.'

Dad's head peered out from the paper and Mum placed her cup on the side table.

'What's happened?' Mum said, her voice edged with concern.

'Nothing serious. It's that ...' I curled my legs further into the contours of the couch. 'I met someone. He's someone I met years ago when I was at King's and then we found each other again while I was Interrailing. He was at Nada's wedding and we've decided we're going to go back—'

'Are you talking about the Turkish boy you met in Istanbul?'

'How did you know he was Turkish?'

'Well ... I ...'

The colour drained from my cheeks. 'You read it. The letter. And the postcards. They *did* get here.'

'I didn't mean to read it, sweetheart. It was addressed to a Ms A. Jones. I thought it was for your sister and I didn't notice it'd been forwarded on from King's. Amy always told us to open mail before sending it up to Manchester. And when I read it ... well.' She settled back into the couch. 'We thought we were protecting you by not showing them to you.'

'*We?*' I turned to Dad.

He remained silent, like he always did in these 'female situations' as he liked to call them, which usually involved Mum and Amy.

'Abbie, please listen to me,' Mum continued. 'You were off to law school, had this incredible training contract. And then suddenly this letter came. There was all this talk of him wanting you to come back to Istanbul, a crazy mother, and some girl who was a drama queen. It sounded like an episode of *Corrie*.'

'But you had no right to hide them.'

She placed her hand on mine. 'You were much younger back then, impressionable. We had seen the mistakes your sister had made by running after the first guy who turned her fancy. We didn't want you following the same path. You wouldn't have known what you'd be giving up. And I should know because ...' She looked down at her lap and pursed her lips. 'Never mind.'

'Because what, Mum? Because you threw your life away for Dad?'

The look on her face made me realise I had hit a nerve.

The scene of my first day of university suddenly came flooding back – when Dad had made me promise to keep on top of my studies. That wasn't the only promise I had given him that day. He had told me that he bitterly regretted making Mum give up her dreams to be with him and made me promise never to let love get in the way of my future. I would always remember these words. 'When the time is right, you'll meet a nice bloke who'll make you happy, but make sure you're not making any sacrifices to be with him.'

But I had been eighteen. Never even been kissed, never known the intense feeling of being in love. I should never have made that promise.

Mum looked away. 'Your situation was nothing like mine. I didn't want you tossing away your dreams for a crush, that's all, when you had such a bright future ahead of you.'

'It might've been a crush back then, Mum, but it's a lot more than that now. We're going to quit our jobs, live in Beirut and join a humanitarian organisation.'

'You're what?' Dad piped up.

'Oh, my stars.' Mum shook her head.

'Stop being so bloody dramatic. I'm twenty-six, for heaven's sake. And I'm stuck in a job I hate. If I'd have got the letter, if I'd known what he'd said back then, maybe I wouldn't be here. I could've taken that charity job and he would've come back to London to work here and ...' It was then I realised I was standing, throwing my arms around, and my voice was probably loud enough for our neighbours to start twitching their net curtains. I hadn't appreciated I had never told them about the job offer from UNICEF, nor that these feelings of resentment had been building.

'Stop it!' Dad bellowed. 'Both of you, stop it!' He pushed himself up from the armchair and opened his mouth to speak. But there were no more words. The newspaper slipped from his grasp as he clutched his heart and tumbled to the floor.

'Dad!' I screamed even before Mum had time to react. I fell to my knees beside him, shaking him, trying but failing to lift him up. Mum sat paralysed on the couch. My hands trembled as I reached for my phone and called for an ambulance before attempting to revive him, guided by the calm voice of the operator on speaker phone.

But resuscitation proved futile. Dad lay unresponsive and there was nothing I could do.

24

Dark clouds rolled in from the north a week later and unleashed torrential rain. Was it too much to ask Wales for a respite from this bleak summer weather? I sat in my car outside Aunt Betsy's house in Mumbles, the windscreen wipers swiping frantically across the glass.

Barry had brought Amy and Mum down from Evesham yesterday but I had wanted to stay one more night in my childhood home, surrounded by memories, at last able to let go of the emotion I had bottled up for Mum's sake. Amy had come down from Manchester as soon as we broke the news, and together we had taken care of Mum while making arrangements for the funeral in Mumbles where Dad had grown up and had wanted to be buried. The service was at three this afternoon at the local church, followed by the wake at the Sailing Club.

Oz had wanted to fly over for the funeral, but I had told him not to. How could I have him here when the argument that led to Dad's death had been about him and our future together? His presence would only serve as a reminder to Mum about what had happened.

I wiped my shoes on the welcome mat and shook out my umbrella. The door was on the latch and I stepped inside.

Aunt Betsy was standing in the hallway and her sympathetic look made me crumble. I sank into her warm embrace. Her perfume was sharp but comforting.

'It's OK. There, there,' she said, stroking my back, my shoulders shaking. 'I'm here for you, pet. It'll all be OK.'

She handed me a tissue tucked away in the sleeve of her cardigan and I dried my eyes.

'You must be starving. I've made some tea and crumpets.'

I shrugged out of my jacket and hooked it onto the coat rack. 'That sounds perfect.'

'Why don't you go into the front room. Your mum's in there.'

The door creaked as I pushed it open and Mum was sitting on the sofa in total darkness. Aunt Betsy bustled in with a tray, poured out two cups and pulled back the heavy drapes. Daylight streamed through the net curtains, highlighting the silvery strands in Mum's auburn hair which appeared more conspicuous. Her cheeks were hollow and there were even darker rings round her eyes. She wore a black cardigan over a long black dress.

'I'll leave you both for a bit,' Aunt Betsy said. 'I want to pop to the church and check on the arrangements.'

I sat down on the couch, blowing away the steam from the cup before placing it back on its saucer. This was our first time alone since that fateful moment.

Mum looked up at me, her eyes swimming with tears. 'I miss him so much.'

I shuffled closer and put my arm around her shoulder. Tears spilled down her cheeks and mine as we sat there.

There were no words, only sobs and gasps for breath. We were both comforting each other, trying to cling to something we knew we could never get back – the moment before everything changed.

Mum wiped her tears with tissues from the box in the centre of the table while I blotted mine.

'I'm sorry, Abbie.' She turned and looked at me, smoothing my hair behind my ear. 'I never should've argued with you that day. I shouldn't have been so disapproving of your plans. We had no idea you were so unhappy.'

'It's not your fault. I should've known it wasn't the right time to tell you.'

'Would there ever have been a right time?' She sniffed and grabbed another tissue.

We sat in silence, grasping each other's hands, and waited for the tide of emotion to subside.

'What am I going to do, Abbie?' Mum said. 'Now he's gone. What am I going to do? I have no job, career, no savings.'

Her words took me by surprise. 'What about Dad's pension?'

'There isn't one.'

'What? But there must be. When we talked about my work pension a while back, he told me of the importance of putting money aside each month.'

'He didn't want you to know.'

'Know what?'

'He was too proud to admit we were in difficulties. There was no big redundancy; the bank made sure of that. Cost cutting, not enough in the coffers, they said. And after the time when they didn't promote him, he didn't like the idea of them managing his pension, for God knows what reason, so he took it upon himself to take it out and invest it, our future, in some overseas tech stocks, or something like that. They collapsed.'

'Why didn't you tell me this before? I could've helped you. How were you paying for the carer?'

'We'd already taken one of those drawdown mortgages on the house. We wanted to support your sister a while ago. Barry's showroom was in trouble and they needed help with some mortgage payments. There was some money left, like a savings pot. But now? I think I'll have to draw down some more or sell.' She turned her gaze to the window. 'But I love that house. It's our home; so many memories of you and Amy growing up. Your dad worked so hard to get it.'

I squeezed her hand and tried to absorb what she had told me.

'I sometimes think he did it deliberately,' she said. 'Left us like that, so we wouldn't go even more into debt with the carer.'

'No, Mum, don't say that. Listen.' I looked her directly in the eyes. 'No arguments. I'm going to help you. I've saved up a lot. Don't draw down any more on the house, the rates are horrendous, and the bank will end up owning more than they should. I'll be a senior associate before the year's out, with a big uplift in pay. I can help you. You'll never ever have to worry about money. And please, don't sell.'

'I can't, sweetheart. You're unhappy. You want to leave your job, move abroad.'

Dad's words to me in the hospital came front and centre into my mind.

'We're family. And family meant more to Dad than anything. And he'd want to know we were sticking together, and you had a future.'

'But what about the future you wanted?'

I blinked away the plan I had allowed myself to sketch out with Oz. 'It was a blip. A midlife crisis.' I laughed inside at the absurdity of that comment when I was only twenty-six. 'My job isn't that bad.'

'And this boy?'

'If he and I are meant to be together, we will find a way.'

The rain pelted my Clapham flat's windowpanes the following Sunday. All week Oz had been trying to coordinate this call, keen to talk to me about something important, but I had been struggling with how to tell him that we could no longer dare to dream our dream. But I hoped that somehow, we could still make a new plan together.

I took a large swig of wine to calm my nerves as I settled in my armchair. The conversation had been strained so far. It was like Oz was talking away from the mouthpiece. I was missing every other word. For all the technological advances, why was a call from Istanbul to London proving so painful?

'There's something I want to talk about,' I said, clutching the glass.

'*Lütfen*, please, let me go first. I have wanted to speak to you before today, and I understand you are in pain and have not had the strength to call. There is no easy way to say this, and it breaks my heart to cause you more sadness, but ...'

My heart thundered in my chest.

'Dima and I are giving our marriage another chance.'

'Oh.' That was the only word I could manage. Numbness was instant. It hadn't ever fully gone away but here it was again, leaving me dumb and immobile as the rain lashed the window harder and faster.

He sighed deeply. 'I never meant to hurt you. Please forgive me. I am sorry, sorrier than you will ever know. I hope one day you will understand my reasons. You deserve to be happy, Abbie, and I can't give that happiness to you.'

I didn't say anything. I couldn't even summon the strength to be angry or hurt, or to urge him to offer me a more credible explanation or even to tell him why I had news too, news that would have tested the strength of our commitment to each other. But it was too late. Liz would have said 'it must have been love'. But what did that matter; it was over now.

25

Now

September

The Istanbul hotel room was bathed in strong sunlight and my dress clung to me in a mass of perspiration and sand. I rubbed my fingers over my forehead, trying to massage away the throbbing in my head. Amy was snoring loudly in the roll-out bed next to mine and there was no movement from next door. I checked the time on my mobile.

'Shit!' I hissed when I saw the missed call and text message that had come through after I had crashed last night.

I would love to see you for coffee. 10 a.m. at the Pierre Loti Café? I hope you can make it. It would be wonderful to see you again. Oz.

As I scrolled back to read what I had written I groaned, and Amy stirred in her bed. I crept into the bathroom and splashed cold water on my face and tied my hair up in a bun. What should I do? Text him back and apologise profusely or see him and explain my hideous inappropriateness face to face?

I looked up the café on my phone and saw it was one of the must-see places in the city for breathtaking views, 'giving you the perfect ending to your stay and leaving you with unforgettable memories of Istanbul'. Would this be the chance for that 'closure' that hadn't happened back in April? If I didn't meet him, would the memory of our time together continue to haunt me?

The café was a fifteen-minute taxi ride from our hotel, set high above the city on a hill. I searched the tables that were set with checked cloths and finally saw him sitting at one by the shade of a tree, looking out to the water.

I smoothed the creases of my green sundress and approached. 'Oz?'

He turned and when our eyes met, I had to steady myself with a hand on the table.

'Abbie.' He grinned broadly and stood up, kissing me on both cheeks. Instinctively I closed my eyes and smelled his familiar scent before shaking myself back to the present. 'Would you like some tea?'

I nodded and sat down. Oz attracted the attention of the waiter and spoke in Turkish, pointing to his glass that was half drunk.

'I am so happy you messaged me,' he said.

I bit my lip hard. 'I'm so sorry about that. I didn't mean to write what I did.'

He laughed warmly. 'It is OK. Nada told me about your celebrations.'

I looked up in surprise. 'She did?'

'Yes. I met her in Ankara at the first part of Yaman's wedding and she told me you were in Istanbul. I wanted to call you, but I only have your old number, and it didn't connect. I was held up at work and by the time I got to the reception you had already gone.'

I puffed out my cheeks, relieved I had left when I did. God knows what I would've done in my drunken state.

'Did you have a good night?'

'Yes and no.'

'Why, what happened?'

The waiter brought my tea, and it was instantly soothing and eased my nausea. 'I had a fight with Liz, and my sister ... well, let's just say the shed lock-up prank when I was eight has been outdone.' I twisted the glass on its saucer, letting my fingers grow warm as I clutched it.

'What did you fight with Liz about?' he asked.

I sighed. 'Remember all those years ago when I came here, and we took that sunset cruise and talked about our dream jobs?'

'Of course, I remember. I remember every single moment of every single day I ever spent with you.'

My eyes met his at those words and my response stuck in my throat. I looked away to the Golden Horn estuary, noticing for a second that the guidebook was accurate in its description of its view, before gathering my thoughts. 'I finally told Liz about the job at UNICEF that I didn't take. She was annoyed at me for not confessing about it all those years ago.'

'I am sure she will eventually understand why you didn't tell her.'

'I hope.' I glanced over at him, my eyes meeting his again. 'Do you ever wonder what might have happened if I had read your letter?'

He nodded. '*Evet.*' He reached out to hold my hand. I shivered at his touch and pulled it away immediately, instinctively playing with my engagement ring.

'I'm sorry,' he said, looking contrite.

'Oz, I—'

'Please, Abbie, let me speak first.' His face looked like he was steeling himself to find the words. 'I know I have no right to say this to you, but if I don't I will always regret it. It has been in my heart for so long and when I saw you in Paris ...' He clenched his jaw and breathed deeply. 'I wish you a lifetime of happiness with your fiancé, but ... *seni seviyorum*. I love you. I still love you. I will always love you. And—'

'Oz, please.' I shook my head. 'You can't say that.' A breeze picked up and I hugged my arms tightly. 'I'm engaged; you're married to Dima—'

'Dima and I separated years ago.'

'What? Why?'

'It is a long story.'

'How did I not know this?'

'When I finally got my life back together, I asked Yusef how you were, and he told me you were already in a relationship and it was serious. And then you came back into my life again in Paris and I could see how happy you were, you got engaged that day; it didn't seem right to say anything. Then in April, I had so wanted to talk to you, but I understand it was a bad time for you and I tried, I really tried to move on.' He looked away to the railing where a pigeon had flown down and was cooing. 'But then you came back here, to my home, and you texted me suddenly last night after I had tried to call you on a number that was no longer yours. When I thought I had lost all hope of seeing you again, there was this message. I had wondered whether maybe ...'

I stood up, suddenly feeling light-headed. 'I told you, Oz. That was nothing more than a drunken text. A mistake. It was a mistake to have come here and let you say those words to me after all this time. You have no right to tell me them.'

The noise of other diners clinking cups, having conversations, laughter – all these sounds dropped away. The only thing I could hear was my heartbeat.

I picked up my handbag from the chair, his words swimming around my brain. 'I have to go.'

Oz leapt up and grabbed my hand. 'Please, Abbie. Please, let's talk. Can't you feel this?' He pulled my hand to his heart – its quick rhythm matched mine. 'This force that keeps bringing us back together is so strong. I can't believe you don't feel anything too. Please. *Beni affet*. Forgive me; for all the pain I caused you. I need you to understand everything.'

I pulled my hand from his grasp. 'Please, Oz. Don't do this. I have a fiancé who I love very much. I only came here to apologise for sending that text. Thank you for the tea, but it's best that I go.' And with those words I walked away and didn't turn around again. I had to get back – to the hotel, to my home and to Charlie.

This wasn't 'closure'. I had opened up an old wound and now it was even more painful. My head spun. I should never have given Oz the opportunity to say he loved me for the very first time. It had taken me over two years to move on after he told me he was giving his marriage another chance. It had hurt so much, I couldn't put myself in that situation again.

26

Seven Years Ago

December

'This feels *so* wrong.' I stretched out an arm to the side, fingertips brushing the glass of fruit punch. Bringing it to my lips, I raised my head off the sun lounger to take a sip.

'Which part? The drinking alcohol at midday, or getting skin cancer before we're thirty?' Liz giggled, readjusting her bikini top.

'Lying on a beach in Thailand in December, when I should be back at work.'

Liz leaned on an elbow, pushing her sunglasses up on her head. 'Abbie, you've been signed off. You've got to rest, take care of yourself.'

I placed my drink back on the low table beside me and rubbed the back of my neck. 'I'm not an invalid, Liz.'

'No, but you had a breakdown and your family packed you off for some R&R with your bestie, so you have no choice but to do everything I say.'

I sat up and hugged my knees, the weight of the memory from a few weeks ago causing me to fold in on myself.

'I'm sorry.' Liz wrapped an arm around my shoulder. 'That was a bit blunt.'

I shook my head. 'No. It's fine. It's just hard remembering that day.'

'I'm here now. We've got all the time in the world to talk it through.'

I settled back down on my sun lounger, the salty air filling my lungs with every breath. Not a single cloud in the sky. Liz was right, this was the perfect place for R&R. For the first time in months, I had slept last night – my sleeping tablet lying on my bedside table unused. But I couldn't escape from my life back home forever.

'This place is amazing, Liz. I no longer resent you for leaving me and travelling the world,' I said with a cheeky smile.

'Hey, you know I wasn't abandoning you. It wasn't my fault Mum decided to sell the flat and give me a large chunk of the proceeds. And I did ask you to come with me, remember?'

I nodded. She had, but there was no way I could have left – not when I had to be there for Mum.

'What time's your next shift?'

Liz scooped up her watch from her bag. 'An hour.'

'Is Mary coming to the beach before you go?'

'Yup.' She flopped back on her sun lounger, twirling her fingers in the sand.

'Hmm.' I studied her.

'What?'

'You've got it bad, haven't you?'

She nibbled her bottom lip. 'I think this is it.'

I sat leaning back on my elbows. 'What? Really?'

'I'm crazy about her.' She stretched her arms dramatically above her head. 'I've never felt like this about anyone. And it's not just because she's this shit-hot barrister who kicks ass in court, but ...' Her face fell.

'But what?'

'I'm not sure she feels the same way about me.'

'I'm sure she does.'

'I think she thinks it's a holiday fling.'

'Tell her it isn't for you. She's probably getting mixed messages. You've always put out this casual vibe with everyone you've dated.'

'Have I?

'It's like a defence mechanism, in case they break up with you, so you won't be left heartbroken.'

'No wonder I've never been with anyone longer than a few months.'

'Talk to her about how you feel.'

'You think it's that simple?'

'Oh, heck knows, Liz. My love life is a disaster. You probably shouldn't be taking advice from me.' I stared out to sea.

'You're still thinking about him, aren't you?'

'Who?' I asked casually.

'You know who. I know it still hurts. But you've got to think of yourself now. You've run yourself into the ground with work and everything else. It's time Abigail Jones took control of her life. Or even, just lived it.'

A waiter appeared to remove our empty glasses, passing over the drinks menu.

'Want another?' Liz asked. 'Drunk on the job wouldn't be the best idea, but you can stay if you want.'

I didn't want our time together to end. It was our first proper catch-up since I had arrived in Phuket two days ago. A trip of a lifetime paid for by the increase in salary from my promotion at work, though I had got a 'friends & family' discount as Liz worked at one of the hotel's restaurants. Throwing myself into work had helped distract me from the grieving process and eventually led to the promotion, given that I had hardly taken a day off in two years. I was getting near to the peak of my career, according to one of the partners at the firm. Only now, it looked like everything was hanging in the balance after being signed off sick.

'Hello, beautiful.' Mary leaned over Liz's sun lounger. With no thought to who was around them, they locked lips. It was long and sensual.

I cleared my throat and waved the waiter away. The kiss continued before they finally broke apart. Mary perched on the edge of the lounger. A shirt was tied loosely over her swimsuit, sunglasses perched on her pixie haircut. Liz couldn't take her gaze off her.

'So, Abbie. Given any more consideration to what I said?' Mary raised an eyebrow, facing me.

'What have you two been conspiring about?' Liz's eyes twinkled.

'I told Abbie that she should think of switching to the Bar. It's not unheard of, changing track. Corporate law is all well and good, but there's no need to be trapped being a solicitor if it doesn't make her happy. I think Abbie would make a brilliant barrister. We had a good chat about it yesterday after lunch, while you were at work.'

'That's fantastic!' Liz exclaimed.

I folded my arms. 'Well ... I haven't yet—'

'And you could put her in touch with the right people?' Liz clutched Mary's hands.

'Of course I would. Our chambers could use some more mature blood.'

I gave a mock hurt look.

'No offence. It's just most new recruits are fresh from their studies, with no real work experience. You'd be a huge asset.'

'But—'

'But what, Abbie?' Liz said. 'These last two years have been shit for you, and I know how much you hate your job.'

'I'll print off some info for you,' Mary said. 'And when I get back to work next week, I'll speak to James Simons QC, our Head of Chambers. Perhaps you could come and do a mini-pupillage with us and follow me on one of my immigration cases; see why I love to talk about what I do all the time.'

She kissed Liz on the tip of her nose which then led to a more intimate embrace.

Suddenly I felt like a third wheel. 'I'll ... um ... see you tonight,' I mumbled, grabbing my things.

Liz gave me a low wave, but her lips remained firmly locked with Mary's. It was great to see her so happy, but a pang of jealousy strummed in my heart. I shifted the beach bag on my shoulder and padded away. The sand burned my feet and I hopped over to the nearest path, which led me back to the resort. There were only a handful of guests dotted around the infinity pool and we'd pretty much had the private beach to ourselves.

I considered what Mary had said. If I did change career track, life would be different. Could I afford to do it?

Mary said being a barrister gave her a lot of fulfilment. She painted a different world to the one I knew. The flexibility of being self-employed sounded appealing, too. But I would have to fund the changeover course myself or apply for a scholarship to help, which would mean using a chunk of my savings I had earmarked for other things.

Dad would question the lack of a monthly salary and benefits of being an employee. But Dad wasn't alive to pass judgement any more. In place of his words, a hollow feeling had nestled inside me; his last voice message sitting on my phone asking how my latest review at work had gone – a message I often replayed to ease the pain of losing him.

A blast of aircon greeted me at the threshold of the hotel. Water trickled from fountains onto seas of pebbles in the centre of the vast atrium. I could happily sit and stare at the rhythmic motion of it flowing for hours. This was the most at peace I had felt since ... my trip to Syria. *Flip. No more tears – I was out of tissues.* I looked skyward to avert their flow.

A lady wearing traditional Thai dress passed by. Her hands were clasped in front of her like she was praying. 'Sawasdee-ka,' she said, with a twang in her voice before walking by.

I took the lift to the third floor and unlocked the door to my room. A heady scent of lilies and ... Another sniff.

Jasmine. My beach bag landed with a thud on the marble floor. There on my bed between two swan-like creatures made from towels was a posy of jasmine. I cradled it in my hands, bringing the petals to my nose. I didn't dare to close my eyes. It would be a winding path down onto memory lane if I did – the scent I associated with my time in Beirut; memories that had long been buried under months of grief and loss.

My mobile vibrated. Another text from Mum. They had increased in frequency since I had come out here. But I couldn't blame her. She was worried. No one wants to see their child collapse and mumble incoherently while waiting for the paramedics to arrive. What had been the trigger that day? A newly pregnant Amy and I had come to help Mum clear out the family home after she had decided it was time to move on with her life and go and live in Mumbles – to be in the one place she believed held Dad's spirit because his ashes had been scattered close to the lighthouse.

Insomnia had plagued me for months and a chest infection I couldn't shift meant I was heavily drugged up, so sharing a bottle of wine while sorting through my childhood memories wasn't that smart with hindsight; the pain of losing Dad coming to the forefront of my mind again with every photograph of him and me in Mumbles – blissful summers and intrepid adventures along the Welsh coastline. I had always been closer to him than Mum.

I sat on the edge of my bed and pulled out the bookmark from my novel on the bedside table. A picture: one of the many I had unearthed from a box under my childhood bed that day we helped Mum move; not of me and Dad but me and Oz; the one of us smiling at the camera on the boat in Istanbul. An ache nestled deep and low in my chest and I brought my locket to my lips as I stared at the image. It was time to let him go and move on with my life.

27

Five years earlier

February

'You look good in that wig,' Liz said, staring at my reflection in the mirror of the ladies at the grand hall of the Middle Temple.

'Really? You think? It's so itchy,' I sighed, adjusting my black gown.

'Here.' She pulled a lipstick from her clutch bag and thrust it at me. 'You're too pale. This will brighten things up.'

I wiped my palms down my black skirt and took the tube from her. 'I'm so nervous. What's wrong with me?'

'Come on, the ceremony's over. Now we get pissed on champagne.'

'I can't.'

'Why not? You've been studying, taking exams and doing whatever it is you trainee barristers must do to get to this point, for like forever. And it's your thirtieth birthday tomorrow. You deserve one night off!'

'I wish.' I thrust out my chin and made my lips crimson. 'All my new colleagues are here. I can't do anything to embarrass myself and champagne always goes straight to my head.'

'All drinks go to your head.'

I smacked my lips together, wrinkled my nose and grabbed a tissue from beside the sink. 'I think I'm nervous because my whole blinkin' family's here.'

Liz readjusted her red dress. 'Can't believe they all came.'

'Neither can I. I was hoping for a polite "congrats, dear, but it's too far for your Aunt Betsy and me to travel" from Mum, and a "sorry we can't leave the kids" from Amy and Barry. But they're all treating it like a mini-holiday and insisting on taking me out tomorrow, too.'

'They're proud of you and want to be here for your big three-oh.'

'They could've sent a card.'

'You're in a grump today, aren't you? Maybe I can ask my *fiancée* to go easy on you tomorrow if you were to let your hair down.' Her shoulders danced, and she puckered her lips.

'You're never going to tire of saying that word, are you?'

'Nope.'

She held her ring to catch the light and caught me staring. 'Your time will come.'

'Oh, stop. I don't have time to be dating. And I don't need someone in my life.'

'Why not? You've finally got the career you want; where's the harm in wanting to share your successes with someone who truly cares about you, someone who makes your insides explode when you're near them?' She had a look resembling a poodle begging its owner for a treat.

'You're incorrigible.'

'I'm in love,' she said with a sweep of her hands, admiring her reflection in the mirror.

'Liz, please stop trying to make everyone as happy as you are. Let me enjoy watching you become a beautiful bride.'

She grinned and applied some lip gloss. 'Think about it. It's fate. If you hadn't joined me out in Thailand you never would've met Mary, and you wouldn't be standing here.'

'It's not fate. I would've come across Mary eventually.'

She shook her head. 'Nah-ah. I was dithering. I wasn't ready to leave Thailand. You encouraged me to follow Mary back home when her holiday ended. Mary would've been one hot, sexy holiday fling if it hadn't been for you.'

I knew I had to get back to the ceremony so there was little point in arguing with Liz about the idea of predestination. 'All right, Liz. It's fate. Fate that I had a nervous breakdown and went to Thailand for a "sabbatical" to figure things out.'

She linked her arm in mine and stared at our reflections. 'Don't say it like that. I hated myself for not being around when you were going through so much.'

'It's not your fault, Liz. And you were there for me in the end.'

The door burst open and heels clacked against the marble floor. 'There you are,' Amy announced, a drop spilling from her champagne flute as the door swung back on her. 'What's going on in here? You've been in the loo for over ten minutes. Barry's chewing the ear off some lawyer person, trying to convince him a second-hand BMW convertible is the car of the season, and I am sooo bored.'

'What lawyer?' My palms grew moist.

'Think his name was James.' She took a swig of her glass.

'God, not James Simons, the Head of Chambers?' I said.

She placed her flute carefully on the side of the sink and adjusted the hem of her pink ribbed dress upward before scooping up her glass again. 'Is he important or something?'

'Yes, he is. He's a Queen's Counsel and a Deputy High Court judge.'

'Ooh, like Judge Judy?'

'You watch too much daytime TV.'

'You try amusing two kids under five every bloody day, seven flippin' days a week.'

She was slurring her words. Clearly, it wasn't her first glass she was nurturing like a newborn.

'I'd better go and rescue him, Liz,' I said. 'Can we talk later?'

She nodded. 'Of course. Go, go.'

Amy grabbed my hand and led me out of the ladies. 'There are some cute guys here.' Her eyes widened, and she nudged me in the shoulder.

'Really? I hadn't noticed. Hard to tell when everyone is wearing a wig.'

'There she is, my beautiful niece,' Aunt Betsy hollered from quite a distance away, her arms outstretched, Mum at her side. She carved her way through the crowd towards me, her lilac dress arranged over her frame like a tent. Her hat had a wide brim which bore a small arrangement of posies.

'We're so proud of you, pet.' Aunt Betsy flung her arms around my neck, unsteadying my headpiece. 'Aren't we, Jean?'

'Yes, we are. More than you will ever know.' Mum's voice was cracking. 'You deserve this, all of this.'

She was going to set me off, but a wolf whistle got my attention. 'Abbie!' Barry was flapping his arm in my direction, his other draped around James Simons's shoulder.

A tray of champagne hovered into view, borne by a waiter, but I excused myself and went over to see what the commotion was.

'Abbie, great news. Jimbo here is a man of excellent taste. He's passing through Manchester next week for a job and said he'd pop by the dealership. I have a rather special vintage Aston Martin I think he's going to love.'

Did he call the Head of Chambers Jimbo? Beads of sweat began to appear on the back of my neck.

James Simons beamed. 'I have to say your brother-in-law knows his cars. I have a small collection, and this would be an excellent addition.'

'Really?' The pitch of my voice rose.

'Don't be so surprised, Ms Jones. We silks know how to let our hair down after our *jobs*.' He laughed. A real belly laugh. I couldn't say I had ever seen him appear so jovial.

Barry slapped him on the back. 'Absolute pleasure to meet you, Jimbo. Here's my card. Give us a tinkle' – he waggled his fingers against his ear, mimicking a phone – 'when you're in my neck of the woods, and we'll sort you out. Excuse me, I think I need to go see my missus.'

'Charming, quite a charming fellow,' James Simons said, as they parted.

I nodded and looked over to where Barry had encircled Amy's waist from behind and given her quite a public display of affection, kissing her hard on the cheek.

'We are delighted to have you at our chambers, Ms Jones,' James Simons said. 'Mary has given me nothing but positive reports about your work. Although I appreciate you are older than some of our new recruits and probably already know which avenue you would like to specialise in, we believe it is important our youngsters get an opportunity to gain experience in all fields of the law our chambers specialises in during their pupillage.'

I nodded, not wanting to say there was only one path I wished to follow – the one Mary specialised in.

'I'd like to introduce you to someone. Charles!' He tapped a tall man on the shoulder. 'Excuse me for the interruption,' he said, addressing an unknown group of people. 'Could you spare Mr Logan for a moment?'

I stood there, my palms stiff and moist, praying no one else from my family would come over and interrupt us. James Simons was not one to talk to pupils, let alone someone who had just been called to the Bar. The guy turned, his green eyes smiling back at me, eyes I had seen before, many years ago.

'Charles, this is Ms Jones.'

We stood staring at each other for what felt like too long. The air between us crackled and fizzed and my heart thundered in my chest. He was even more handsome than I had remembered.

'A pleasure.' Charles extended his hand and shook mine. The side of his mouth turned up at the same time as the eyebrow above.

We were still shaking hands. I couldn't believe it was him.

'I've heard a lot about you, Ms Jones,' he said, with a hint of a teasing tone, 'but I haven't had the opportunity to meet you since ... you came to our set.'

'I am entrusting you to Charles for the next couple of weeks,' James Simons continued. 'He's our number one corporate barrister, and you'll be working with him for a while. Then you'll rotate on to someone else. I haven't yet decided. I believe once you make your decision for specialism, it will be a well-informed one. Ah, Gerald.' He extended a finger as someone passed by. 'Excuse me.' He nodded at us and walked away.

I peered up at Charles, tucking some stray hairs beneath my wig.

'It must be fate,' he said, his eyes sparkling.

'I'm sorry I didn't call. I ... I lost your card.'

'No need to apologise. It was a long time ago. About nine years if I remember correctly?'

I nodded, remembering the time at the recruitment fair when he had sat in a booth and tried to tempt King's students to consider training as a barrister.

He smiled. 'I see my art of persuasion needs some fine-tuning if it's taken you this long.'

'I was dead set on being a solicitor back then, and I did become one. But I had a bit of an epiphany on a sabbatical in Thailand a while back.'

'Did you turn Buddhist?'

I laughed. 'No, nothing like that. But I did meet Mary Baker, and she was inspiring to say the least.'

'Ah, so you're Mary's prodigy. I've heard a lot about you. Looks like I'll have my work cut out trying to convince you corporate law is where you should be.'

'You can try,' I said, before realising I was coming off too flirty for a setting like this. He dipped his head before looking back up at me.

I grabbed a glass of champagne from a passing waiter to steady myself at the same time as he did, and our fingers brushed together. Mine tingled at his touch.

'And who do we have here?' My sister materialised beside me, breaking the moment. She was sashaying from side to side and held out her hand as though she were waiting for it to be kissed. Charles took it awkwardly and shook it.

'This is Charles Logan, and this is my sister, Amy,' I said.

'A pleasure to meet you,' he said, blinking rapidly.

Amy giggled. 'Everyone in this room sounds like Colin Firth, all posh and hoity-toity,' she said, grasping my shoulder, causing my wig to fall off my head. I spilled some champagne as I picked it up off the floor.

'It was lovely to meet you again, Mr Logan. I look forward to working with you. But if you'll excuse me.' I took Amy's arm and led her away, peering over my shoulder to catch another glimpse of Charles. We held each other's gaze until I had reached the doorway.

'Are you trying to humiliate me?' I hissed, putting my wig back on. 'Can't you see how important this night is for me?'

'Yes, I can. It's all I've heard about from Mum for weeks, months even. In fact, it's all I ever hear. Abbie's big achievement, Abbie's law school graduation, Abbie's twenty-first birthday,

Abbie who saved her sister from drowning. No one ever came to Manchester for my flipping birthdays, no one cared when I got my hairdressing certificate. And why?'

I shrugged, taken aback at her admission.

'Cos nothing I ever do is good enough, not when I've got a little sister who walks on water. Little miss big-shot solicitor turned big-shot barrister, mixing with all these posh, rich nobs. You're just like them, too. Your family isn't good enough for you.'

She raised a hand, silencing my attempt at a retort.

'Don't tell me you don't think it,' she continued. 'We're an embarrassment to you. You couldn't wait to leave home, go to London, mix with all these Oxbridge types—'

'At least I made something of my life, made Dad proud,' I shot back. 'And I didn't cause him unending stress for years, not finishing school and running off with a drug dealer and then turning up back home knocked up by some car salesman.'

The sting was instant. I hadn't seen her arm move until her hand had whistled past my face.

'Get lost,' she spat. 'You can stick your thirtieth birthday up your arse. I never want to speak to you again.' She turned and stormed back into the hall.

Out by the cloakroom, Liz was beckoning me with her hand. I could still feel the tingling from the slap on my cheek as I went over, and I prayed there was no red mark to show it.

'Quick,' Liz said, tugging the sleeve of my gown.

'What's the rush?'

She dragged me over to the coat attendant. 'Got your ticket?'

I handed it to the lady as Liz passed across hers. 'But I haven't said goodbye to Mum and Aunt Betsy. And Amy and I had the biggest fight with—'

'I heard it. We all did. But you haven't got time. It's gone half six and it'll take us twenty-five minutes to get where we're going and it's icy on the pavements.'

'Get where?' I asked, putting my arms into the sleeves as Liz held my coat open for me.

'I'll tell you on the way. Give me your wig and gown. I'll write a note asking Mary to take them back to chambers for you,' she said as she scrawled on a scrap piece of paper, handing it over to the attendant.

'Ms Jones?'

I turned around to see Charles Logan coming towards me.

'Give me a minute, Liz. I'll meet you outside.'

'Make it quick,' she said before heading out. I guessed she had some secret early birthday treat planned for me.

I looked up at Charles expectantly – his deep-set green eyes not leaving mine. He removed his wig and shook out his sandy hair from its flat state. 'I was wondering … umm … if whether … umm. Would you like to have coffee with me sometime?'

A date? It had been a long time since I had been on a date and there was no denying there was an attraction between us. A flutter tickled my stomach. Maybe now I had qualified, I could finally relax and focus on other aspects of my life.

'I'd like that,' I said finally, and his instant smile warmed my heart.

Twenty-five minutes later, I was facing Liz and didn't dare look round at the crowd gathering outside the Prince Charles cinema, north of Leicester Square, waiting to watch a Valentine's special of *An Affair to Remember*.

'Oz won't be here.' I sighed, still in utter disbelief this was what Liz had dragged me away for. It was the day before my thirtieth birthday – nine years since we first met, and the day Oz and I had jokingly arranged to meet for a date.

'You've said that every minute since we left the Middle Temple.'

'Liz, he ended it between us. This is ridiculous. I'm over him.'

She folded her arms and looked at me with eyebrows raised. 'Really? If you were over him, you wouldn't be constantly comparing every guy you meet to him, always finding fault, giving lame reasons why you're not ready to be getting serious with anyone. Look at you. I know you're secretly hoping he's going to be here.'

'That's not true. In fact, someone asked me out tonight, and I said yes. And maybe it could be the start of something serious.'

Liz's eyes suddenly widened as she looked over my shoulder. 'Oh my God. He's here.'

28

Now

October

I picked up the note from the box.

I pulled these down from the loft for you. Hope you have fun reminiscing. Love you x

We were moving into our new house in a week and Charlie had asked what was in these boxes that he had never seen me open. I had told him I would go through them and toss out any rubbish before the movers came next week. It was a Sunday and he had left early to get some papers from chambers before heading up to Birmingham, ready to meet the solicitor on his case which was beginning tomorrow.

Cradling a bowl of cereal, I surveyed the scene in front of me. My life in four boxes. Three of them I had filled myself – they were the contents of my bedroom in Evesham and other stuff I had collected from my life in London before I'd moved in with Charlie. The last one Mum had filled for me with items from my childhood. None of them had been opened in years.

With a pair of scissors, I ripped off the tape to the box which was marked 'Bedroom'. From inside, I pulled out six guidebooks: one for each of the places Liz and I had visited on our Interrail holiday. I still couldn't believe she had bought these in advance of our trip – so thoughtful – and had lugged them around, delighting every time she brandished a new one as we headed off on our next adventure. Each one well thumbed, the spines cracked, pencil marks lining the margins.

Beneath the books were a collection of pages and leaflets from some of the rallies Liz and I had joined during our time at King's and after. There was a whole folder dedicated to the volunteer placement we had done with UNICEF. Buried underneath it, I found a letter from the same organisation – the letter that offered me a place on their graduate scheme. I had never shown this to anyone. A secret I had hidden away after I returned from my first trip to Istanbul.

Liz and I had made amends after our bust-up on my hen do. She blamed the alcohol and I had apologised for not confiding in her. But it wouldn't have made a difference if I had told her all those years ago. I was on a set path back then – determined not to veer from it.

Unearthing Merriam-Webster's Law dictionary, I sighed. Passing more exams in the year following graduation had pleased Dad no end. And that's all I had ever wanted, to please him; to never cause him any stress in the way Amy had. Only I had.

My eyes brimmed with tears as I slumped on the floor, holding one of the many certificates I had received from school – this one a debating competition from my time in the sixth form. It was only a record of attendance, but Dad had wanted to frame it. He put all my achievements in a frame.

'I miss you, Dad,' I cried into the silence. 'I miss you so much.'

Two hours went by and all I had gone through was the contents of one and a half boxes and a giant packet of tissues. A handful of postcards slipped out of the third box. Liz's postcards from Thailand; the ones she had sent me before my trip there, begging me to join her. That had been my turning point. Visiting her and meeting Mary. I owed them everything for setting me back on the right track.

Beneath the sun-filled images of south-east Asia was an old shoebox. My heart skipped a beat and my hands shook as I opened the lid. Inside was the Türkiye bracelet Oz had given me, along with other mementos of my first time in Istanbul. I put the bangle on and rolled it round and round my wrist thinking back to the conversation I'd had with him last month in Istanbul. Had it changed anything?

Tucked deep within the box lay a small pocket album. I clutched it tightly to my chest and breathed in and out to steady myself. Beneath the plastic sheets were all the pictures ever taken of me and Oz: the Photo-Me ones, us dancing at the Valentine's dance, sightseeing in Istanbul and Damascus and the one where we were watching the dawn in Beirut.

Here was our storyboard. A handful of days spent together – each one preserved in those smiles, embraces and kisses with a narrative of hopes and dreams.

I had thought that shutting them away in an album and hiding it in a box would mean I wouldn't ever have to deal with that part of my life again.

I suddenly grew even more curious about the contents of the fourth box. Mum had filled it for me the day I had my breakdown and I had never even opened it. Inside were school reports, more certificates, and … my eyes widened. A letter addressed to me at King's and forwarded on to my Evesham address, along with six postcards filled with all the sites I had visited in Istanbul. Oz's words. Words I had never had the chance to read.

It was suddenly hard to swallow. I grabbed my inhaler from beside me and pumped out the medicine, but my heart continued to thunder in my chest. I turned over the letter, where the seal had been ripped.

The sound of the doorbell ringing made me jump and I leapt to my feet, shoving the letter and postcards into the guide to Istanbul which I placed on the box before heading to the front door.

I opened it a fraction and there in the doorway stood Amy. Her hair was piled up in a messy bun, large hoop earrings dangling at her ears, her arms crossed over her denim jacket. This was the first time I had seen her since my hen party.

'What are you doing here?' I asked.

She shivered from the cold and hopped on the spot. 'I've come to apologise.'

'For what?'

She gave a slight shrug. 'For what happened at your hen do … and yeah … generally being a shitty sister. Sorry I haven't come before. It's been hard to get away with the kids and the business, but Mum made me realise I have to make things right between us.' She reached into her bag and pulled out a bottle of red. 'Can I come in?'

I let my initial frostiness thaw. 'Sure.'

She surveyed the scene in the living room: boxes overturned, paper littering the carpet and balls of damp tissues strewn around.

'I see you started without me,' Amy said.

'How did you know I was going through these today?'

'Mum told me, and she was worried.'

'She's got no reason to be.'

'Come on, Abbie. Take a look at yourself. You look like hell and the last time you cleared out our family home, you ...' She shook her head, her earrings dancing around her face.

I sat down, the weight of the memory of my breakdown pulling me into the couch. 'That was a long time ago. And this is different.'

'Is it?' She lifted up the empty packet of tissues. 'Mum knew sorting through these boxes might stir up memories about Dad. We were talking and I confessed what happened at your hen do. She was so mad at me – said she'd look after the kids and that it was about time I made amends. It's taken me three hours to drive here and I don't have the energy to drive back now.'

'I'll go and get some glasses then,' I said, unable to argue with that line of defence.

Amy poured us each a glass and stretched out on the floor, resting her back against the sofa, smoothing out her plaid skirt. I sat down in front of her.

She picked up a picture of me in my wig and gown, kneeling in front of the chancellor – the day I became a barrister. She groaned. 'God, I'm sorry about that night as well. I said some horrible things to you.'

My shoulders slumped. 'It's old news.' I took the frame from her and laid it back in the box. 'And I said some horrible things back, remember?'

'I guess we were both pretty awful to each other that night, and both too damn stubborn to apologise.' Her eyes glazed over as though she was back there. 'I was horribly drunk, and I knew something was going on with Barry. I was on edge.'

'That was the weekend you caught him cheating?'

'I'd had my doubts for a while. It was dead suspicious when he bailed early to go back to Manchester. In a bizarre way our fight saved me. If I hadn't decided to leave London not long after him because of that spat, I wouldn't have caught him and his secretary doing that *karma sutra* move he and I had *never* done.'

'I'm sorry,' I said, stroking her arm.

'What have you got to be sorry for? Best thing that ever happened to me.' She took a large sip of her wine.

'But I thought you loved Barry. You said you knew instantly he was "Mr Forever".'

'I loved the fact he owned a car dealership and I got to live in a nice part of Manchester and drive a BMW.'

I gave her a look, part critical, part pitying.

'Yes, I am *that* shallow.' She giggled before draining her drink and placing the glass on the floor. 'Did you think Charlie was your "Mr Forever" the moment you met him?'

I thought back to that day of the recruitment fair and then our first date. 'No. It wasn't instant. It was his thoughtfulness that attracted me to him initially. We were friends before we were lovers.'

'A slow burn, eh?' She topped up her glass. 'I'm still a firm believer in that instant chemistry, the feeling that you can't wait to tear each other's clothes off. In fact, there's someone new in my life.'

'There is?'

She nodded and looked suddenly bashful as she hugged her knees tight. 'His name is Dylan. He owns the pub next to the salon. Divorced, one kid. He's the reason why I didn't hook up with anyone in Istanbul. Wouldn't have met him if it hadn't been for you.'

'What have I got to do with anything?'

'Do I have to spell it out?'

I looked away, distracting myself with a few school reports which were lying on the floor. 'I don't know what you're talking about.'

Amy grasped my hand. 'Mum told me the whole story, which makes this apology visit even more important to me. All these years I thought the sale of our childhood home had paid for Mum's shop and my business. But it was you. *You* gave up all *your* money for us. That was money Dad told you to save for a place of your own but you gave it to me and Mum so we could both have a fresh start.'

'I didn't give up everything.'

'For two years you worked yourself to a breakdown to support Mum after Dad died and then you stood by me when my marriage collapsed and made sure I had a place to live with Mum by helping her buy a bigger place in Mumbles and then setting me back on my feet with my own business. I can't believe you did all that. All that money; money that was for your future.'

'I didn't need it. Carrying on renting wasn't the end of the world. And look at me now.' I swept my arm around the living room. 'This isn't too shabby, and I'm getting married in a castle and moving to Belsize Park.' I raised my glass and drained it.

'That was the saddest speech I have ever heard.'

'I am lucky, Amy. Can we leave it?'

She shook her head. 'Why did you do it, Abbie? I've been a crappy sister all these years. Come on, admit it.'

'Well ... if you exclude the time you locked me in the shed, cut the hair off all my favourite dolls and slapped me in the face at my call to the Bar ceremony, you haven't been that bad,' I said with a hint of sarcasm.

'What about when I almost got us both drowned and you saved me?'

I shook my head. 'I don't remember it like that. There was only one life jacket on that boat, and you gave it to me. You put my life ahead of yours. *You* saved *me*.'

'Mum and Dad didn't see it like that.' She cupped her hands in her lap. 'Nothing I did was ever good enough. I was a constant source of disappointment. You were right that night of your call to the Bar when you said I had caused them so much grief over the years. Dad never forgave me for that.'

'At least you weren't the one who killed him,' I whispered, my eyes blurring with tears.

The force of Amy's hug knocked my glass out of my hand, the last few drops spilling onto the carpet. But I didn't care.

'Oh, sis,' she murmured as she stroked my back, soothing me. 'You didn't kill him.'

I let the tears roll again and the relief was enormous.

'If Mum and I hadn't been arguing that day, then—'

'That's not true,' Amy interrupted. 'The hospital said as much. His heart was weak. He'd been a ticking time bomb since the first heart attack after he and I had that big spat. So, if you believe you killed him, then I was as much to blame. But we can't keep beating ourselves up over it.'

I breathed deeply. 'I think that's what I had been doing until the breakdown – blaming myself. When I went to Thailand to be with Liz, I didn't want to come back. She and I seriously considered running a bar over there.' I laughed at the absurdity of it.

'And what would've been wrong with that?'

'Nothing. Everything. Dad would've been horrified.'

She sighed. 'That's it. Anything you do, you hear Dad's verdict, even though he's been dead for almost a decade.'

I nodded. 'Didn't matter anyway. Liz was crazily in love. I encouraged her to come back for Mary, but the truth was ... I was being selfish. I did it for me. I missed her. I'd lost Dad, her and ...' His name stuck in my throat.

'And?'

'A dream of ... well, a dream of doing something different with my life.'

'Yet you chose to stay in law when you could've gone and done anything. Like run a bar in Thailand.'

'A fantasy, Amy. Once London life sucks you in, it's hard to escape. And yes, I'll admit it, I was desperate to keep on making Dad proud, even though I'd never sense pride, or anything else, from him ever again. And I guess I panicked. Switching to being a barrister wasn't a huge step from solicitor and I wanted to make sure I'd be earning enough to keep helping Mum. But I'm glad I did it. I get to help people, reunite families; it's rewarding, most of the time. Meeting Mary and hearing about her work was inspiring.'

We sat in silence for a while, letting our words sink in. It was a huge relief opening up to Amy. The pain at losing Dad had been growing in intensity since I got engaged, building to a crescendo when I had my asthma attack at Browns Bride as the owner painted the picture of Dad walking me down the aisle – an image that would never be realised. But seeing Oz again in Istanbul and unpacking all these memories had brought grief and sadness to the forefront of my mind yet again.

'Do you regret having kids with Barry?' I asked after a while.

'God, no.'

'Really? You always moaned about them when they were babies.'

'Barry never lifted a finger,' she said, reaching for the bottle again and shaking it before placing it back down when she found it empty. 'I did all the childcare; he expected me to be the perfect housewife. It was a lonely time.'

'I'm sorry. I had no idea.'

'But they're my little angels. I adore them. And now they're older, they're easier to manage, especially as I have a live-in babysitter in Mum. My life's back on track and I love bringing them up in Wales. Why d'you ask? Getting broody?' She nudged me in the arm.

Her question caught me off guard though it shouldn't have. Ever since the engagement it was all friends and family – and even those I didn't know well – had asked. An innocent question but so personal, so intrusive. And the truth was, Charlie and I still hadn't talked about it, not since that time a few weeks after we had got together – a conversation that we *had* to have even though our romance was in its early stages.

'Still got the wedding to get through first,' I managed to say with a half-smile, hugging my arms around my stomach – an empty feeling lying there.

Amy laughed suddenly.

I wiped my wet cheeks with one of the last remaining tissues. 'What's so funny?'

'I was just thinking. Mum's going to be dead pleased when she finds out we've cleared the air. And I really am sorry for what happened on your hen do. Life does get a bit stressful and I was letting my hair down. But pretending to drown so you would let yours down was a low blow.'

I nudged her with my shoulder. 'You're forgiven.'

'I'm starving,' she announced, 'and we need another bottle.' She shifted her position, knocking the guide to Istanbul over. The letter and postcards slipped out. 'What are these?' She turned a couple of the postcards over and read them.

'They're nothing,' I said, grabbing them from her.

'They're from that Turkish guy, the one you were going to run away with. These are the postcards and the letter Mum and Dad hid from you.'

'How do you know about all that?'

'The day we were packing up our home in Evesham, when Mum went with you to the hospital after you collapsed, I cleared up. There was this small box and I'm sorry, but I looked in it. Saw all these cute photos of the two of you in an album. I asked Mum about it a while after and she told me about how you wanted to live abroad with him but that it hadn't worked out and that she and Dad hadn't shown you something he'd written ages ago. I got well huffy with her – told her it was out of order, that she had no right to have done that. I know they were only protecting you cos they thought they'd failed me, but you are nothing like me and they should've trusted you to follow your own mind. But I didn't see these.'

I clutched them tightly in my hands, noticing the beautiful images that adorned each postcard.

'Have you read them?' she said.

I shook my head. 'I only found them just before you came. They were buried in one of the boxes. I think I'm scared.'

'Why?'

'Because ...' I swallowed. 'Because I'm worried it will bring back all these memories of a time when I thought my life was going to be different. I thought I'd buried my time with Oz. I'm meant to be moving in a week, getting married in three months and focussing on a future with Charlie, but Oz keeps turning up in my life. I saw him in Paris last December at the immigration conference and then again for a coffee on our last day in Istanbul when I left that note saying I had gone sightseeing.'

'Did anything happen between you?'

'No, of course not.' My eye twitched at the question as I thought back to what Oz had said and how it had felt when he held my hand to his heart.

Amy hugged her knees. 'OK, seeing as this is confession time, I'll admit it, I picked Istanbul for your hen do deliberately.'

My eyes widened. 'What?'

She shrugged. 'I didn't want you to regret anything in your past before you made this big commitment. When I got in touch with your Lebanese mate, I asked her about him. His life sounds pretty complicated. I knew he was going to be at that wedding reception and I thought maybe ... Oh no, you're pissed with me, aren't you? Shit, why do I always get things so horribly wrong with you?'

I slumped back on the carpet and stared at the ceiling. 'Oh, Amy, what am I going to do? I love Charlie more than anything, but I can't get Oz out of my head. In Istanbul he told me he was divorced and that he still loved me. But I could never do anything to hurt Charlie.'

She grabbed the letter and postcards from my grasp. 'Then let's burn these.'

I shot up. 'No!'

Amy looked startled by my reaction. 'I mean, not yet. I want to know what he said.'

'Want me to read them?'

I nodded and took a deep breath to steady myself. She pulled out the letter and unfolded it.

Dear Abbie,

By now you must be home. I don't even know where to begin. If I could write in Turkish, then it would be easy to express what I am feeling to you. I hope this reaches you. Your university said they would forward it on.

Why did you leave so sudden, Abbie? I had hoped to find you at your hotel to explain everything, but you had gone. I confronted my mother and she said she told you about the business deal between my family and Dima's family. It is complicated. I need to see you or talk to you to explain. And I am sorry you had to see that display from Dima on the stage. She can be, how do you say, a drama queen sometimes.

Please, Abbie, all I ask is you contact me. My phone number is at the top of this letter. I want to see you again. The day we spent together: the meal in Arnavutköy, the boat ride – they will forever hold a place in my heart. I wondered if there was something between us? Please tell me I have not imagined it. When I said I wanted to come back to London again, I meant it. I want to find a way to see you again. Please also consider coming back to Istanbul.

You told me you had not made a decision about law school. Don't make any choices with a sad heart. I want you to know your visit meant so much to me. That you came to see me, it gives me so much joy. Please contact me so I can speak to you and explain everything.

Love,

Oz

A feeling of longing and regret hit me.

Amy turned over the first postcard and read each one in turn.

The fishing village I took you to on the bike. Remember the meal we had? Please write to me. Love Oz

The palace of Dolmabahçe. Such opulence. Your judgement of this place was so true. Please write. Love Oz

The hotel Sarniç. I went there today and said hello to the concierge. He remembers you fondly. Please, Abbie, please write to me. Love Oz

The bazaar. Do you still have your bracelet? Please look at it and remember me. I never meant for you to be hurt by the actions of my family. Love Oz

The boat we took around the Bosphorus. I want to take that ride with you again. Love Oz

Blessings for the New Year. I won't send any more postcards. I must respect your decision. It is best I follow my path. Maybe we will meet again in London in nine years on the 14th of February for our cinema date? It would be destiny if we did. Love Oz

I sighed deeply as I held my hand over the bracelet. How could I ever burn these?

Amy put her fingers to her open mouth. 'Nine years after this letter on February the fourteenth. Was that the night of your "call to the Bar" ceremony?'

'Yes. Yes, it was.'

That had been the last time I saw him before he walked back into my life again in Paris. Too much time had passed in between; I had moved on, and for good reason.

And now? I couldn't let him keep coming back into my life like a wrecking ball. This letter, these postcards, the photo album with those brief snapshots of the handful of days we had spent together didn't change anything.

29

Now

November

The door to Liz's house swung open.

'Hi,' Liz whimpered.

I threw my arms around her and stood in the doorway holding her, the muffled sounds of her sobs at my neck.

'It's going to be OK, Liz,' I said, stroking her back.

I came over as soon as I had spoken to her after the desperate text message popped up on my phone. Charlie and I had been sitting at our dining table with paper cut-outs representing our wedding guests, working out the possible seating plans. Initially, I had been relieved by the interruption. I had already swallowed two paracetamol because arranging 160 guests had given me a splitting headache. But when I had called Liz to find out what the matter was, my relief had turned to heartache.

'How is your mum?' I asked as we stepped inside the kitchen, my arm still firmly clasping her shoulder. We sat down at the table next to each other.

'In shock, denial.'

'And you?'

Her bottom lip quivered. 'I don't want to lose her. She's all I've got.'

Liz grabbed a tissue from the box in the centre and blotted her face.

'That's not true.' I reached over to squeeze her hand. 'You've got Mary, me, Mary's parents. We'll all step up, help you in any way we can. I'll take some time off to look after Maddy.'

'Thanks, Abs. I can't even think straight. I mean, breast cancer. You hear the "c" word all the time, but you never think it might happen to you or your family. And then the diagnosis comes and it's like your world falls apart.'

'When does she start treatment?'

'Next week. And Mary has a big case coming up, then she's attending that conference in Paris, remember, the one you went to last year. Plus, there's all your wedding prep.'

'That should be the least of your concerns. Give it all to me and I'll get it done. Your mum should be your priority. And she'll get better. She'll get the treatment she needs, and she will fight it.'

She looked up at me with expectant eyes. 'You think?'

'I do. She's been in so many scrapes in her life and got through all of them. And with you by her side, she'll get through this.'

A thin-lipped smile broke on Liz's face. 'Hard to believe we're closer now than we ever were. If it hadn't been for you getting me to call her that day . . .' She broke off and held onto my hand tighter, staring at my engagement ring. 'I'm sorry for dragging you away from Charlie. You were meant to be spending time doing wedding stuff.'

'It's fine, he'll understand.'

At least I hoped he would. We had been trying and failing to find time together to plan the seating since the day his mum set it as a task a couple of weeks ago.

The front door opened, and I peered down the hallway to see Mary pushing the buggy inside. She left it parked by the entrance and came into the kitchen, giving Liz a kiss on the cheek and me a hug.

'Maddy finally drifted off to sleep,' Mary said, flipping the switch on the kettle. 'I'm glad you're here, Abbie.' She unwound her scarf and placed it along with her coat over one of the kitchen chairs. 'There's something rather important I need to ask you – it's a favour. I was thinking about it on my walk.'

'Anything. I'll do anything,' I said without hesitation.

'I have a long case coming up next week and don't want to be gone from Liz the whole week plus the weekend. I'd very much like you to take over from me again at the immigration conference in Paris.'

I was shocked. 'Run the workshop?'

'Yes. After all, it was thanks to you we got asked back in the first place. You made the connections. Going from being an attendee to hosting an event is a big deal.'

'I'm flattered, Mary, but I'm not sure I'm the right person for the task.'

'Nonsense, I can't think of anyone more qualified to run it.'

I hesitated. Next weekend Charlie and I were meant to be heading up to Auchen Castle to do some wedding preparation with his mum, including a run-through of the service. And the week after I had a difficult case that needed a lot of prepping for.

But this was the opportunity of a lifetime. Maybe there was a chance we could postpone our trip to the following weekend. I had loved the buzz of the last conference, the opportunity to talk to people and network. And to run something high profile would be the highlight of what had proved to be a difficult year for me. I had lost more cases than I'd won and some of the losses had hit me hard. Seeing families ripped apart always affected me deeply.

Another thought popped into my mind. Would Oz be there? Could I ever face him again after what he had told me in Istanbul? Did it even matter?

I pulled my locket back and forth on its chain.

'I'd be honoured, Mary.'

After spending the rest of the day with Liz and Mary, I returned that evening to find Charlie in our expansive kitchen reading through some papers at the breakfast bar, sipping a glass of red wine, his dinner plate empty. The rest of the house was cold and dark. I had persuaded Charlie that it was a waste of money to keep heating and lighting parts of the house we never went in.

'There you are,' he said. 'How are you feeling?'

'Like a rocket exploded in my brain,' I said, rubbing my temples.

'Is there anything I can get you?'

'No, I'll be fine.' I padded over to the sink and ran some water into a glass. A packet of paracetamol lay on the window ledge and I popped out a couple and swallowed them. 'Sorry about today.'

'Come and sit down, Abbie,' he said, patting the bar stool next to him. 'Let me warm you up some dinner.'

I shook my head. 'Thanks, but I'm not that hungry.' I laid my mobile on the counter and pulled at the sleeves of my jumper.

'How's Liz?'

'A little better. She's had such a tough year, and just when life was back on track with Maddy, this happens.'

Charlie stood and enveloped me in his arms, kissing the top of my head. 'Don't worry, she'll be fine; she's got a good support network.'

I let his embrace soothe me before clocking the finished seating arrangements on the kitchen table. 'I'm sorry about not helping with those,' I said, tipping my chin in the direction of the charts.

'It doesn't matter. There are a few positions I need to check with you, so we avoid World War III breaking out between various members of my family.' He smiled. 'But we can do that tomorrow.'

'Actually,' I said, turning to face him. 'I promised Liz I would go over again, and I need to see Mary.'

'Why do you need to see Mary?'

I took a deep breath and braced myself for what I was about to tell him. 'She's asked me to take over from her in Paris next weekend. I'm going back to the immigration conference to run the workshop.'

He sat back down on the stool. 'You're what?'

'I hoped you would understand that I have to do this. Not only am I helping Mary; it will be a huge opportunity for me.'

He tilted his head to the side. 'And our wedding plans?'

'I thought we could postpone the trip until the following weekend.'

His jaw visibly clenched and a vein on the side of his forehead popped. 'I don't want to appear selfish, but there are other people who could fill in. It's just a workshop.'

I bristled. 'It's not "just" a workshop. It's my chance to prove, to prove ...'

'To prove what, Abbie?'

I cradled the glass of water, unable to finish that sentence.

'I know Liz is your best friend and I completely understand your need to be with her right now, but I don't see why you have to be the one to go to Paris when there are three other equally qualified immigration barristers at chambers who could step in.'

Mary had asked *me*. Me. And I truly wanted to believe I was chosen because she had faith in my ability, not just because I was Liz's best friend.

Charlie took the glass of water from my hands, placing it on the side before clasping them tightly. 'Abbie ... I feel like we're slipping away from each other. We've both been so preoccupied with work, and now you're caught up with Liz and Maddy again and you're adding the workshop to the mix because you'll always feel you owe Mary something.' He shifted closer. 'I want to feel like I matter too, that *we* matter. Ever since you came back from Istanbul, it's like you've put these barriers up. I thought you'd be more excited about moving into this house, but your clothes are still in a suitcase as if you're a guest.'

It was true. There hadn't been any weekends free to give the house a second thought. Life was spinning out of control and I didn't know how to make it stop. But I hadn't noticed that most of my clothes were still left unpacked.

My phone vibrated on the counter. I glanced over at the screen. It was a Breaking News alert. The headline made me sit bolt upright. 'Terror strikes at the heart of Istanbul.' Underneath the captions the following words stood out: bombs. Beşiktaş stadium. Twenty-nine dead. One hundred and sixty-six wounded.

I pushed back my stool, scraping it along the marble floor, and leapt to my feet. 'I changed my mind. I am hungry,' I said. 'Think I'll pop out and get a Chinese.'

'Why don't you order a delivery?'

'I think I need some fresh air, clear my head.'

I walked past him to leave, but he grabbed my hands, squeezing them tightly. 'Abbie. I'm just worried that you're taking on too much and I don't want to see what happened to you all those years ago happen again. Liz has Mary, her wife, someone who can step up and be there for her more. Remember that. It's not your job to rescue everyone.'

I didn't respond; merely nodded before racing out the door, the guilt for not saying why I was leaving growing exponentially.

Weaving my way down the road and around the corner to our local Chinese, I pulled out my phone as I neared the entrance. Scrolling through my list of contacts, my finger hovered over Oz's name as I caught my breath. The rings were endless.

'Abbie?'

At that point, I should've hit 'end call'. All I wanted to know was whether he was alive, didn't I?

'*Allo*? Abbie?'

His voice at my ear was like a cube of butter on hot toast.

I licked my lips which had dried to a crisp from the current cold spell. 'Hi.'

He sighed. 'It's so good to hear from you.' There were sirens and cries in the background.

'The bombs. I just saw the headline and I ... I had to know straight away if you were OK.'

'Thank Allah, I am fine. I was at the game.'

A sharp intake of November air caught at the back of my throat. 'You were?'

'But the match was already over. I was heading home instead of going out after with my friends. But they are also safe.'

Silence fell between us, but his breathing was audible.

'I want to see you again,' he said finally. 'I need to say sorry for what I said at the café and to properly explain what has happened these last few years, but, on a phone, in an email ... It is too hard. I need to see you. *Lütfen*. Please. I can't move on until you know everything.'

Cars went past on the road and people shuffled along the pavement. Their figures blended into the backdrop, words from snatched conversations barely comprehensible.

'The immigration conference in Paris,' he said suddenly. 'Will you be there?'

I held my breath. 'I might be. My colleague has asked me to run a workshop there.'

'Really? I am giving a speech again. Perhaps we can have a coffee. I promise I won't say anything to upset you.'

What could I say to that? Could I honestly see him again and not be reminded of what he had said to me in Istanbul? But he was right. There was still so much to talk about. And deep down I was aching to know what had happened in his life after I saw him in Leicester Square, the night before my thirtieth birthday.

30

Five years earlier

February

'Stop teasing me,' I said to Liz as we stood in front of the Prince Charles cinema as crowds gathered around us. 'Oz isn't here.'

Liz looked at me in a way I hadn't seen before.

I turned around slowly and met his eyes before rapidly looking back and clutching Liz's arm. 'What do I do?'

'Well, you're rumbled. He's seen you. You have to go on a date now.' She bound me in one of her bone-crushing hugs.

'Shit,' she said, pulling back. 'It is fate. I didn't think he'd be here. This was going to be an intervention. I was going to tell you to let the memory of him go; that you can't keep going through life comparing every guy to him. But here he is.' She smiled and tucked a few strands of hair behind my ear. 'And you told me you'd agreed to meet if you were both single. I bet it didn't work out with the crazy Turkish girl. I bet he'll be horribly apologetic for breaking your heart, and you can tell him from me, if he dares do something like that again, he'll have me to contend with. I want you to have what I have with Mary, Abs, cos it's flipping incredible and you deserve it.' She squealed. 'This is like a movie – a fairytale ending.'

I allowed myself to get caught up in her enthusiasm for a moment and a broad smile broke across my face before I remembered the date I had agreed to with Charles. Oz had come back into my life when I had finally been ready to move on. Was this fate playing a cruel joke?

'I'll go back and tell your family you're tied up. OK? Go meet him. Go be happy.'

Oz had a suit carrier over one shoulder and held a small case in the other. He looked sad; his eyes were sunken and tired-looking and my smile faded.

'You came,' we both said, laughing as we spoke over each other.

'I have a stopover in London for a few hours. I came from the airport. I go to New York tonight.'

'Oh.' It was hard to conceal the disappointment in my voice.

'I wanted to see you.' He swallowed a gulp of air as his eyes grew misty. 'I needed someone to talk to.' He shivered, even though he was bundled up in a smart coat and scarf.

'Let's go in then.'

We bought two tickets to the movie and made our way down to the bar, ordering a whisky on the rocks and a gin and tonic from the bartender as we sat on a couple of stools, draping our coats over another. The area around us began to fill with pre-movie revellers, and a low hum of conversation and excited chatter arose.

I stared long enough at his hand to see he wasn't wearing a ring. But my eyes were still drawn to the anguish on his face.

'Is everything OK?' I asked.

He said nothing and stared at the depths of his drink, rattling the ice cubes against the sides.

'Talk to me, please, Oz. What's the matter? Why are you going to New York?'

'My life is a lie. One big lie.'

I twisted on the stool so I could look at him more closely. 'What happened?'

'You never asked me why I registered at UCL in a different name.'

'No, I don't think I ever did.'

'Around that time, my mother caught me going through some papers in her office. Bank statements. Payments to someone in New York, someone called S. Demir, my father's name. I challenged her about them, but she said it was a common name and had to do with a property they were leasing in America. But I still registered with his surname to annoy her. Like a child. I wanted a reaction from her.'

I took a sip of my drink, wondering where this story was headed. It was like we had picked back up from a conversation we'd had in Damascus, as if there hadn't been a gap of four years.

'She once said to me, something I could not forget. She said she was glad he was dead because she would never forgive him for the accident. But he never felt dead to me.' He pushed his glass to one side and held his hands behind his head, threading his fingers backwards and forwards through his hair before pounding the bar with his fists, causing both glasses to rattle.

'But she lied. He's not dead. He is very much alive.' He looked at me, his eyes wet with tears and anguish.

'What?' I held my hand up to my mouth.

'Yirmi yedi yıl. Twenty-seven years. Twenty. Seven. Years. I have not had the love of a father for twenty-seven years.'

What could I say? How on earth could I ease his pain? I placed my hand over his, giving it a gentle squeeze, willing him to continue.

'Two days ago, I received a call from a friend in America. He rang to say he had met a Turkish professor at the University of New York, where my friend is a research fellow. He said this man, this man he'd met by chance ... was my father. *Yani,* I thought he was crazy,' he said with a half-smile. 'But then he sent me a photo of him, from the university website.' He closed his eyes and wiped his other hand across them, removing every trace of tears.

'I don't know what to say, Oz. I can't begin to imagine how you must be feeling. Are you on your way to see him?'

He nodded. 'No one knows. I haven't shared this with anyone ... except you. This will tear my family apart, but I have a right to know. Yes?'

'Of course you do.'

'You do not think me foolish to want to dig up the past? Do you think I should have told my family what I had found out? Give them a chance to explain?'

'If it were me, I wouldn't want to waste a single second not being with my father. I would do anything to see him again.'

'I'm sorry, Abbie. I did not mean to bring you sad feelings.'

'It's fine. It's been four years. Time heals.' I gave a slight shrug.

'I did not want to take a direct flight. I wanted to see you.'

'How did you know I'd be here?'

'Destiny?' His weak smile brought an ache to my heart.

'You mean "chance"?' I knew my attempt at humour was not what he needed but his demeanour softened.

'I had a plan B. I hoped your number would still be the same. I couldn't quite believe this happened now when we had made that promise to be here on this day.' He clasped my hand which was still resting on his other one and looked at it wistfully. I stared at his fingers and looked back up into his eyes. He broke contact to reach into his trousers. 'I sometimes forget to put it back on after football practice.'

I felt a stab of pain in my chest. 'Yes, of course.' What was I thinking? He was here to share his news, his pain, nothing else.

As he pulled open his wallet, there behind his wedding ring was a photo of a young girl.

'Who's that?'

His lips thinned as he pulled out the picture and handed it to me. 'This is Eda, my daughter.'

I held the photo and looked at it, wordlessly.

'She is nearly four.'

I was breathing in and out deeply, trying to compose myself. Oz had a daughter. The walls of the bar began to crumble around me as I took in this little girl in the picture. 'She's beautiful,' I whispered.

He sniffed. 'I am so sorry, Abbie. When I found out Dima was pregnant, I couldn't leave, I couldn't do that to my unborn child. It wouldn't have been fair on anyone, especially you. I knew then we could not have the life we talked about in Beirut. Eda is the most precious thing to me. I have made many mistakes over the years, but she is not one of them. And Dima is her mother. I can't not have her in my life even though I will never forgive her for how it came to be.'

I looked back at him. 'What do you mean?'

'We weren't able to have children naturally and there had been pressure from our families for a child, so we had sought other methods. Dima visited the special clinic after I filed for divorce without me knowing. Despite my anger, I had to stand by her.'

A general commotion behind us indicated the film was about to start. These revelations buzzed around in my mind like a swarm of bees and I had no headspace to even begin to comprehend them.

'We'd better go in, I guess,' I said lightly, picking up my coat, hoping he had not noticed my thunderstruck expression.

I couldn't look at him as the lights dimmed and the film began. I cursed myself for even thinking this was anything more than a heart-to-heart. What was I even still doing here? This wasn't a date.

Our arms touched on the seat rest. I hated the fact I still felt alive at his warmth. His little finger twitched and gently nudged mine. I didn't pull back. My focus was no longer on Cary Grant and the big screen, but our hands.

It was a gentle movement at first, and I was transfixed. He stroked my little finger with his before working each of his fingers between mine, squeezing them tight. He brought my hand towards his mouth and stopped. His breath was on my skin, his lips tantalisingly close.

I stood up abruptly and grabbed my things, feeling my way out of the cinema in the darkness.

'Abbie,' Oz called after me.

He caught up to me in the empty bar. 'Please don't go. I'm sorry, I didn't mean to do this. Any of this. Please. Forgive me. I am not thinking straight right now. Perhaps on my way back from New York, we can meet?'

I took a deep breath, pulling my locket back and forth along its chain. 'I don't think that's a good idea, Oz. I can't be there for you. It's not fair on me. I wanted a life with you, and I can't be in the one you have now.'

With those words I left, knowing that I was right, and Liz was wrong. The only happy endings were in the movies. I knew the direction I wanted to take. My new career would be my focus. I didn't need anyone in my life. Not right now.

31

Three years earlier

December

My ticket beeped as I placed it on the reader and 'Seek assistance' flashed up, the barrier remaining firmly closed.

'No, no, no!' I cried out.

In the distance, the train from Birmingham New Street to London's Euston station began to pull away.

My shoulders slumped and I could feel a lump in the back of my throat. I wouldn't normally be upset about missing a train but today I had lost a five-day case I had worked weeks on, and it had hit me harder than I expected. All I wanted to do was curl up in my bed back at my flat and drown my sorrows with a bottle of wine. It was six o'clock. By my calculation it would be another four hours before I would be slumped under the covers, judging by the time of the next train. The idea of crawling into my cold, damp flat that late didn't fill me with much joy. The landlord had promised to fix the radiators, but my pleas had fallen on deaf ears. I wished I could go to Liz's, but she was moving into her new Notting Hill house with Mary this weekend.

'Abbie?'

I turned to see Charlie Logan standing beside me. I attempted a smile. 'Hi.'

'Is everything OK?' He looked at my face which was rapidly crumbling.

'I'm fine. Only ...' I looked up into his eyes. I had never noticed quite how intensely green they were. He usually wore glasses but not today. The concern in his face made me fall apart. My bottom lip began to quiver.

Suddenly I found myself enveloped in warmth as his arms encircled me and I let a few tears soak into his cashmere coat, the fabric soft on my cheek. I inhaled a comforting scent close to his neck – a mix of aftershave and shower gel. He held me and it was the most at peace I had felt in a long time. It was soothing and very much needed.

Charlie and I had become firm work friends over the last two years. On our first coffee date he hadn't made a move. It was probably because I had come across a little frosty and spouted off about office relationships not being a good idea. Our paths rarely crossed because we had different specialisms, but every time they did, I couldn't deny I was always happy to see him. He made me laugh with his dry sense of humour and was a real gentleman.

I pulled back and accepted the handkerchief he offered up. It was monogrammed with his initials.

'Terribly old-fashioned. My mum insists on sending me them for my birthday every year. Very embarrassing.'

I laughed through my tears. 'What are you doing here?'

'Just arrived for a case which starts early tomorrow. And you?'

I looked over my shoulder at the empty platform. 'Missed my train home and ... lost my case.'

'Ah.' He gave a knowing nod. 'Looks like you need a drink to drown your sorrows.'

My heart began to pick up speed and I held his eyes steady with mine, not daring to look away. 'You know what? That's exactly what I need. Would you like to join me?'

'I thought you'd never ask.' He smiled and gave me a cheeky wink.

Over wine and dinner at All Bar One, Charlie let me unpick every detail of my case. He listened and didn't judge and told me not to let this one defeat overshadow my past victories. We chatted about other topics as well – our families, personal lives, likes and dislikes. Three hours slipped by until we found ourselves standing back on the exact same spot as we had met – under the departures board. My face ached from smiling so hard.

We stood inches apart from each other, the warmth of the wine heating my cheeks.

'Thank you, Charlie. I feel—'

And then his lips were on mine. The kiss was urgent and sensual, and my body arched into his. He held the back of my head with one hand and the other firmly clasped my back.

I didn't hear the whistle of the guard signalling my train was about to depart, nor did I notice the passengers pushing past us to get through the turnstile. What did it even matter if I missed the last train home?

Time stood still. I knew then this was the start of something special.

32

Now

November

'Four attendees!' I exclaimed as I stood outside the meeting room where I was due to run the workshop in a couple of hours, scanning the sign-up sheet. That was *it*? I had four people coming to my workshop. So much for making a name for myself. Charlie had finally agreed to postpone the trip to Scotland so I could come to Paris and for what?

I had hardly seen him during the week as I had juggled work, conference prep and visits to Liz's to look after Maddy so she could be with her mum. Each night I would crawl into bed long after he did, and he was always up before I rose to get to court. He had seen me off at King's Cross station this morning with a hug and wished me good luck, but his goodbye kiss barely touched my lips. I tried to park any thoughts of what that meant on the train ride and focussed on my workshop ahead.

I buttoned the jacket of my dark grey trouser suit and fanned my face with the conference pack.

'Abbie.'

I froze before slowly turning around. There he was. Oz. Dressed smartly in a navy-blue suit. I accepted the welcome kisses and cursed myself for the way it made me feel. He looked over my shoulder at the sheet.

'Looks like word got out my colleague wasn't running the workshop.' I sighed.

'I am sure that's not true.' His eyes focussed on my bottom lip which I was chewing voraciously. 'Are you worried about running it?'

This was a work setting and I was more than used to dealing with a few butterflies. I did so each time I stood up in court, with a surge of adrenaline. But something in Oz's expression was causing me to be honest about my true feelings. 'I'm bricking it.'

'This expression I don't understand.' He smiled sympathetically.

'Let's just say yes, I am more than scared. I feel like I have a lot resting on it.'

'I am free if you would like to run through it. You can practise on me.'

And in an instant, I was transported back to the first time we met: the small café in London, the earnestness of youth, the flushing of my cheeks every time something was said that could possibly have a hidden meaning, the thoughtful way in which Oz had offered to help me salvage my dissertation.

'You'd do that?'

'Of course. For you, always.'

We found an empty meeting room and I switched on my laptop. I felt calm in Oz's company. Even though I couldn't erase the memory of the last time we had met, my full concentration was on the task at hand. I stood up and straightened my jacket, mirroring Oz's smile as he sat on the other side of the table waiting for me to begin.

I worked through the material, showing him the slides I was going to use and how I planned to break my presentation into sessions to let the attendees come up with ideas of their own. Though with four people due to turn up, I feared any discussion might be strained.

'Well?' I said, once I had finished my closing speech.

'This is good work. I have only one concern. So much of what you say is from here.' He pointed to his head. 'And not from—'

'Here?' I finished his sentence for him, laying my hand over my heart.

'How did you know what I would say?'

'You said something similar to me when you were looking through my dissertation all those years ago.'

He leaned forward on the table. 'I heard about Mary's stories in your words, but not yours. You may not have Mary's career in years, but your experiences are still important and valid. People will be interested.' It was true. Mary had forwarded me a lot of the material I had used.

Oz took a quick look at his watch. 'You must forgive me,' he said, 'but I am meeting someone in a few minutes. Perhaps we can meet later on? For a coffee?'

'Sure.' I didn't give my response much thought because my mind was churning with ideas and stories, cases I had experienced, interesting junctures in my career I could talk about. I sat down and wrote some more notes and didn't even notice Oz leave.

A while later, I was sitting in my meeting room ready to go, my welcome slide up on the projector. The door swung open and four people stepped inside. I greeted them and was about to begin my presentation, when five or six more walked in. Who were these people? Before I knew it, the room was filled, and extra chairs were required.

My face glowed with excitement. Then I saw him. He had tried to be inconspicuous, but I could see him beyond the doors, out in the foyer. Oz. My heart swelled. There had been no meeting he had to attend. He had been drumming up people to come to my workshop. A murmur of Turkish, French and other hard-to-follow languages filled the tight space as I welcomed everyone.

By the time the two-hour session finished, I was buzzing. Buzzing. The last of the delegates left, having shaken my hand, saying it had been an invaluable experience. Beaming, I did a fist pump as I turned around to my laptop.

My phone buzzed on the table. It was a message from Oz.

How was the workshop? I am sitting at Café L'Ecir on the corner of Rue de la Tombe Issoire. It would be lovely to see you if you have the time.

I hesitated. What would Charlie say if he knew I was having coffee with him? Nothing. I still hadn't told him who Oz really was. But Oz and I needed to clear the air after our last meeting. Too much had happened between us to let it end like that. And I was confident that I could finally get the 'closure' that I hadn't had in Istanbul.

Having changed into flats, my black jeans and green wool jumper – which were warmer against the Paris chill – I walked to the café and saw Oz through the window. He was hunched over a newspaper in dark jeans and V-neck navy-blue jumper over his work shirt.

He saw me and smiled. My heart flip-flopped, but I shook the feeling away. It was probably still the excitement I was feeling; the high.

A waiter directed me to the table, having taken my coat, and Oz stood up as I approached.

'How was it? Ah, I can see by the smile it was good.'

I sat down straight away, keen to avoid his usual greeting. 'It was amazing. Thank you, thank you so much for getting all those people to come.'

He shrugged. 'I don't understand what you mean,' he said, sitting back down.

'Come on. I know it was you. Or was it a coincidence a third of the delegates happened to be Turkish?'

He looked shyly down at his coffee. 'Busted. Is this the word British people use?'

'I don't think your crime will get you arrested.'

'Ah, OK. Then I am guilty of you finding me out.'

'It was really thoughtful, Oz. It went incredibly well.'

'I see from your face. What would you like to drink?' he said, as the waiter appeared again.

I scanned the menu on the table, enjoying the smell of roasted coffee beans and warm pastries. *'Un cappuccino, s'il vous plaît,'* I said to the waiter.

I breathed out deeply. 'I can't get my heartbeat to slow down.'

'Then you must do more of these workshops.'

'I think I will.'

He stirred his coffee with a small spoon, lost in thought.

'So ...' I said. 'When I called you last week, you said you wanted to talk.'

He pulled at the sleeves of his jumper before taking a sip of coffee. 'First, please let me apologise for saying those words to you in Istanbul. It was inappropriate and I am sorry. I also never properly thanked you for being there that day in London when I was on my way to New York. It wasn't until a long time after, I realised I had not asked you anything about your life, or why you had come.'

'Liz. She's a believer in fate. And she convinced me that even though our little joke about meeting again in nine years was nothing more than that, I wouldn't be able to live with myself if I didn't find out if ... if ...' The words got stuck.

'If I was single?' He slumped in his chair a fraction.

The waiter brought my drink, and I skimmed a bit of the chocolatey foam off the top.

'I am sorry, Abbie. If I had not been on my way to New York that day, I would not have been there.'

'I know. You and Dima had decided to give your marriage another go, you had a beautiful daughter. It was silly really, me being there.'

He tutted. 'Not silly at all. I was so happy you came. It was our destiny to be there at that moment.'

'So ...' I twisted my cup. 'What happened after that night?' I looked into his eyes, those caramel eyes that had become so familiar to me – those eyes that appeared sad and listless under the lights of the café.

'I went to New York and met my father.' A smile broke free in the corner of his mouth. 'Ah, Abbie. The feeling was ... *eh*. No. I do not have the right words in English. It took me a few days to absorb what had happened. He was as surprised to see me as I was to find out he was alive. I didn't want to leave New York. I didn't sleep. How could I? I was scared if I shut my eyes and woke up, I would find it all a dream. We had a lifetime of memories to discuss. I went through all the emotions; anger, joy, frustration.'

His eyes misted over, and he reached out to cradle his mug.

'What happened then?'

'He didn't want me to tell the rest of the family, but how could I not? My brother and sister had a right to know. But the news tore the whole family apart. It was then my grandfather admitted he was behind the whole secret. My mother had gone along with the lie too. They paid my father to leave. They ensured he could start a new life in the US away from us. Not only because of the accident but because he had brought so much shame to the family with his drinking and his bad business decisions. My mother justified her actions by saying he was dead to her as she would never forgive him for almost killing me. She and my grandfather were both furious I had found him. I left the family business; cut myself off completely. I had nothing. Dima was unhappy with the life we began to lead, and she left me, taking Eda to live with her parents.'

'I ... I don't know what to say.'

'In an instant I had lost everything; my family, my daughter, but I had gained a father.' He shook his head. 'I ... how do you say ... Ah, my English is failing me. I hit rock bottom.'

'I'm sure you did.'

'It took me a very long time to accept it all. But a good friend of mine, he took me in. And I stayed in contact with my father who was supportive. I finally got a job through an old university friend who works at the charity with me. And I fought for a long time to have Eda back in my life.'

'I'm so sorry, Oz.'

'Don't feel sorry for me, Abbie. I should've had the courage many years ago to stand up to all of them. But when I found out Dima was pregnant, I thought the right thing to do was to be by her side and support her. My happiness was again the sacrifice. It is me who should apologise to you, for the pain I caused you. Every time I put my family first. I have so many regrets. You and I had made a dream together, and it was destroyed by the actions of others and the lack of courage from me. Even though it was the beginning of a dream, it was still one I'd wanted with all my heart. And now ...' He glanced at my engagement ring. 'It is too late. I wanted to tell you all this back in April when you came to the property exhibition.'

'I couldn't go in. I saw you with your family and Dima.'

'Dima wasn't there.'

'What? But there was a woman with her arm draped over you.'

'My sister. She organised for me to be there, to try and help heal the family.'

'Oh,' the only word I could muster. I focussed on my cup, the murmur of other diners and the hiss of the coffee machine surrounding us, questioning what would have happened if I had known he was no longer with Dima all those months ago.

'I read your letter,' I said finally. 'The one my parents hid from me. I found it in a box my mum packed for me years ago. I read it last month and your words stayed in my mind for a long time.'

He looked at me expectantly.

'I'm not sure what I would've done if I'd read your words back then; possibly I would've written back to you. I would've let you explain what had happened that night. Who knows? We can't change the past.'

He held onto his cup, letting his coffee grow cold.

'The night when you told me you were giving your marriage another chance, a week after my dad's funeral, I never had the chance to tell you what *I* was going to say. It would've hurt you too. Our dream could never have happened. My mother had told me she was in financial difficulty. I knew then I could never leave her, my job or England. We would've come to the same impasse even if you hadn't said those things to me. It wasn't only the actions of your family or your perceived lack of courage that destroyed our dream. I would've destroyed it too, Oz. I never told you, but Mum and I had been arguing the moment Dad died and it was about me running away to Beirut with you. That's why

347

I hadn't wanted you to come to the funeral. I was scared. Scared of hurting Mum even more with your presence.'

He held my gaze and the look of anguish on his face mirrored the turmoil churning inside me as I remembered that time.

'You changed your name to Demir, I noticed,' I said, wanting to move on.

He nodded. 'I cut off all my ties to the Arsel name. I have restored my relations with my brother and sister. They met with our father two years ago. We are healing but I cannot forget all that has happened. And you will change your name soon?'

'Actually, I won't. As a barrister you tend to keep your maiden name. But yes, the wedding is next month.' I twisted the ring round my finger. 'Why didn't you contact me again after that cinema night?'

'You told me not to. You didn't give me your new number. I wanted to respect your wishes. My life moved on and one day when I was catching up with Yusef, he told me you were with someone and it was serious. I had to be happy for you.'

I sighed. Why didn't I contact him? Why didn't I call him to see what had happened with his father? Liz had given me the 'intervention' talk again once I had told her what had happened the night we went to the cinema. She had told me she was sorry for getting my hopes up and agreed that I should move on. And I had.

'You know what I wish?' Oz said, breaking into my thoughts.

I looked at him, eyebrows raised.

'I wish we could go back to that day. The day we met, when we went to the art gallery, walked the streets of London and we went on the top deck of the bus. We were tourists. I want it to be like that again.'

'It would be lovely. Liz and I visited Paris on our Interrailing trip. We crammed in so much in those three days. I don't like being here and only seeing the inside of a conference centre.'

'Why don't we?' Oz said, his voice suddenly charged.

'Why don't we what?'

'Tour the city. Let's jump on one of those tourist buses. Why waste our time going over the past? I don't have any appointments this afternoon. Let's have this one time together.'

A pulse of guilt ricocheted inside my chest at the thought of heading off with him. I hadn't even told Charlie he would be here and my continued omission of that fact suddenly made me feel like I had come here to conduct an illicit affair. No, I could never do that to Charlie. My sweet, uncomplicated Charlie.

But all Oz was asking for was an afternoon of sightseeing, a chance to see Paris again, a treat for the huge success of the workshop. Nothing more.

'As friends,' I said firmly, feeling the need to clarify.

'Of course,' he said, ruffling the back of his head. 'I am happy for you, Abbie. You were strong. You changed your life and found a job and a partner who make you happy. And I am happy too. My work and my daughter bring me much joy.

But let us have this one last afternoon together, for … old times' sake, yes? This is the phrase? Please don't think of what I said before in Istanbul. It is an afternoon as friends.'

After all we had been through, could Oz and I really go from lovers to friends?

33

The yellow sightseeing bus pulled away from Notre Dame with a sudden jerk, and I fell backward into Oz's arms on the windy staircase to the top deck. I apologised and regained my balance, holding onto the rail to steady myself. We chose seats at the front, where we had an uninterrupted view.

Paris from this vantage point was even more breathtaking than at street level and a welcome respite from the stuffy conference hotel. Oz pointed out some of the places he had been to before as I reminisced about my favourite spots Liz and I had visited. I pulled up the collar of my coat and sank into it.

'We can go downstairs if you're cold,' Oz said.

The bus stalled in some traffic and the chilly wind dropped with it.

'I'll survive,' I said, rubbing my hands together. 'I don't want to miss out on this view.'

After a while, we drove along the Champs Élysées, past the Arc de Triomphe looming larger as we made our way down the avenue. The bus swung round some of the countless roads fanning out from the monument and I unwittingly leaned against Oz.

We took a few photos with his phone, determined to get the perfect selfie of us with the giant arch in the background, but it was nigh on impossible with all the dumb faces we kept pulling. A thought popped in my head. Here I was creating even more memories with Oz like the ones in that secret photo album I had kept hidden – an addition to our storyboard. But these were on Oz's phone. They would be a distant memory once I left Paris, never to be developed and laid inside the plastic sheets. The thought made my heart sink a little.

We grabbed our separate headphones and connected them to the tourist information system but mine weren't working. Oz passed me one of his buds, but I wrinkled my nose. Turkish was blasting in my ears. I could barely understand a single word, but then I never did make it past the top must-know phrases in my Lonely Planet guide.

He shrugged but didn't change the channel, trying to hold his laughter back.

I folded my arms in a sulk before poking him until he changed it to English.

The bus paused at the Trocadero. 'Can we get off here?' I asked.

'*Hadi*,' he said, and began to make his way to the staircase. He turned around to offer me a hand so I could navigate the narrow descent safely without sending him flying down to the bottom, but I laughed and said I would be more careful this time.

We hopped off the bus and I spun around, taking in the jaw-dropping view of the Eiffel Tower.

'Come with me,' Oz said with a flick of his head.

He stepped into a shop overflowing with tourist tat. I waited outside, twisting a carousel of postcards. He came out a couple of minutes later brandishing a plastic bag. 'I got you something.'

'You did?' I squealed. It was hard to contain my excitement; even though it was only mid-November, the city was decked out with Christmas decorations and the festive feeling was infectious.

'As a Beşiktaş supporter, it makes me sad to buy this, but your need is more important.' He pulled out a Paris St Germain scarf and wrapped it round my neck. It was soft and immediately warming.

'Thank you.' I beamed, pulling it over my mouth, enjoying the feeling of hot breath on my chin.

'And these as well.' He held out a pair of thick woollen gloves.

They were huge and garish, engulfing my hands. I felt like a mascot at a football game. 'Umm, thanks.' I stifled a giggle.

'You don't like them?'

'No, I love them. They're a little … big?'

'At least you'll be warm.'

'I'm all toasty,' I said, as we walked away from the shop.

'Ah, like a piece of toast. So many English expressions. Too many to learn.'

'I'm as snug as a bug in a rug.'

'*Niye*? Why would a bug be in a rug?'

'No idea. They're expressions, you're not meant to question them. Ooh.' I stopped when I saw the carousel in the distance. 'Can we go on that?'

'*Hadi.*'

We headed over to the fairground attraction and spun around several times, hopping on and off different horses and squeezing into a carriage. There weren't many others riding, so we were free to move around as we pleased. A tune played as we swung around – '*La Vie en Rose*'. Its gentle melody cast a magic spell around me, and I closed my eyes for a second as I clutched the pole and smiled to myself. What was this feeling? Life through rose-tinted glasses as the song suggested, a feeling of contentment, achievement, pure happiness. But this wasn't real life.

After strolling through the Jardins du Trocadéro, we bought warm crepes from a food truck at the foot of the Eiffel Tower. We polished them off, washing them down with hot chocolate from Styrofoam cups – the boost we needed before climbing the 674 steps to the second floor of the tower.

My skin prickled with heat once we reached the top, and I removed my coat to relieve the sweat building up beneath my jumper and unwound the scarf.

We walked around the perimeter, catching our breath, until we stopped on the side where we could watch the sun dip low in the sky. It was late afternoon, but the early sunset was a reminder our time together would soon come to an end.

Lights began to twinkle below as the daylight faded.

'It's beautiful up here,' I said, leaning on the barrier. I turned to peer at Oz, who was staring at me intently. 'What? Why are you looking at me like that?'

He shook his head. 'No reason.' His jaw visibly clenched. 'It's just … I've been here so many times before, but being here with you ... never mind.' He stared out into the distance, his shoulders appearing to tense beneath his coat.

'No, tell me.'

He looked back. 'Paris is magical. There is a heart beating beneath its roads. It has an unmatched vibrancy. You and I have been together in London, Istanbul, Beirut and Damascus, but here in Paris ...' He pursed his lips and lost himself in his thoughts.

I dared not ask him to complete the sentence. It was getting too hard; reviving all these dormant emotions, feelings that had to be suppressed. And it was taking all my resolve not to allow pictures to pop into my head of us together. Image after image: the photo booth, the sunset cruise, sunrise in Beirut, the mosques in Damascus. I twisted my engagement ring and clenched my fist so it would leave an imprint on my palm, a reminder of my commitment to Charlie.

'It's been lovely to be in your company again,' he said. 'That is what I wanted to say.'

'I ... I guess we should think about going back,' I said, not wanting to admit how lovely the afternoon had been. 'I need to get ready for the reception this evening. I've been invited to sit with a table of judges. One of the delegates who you persuaded to come to my workshop invited me. I can't quite believe it.'

'*Harika*. How wonderful! I am so happy for you. Sadly, I will miss the dinner. I am meeting up with a friend tonight. He is a fashion designer and is taking me to a bar – L'Espace B – near to the Parc de la Villette. There is a Turkish folk singer who will play tonight. Then my flight leaves at eleven.'

This was it. Our time was over. It was time to say goodbye forever.

We carried on walking until we reached the entrance.

'Today has been lovely,' I said, echoing his earlier sentiment. 'Really lovely.'

'It has.'

God, why was this feeling like the end of a first date? I needed to shake those thoughts away as quickly as possible and lighten the mood. The earlier guilt I had felt was growing tenfold.

As we stepped inside the conference hotel and walked up the small flight of shallow stairs, wearily, my shoe missed the final step and I tipped headlong towards the marble floor of the lobby.

Yet again, Oz was there to catch me. That romcom we kept re-enacting had a new chapter. But instead of feeling embarrassed I began to laugh, not quietly but huge peals of laughter.

As I lay on top of him, he began to laugh too. We laughed so much I hadn't realised everyone around us had stopped what they were doing. For a second, Oz's gaze moved from my eyes to my mouth and my gaze moved from his dimples to his lips. The world stopped.

I hastily pulled myself up, fiddling with my hair, at a loss what to do next.

My mobile buzzed and I saw Charlie's name flash up. *Flip*. I had promised to call him after the workshop to tell him how it had gone and had completely forgotten.

'I have to go,' I said, not daring to look Oz in the eyes. 'I need to take this.'

Oz stretched out his hand. 'Goodbye, Abbie,' he said sadly.

I shook it tentatively, looking back up at him. 'Goodbye, Oz.'

As I accepted the call, I unwound the enormous scarf and sat on one of the couches in the lobby.

'Hey, finally I get hold of you. How did it go?'

'Great. Wonderful in fact.'

'I tried calling you several times. I was getting worried. Was even thinking of getting the next train out to see if you were OK.' He laughed but it sounded a little hollow.

'I was sightseeing.' The words tumbled out without hesitation – the need to be finally honest overwhelming me.

'What?'

'I went sightseeing with a friend.'

'Sightseeing? I thought it was back-to-back meetings the whole day. What friend do you have out there?'

I swallowed hard. 'The one you met at the conference last year. Oz.'

'The Turkish guy whose property event I went to?'

'Yes.'

The silence was unnerving.

'And you spent the afternoon with him instead of going to meetings?'

'Yes.' Suddenly it was hard to breathe. 'Charlie, it's not what you think. There's nothing between us.'

'But there was?' His voice cracked.

My fingers fanned out across my neck. 'A long, long time ago. Not now.'

I could hear him breathing in and out down the line. 'I don't understand. We cancelled our trip so you could attend this conference, to prove … I'm not really sure what you're trying to prove, but now I find out you've not even been there all afternoon. Tell me, Abbie, what exactly am I meant to think?'

My mouth opened, but it was as though a large weight was sitting on my chest restricting my ability to speak.

'Come home, Abbie. We need to talk. Why don't you take the next train back to London?'

I dreaded saying the next words. 'I can't. I've got the big dinner tonight and I've been invited to sit at a really important table with several judges. And there are other talks tomorrow.'

'Abbie. Why do I have this sinking feeling that I'm losing you?'

'You're not, Charlie,' I said, squeezing my eyes shut.

'Then please, come home.'

34

I stood outside L'Espace B, trying to steady my heartbeat. I was running out of time. The conference dinner was due to start in an hour, but something had drawn me here first, something inexplicable.

A bouncer clicked a tally counter and let me step inside, into a dimly lit room. In one corner a bar was lit with neon lights, and crystal decanters lined a mirrored wall. A stage was set in another, with a single microphone and a chair on it. A few tables were scattered around the wooden floor.

Searching every booth in the room, I finally found him, sitting alone. He was holding a tumbler, staring into the depths of the liquid.

'Can I join you?'

'Abbie!' Oz's look was one of bewilderment. 'What are you doing here?'

'I—'

'*Vous désirez?*' a waiter said, appearing at our table as I took off the scarf Oz had bought me and unbuttoned my coat.

I shrugged and looked over at Oz, glad I could remember some of my basic French. 'Whatever you're having.'

'*Un armagnac, s'il vous plaît,*' Oz said, and the waiter retreated. 'It will warm you up.'

I settled back. 'Who's singing tonight?'

'Mazhar Alanson. He used to be a member of a famous Turkish pop group called MFÖ but now he is a solo singer.'

I nodded and looked around the room; couples sat close together, talking animatedly, friends laughing, faces glowing in the soft light.

'I thought you had to go to the conference dinner tonight.'

The waiter brought my drink, and I took a sip. The thick liquid coated my lips and slipped down with a burn.

'I am. I can't stay long.' I looked at Oz's face, illuminated by the flickering candle on the table, and could see the disappointment in his eyes. Those eyes. *Someone, please throw me a life jacket before I drown in them again.* 'I didn't want that goodbye at the hotel to be our last goodbye.'

Another few sips and my insides felt like smouldering embers. A voice in my head said: *Why are you here, Abbie? You've already said goodbye so many times.*

The room plunged into darkness and I looked at the stage where a bald man with a thin white goatee had appeared under a spotlight. A ripple of applause broke across the room. He sat down, lifting a guitar into his lap, and spoke Turkish into the microphone – his mouth so close, his voice reverberated deep and low. A few wolf whistles followed before his fingers began to strum. The first song was slow and mournful. A song about unrequited love, or love lost?

I froze when he got to the chorus. I tapped Oz on the arm, and he raised his eyebrows. I inched forward. 'The rowing boat, in the harbour in Istanbul. You sang this to me.'

Holding my gaze, he mouthed along to the words, his voice audible, as if he was there on stage accompanying the singer.

An ache nestled in my chest.

'Abbie, please don't be sad,' he said, leaning in.

He reached out with his fingers towards my cheek before catching himself and pulling back.

The song came to an end and I was glad for the darkness, and a pause, so I could fish out a tissue and wipe moisture from my eyes before clapping along with everyone else.

'I'm sorry I forgot about that song,' he said.

'It's OK. It was a long time ago.'

Oz's phone buzzed on the table and he picked it up. 'My friend is going to be late.'

He looked back up at me and the backdrop faded. His features glowed in the candlelight and a strange thought crept inside my mind – that this moment had been captured in a photo and placed inside my album; our storyboard had a new addition.

The music started again but neither of us turned to the stage.

'Dance with me?' he said.

I knew I shouldn't, but I nodded. I took his hand as we headed to an area by the stage. A few other couples were already swaying to the beat. He drew me in, his arms wrapping around my waist while I reached out to hold his shoulders. We moved to the music as we held each other. The meaning of the words was indecipherable to me, but as I closed my eyes, Oz translated them into English against my ear. His body was closer and the heat emanating from it was like standing in front of a bonfire. It was a song of second chances, forgiveness and asking for one more try at love. His lips caressed my ear for a second, but it ignited something in me which shook me to the core. It took all my strength to break free from his touch.

'I'm sorry, Oz, I can't,' I said, dropping my hands from his shoulders and taking a step back. 'I can't do this. *We* can't do this.'

'Abbie, please, don't go.'

Turning on my heel, I grabbed my coat from the table and made my way to the exit. Charlie didn't deserve this. I loved him too much to hurt him in this way.

It was only once I was back on the Metro that I realised that I had forgotten to pick up the scarf Oz had bought me. But I couldn't go back. I had to get to the conference dinner before I shattered another promise I had made to Charlie.

35

The door to our Belsize Park house opened. Charlie stood behind it in his dressing gown, his eyes sad and tired behind his glasses. It was almost ten in the morning. I hadn't taken the train Charlie had wanted me to last night – the dinner was too important for me to miss – but I had promised him I would be on the first one this morning.

'I forgot my keys,' I said.

He stood aside and let me in. I stood awkwardly in the hallway while Charlie closed the door, but he didn't turn to hug me. I was rooted to the spot not knowing which room to go into. Charlie nodded to the sitting room.

'I'll bring you a cup of tea.' He headed for the kitchen.

As I sat down on the corner of the couch, I looked around the room. Pictures lay on the floor unhung, boxes of books still unpacked sat under shelves; paint swatches were propped up on the mantelpiece with no choices made. Charlie shuffled in with two mugs and placed them on the coffee table before sitting on the other end of the sofa – a large expanse of grey velvet between us.

I wrapped my hands around the cup to warm my fingers.

'Charlie, I ...'

'You have feelings for him, don't you?'

I put the cup down and sat back. 'I can't deny seeing him again has stirred up some old emotions.'

'You once told me someone had broken your heart. You said he was the reason why you were so hesitant to get serious with anyone again. I had forgotten you told me he was Turkish. It's him, isn't it? You're still in love with him.'

The answer stuck in my throat as I turned to him. 'But I love you, Charlie, and I hate myself for still having these feelings.'

His jaw visibly clenched. 'Did you know he would be in Paris? Is that why you insisted on going?'

'No. I said yes to the conference before I knew he would be there … But I confess, I called him the day of the football stadium terror attack to see if he was OK and he told me he was going to be a keynote speaker. But I went for me; to prove I could do it, to further my career. I want to be so much more than just "approachable and patient".'

'And this was the first time you had seen him since the last conference?'

Heat burned my cheeks, and I slowly shook my head. 'I saw him at my hen do. We had coffee. But nothing happened, I promise. And very briefly outside the property exhibition.' I reached out to clasp his hands, but he moved them out the way.

'I knew it. When I told him you were feeling unwell, he dashed outside suddenly. It was to see you. And your hen do. I saw a change in you after that trip; told myself I was mistaken, that you were probably just exhausted. But it was because of *him*.'

Charlie raked his hand through his hair. He could no longer look me in the eye, and I felt an acute pain in my chest like a hot iron poker stabbing me.

'Do you want to know something ridiculous? Before you told me about the conference, I was going to suggest spending next weekend looking after Maddy – give Liz and Mary some space. I was hoping we could see what it would be like to have a little person around the place because I have been so desperate to talk about when we might try for a baby.'

'No, please, Charlie. Don't mention that now.' Tears welled as I tried to keep control.

'Why, Abbie? I can't go on being silent any more. Losing our baby hurt me just as much as it hurt you. I know I will never understand physically what you went through and why you keep blaming yourself for what happened.'

'But it *was* my fault.' I choked on a sob. 'I didn't want it. It was my fault it died.'

'It wasn't your fault.'

I began shaking. 'I was so scared of what it would mean, the sacrifices I would have to make so early on in my career, and we had only just got together. It *was* my fault.'

Suddenly I was in his arms, my head buried in his dressing gown. The tears flowed, almost four years of hurt and loss flowing freely. How could I ever forget that time? In the space of a few weeks I had gone from an unwanted positive sign on a stick to a miscarriage. No one else knew. It was a secret we had kept between us. A secret we hadn't discussed but had let slowly chip away at our relationship. It's not that I never wanted to have a baby, it was that I hadn't forgiven myself for the one I had lost or got over the physical and mental pain I had endured losing it – doubling over in the middle of rush hour one wintry morning, Charlie rushing me to hospital to have a scan that showed I was no longer pregnant. Surely it shouldn't be that hard to want to try again with the man you love. Why was I so reluctant to even talk about it?

Charlie handed me a monogrammed handkerchief from his dressing gown and I blotted my face.

'So, what now?' he said. 'I still love you, Abbie, even though my heart is shattering, the more you tell me.'

I let more tears fall. 'I don't know.'

'You're in love with us both?'

'Yes,' I whispered.

But I only have one life to live, not two.

'I don't deserve you, Charlie. I don't deserve anyone.' I twisted my engagement ring round and round my finger. 'I can't hurt you like this any more.' I slipped it off and placed it on the table between us.

We sat in silence for what felt like an eternity. The clock on the fireplace ticked. Charlie finally got up and walked to the door. 'I need some fresh air. And I think it's best I leave for Birmingham today, not tomorrow. I'll work up there for a few extra days. I can't be around you right now.'

Ten minutes later I heard the front door close. I found my phone and scrolled through my contacts, another wave of emotion choking me.

'Hey, little sis.'

Yes, she was the first person I wanted to call. Amy and I had become closer than ever since her visit last month, and because Liz was going through so much with her mum, I was thankful to have someone else to turn to.

'What's the matter?' Amy asked.

'Charlie and I just broke up,' I said, a little raspy.

'Oh, Abbie. Want me to come down to London?'

'Yes. I think I'd like that.' I sniffed. 'I hurt him really bad, and I have to call so many people to tell them the wedding's off, I—'

'Hey, shh. It's all going to be fine. You've done the right thing.'

'How do you know that?'

'You're in love with Oz. Always were and always will be. I saw it in your eyes when I read you his letter. Things might hurt now but they'll come good in the end. I know they will.'

36

Now

December

I lay on my bed in the Streatham flat I had signed a lease for a few weeks ago. It had been an emotional time. Disentangling myself from my life with Charlie after four years together had been hard. We hadn't spoken much except for brief exchanges about the house, cancelling fees for the wedding and honeymoon and arranging for my things to be packed up. Whenever we met, I was reminded of the hurt I had caused him – the pain I wished I could have spared him.

Boxes still littered the perimeter of my new bedroom, some of them empty, clothes spilling out of others. The radiators needed bleeding, so I was bundled up in my warmest green turtleneck that Mum had knitted me which fanned out over my black leggings. Rain lashed the windows and I hoped it would abate in time for my trip to Mumbles tomorrow where I was to spend Christmas. I couldn't wait to go; the longing to be in the heart of my family had grown each day since Amy had come down to visit. Mum didn't know the full details of the break-up. She said she would be there when I was ready to share. The truth was I was still processing everything.

The doorbell buzzed and I looked at the time on my mobile. Who would be calling round so late at night? Liz was with her mum and no one else knew my new address. It was no doubt someone wanting another flat who had pressed it accidentally.

It buzzed again. I swung my legs over the bed, passing through my small kitchen which I had furnished with the basics and the dining table that had my paperwork for my first case of the new year. The intercom was broken, so I grabbed my keys and slipped into a pair of flats before padding down the stairs to the front door.

I pulled it open and stopped suddenly. Standing there with no umbrella, bathed in the porch light and getting soaked to the skin, was the last person I expected to see. He was breathing heavily, and raindrops ran down his face.

'What are you doing here?' I asked in disbelief.

He reached into his messenger bag and pulled out a plastic bag, handing it over to me. 'You forgot your scarf.'

I took the bag and reached inside, pulling out the Paris St Germain merchandise. 'You came all the way to give me back the scarf?'

Oz smiled and nodded.

'Did you run from Istanbul?' I returned his smile which broadened.

'I rang Nada to get your address so I could send it. And she told me … she told me you had moved and that you now lived alone, that you were no longer getting married. Maybe I should have waited, given you some space. But I couldn't. I booked a flight straight away and ran here from the station.'

He looked up as he continued to get soaked. His dark hair glistened in the rain and I studied his face, those eyes as he looked at me in earnest.

'I know I should have called you or emailed you,' he said. 'But I have waited so long for this moment. I couldn't wait another second to tell you again ... I love you.'

I stepped out into the rain, my heart swelling – not caring that I was getting drenched too. We stared at each other, not daring to look away; the rain falling on me, my lips, his lips, our lips as they merged together.

Early morning light flowed through the window, the rain easing up a little now. The warmth of Oz's naked chest against my cheek; the feeling of belonging, connecting. I sighed and stroked the tattoo which now covered the scar on his arm. It was sexy as hell, but when he had told me his reasons for getting it – the pain he had wanted to feel for what that accident had represented in his life – I felt an ache in my heart.

'What is this, Oz?' I asked. 'What is it between us? When I'm with you, I no longer feel lost, I feel home.'

He laced his fingers through mine. 'I'm not sure. My English fails me.'

I rested my chin on his chest. 'You always use that as an excuse. Your English is flawless.'

Those dimples appeared. 'Flattery will get you anything.'

'Perhaps it's the years apart that make it more intense when we find a way back to each other.'

He placed my hand to his heart. 'For me, this is whole when you are in my arms.'

My fingers trembled beneath his hold. Thoughts crowded my mind, and I couldn't think of a response. Instead, I buried myself against his chest and choked back my emotion.

'Hey, it's OK.' He placed his arms around me. 'Don't be sad, Abbie.'

'Why do our lives have to be like this?' I looked back up at him. 'Why is everything so complicated?'

'Because we have built our lives apart from each other.'

I stroked his chest and let the warmth of his body soothe me.

'Where are you spending Christmas and New Year?' I asked finally, trying to lighten the mood.

'Christmas is a working day in Turkey. My sister wants me to visit for a family weekend on the twenty-ninth and thirtieth, and I promised my brother I would go to the opening of a new nightclub called the Zehra on New Year's Eve, though I'd rather be with Eda, but Dima is not sure of her plans.'

'I wish things could be different for us, Oz.'

He suddenly sat up in bed. 'Come with me. Come to Istanbul. Live with me.' His look was pleading. 'I know I don't have much to offer you. My apartment is small. But what I can give you is my heart.'

My locket suddenly felt like a dead weight hanging round my neck. 'I can't, Oz. My family, my job, my life is here. It's the same reason why you can't come and live in England. Eda is your world; you can't leave her. And you love your job.'

Oz closed his eyes.

How could we ever build a relationship when we led such separate lives so far from each other? When we were younger, it had been easy to imagine packing up and leaving. That couldn't happen now.

But I didn't want it to end like this with Oz. I kissed him, hard. And in the half darkness, we reached for each other, willing the light to stay shut out, for the day not to begin. We made love for the second time, finding each other, exploring each other's bodies, knowing this was going to be the final chapter in our story.

As I waved him goodbye the next morning, my heart split in two. I held my locket to my lips and let the tears fall.

37

The taste of chickpea, garlic and olive oil was tart on my tongue and that night in Damascus, almost ten years ago, came flooding back – the downtown café recommended by Yusef that Oz and I had dined at. Who knew a pot of hummus could trigger memories from so long ago? As I savoured the images, I held a piece of warm flatbread, the remnants of the pale yellow dip drooping off it. My time with Oz was all that had preoccupied my mind since he'd left on Christmas Eve.

'I think you're meant to eat it before it falls to the floor.' Liz nudged me as we sat on her couch in front of the TV.

Christmas lights twinkled from the tree in the corner. Maddy and Liz's mum were both napping upstairs, and Mary was at the chambers' New Year's Eve party while Liz and I sat waiting to see in midnight from her front room.

Liz took the plate away from me and laid it on the table. 'What's the matter, Abs? You look so troubled – like the weight of the world is on your shoulders.'

'I'm trying to make sense of everything, but I can't. How did this all happen? I should be in Brazil on my honeymoon, but instead Charlie's gone on his own. I keep replaying the past year over in my head, wondering where it all went wrong. But the truth is … I don't think I ever wanted to get married or start a family—'

'Unless it was with Oz?'

She held my gaze and reached out to grasp my hands.

'Why, Abbie? Why is it so hard for you to say? I still can't believe you never confided in me about seeing him in Paris twice and at your hen do and then hooking up again before Christmas.'

'You were going through so much, then and now, and I think I was scared of being honest about my feelings and having you validate them. You said something to me once about getting in touch with old girlfriends after you got engaged. You said you felt nothing.' I tipped my head back and stared at the ceiling. 'When I saw Oz that day in Paris last year, in the crowd, the rush of emotion was so forceful. I even hesitated when Charlie proposed because Oz's face was so clear in my mind. And then when he spoke on the podium, all those memories of us together came flooding back like a tsunami. I should have been honest with how I felt back then. Maybe I could have spared Charlie all this pain.'

Liz clutched my hands tighter.

'I just assumed that I would eventually get over Oz; that I knew what I had with Charlie was good, strong, long-lasting.' I shook my head. 'But each time Oz kept coming back into my life it became harder to suppress my feelings towards him.'

'Why did you say goodbye on Christmas Eve, then? He *loves* you; he wants to be with you, and I know you want to be with him. What's holding you back?'

'My life is here, Liz. I almost gave up everything once before and look where it got me.'

'You're scared of getting hurt again?'

I nodded before letting a small smile break free in the corner of my mouth.

'Wait, there's more, isn't there?'

'Oz called me this afternoon.'

Her eyes widened. 'He did?'

'But I missed it and before I could call him back, he sent me a long email. He's coming to London. January the fifth. He wants us to be together even if it means he has to make sacrifices for it to happen.'

'Why is there nothing but anguish on your face? This is fucking brilliant!'

'No, it's not. I haven't called him back because I don't know what to say. I wasn't prepared to go to Istanbul, so why should I expect him to come here? His daughter, his life, his job. They're all in Turkey. But … at the same time I want him to come, but also, it's too soon. Charlie and I only broke up just over a month ago.'

'Abs, please stop being so hard on yourself. It's not too soon. If anything, it's fifteen years too late.'

'Why is he the only guy you ever truly liked?'

She smiled coyly. 'I was going to save this little speech for your wedding.'

I raised an eyebrow. 'With Oz? You really believe he's still "the One"?'

'Ever since the first time I met him. When you went up to change the night of the Valentine's dance, I asked him how you'd met and what you'd been up to that day. He said he'd never met anyone as smart or independent as you. His face had this look, a mixture of love and admiration. He was clearly smitten. It was adorable. He said you falling into his arms at the march was destiny.'

'I still don't get the difference between destiny and fate.'

'Come on, Abs. Everyone knows that. With destiny there's an element of choice, and each time, without you realising it, you choose him. You knew he'd be at the conference and you chose to go.'

'But Mary asked me to—'

'And Mary would've understood if you'd changed your mind. You said you did it to further your career, but you could've found other ways to do that. And you chose to see him in Istanbul when you could've sent a simple apology text.'

My eyes suddenly caught the 'Breaking news' flashing up on the TV. Another attack in Istanbul. Thirty-nine dead. Zehra nightclub.

'No,' I choked out.

'What?' Liz said. She clocked the news on the screen and turned up the volume.

'No, no, no, no, no. Oz is at that club.' I bolted out the room to grab my mobile. As I brought the screen to life, I rang his number. The rings were endless. 'Come on, come on.' A blast of Turkish hit my ear – voicemail. I clicked 'end call' and tried again. Once. Twice. Three times. No connection. No comforting voice telling me he was OK.

My throat tightened. I didn't even notice Liz placing my inhaler in my hand but instinctively I brought it to my mouth and drew out two deep puffs. But the medicine did nothing to soothe my mind which was running at breakneck speed with all possible worst-case scenarios. The TV blared in the background – horrific images of bodies being carried out on stretchers, people wailing and the continuous blast of ambulance sirens.

Then, suddenly. Ping. A message on my phone. Oz.

Happy New Year! See you in London soon.

He wasn't there. He must have spent New Year's Eve with Eda after all. My sigh of relief passed through every extremity of my body. I switched off my phone and glanced at Liz.

'Good news, I take it?' she said.

I nodded, a smile spreading across my face. She enveloped me in a hug which almost knocked me sideways. But her warmth was soothing.

'Abigail Jones, will you stop having so much bleedin' drama in your life. What are you going to do now?'

'I love him, Liz. I've always loved him. And I can't bear the thought of never seeing him again. It's our destiny to be together, right? That means we'll find a way.'

38

Now

January

Heathrow terminal two. Passengers from Oz's flight began to pass through the doors. I chewed the inside of my cheek, drumming my fingers against my legs. I had no idea how this was going to play out, but it would be so much easier to talk it through face to face.

Suddenly in the sea of passengers I could see him: the mass of dark curls, the familiarity of his features. His head was tipped back so he could scan over the crowd. When his gaze met mine, he stilled.

The photo. The one the photographer had taken in Istanbul almost fifteen years ago at Oz's brother's birthday party. It was imprinted in my brain, singed there by a flash which had momentarily dazzled me. I had commented on the similarities of the brothers at the time.

I didn't move. I couldn't move. Oz's brother Sinan approached and stood on the other side of the barrier, a case at his feet.

'Abbie? Do you remember me?'

There was a sallowness to his skin, eyes sunken, darkness haunting them.

'Yes.' I wasn't sure if I had said the word out loud. 'Where's Oz?'

'Can we go and sit somewhere?'

We weaved through the crowds and found our way to the nearest coffee shop. My throat and mouth were dry as I sat down, but I waved off the offer of a drink.

Sinan went to the counter before sitting down next to me with his cup. He stared at it for a while, clearly gearing himself up to say his next words. 'Oz can't be here today.'

My heart began to crack, like a glacier carving off a big chunk into the sea. 'What? Why?'

'You'll have to forgive me. My English is not good like Oz. He can never come.' His eyes misted.

All sounds dropped away except a thundering in my ears. I focussed hard on his lips.

'This is not easy to say. The shooting at the nightclub. We were there. And ... Oz was shot in the back. It was a long time for the ambulance to arrive. There was a lot of blood, and he was unconscious in the hospital for hours. They had to perform two operations and found that the bullet hit some nerves, so they had to put him in an induced coma. And ...'

'No.' The word came out like a whisper.

It didn't make any sense. Why was this the first I was hearing of this?

'But he texted me. He sent me a happy new year message. And then there were other messages he sent the next day with his new phone. I ... I thought everything was fine.' My hands began to tremble, and my voice was thinner. Scrolling through the texts on my phone, I found the words I'd received that night. The time. Why didn't I look at the time it was sent? Before the attack. It must have been caught in some internet waiting room with everyone trying to send new year messages at the same time. When I had tried to call him, I couldn't reach him until these messages had come through from a strange number.

'I'm sorry. We were in shock. It was – how do you say?' He mumbled something in Turkish. 'It was a hard time. It was something we could not say in a phone message or a text. I'm sorry. I sent you those messages after the attack from my phone.'

Numbness crept over me. Tears didn't flow. Was I breathing? There was nothing at all going on in my chest.

'When he woke up—'

'Wait, *what*?' It was like I had suddenly been brought back to life. 'Oh, thank God,' I screamed, clutching his hand tightly. 'He's alive,' I whispered, but the ache in my chest soon returned. 'But I don't understand. Why didn't he call me?' I stood up abruptly. 'I have to see him. I *need* to see him.'

Sinan stood and gently grasped my arm. 'Abbie, please. That is not all.' He pulled me back down onto the chair. 'There was a lot of nerve damage from the bullet. When he woke, the doctors did many tests … but … they think he might never walk again.'

I froze.

'It was all my fault.' He clenched his jaw. 'I asked him to come, to the club. He should have been with his daughter, but I had not seen him in many weeks and wanted to be with him. I'd arranged a party at the nightclub. It was fun, until …' He swallowed hard. 'Someone started shooting. It was like fireworks inside. And then … Oz stepped in front of me … he saved my life.'

Stop. Closing my ears, I willed him to stop. I wanted to scream at the excited passengers around me, reuniting with their loved ones. 'This can't be. He was coming here; we were going to try and find a way to be together.' I shook my head. 'I have to see him. I have to get a ticket right now and come.' I began rooting around in my handbag for my purse before Sinan's hands covered mine.

'*Hayır.*' He shook his head. 'You can't. He doesn't want to see you. He doesn't want you to … throw away your life for him.'

'He can't mean it. All the things he wrote to me in his email. You don't understand.'

I didn't realise how much my hands were shaking until Sinan released his grip. 'Please, Abbie. Please accept the wishes of my brother and my family. This is a difficult time for us, and we are accepting some hard things. We were broken even before this and we want time to heal. There is no place for you. Oz asked me to come here to tell you he can never be with you again.'

39

It was the second time I had thrown up that morning. The toilet at chambers reeked of the smell of bleach – my feeble attempt to mask the odour. It must've been that breakfast burrito I had picked up on the way to work from the food truck outside Temple tube.

A knock at the door.

'Abbie?' Mary called from the other side. 'Is everything all right?'

I leaned on the sink. 'I'm fine. I'll be out in a minute.'

The reflection in the mirror made me take a step back: pale cheeks, lank hair, dark rings under my eyes. I popped a mint in my mouth and sucked it hard.

Mary was waiting at the other side of the door, eyebrows drawn together. 'Are you sure you should be at work?'

'I think I ate something off this morning.'

'I don't mean that.' She held my elbow and took me over to the windowsill, the bright winter's day warming the area in front of the glass. 'Liz told me what happened. Perhaps you'd like to take some time off. I can't imagine it'd be easy to focus on work today. We have your notes for Wednesday. We'll muddle through.'

'No, I'm fine. Liz overreacted.'

'Are you sure?'

'Absolutely sure. I'm meeting her later for lunch and I will tell her she worried you needlessly.'

She looked at me with a sympathetic smile, unbuttoning her jacket. She pulled me down to sit beside her in the window seat.

'Listen, Abbie. I never properly thanked you for taking over from me in Paris. I know there have been rumours circulating about why I chose you. We'll probably never be able to shake the nepotism label, but it doesn't mean we can't try. I picked you for a reason. You're smart, dedicated, a natural facilitator. The feedback on the event was excellent. They've asked you to run some similar events up in Oxford. And James Simons can see how hard you're working, too.'

I nodded, not letting the compliment or the request sink in. It never registered when Mary said something nice to me. She was my best friend's wife. But now wasn't the time to tell her I had been thinking long and hard about changing chambers. It was the only way. Partly to avoid having to bump into Charlie but also because I needed to fly on my own. How could I ever do that here with everyone always assuming I was Mary's pet?

'But sometimes, Abbie, it's easy to let all this take over. Recently, I've realised the importance of having a balance. Liz and Maddy are my world. I will always put them first. We're a team, and it's my mother-in-law's illness that has made me realise I need to make changes to make the balance a reality. That's why I am going to cut back on the cases I'm taking on.

Liz misses working and she deserves a partner who can support her to be able to handle a working and family life. I know you've had a tough year. Losing cases never gets easier to bear, but sometimes it's better to take on fewer and not overstretch yourself. Find a different way to cement a good reputation. Do you understand what I'm trying to say?'

Her words floated into the air, my mind elsewhere. 'Yes, I do. Thanks, Mary. I appreciate the chat,' I said, probably too abruptly. 'I'm sorry. I do understand. I've just got a lot of work to do, so I'd better get back to it.'

I sat at my desk; files laid out for my case in front of me. Words skipped across the lines – fuzzy one minute, nonsensical the next. I rubbed my temples and willed my head to stop throbbing.

Air. I needed air. Grabbing my coat and scarf from the back of the chair, I headed out. One foot in front of the other. I had no idea where I was going, but I kept on walking – along the Strand, through Piccadilly, cutting my way through Mayfair, until I reached Edgware Road.

I unwrapped my Paris St Germain scarf from my neck as I walked into Maroush. The layout of the restaurant was different; glass tables and mint walls lined with framed photographs. The counter was on the other side of the room. A young man stood behind it.

'*Ahlan wa Sahlan*. Would you like to see a menu?'

I took a seat in front of him on a bar stool that was tucked underneath the marble counter. 'I'd like a coffee, please.' I glanced to my left where a glass frontage revealed rows of pastries heaped high on plates. The smell was sickly sweet.

He fiddled with a pot, spooning three scoops of coffee into it while I slipped off my coat and laid it on the stool next to me. 'Excuse me, is there an older gentleman who works here as well?'

The waiter set the pot to boil. 'Do you mean Rafik? He is retired now. Moved back to Beirut a few years ago. I am his grandson. Do you know him?'

'I came here many years ago, fifteen years in fact. I had the most wonderful meal with a group of international students.'

He passed me the small coffee cup with a bowl of sugar.

'Thank you,' I said.

'*Tikrami*. Wait, I think there are some photos of my grandfather from around that time.'

'Really?'

'Yes, just a minute.' He wiped his hands on a cloth and walked out from the counter, scanning the photos on the wall and rubbing his chin. '*Na'am*. Here are two.'

I slid off my stool, catching it before it wobbled to the ground, and looked to where he was pointing. One photo was of Rafik with someone I didn't know, and next to it ... There he was. Rafik flanked by Yusef, Yaman and Oz. He was wearing something I didn't recognise so it must have been taken on a different day. My finger reached out and touched him.

'Do you know them?' he asked.

I nodded. 'Yes, I do.'

The waiter unhooked the photograph from the wall. He unpicked the clasps and removed the backing. 'Papa Rafik always kept other photos behind each one. He could never decide on the picture he liked best and didn't want to throw any away. Here' – he gave me three photos – 'please have them.'

Each one included Oz; that irrepressible smile; so young in faded jeans and a V-neck blue jumper. *Why, Oz? Why won't you let me come to you?*

'These mean a lot to me, thank you.'

'*Tikrami,*' he said, returning behind the counter.

I held the photos to my lips, thinking about all the things he had written in his last email to me. The one on New Year's Eve. I still couldn't make any sense of everything that had happened since.

I made my way back down Edgware Road. Tucked inside the entrance of Marble Arch tube lay the Photo-Me booth. Graffiti lined the exterior and an out-of-order sign was stuck to it. A heavy heart dragged me down the escalator to the Central line. The platform. The place where I made that decision to stop him getting on that train. I chose Oz. But why didn't I call him the next day or even the one after that? How would our lives have played out if I had? Or was there no point even speculating because this was our destiny?

At the corner of the Strand, I waited, raising my face to the sky, the sun warming my skin. This should've been a happy day – the start of a new chapter in my life.

'Abs?'

Liz walked towards me, bundled in her sheep-like black coat. I was grateful her presence didn't cause anything to come apart within me.

'I'm in shock. That's all. I can't get my head around it,' I said.

She steered me away from crowds of tourists thronging around us and led me down an alleyway in the direction of the river.

'I don't know what to say,' she said. 'I can't believe it happened. Are you going to see his brother again?'

'I want to. But Oz has made his decision. He doesn't want me, and his family certainly don't either. I have no clue what to do. My body feels numb.'

We walked in silence for a while, my head resting on her shoulder. 'I keep staring at my phone, hoping it will spring to life, and for him to tell me it was all a mistake, and he missed his flight. Wanting to rewind to a couple of weeks ago, wishing I'd never let him leave my flat. Why didn't I call him the second I got his email? Why didn't I tell him to come straight away? He wouldn't have been at the club then. He'd have been here in London.'

She squeezed my arm and we continued walking, letting my questions hang unanswered in the air between us.

We slowed as we reached the Middle Temple gardens. 'Abs. I will always be there for you, but I think there's someone else you need. And when you got me to call mine, it was the best thing I ever did.'

I peered over her shoulder. 'Mum?'

'I called her. Told her everything. About you seeing Oz again over the last year and what happened on New Year's Eve. She was shocked you kept this all to yourself. We all want to make things better, but I have to get back to Maddy and Mum. You've always been by my side and I couldn't have survived this past year without you. I'm stronger now and I want you to promise me you will always confide in me.' She blew me a kiss and walked out of the gate.

Slipping my hands into my pockets, fingers curling around the big, crocheted gloves Oz had bought me in Paris, I walked over to where Mum was sitting – a bench surrounded by bushes, early buds in their branches.

'Hey, Mum.'

'Oh, love.' She stood, the lines on her forehead intensifying. She wrapped her arms around me. 'I'm so sorry, so, so sorry,' she whispered into my hair, stroking my back.

We settled on the bench and she held my gaze. 'This is all my fault.'

'How is this your fault?'

'The letter and the postcards.'

'Please, don't bring those up.'

'But if I hadn't been so protective, hadn't hidden them from you, things wouldn't be like this.' She sighed heavily.

'Why did you hide them, Mum? Was it really because you were worried I would make the same mistakes as Amy?'

She pursed her lips, drawing the collar of her grey coat closer to her neck, her hand-knitted purple scarf peeking out from inside. 'That was part of the reason.' She looked down at her clasped hands. 'I had dreams once. When I was doing my design apprenticeship, I got an opportunity to work at a fashion house in New York.'

'You never told us.'

'But I had just met your father ... and I've told you how he swept me off my feet.' She gave a half laugh.

'You had to choose?'

She toyed with her wedding ring. 'Your dad was terribly old-fashioned. Wanted to start a family right away and for me to be at home. He'd had an unsettled childhood – his dad working down the mines in Wales, always absent. And after his mum passed when he was fifteen, he'd had to fend for himself. He fancied a traditional life, and I was too in love with him to say otherwise. And he didn't want to move to America. What job could he have got out there?'

My shoulders sagged. 'I didn't know that. He never liked to talk about his childhood. And you never told me about New York, only about the romantic way you got together. So, you were worried I would be giving up everything if I read that letter? You didn't trust me to make my own informed decision?'

She nodded. 'And that we'd never see you again.'

'That would never have happened.'

'You don't get it, sweetheart. We almost lost you the day you had your first asthma attack, when you were seven. It was ... I can't even begin to describe what I went through that day in London. Afterwards I swore I'd do whatever I could to shield you from harm, never let you take unnecessary risks. You were so dedicated, so sure that it was your goal to go to law school. But now I know how miserable it made you in the end, I should've trusted you to make your own choices back then. I understand now.' She bowed her head.

'You knew what you'd be giving up, but you still chose Dad. Did you regret it?'

She shook her head. 'Not even for a minute.'

'Dad said you did.'

'What? When did he say that?'

'On my first day of university. He made me promise never to let love get in the way of my future because he felt guilty making you throw away your dreams.'

She tutted. 'The silly fool. He should never have said that to you. I won't deny some days I wished I'd done something more with my life, but I could've, if I'd wanted to. And I am. Thanks to you.'

'A craft shop in Mumbles? That's hardly a design house in New York.'

'Is this why you push yourself so hard in your work? You still want to make your dad proud? You think he would've been any less proud if you'd gone to Beirut to work for that charity?'

I nodded, scanning the sky, trying to hold back the tears. But the pressure was building.

'This is why you continued working to support me and then your sister? Why you became a barrister? When all you wanted was to be with Oz?'

My lip wobbled and I breathed in and out to steady myself.

'The day when Dad got the letter telling him he hadn't got the promotion, I overheard him fighting with Amy. He'd told her I'd be the one to make something of my life, get a profession. And then he had the heart attack, and you went with him to the hospital. I thought he'd died. When you came back, I knew I'd do whatever it took to make him happy, so it would never happen again.'

'Why didn't you ever say? That's so much responsibility for a teenager. I am so sorry you felt that way, sweetheart.'

'It didn't matter. Once I came back from Istanbul, it no longer seemed right to change course. And I was afraid he'd be bitterly disappointed if I'd even mentioned it.'

'Oh, love. He would never have been disappointed in you. You were his world. There was nothing you could've done to make him think otherwise. He was set in his ways. I guess he believed he'd stifled my dreams and hoped things would be different for you; to have a career, be your own person. He set his heart on the best for you, we both did, but along the way we failed to see what we thought was best for you wouldn't make you happy.'

'Really? I assumed he'd be crushed if I told him I didn't want to go to law school.'

She pulled back. 'I'm so sorry. What else can I say? We should've been more understanding back then, not put so much pressure on you. And I'll never forgive myself for leaning on you so much when he died.'

'Mum, please, we've been over this.'

'No, we haven't. Not enough, anyway. All the sacrifices you made for me and then your sister. It broke my heart to see you suffer. You kept your feelings so hidden; I'll always feel guilty for not realising how much you were hurting. Everything was focussed on me losing my husband, your sister having the baby. We all failed to see you'd lost a father and then someone you wanted to build a future with.'

'That was never going to happen. And Dad told me to always look after you and Amy when he was in hospital and I promised him I would. But that wasn't the only thing standing in our way. There have always been so many other obstacles between me and Oz. His family, distance ... We've been together, in the same place, for only fourteen days in total. Fourteen days in fifteen years. Crazy, right?' I swallowed a laugh.

Mum tilted her head to the side. 'Tell me about those precious days. Tell me everything, sweetheart. There are so many gaps. I want to hear all about him. Every day you spent together, the dreams you created, the life you once hoped to create with him. Then maybe you can figure out how to move forward.'

I leaned back on the bench, the sun warm on my face. I began with how we met, her eyes bulging at the mention of me fainting, the crazy way Liz had engineered our Interrailing to get me to Istanbul, his family ruling his life, the road trip to Damascus, the mosques and the restaurants. Syria was a place that had been battered by civil war for years. Incredible to think I had been there before it all began. I then filled her in on all the chance meetings over the last twelve months.

'Why didn't you tell me about seeing him again this last year?' she said.

'I didn't know how you would react. I've always assumed if you heard his name, it would take you back to the day Dad died. The guilt is still there for me.'

She grasped my hands again. 'You need to let it go, Abbie. I don't blame you or Oz for what happened to your dad. And

I wish we had spoken about that before today.' She stroked my knuckles. 'You said goodbye to him when he last came to see you, though. Why?'

'Charlie and I had only broken up a few weeks before, and Oz and I agreed our lives in our own countries were too important to us, that we—'

'Couldn't make the sacrifice for love?'

I stroked the ends of my scarf. 'When Oz talks about his work, his eyes light up. It's taken him years to find that satisfaction. And he adores his daughter and cherishes what little time he gets to spend with her.'

'And it didn't feel right with you that he was willing to sacrifice it all – for you?'

I shook my head. Reaching for my bag, I pulled out my phone. 'When he sent me this email, I hesitated.'

'What did it say?'

'Can I read it to you?'

'Of course.'

I scrolled through my inbox until I reached his message.

Abbie, aşkim, my life, my soul. When you lay in my arms that Wednesday morning, I knew then I couldn't let you go. I don't care what sacrifices I have to make. There have been so many obstacles. They have stood in our path, but they must be overcome. We can do it, together.

I will speak to my boss and try and organise a sabbatical and talk with Dima to see how I can continue to see Eda. I am not sure how, but even if it means I fly back every week between Istanbul and London, I will do it. I will do anything so we can be with each other for longer than a couple of days at a time. Once we are together, everything will be changed, and we can work things out.

When you walked into my life fifteen years ago, I was a confused young man, living a privileged life. London taught me so much, that there was a bigger world outside my family. I was no longer living in my goldfish bowl but had broken out into a stream. But then you fell in my arms. So bright, so lovable, so lively, and then I was out in the ocean, swimming free. You pushed me to make changes in my life, to seek happiness and do what I wanted and not what would only please my family. I wish I'd had the courage to make those changes.

The list of regrets is so great but now it is enough. There are no more. I have made my decision. I will come to London on the 5th of January. We will sit and talk and see where we go from there. Please, Abbie, think about what I have written. You do not have to give me a decision straight away.

We both have lives apart from each other. Distance is our enemy, but let's find neutral ground. I don't want you to give up your life in London, but maybe one day, you will want to experience life abroad, with me.

See you soon.

Love always,

Oz

My voice cracked as I read his last words, the ache that had settled deep in my chest returning with increased strength.

'Wow,' Mum whispered. 'That was beautiful.'

'He attached a photo of us in Paris. Do you want to see it?'

She nodded and I held my phone out to her.

'He's a handsome man. Such a warm smile. And the two of you together ... well ...'

'What should I do, Mum?'

'I can't answer that for you. He's endured something horrific, sweetheart. He's right. Your life would have to change to be with him. We can't even begin to imagine what he's been through, but I can sympathise with his family. I at least know what it's like to almost lose a child. And he has a daughter. He needs to be with her. He can't travel back and forth right now.'

She patted my hand. 'I will tell you this, though. Sacrifices often have to be made for the one you love because relationships are hard work. Being with someone you'd do anything for means you have to make choices, tough choices sometimes. But when it's for the right person, they become easier to make. You might not know it in here,' she said, pointing to her head before placing her hand on her heart, 'but you'll feel in here that it's the right decision.'

I smiled at the memory of Oz saying something similar.

'And Amy and I can manage on our own. We don't need you to always rescue us.'

'Mum, that's not all.' I chewed the inside of my cheek and willed the sickness to subside. The nausea had grown in intensity over the last two days. 'I think I might be pregnant.'

40

Now

March

The taxi came to a stop outside a cobblestone path in front of the OCM building – a white four-storey structure in the outskirts of Munich. I wasn't sure what the letters stood for, but I knew it was one of Germany's leading orthopaedic surgery and rehabilitation centres.

'*Danke*,' I said to the driver as I handed over twenty euros and waved away the change.

My weekend suitcase bumped over the uneven surface until I reached the glass-fronted entrance.

At the reception desk, a woman sat tapping away on a computer, a pair of spectacles teetering on the end of her nose. Rows of white cabinets lay behind her, a stack of files by her side in a Jenga-like structure.

'*Wilkommen*,' she said, her voice sharp and clipped.

'Um … *Guten morgen*,' I replied, no clue as to whether it was the correct greeting for the time of day. 'I am here to visit a patient at this hospital.'

She wrinkled her nose. 'Are you family?'

'No. No, I'm not.'

'Then, no,' she snapped. 'We cannot permit you to enter.'

'But you see—'

'*Fräulein*. This is not a hospital. It is a specialist clinic for some of the worst spinal injuries in the world. It is not a place to …' She mumbled in German. '*Rumhängen*, hang with your friends.' Her glasses tipped off the end of her nose, the beaded chain around her neck stopping them from clattering to the floor. She resumed typing.

I pushed the handle of my case down until it clicked. 'No.'

The woman stopped and raised her eyebrows.

'I have come to see a man called Özgür Demir. I've come all the way from London. It's important I see him. In fact, I am not leaving until I do.'

She opened her mouth before pinching her lips.

'Abbie?' someone called out, with a Turkish inflection.

Sinan was walking along the corridor towards me, passing through an automatic barrier.

'Hello, Sinan.'

'What are you doing here?'

'I came to see Oz.'

'But I said—'

'Yes, you did. But there's something you need to understand. And he needs to understand too. I love him. I love Oz. And I refuse to let him go. I appreciate the messages you've sent me and all the updates on his condition. I know I said I wouldn't bother your family in return for the information. But I lied. I refuse to believe it has to be over between us. I love him, for heaven's sake, and I'm not leaving until I see him. I don't care if he never walks again. I don't want to be protected from a life he thinks I shouldn't have. That's not his choice to make. I want to see him, Sinan. Please. *Lütfen*,' I added for good measure.

Sinan sighed, his shoulders dropping. He moved over to the reception desk and spoke to the lady in broken German and she opened the barrier so we could enter.

A ripple of excitement pulsed through me but soon the tic in my eye was off again, doing its merry dance. Thankfully, my morning sickness had subsided and wouldn't return until later in the evening.

Once I had spoken to Mum, a plan began to take shape in my mind. I had immediately called Sinan and begged him to see me again and subsequently persuaded him to keep me updated on Oz's condition. In return, I had agreed to not bother his family. But when Sinan messaged to say Oz was scheduled to go to Germany for some aggressive rehabilitation, I began to hatch a plan to see him again. Turkey was still considered a high-risk country for Brits to travel to, so the news of his transfer gave me hope. When the pregnancy test came back positive, I was filled with conflicting emotions.

But when I had reclined on the doctor's examination bed during my twelve-week scan a few days ago my apprehension turned to joy. To see the life growing inside me on the screen made me more determined than ever that I wanted to be with Oz. Not being able to share this precious moment with him had been hard to take but had healed the pain I had buried for so long. Oz needed to understand I was willing to upend the life I had created for myself to be with him, and I hoped to conquer everything standing in our path, together.

The road ahead was uncertain and shrouded in mist, but it was a road I wanted to travel with him. The question was, would he want to travel it with me?

Sinan stopped outside a room on the third floor. 'He is not the same man you say you love. The doctors did some tests yesterday and we do not have the results yet. But his recovery will be long, and his spirit is broken. *Yani . . .*' He shrugged his shoulders. 'You are stubborn like my brother. Maybe you are what he needs. Before the shooting, he told me his plans to be with you. He was happy. He is only sad now.'

The door swung open and a doctor stepped outside, murmuring a greeting as he passed us.

I took a deep breath. Sinan spoke in Turkish while I cowered behind his large frame. My body felt heavy all of a sudden, my feet glued to the spot.

Oz's voice sounded frail and I couldn't make out any of the words he spoke. The tone was unfamiliar, too.

'Listen to her. Don't send her away,' Sinan said, finally reverting to English. He bowed his head low so he could whisper the next bit to me. 'Good luck.'

The door shut with a sucking sound. Oz turned away towards the window. Rain had started to hurl itself against the glass, a spring-like day made wintry in a matter of minutes. Branches tapped against the window.

I pushed my suitcase into the corner of the room before moving behind the chair. As I pushed it closer to him, its feet scraped noisily on the linoleum. I draped my coat over its arm and sat down. Munich was colder than I had expected it to be and I shivered a little beneath my thin pale blue jumper and rubbed my hands against my jeans to warm them up.

The head of Oz's bed was elevated. A machine was hooked to one side of him, numbers displayed in neon blue against a black background. There were bruises around the tube in his hand which connected him to the monitor. His hair hung low over the neckline of his gown – longer than when I had last seen him in London. He was covered in sheets and a blanket from the waist down.

'Oz—'

'Abbie, please. I don't want to see you,' he said dully, still facing the window.

I gritted my teeth, determined to carry on. 'You don't have to look at me. I can't even begin to imagine the pain you are going through. But I beg you, please hear me out.'

His head didn't move. That's when I noticed a wheelchair folded up on the other side of the bed.

'Lütfen,' I said, reaching out to grab his hand and stroke his knuckles. The feeling of the tube inserted into his skin made me queasy. 'Lütfen.'

Finally, he turned his head. Those eyes. The eyes that had enchanted me on so many occasions, were clouded in pain. I longed to reach out and stroke his hair, to tell him everything would be OK, that we would figure it all out. Words began to form in my brain but were overwhelmed by images of him in the club that night; images that had surfaced in my nightmares over the past few months. I couldn't imagine what he and his brother had lived through. How do you even begin to put your life back together after such an atrocity?

I licked my bottom lip, the chapped skin rough against my tongue.

'I had to see you, Oz. I don't know if you knew Sinan has been keeping me up to date with how you are. I had to come.

I wanted to come the day I heard about the shooting; to fly out the second Sinan told me the news. But he pleaded with me not to. He said you didn't want to see me.' I shook my head. 'I refuse to believe it.'

He stared off into the distance, breaking eye contact.

'When you sent me the email,' I continued, 'my world spun off its axis. I was so sure you'd regret making those changes in your life to be with me. Then when I heard about the shooting, when I thought you had been killed, I knew a life without you wasn't even worth thinking about.'

'Stop!' he said sharply, looking at me. 'Please, Abbie. I don't want to hear this. We can't be together. You don't understand how your life would be. Look at me. I can't walk, I can't dance with you. I don't want your pity. I'd be a burden on you. All the things we could no longer do together. Our relationship has been played out across the world, and we could never do that again. I can't come and live in London. And my family is in Turkey, and I need them. Since the accident, my mother has been full of remorse and we have become close again.'

I nodded. 'I know that, Oz. I'm not asking you to move to England. Hell, I have no clue how this will work. I'll travel between England and wherever you are. I'll retrain; I'll use my experience to find something to do in Turkey.' I shrugged. 'I don't have the answers, but I love you, and I'll never stop loving you. And that is not going to change, whatever you or your family might think.'

'But your job. You love your job.'

'I love you more.'

He swallowed hard and a single tear trickled down onto his pillow.

'I don't care if we never dance again. We can hold each other and listen to the music. We can still travel when the time is right. We can …'

I leaned in and kissed his cheek, my lips growing wet as he continued to cry. I stroked his hair. 'I thought I'd lost you forever.' I couldn't bear seeing his tears any longer and buried my face in his neck.

A squeeze of my hand; a signal. I looked back at him and he squeezed my fingers even tighter. 'I imagined it was the end.'

I stroked his cheek, the anguished look on his face mirroring mine. 'You're a hero. You're my hero. Please don't send me away. I want to be with you, forever.'

My mouth settled on his lips and I felt suddenly weightless, as if a great burden had been lifted. I leaned back, clutching his hand in both of mine.

His gaze fell on my suitcase. 'How long are you here for?'

'As long as it takes for me to convince you I want to be a part of your life, no matter what that means.'

'I hope you will stay longer than that. You only just got here.'

I smiled at his words. Was this a hint of British humour? 'You mean it?'

He nodded. 'My heart has been in pieces since the incident. But seeing you, hearing you say what you'd give up for me, it gives me a new hope, that maybe, *inşallah*, what the doctor believes could happen, will.'

I blinked. 'You've lost me, Oz. I think I'm still delirious from you saying I can stay. What does the doctor believe?'

'The test results just came back. It is a slim hope. It is not impossible ... I might walk again.'

I pulled back, a tentative smile breaking across my mouth.

'Wait. It is still a long road. I will need a couple more operations, the first one in a few days. The physical therapy could last a year, maybe two, or more. When he told me, the words didn't make sense to me. But then ... but then you appeared. You have given me reason to want to believe it can happen again.'

'You bet it will.' I stroked his hair and cradled his head. 'And one day ... you will walk and run with Eda and our kids in the park and kick a ball with them.'

'Kids? *Inşallah*, Abbie. *Inşallah*.'

I raised an eyebrow. 'For once I know this will happen.'

'*Ne?*'

'I'm having a baby, Oz. Our baby.'

'*Yok artık!* No way. *Asla*.' He searched my eyes, his mouth wide. 'It's true?'

I nodded.

'*Vah, vah, vah,*' he cried, pulling me nearer. The familiar citrus scent stirred my senses once more. 'You have made me the happiest man, Abbie. You have given me another reason to fight.'

I slipped off my shoes and shuffled onto the bed beside him, careful not to cause him any pain. I laid my arm across his chest and settled, the warmth of his body beside me. It was all the comfort I needed.

Epilogue

Thirteen Months Later

April

I get it. The difference between fate and destiny. Fate is fixed, implacable. But destiny is something we can shape and change. There's an element of choice in it. And I had chosen Oz. I had always chosen him. 'It must be love,' Liz had once said. And because of love, it had been our destiny to be together.

'I found her,' Liz announced as we stepped inside Aunt Betsy's dining room, having completed the short walk back up from Bracelet Bay, a stone's throw from my aunt's house in Mumbles.

Mum bustled in, bringing silver platters of cucumber sandwiches, fairy cakes and scones, all lined with paper doilies.

'Good. We thought you'd run away.'

'Never, Mum. Never. I just needed a breather.'

A cake was laid out in the centre of the table, laced with white fondant. Mum had also tried her hand at an array of Turkish dishes, having studied a cookbook.

'Boiling object, incoming,' Aunt Betsy sang out as she came into the room. She laid the china teapot out at the back of the table, away from little hands. And today there were quite a few of them. Amy had brought her two and Maddy was somewhere on the premises, probably playing hide-and-seek. Liz's mum was here too, looking resplendent and continuing to battle her illness with dignity.

There was a row of chairs laid out by the bay window with a space between the middle two for Oz's wheelchair.

Amy came in holding Oğhuzan in her arms, his head flopped on her shoulder. I melted. The same reaction every time I saw him. His first smile had destroyed me even more when little dimples had formed in his cheeks. Yes, his name was not easy to say, but thanks to Maddy, his nickname – Oggie – had stuck. He was named after Oz's favourite Beşiktaş player. His middle name – Philip – was a tribute to my father.

I brought my locket to my lips and kissed it. Inside was a picture of Dad, and when I got around to it, I would put a picture of Oz with our son in the other side.

'He's fast asleep,' Amy said. 'I'm going to put him upstairs and bring the monitor down. With a bit of luck, he'll sleep through the ceremony.'

'Thanks,' I said, leaning in to place a kiss on his forehead.

I laid my shawl on one of the chairs and sat down. In the corner of the fabric, three names were embroidered – mine, Oz's and our son's. It was a beautiful creation. Mum had posted it online and orders had flooded in. It was easier to reach a wider audience now that Amy and her new husband Dylan were handling internet sales. Several of Mum's creations had become bestsellers and the business was thriving. I had used the shawl to carry Oggie home from the hospital. It was a good match with Mum's wedding dress, which I was wearing – the perfect outfit for today's occasion. It held so much love within the lace trim.

Oggie was already a well-travelled little boy, with nearly as many stamps in his passport as I had. There were days when I didn't know where I lived. I was on maternity leave but not for much longer. In a month, we would pack up our things in Istanbul and would be starting a new life in Oxford. Oz had got a part-time job with the university at the Refugee Studies Centre, and I was transferring to the annex of Greencourt chambers which was based in the centre of town. With most of my cases across the Midlands, in Birmingham, Coventry and further south in Reading, it was the perfect base. The days Oz was working, I would look after Oggie. The clerks at the office knew not to book me on cases for that part of the week. I had also run several workshops similar to the one in Paris. Even better news, Eda was starting secondary school in England and would be living with us. Dima had given birth to twin boys and she and her new husband had agreed to the move on condition that Eda went back to Turkey for the holidays. Last I heard, Charlie had met an American sculptor in Brazil and got married in Vegas a few months later before settling in Cambridge, and I was happy for him.

Oz and I had found a small bungalow on the outskirts of Oxford and put down a joint deposit on it. Mum would be happy. She had longed to spend more time with her grandson and was taking every opportunity, since we had come back a few days ahead of Oz.

Both sides of the family were about to meet for the first time because today was our engagement party. We were following the traditional Turkish custom. Things had already been agreed in principle back in Turkey, where I had made the perfect cup of Turkish coffee for all Oz's relatives to gain their approval, adding salt to Oz's cup. And yes, he had drunk it and smiled appreciatively. But now we were on my turf, awaiting him, his mum, siblings, daughter and his father for the second part of the proceedings – the exchange of rings. Two gold bands tied together with a red ribbon would be placed on our ring fingers. Then the ribbon would be cut by his father to mark our union, swiftly followed by a big party out in the garden under a pop-up gazebo. Then in a week, we would have our official wedding back in Turkey – a huge affair, if Oz's family had anything to do with it. But I didn't mind. Nada and her family would be there to celebrate, too.

Oz's dad had already met his grandson back in Turkey. It had been tense when he had arrived in Istanbul, but relations between him and the rest of the family were beginning to improve. Oz's mother was a changed woman, full of regret for how she had treated her son. And the birth of her first grandson had helped strengthen their bond. Oz's sister Eylül had two daughters and his brother was divorced with no kids, so the arrival of an heir to the Arsel family was a big deal, not that Oz would describe it like that.

The day Oggie was born, I saw a change in Oz. He became even more dedicated to his gruelling physiotherapy. The idea of chasing our little boy around our new home was the extra impetus he needed to continue with his treatment. He'd had another two operations over the year, and the annex to the Arsel compound in Istanbul had been converted into a clinic for his therapy. But we ached for our own place, to start our new life as a family, meeting life head-on together, the four of us.

The doorbell rang, and I took a deep breath. I heard the squeak of the door hinge and a series of gasps. God, I hoped no one was making a fuss about how we would get the wheelchair through the hallway.

Liz peered her head around the doorframe of the living room. 'Stay right there,' she said. 'You're never going to believe this,' she chirruped, before disappearing again.

I could hear a clicking sound, which became progressively louder. I stood and smoothed the creases in my dress. As Oz entered, dressed in a smart navy suit, I gasped, my hand reaching to my heart. He was on crutches.

'You're, you're ... walking?'

He bit his bottom lip, straining as he took some halting steps. He stopped in the middle of the room, breathing heavily. 'It's a special day. I wanted to make an effort.'

I leapt towards him, flinging my arms around his neck. One crutch clattered to the floor and he fell into me, out of breath, as he slipped his free arm around me. A wave of pure happiness washed over my body. I squeezed him tightly before pulling back and searching his eyes.

His smile mirrored mine.

'I got you something.' He steadied himself, reached into his jacket and pulled out two tickets. Train tickets.

'Vienna?' My eyes widened.

'I thought it would be a nice place for a honeymoon. When we first met, you told me at the café that you wanted to go. Maybe you will want to get off the train there with me?'

'For you, always.'

Thank you to...

Kate Burke, my extraordinarily brilliant agent. Your belief in this book has meant the world to me, and I am looking forward to many collaborative writing years ahead. A big thank you to Sian Ellis-Martin, James Pusey, Hana Murrell and the rest of the Blake Friedmann team for your thoughtful edits, getting the book into international hands and making sure I stay on top of tax issues!

I am fortunate to have not one but three incredible editors at Penguin Random House. Jennie Rothwell – you fell in love with Abbie and Oz's story and carried the book to new depths. Your compassion, insight and hilarious edits made the start of my publishing journey an absolute joy. To Emily Griffin, thank you for having faith in the book and for all your hard work, and to my new editor – Katie Loughnane – I am beyond excited to have you in my corner. You have championed the book from your first day at Cornerstone. All three of you have made me a better writer and shared my love of my favourite Turkish actor! Thanks also to Ajebowale Roberts and Sania Riaz for your edits, and the rest of the amazing team at PRH: Natalia Cacciatore (marketing); Sarah Harwood (PR); Mathew Watterson, Claire Simmonds, Jade Unwin, Olivia Allen, Evie Kettlewell (UK sales); Richard Rowlands (international sales) and Helen Wynn-Smith (production). Amy Musgrave's cover design is simply gorgeous, and I couldn't be happier with Lucy Truman's exquisite cover illustration. To Sarah Bance for saving my blushes with her expert copy-edit, and a multitude of thanks to Mehmet Munzur and Hilda Pressdee for your translation edits. And to my wonderful sensitivity reader, Peru Boro, thanks for your comments and support.

I am very grateful to my early readers and proof-readers for their plot suggestions, editing nous and encouragement: Ben McLannahan, Katie Golding, Sue Fortin, Fiona Schneider and Jen Thompson. The Pressdee girls (my nieces) – Charlie, Georgina, Ellie and Alex, your youthful comments on the story were on point. Immense gratitude to my brother Piers for his legal expertise and continuous confidence boosting, and my sister-in-law Sally for her equally insightful guidance on the legal profession. To my late father who would have been ridiculously proud that I am a published author – thanks for all those family holidays to Mumbles.

My fellow writer friends: Lucy Keeling, Emma Hughes, Meera Shah, Sara Jafari and Lia Middleton, I appreciate you keeping me sane on this crazy publishing journey; and to my best friends Sarah Brett, Hannah Tigg, Dee Spence and Katrina Webster Stamas, thanks for propping me up when life has thrown curveballs. To my Bake-Off book club girls: Amy, Beth, Emma, Hannah, Jess, Lisa, Nicole and Vicky – you are the best thing to have come out of Instagram for me. And to all the other wonderful #bookstagrammers with whom I have shared my love of romance and reading – you are all superstars.

To my Turkish muse, the hugely talented actor Çağatay Ulusoy, I have loved every show you have acted in. The character of Oz was inspired by you and my love of Turkish soap operas. Abbie and Oz's chance encounter came to me on the Women's March in NYC when I was living in the US. Thanks to my friend Sam Harley-Smith, who marched with me and steered me away from the crowds when I was overcome with outdoor claustrophobia, like Abbie. What a momentous day that was. And thanks to Alex Campbell, my old school friend, who happened to be visiting the following week and encouraged me to start writing this novel.

The Khoury family: my late grandfather Bishara, I am indebted to you for instilling a love of books; and to my aunts – Mira, Lila and Leila, thank you for cheering me on from Beirut. I hope I have done you all proud. Carrying the Khoury name is a badge of honour for me.

My writing stints are always fuelled by coffee. Thanks to the Crazy Mocha in Montclair, New Jersey where I first penned this novel and 63 High Street in my current hometown of New Malden where I have edited during countless mornings. Across the road is Suttles, a shop that has indulged my stationery obsession since I was a little girl and now provides me with all my printing and publishing needs – thanks, Andy.

To my mother, words can't express how much I appreciate all that you have done for me. My three pets (aka the ones I exploit on my Instagram page): Flair, Eloise and Biscuit, thanks for all your unconditional love (well, as long as you get treats). To my girls – Miranda and Rose. Mummy did it! I love you more than you will ever know. I hope I have shown you through my sheer grit and determination that anything is possible if you believe in it.

And finally, to you! Yes, you. For buying this book and reading it. I am so grateful. Please do get in touch on social media and let me know what you think – I'm @carolinekauthor on Instagram and Twitter.